LINNET MCLAUGHLIN

REBORN

The Allies Of Old

This book is a work of fiction. Any references to historical events, real people, or real places are used fictitiously. Other names, characters, places, and events are products of the author's imagination, and any resemblance to actual events or places or persons, living or dead, is entirely coincidental. McLaughlin, Linnet. Reborn (The Allies Of Old Book 1)

Copyright © 2018 by Linnet McLaughlin All rights reserved, including the right to reproduce this book or portions thereof in any form whatsoever.

Cover Art by Paul Burnham

Acknowledgments

To Howie, my love in this life and all the lives hereafter, the hero of every dream both sleeping and waking; without you the incredible wanderings of my imagination would have remained locked inside my mind. I can never thank you enough.

To Jeanette, Judie, Mary, Maria, and Heather, the soul sisters I've been blessed to call my friends since adolescence- you rock girls, and now all the world can see how much.

Special thanks to Paul for capturing the image in my head and breathing life into the perfect cover, and Scott for the incredible finishing touches.

Chapter One

Anna awoke to agony. Her entire being was on fire, the blood flowing through her veins a river of lava. There was a strange whimpering noise coming from somewhere...*me, it's me*. She felt panic rising in her chest and bit down hard on her lip, forcing the eerie sound to cease. She slowly opened her eyes then quickly shut them against the excruciating pain of light hitting her pupils.

She managed to drag her hand to her face and massage her eyelids before hesitantly cracking them open again. Little by little she widened them and her ears seemed to pop and all at once she could hear sounds above the dull roaring in her head. She was accosted with voices-screaming, shouting and...cheering? *What the hell*, she thought feverishly, and believed that fitting. She was on fire, people were screaming, she was in hell.

Panic gripped her as she heard the eerie keening again and she bit down on her lip once more, forcing herself to reason. If she was in hell, wouldn't she be filled with bitterness and hatred? She pictured the faces of her friends and love for them burned fiercely inside her. She calmed and made herself focus.

She was lying on a cold cement floor and appeared to be facing a wall. The loud and terrifying sounds were coming from somewhere behind her. She knew that when she turned she'd be in the middle of a nightmare, but unless she planned on lying here forever she had to figure out where she was and what to do, and that required facing it. She took a deep breath and nearly screamed, her body hurt so badly. Clenching her teeth she slowly turned and immediately wished she hadn't.

Oh God help me, she thought desperately.

There were people in the center of the room and they were fighting like feral cats, clawing and ripping, biting and tearing into one another. Flesh was splattered with blood in pieces scattered across the cement floor. *Not real*, her mind whispered in horror, *this can't be real*. Panic began to build once more and she tore her eyes away from the gory scene to look at the others in the room, those on the sidelines cheering. It was as if they were gathered around a dog fight, but instead of dogs they were people who now behaved like rabid beasts.

She heard more keening noises and bit her lip again, then realized it wasn't coming from her. She slid her gaze down the length of wall and there were other bodies, mostly female, lying in fetal and contorted positions.

Ten feet away a pair of sightless eyes were facing her...*dead* her mind supplied, *he's dead*.

Suddenly a girl leapt up from her place against the wall and started spitting and hissing, saliva flying from her mouth as she snapped at the air. She did not appear human and Anna was filled with a bone numbing dread as the taste and scent of blood overwhelmed her every sense and she was *sooo hungry*, and she wanted to *eat*, and *Oh God ravenous*....

NO,NO, NO! I will Not become that, I will Not become that, I will Not become....that.

The alien craving finally receded and she took a long breath, exhaling slowly before returning her attention to the center of the room. She saw the snapping girl in the midst of the carnage and recoiled in horror as the crazed female jumped on another girl's back *tearing half of her neck away with her fucking teeth*! Revulsion writhed in her stomach and for a terrifying moment she feared she would start retching and alert others to her conscious state.

She was blessedly distracted by a wheezing sound a little to her left and turned slightly, staring into the eyes of a girl who smelled of death.

Smelled of death? The girl was still holding on, but somehow Anna knew it wouldn't be long. The pain and fear reflected in the unfocused gaze tore at her heart and she wished she could comfort her. But self-preservation was a powerful thing.

She turned away from the girl and an image came to her. *Jake,* her memory hissed, and she searched the room for the one who had done this. The lying, deceiving, monstrous bastard who had done this.

She located him standing on the sidelines, laughing and taking money. *He's taking bets*, her horrified mind whispered. A tremor vibrated her body as tears of devastation burned the insides of her lids.

She had to get out of here. Get away, lose her mind or die, those were her options. She tried to turn in another direction but a fresh wave of pain scorched her insides and she gasped silently, squeezing her eyes shut and rocking back and forth. After an eternity the feeling waned and she could breathe again.

When she re-opened her eyes the only thing that had changed was the now empty stare of the girl lying dead beside her.

She caught movement to her left and turned to see a few more men entering the room. Her brain finally processed that she was lying in a corridor. She was facing the large basement where the carnage was taking place but she wasn't inside the room and she could now see the exit which was twenty-five feet down the length of wall.

If she could just crawl past the entryway she would be out of sight to the observers inside, and then if she could just get through the door...

As she eyed her destination an enormous male burst through the entrance. He was over six and a half feet tall with a black coat stretched across his broad muscular back and shoulders. He stood on the threshold, his huge hands clenched into fists, and she could *feel* the fury rolling off him.

He turned slightly, glancing down the length of wall, and she saw eerie lights flashing in his eyes before they came to rest on her face. For just a moment the fury was replaced with something else.

Never in her life had she seen someone so beautiful, his eyes were shimmering ice blue with gold flecks set in a face that appeared to have been chiseled off a statue of a Greek God. Even his hair seemed to shimmer with different colored golden highlights. His gaze continued to rest on her, his eyes flaring with an intense despair that sliced straight through her heart.

The look faded as quickly as it had come, replaced by rage, and his lips pulled back from his teeth in a snarl as he leapt across the space into the room, throwing bodies out of his way with so much force they flew in every direction. He stopped in front of her enemy and roared in a language she had never before heard.

Jake cowered, and as he attempted to speak the god-like man *ripped his head from his shoulders* and threw it into the far wall where it *Exploded.*

The violence of the act stunned her already overwhelmed senses, and she was certain what she had just seen could not be real, that this was all just a vivid nightmare. She may have been able to convince herself of it, if not for the pain slicing at her nerves and thrumming through her blood.

Her eyes were glued to the scene and with the exception of the mutated humans everyone had flattened themselves against the wall, none wanting to be a bi-product of the god's fury.

He stalked up to another group of cowering males and growled. With a wide swing his enormous fist caved in the side of a man's head while he grasped another by his neck and lifted him. He hurled the dangling form into a wall and Anna could hear bones shattering. He turned and wiped his hands off on the shirt of yet another and spoke with a sneer curving his lips.

As she watched she began to feel a glimmer of hope. This terrifying male was one of them and it appeared he did not approve. Maybe they weren't all evil, maybe he was going to break this up and take her somewhere safe. She held her breath and watched him step away from the men. He took one last look around the room, and she saw that the flames in his eyes had extinguished, leaving shards of ice in their wake. He strode away and the fighting resumed.

He didn't stop them, she thought miserably, as her small sliver of hope died.

The pain returned with brutal force and as she felt her life ebbing she sensed a presence looming over her. *He* was standing there watching her die. After a moment she heard him walk away and felt her heart skip, then stop all together.

NOOOO, her mind bellowed, NOT MY TIME! With every ounce of strength she possessed she willed her heart to beat. *You will NOT DIE and leave Jenna and Austin to shoulder that kind of guilt! You will NOT DIE and take the last piece of your father's heart! You will not die, you will NOT. DIE*.

Her heart stuttered back to life and resumed its steady beating, and gradually her body grew stronger, fighting off the pain.

*I'm going to make it, s*he thought with a sudden rush of immense gratitude.

Another group came through the entrance and walked up to the opening of the room. Their backs were to her, blocking the view of the people inside. Ever so slowly she began crawling her way past them.

Please don't let anyone choose this moment to spring from the wall, she prayed fervently. It felt as if it was taking too long but she was afraid any sudden movements would catch in their peripheral.

Finally she reached the entrance and dragged herself through it. She moved out of sight and used the wall to pull herself to her feet. There was a stairway straight ahead and as she was gathering strength to climb it she heard footsteps above her. She looked around wildly and spotted a crawlspace under the stairs. Throwing herself in it, she drew her knees to her chest.

The pounding of feet over her head as they thundered down the steps nearly stopped her heart once more, but they continued forward into the melee without a backward glance.

Exhaustion overtook her and she knew she had nothing left. She could only hope to go unnoticed. She felt her eyelids sagging and sleep came like a down comforter floating her away.

Chapter Two
Seven Weeks Earlier

Anna mused that there were few things, at least in her limited experience of life, that were more beautiful than a waterfall. She closed her eyes against the fine mist blanketing her face and listened.

It was a combination of things really. The constant thunder of its endless pour over the sides of well-worn rock, but when you listened closely it was as if there were hundreds of individual streams all calling out their own unique, triumphant cries as they jumped over the side in complete and joyous abandon, and when you put it all together it became one voice, like a well-trained symphony.

And that was what she saw of it with her eyes still closed and her head thrown back, breathing in the chilly vapor that seemed to refresh her to her innermost core, yet another element of its glory.

She slowly opened her eyes and began moving backward out of its delicious spray to fully take in the sight. She drew in a breath and experienced a shiver of pure pleasure. It was mesmerizing to watch and she grinned foolishly at the thought that those hundreds of slivers of water looked like strings of diamonds leaping into the shimmering robes of an angel, rippling the gown as they flowed to the bottom.

She heard voices headed her way and it broke apart the magic of the moment.

What is it about people that they can rarely be in tune with nature? She thought in exasperation. *They're always loud and oblivious to everything around them except the sounds of their own voices.* She watched as the group came stomping over, somehow managing to be heard over nature's thunderous music. As they reached the rocky edge they stopped in unison, and in that brief moment there was absolute silence. *Hmm, perhaps not so unaffected after all*, she thought with a small smile. She watched them for a few more seconds before making her way back to the park's expansive lawn.

As she walked she laughed to herself thinking that her ungenerous thoughts of the group were just a *mite* hypocritical. In a few minutes her friends would be arriving and the six of them would hardly be pensive and quiet as they made their way down the river bed to the main waterfall. Giving her head a shake she focused on her surroundings and smiled widely. It was a beautiful day, the sun was out in full force and she knew the grass would feel amazing on her feet, so she slid her sandals off and curled her toes in the soft green blanket. She dropped down on the spongy warmth and stretched out on her back, closing her eyes blissfully as the breeze from the falls tickled across her face. *Just give me a pillow and I could easily take a nap,* she sighed. She entertained the thought for about two seconds before deciding against it. The girls would be there any minute and she shuddered to think of the different methods they might use to wake her up...cold water in the face, a spider on her chest, shouting in her ear, hmm, yeah, staying awake was definitely safer.

She stared up at the sky and decided to play her favorite childhood game while she waited-cloud animation. There were large pieces of white fluff scattered and floating across the great blue and she found her first cartoon immediately as a Viking ship came into focus, proud sails billowing in the wind chasing after a...large dog? Yup, complete with a lolling tongue. To the west a clown on stilts was bending down to pick up....nooo, not a clown, a transformer, and he was stepping out of another dimension. *Good one*, she mentally applauded...

"Anna bo banna fo fanna!"

She sat up and grinned as she spotted her friends making their way across the clearing. Her lip twitched at the sight of Jenna singing and bopping her head, her wavy long black hair swishing back and forth. She bumped her generous hips against her sister Jess who laughed and bumped her back, though when Jess did it the motion was far more sensual. With a classically beautiful face and an hourglass figure that tapered into long legs, Jess always looked like she'd just stepped out of a magazine. The siblings did a dance skip and Anna grinned before shifting her focus to the others.

Macey was watching the sisters with an expression of mock hilarity, a look that was often seen on her exotically attractive face. She was smiling from ear to ear, and God Anna loved that smile. White and wide and genuine, it was nearly always present. She giggled as she watched Macey reach out and goose Jenna, laughing loudly as she dodged retaliation.

"Hey, what about me?" Jess sulked teasingly.

"Ooh baby, get over here," Macey made a kitty sound.

Anna grinned as she caught Holly's eye roll in her peripheral.

Marina caught it as well, "Oh come on Hol, you know you want some!"

Holly looked up at the much taller blonde and smirked, "Don't even think about it," she warned.

Marina made a move towards her and Holly darted away with a squeal, her wavy brown hair streaming out behind her.

God I love my girls, Anna thought. All so different yet they complemented one another perfectly.

They reached her and she hopped to her feet, joining the two sisters of the group in song, doing a little shimmy shake.

"Party tonight!" Jess clapped Anna five and bumped hips with her, still dancing.

"You know it! So what guy are you lusting after today?" She raised an eyebrow, her lip curling in a teasing smile.

Jess smiled back at her in a very impish way, so Anna prodded, "Who is it, spill!"

"Nathan Ryden," Jenna stated, "she totally made out with him the other night at the pier."

"I did not make out with him, it was just one kiss!"

"Uh huh, is that what we're calling five minute long tongue action these days?"

Jess glared at her sister, then gave it up and grinned. "Okay," she confessed," I guess I made out with him a little."

"Nathan, really? Since when do you like him?" Marina piped in as she tied her long blonde hair back in a lopsided ponytail.

"Do you really need to ask that question," Jenna rolled her blue-violet eyes, "it was just a matter of time since he's one of the last remaining cute guys in our town that she *hasn't* had a fling with."

"You are so mean to me, and you make me sound so bad!" Jess pouted.

Anna draped her arm around her shoulder. "Don't listen to her, there is absolutely nothing wrong with being boy crazy Jenna just likes giving you crap."

"Oh pu-leeze," Jenna drawled, "this coming from you? You've kissed exactly two people and it took eons for you to get to that point both times!"

Anna blushed and shook her head. "It's not my fault that guys look at me and see a cute little sister."

That earned her a chorus of boos.

"Anna, what are you talking about, you're gorgeous!" Jess put a hand on her hip, a frown creasing her brow.

"Yeah, false modesty is very unattractive," Jenna added.

Anna smirked. "Hey, I'm not being falsely modest, I just happen to know that my pixie look does not elicit strong sexual urges from the opposite sex. Since some of my friends have guys eye-screwing them everywhere we go, I should know." Being five foot three and petite of build she was convinced she was too tiny and childlike to ever be considered sexy. It was only her silvery blonde hair and unusual turquoise eyes that allowed her to admit she was attractive.

"What about Austin?" Holly offered.

"He doesn't count."

"And why not?"

"Because he's like a brother to me," she held up a hand to stop the objections, "yes I know he feels differently, but I just...I don't know."

"But he's tall and handsome, and obviously does not think that you're too childlike," Jess pointed out.

"Well that's just because I have such an amazingly sexy personality! See, I'm not falsely modest, in fact I find myself fantastically awesome." She stuck out her tongue and laughter filled the air around her.

"Eh hmm," Holly cleared her throat as the laughter died away, "if you want to talk about pixie-ish, let's talk about me instead." She waved her hand over her body and raised her eyebrows.

Anna shrugged smiling, "We're both pixies." Holly was a little taller but even slighter in stature if that was possible.

"So," Marina chimed in, tapping her foot in mock impatience, "are we going to stand around all day discussing our looks, or go see our waterfall?"

"Eww Mar, you be-otch," Macey laughed and poked her in the side.

They headed down to the river bed and began their trek towards the great falls, a much taller version of the one Anna had been soaking in before they arrived and therefore the main attraction, although privately Anna preferred the entrance falls. There was just something less tame about them-explosive and wild, the way she secretly wanted her life to be. Glancing around at her friends she wondered if any of them felt the same.

Over the years of their friendship, particularly once they'd turned sixteen and could drive themselves, they'd spent a great deal of time at this particular park. So much time it had begun to feel like an extension of their backyards. The previous year had rend some changes in that routine however, since she and Holly had graduated a year before the others and Holly now resided in the state of North Carolina where she attended college during the school term. Their group of six had become five for a time and they'd all felt the loss.

Anna had continued to live at home, taking some courses at the local community college, but she was currently toying with the idea of moving to California once the summer ended. Macey would be relocating to Buffalo for university and Jenna was considering the same....soon they would be living separate lives. It was equal parts exciting and profoundly sad, the duality giving her a head spin.

When they reached their destination they all stopped to pay homage to the great waters rushing down from high above. Though it was narrow, the sheer height from which it fell was greater than that of Niagara Falls making it impressive in its own right. Sometimes, when there were few people around, they would swim at the base of it. Today the park was busy and they would not escape notice if they were to jump in with their typical banshee cries so they restricted themselves to the benches that lined the wooden railing.

Their conversation consisted mainly of their impending trip to Europe. The journey overseas would begin in two weeks, a mere two days after the remaining four girls received their diplomas. They had been planning their great escape for a year and it was hard for them to believe it was almost here.

The vacation would center in London, with side trips to France, Ireland and Italy. At first they had thought to stay in Paris for the greater part of it, but the language barrier presented a problem. They'd finally agreed on five days each in Paris, Venice, and Dublin, the remaining two weeks would be spent partying at the famous English pubs and clubs in and around London town. Initially they'd intended for their trip to last the entire summer, but Holly had an internship, Jess a job obligation (bleh), and Macey's parents wanted her home for a bit before she moved into the college dorm-so they'd narrowed it down to a month.

"Sooo, are we ready to head back?" Macey inched in that direction indicating that *she* was and they all stood. Macey was never overtly demanding, she would always tell you what she wanted in a question, but after years of friendship they all knew that when she was done with a particular place she would become mildly and increasingly irritated if they continued to stay.

They walked back through the canyon continuing their discussion of Europe. Holly had been doing her research (she could always be counted on for that, organization and planning were her specialties) and she had an itinerary made up for them. Anna insisted however, that they leave some things blank. She liked surprises and doing things in a fly by night fashion, as did Marina which was evidenced in nearly every one of their excursions.

When they were once again at the grassy field that led to the parking area, Anna halted to salute her entrance waterfalls and turned to the girls with an expression of thoughtfulness. "Isn't it amazing how two hundred years from now, barring any major catastrophes, that water will still be pouring down over those rocks?"

"You think too much," Marina grinned, pushing her playfully.

She shrugged, smiling back. *Well I think it's cool*, she thought defensively, *it's just too bad I won't be around to see it*.

Chapter Three

When they arrived at Anna's house the girls busied themselves getting ready for the party.

They were having a pre-graduation bash since they wouldn't be around long after the momentous day-and because Anna's dad was not at home her abode was the logical choice.

Anna brushed a hand over a picture of her father as she made her way to her bedroom to change.

As a photojournalist Marty Preston had once spent most of his time in the remote areas of the world, a lifestyle that had abruptly changed when he'd met Anna's mother Emma. For sixteen years he had stayed local to be with his little family, until three years earlier when an accident had taken Emma's life and he'd become a shell of the man he once was. In the months following the accident he had tried to be there for Anna, but after awhile it had become apparent that he was more dead than alive. So he'd re-established some old connections and went back to working all over the globe. At sixteen years of age she had been able to care for herself, but it was still hard, she often felt as if she'd lost both parents instead of only one.

It was lucky for her that her mom had been the kind of person who believed that life was not a given and had taught her to expect the unexpected and deal with all that came her way with optimism. "It's all in how we perceive it Anna Banana," she would say, "if your house burns down you can be devastated by the loss or excited at the prospect of building something new. Personally I strongly believe in the latter, and that my darling is how I expect you to live-with great hope and a sense of possibility, always seeking the light at the end of the tunnel or a glimpse of the sun breaking through the clouds. Because believe me there will be plenty of cloudy days. You can wish the rain would go away, or you can dance in it." And the two of them had danced in the rain often in her young life, both literally and figuratively. She missed her mom desperately but refused to give in to the grief, wanting to honor her life and memory by following her advice. She often wondered if somewhere deep down her mother had known that she would be taken early, if perhaps she'd lived and believed the things she did because of it. She also wondered if her mom would approve of the trip she was taking.

Shortly after her mother's death she'd learned that the grandparents she had never known had been deliriously wealthy and had left every penny of their vast inheritance to her. George and Karen Tyler had been bluebloods, coming from "old money" and when their only child had decided to marry "beneath" her they'd all but disowned her. Apparently they had completely changed their position once Anna had come into the picture, but right before her second birthday a sailing accident had claimed their lives and a reading of the will had named her their sole heir.

The money had been held in a trust by her mom until her death, then it had transferred to Anna's father who wanted absolutely nothing to do with it. He had immediately hired a financial manager and the moment Anna turned eighteen it had been transferred to her. Her dad had simply said "It's yours by birthright sweetheart, it's more than enough to keep you living large for the rest of your days. Just try and always keep in mind that money isn't everything. I trust I've trained you well as to the important things in life, I'm sure for you it will only make life sweeter."

After that brief little pep talk he hadn't spoken of it again, and when she'd tried to ask him for advice on spending he'd simply shaken his head and shrugged. The financial manager had a lot to say about it on the other hand, but he was so boring and practical she ended up deciding she would figure things out as she went.

Her first big spending spree had occurred the previous summer when she and the girls had rented an R.V. and toured the country. They had alternately stayed in campsites and fancy hotels making for an incredible experience, and it was during that trip that they had begun planning this one.

She finished dressing and headed back downstairs, hearing Macey's happy voice coming from the kitchen.

"I have ten CD's of party music set and ready to go," her friend announced.

"Awesome, Jess is talking to Jim who is picking up the alcohol as we speak," Jenna stated with a grin as Anna walked into the room.

Anna grinned in return. She strongly believed there was something about drinking under the legal age that made it more fun. She also felt if they were to change the age to what it should be (either 18 or when your parents gave the okay) there would be a lot less problems associated with it. She never could understand how a person could be old enough to fight in a war but too young to drink a beer. In Europe it would not be illegal, in fact she'd heard that in places like Ireland you could order a drink if you could see over the bar.

"So what's he getting?" she asked.

"Everything we asked for-a keg of amber, wine coolers for the wimps like Jess, and a variety of bottles of liquor and soda." Jenna dodged Jess as she attempted to smack her for the comment.

Anna laughed, shaking her head. "Okay let's see...I have the table set up for beer pong on the second deck, the hoist deck is set with the stereo, the neighbors are apprised of what's going on and the food just needs to be brought down along with the coolers of ice." She ticked each item off on her fingers.

Her house was located across the street from the lake and they had a two story set of stairs complete with decks leading down to the rocky beach. They also had a deck on top of the boat hoist that her father had ingeniously built at the end of their long dock.

"What about karaoke?" Jess asked.

"Oh yeah baby, that's set up with the stereo," Anna winked at her friend. The girl really loved to sing.

"I can't believe your neighbors don't care that you're having a big party," Jess stated.

"Well my dad talked to them, and as long as everyone who comes either has a D.D. or stays the night, it's A-OK."

"I'm surprised *your* parents are okay with this," Marina said to Macey.

Macey smiled her typical mischief smile. "They don't mind if I drink as long as I'm responsible and I don't get in a car, and since I can walk home from here that's obviously not an issue."

"Walk? You could crawl home from here," Anna interjected. Macey's house was located about a hundred yards away on the lake side of the street. "Which is exactly what you'll be doing if I make your drinks," she joked.

"Still, they always seem to treat you like a child," Marina insisted.

Macey waved her hand dismissively, "Nah, they're getting better, I'm graduating after all."

Holly clapped her hands for attention, "Okay girls come on, we have to start bringing the food down."

There was a chorus of "yes ma'am's," and they got to work.

On their second trip down the stairs Anna found herself being lifted into the air from behind.

"Austin, put me down," she laughed.

"Give me that," he took the cooler from her, "as klutzy as you are I would hate to spend your party at the hospital for a broken leg." He mock played falling down the stairs and she made a face at him. He laughed and waggled his eyebrows before jogging down ahead of her.

"Yo Anna, where can I set up the horseballs?"

Anna turned to see Nate, Austin's closest friend as well as the guy Jess was currently crushing on, calling to her from the top of the stairs.

"The shore is wide enough, just bring the equipment down, you can bury the posts in the rocks," she called back.

"A'ight."

She continued down the stairs musing about whether or not the twenty first century version of horseshoes would end up replacing the much older game. Anna personally preferred it because it required a little less accuracy, though she imagined veteran players would turn the nose up at it for the same reason.

The small group quickly finished setting things up as more people began to arrive.

Anna bent down to retrieve a cup and a blush spread over her face as she sensed Austin's eyes on her. She wasn't the type to be easily offended, but embarrassed? Yeah, every little thing of a potentially sexual nature had her reddening instantly. Annoying, that's what it was. She made a production of straightening stuff out on the table so he wouldn't see her burning face.

"Your ears are all red," he stated.

Busted. "Yeah well, if your eyes had fingers, my bum would be red," she shot back.

He laughed. "I can't help it that my eyes have such good taste."

He was hovering over her shoulder so she pushed back against him. "Personal space, ever heard of it?"

"Okay, all right, you don't have to get all snippy."

"Snippy? Did you seriously say snippy?" She giggled and faced him. He was smiling back, but he had a peculiar expression in his eyes that belied his feelings to be other than light. She shifted uncomfortably hoping this was NOT the moment he chose to bear his heart. He reached around her and grabbed two cups, the look disappearing.

"What's your poison today?"

"Beer, definitely no liquor for me."

"Aww, come on, do you mean to tell me that a little bitty hangover has got you scared?"

"That was no bitty hangover, it was a mongo hangover from hell thank you very much, and it's not fear but self preservation. I would really like to get up tomorrow without puking."

He grinned at her as they headed over to the keg. Nate and a couple of others had beat them to it, so Anna left it to Austin to get her drink. She made her way over to Jess who was making eyes at Nate in a less than subtle manner.

"Obvious much?" Anna whispered, raising a brow. She took Jess by the elbow and led her down the beach.

When they were far enough away Jess burst out, "God, I know, I can't stop staring at him! I never noticed how freakin' cute he was! I want him to kiss me so bad right now."

Anna rolled her eyes, her lips twitching in amusement, "Weren't you just saying that about Brent Regault?"

"Oh yuck, I don't know what I was thinking, he is *so* gross."

Anna tittered. "Gross? I don't know if I'd go that far, he's kinda cute."

"Yeah, until you kiss him and he slobbers all over your face!"

"Oh, eww, that is gross. So I take it Nate is a good kisser?"

"Yes!" Jess grabbed her arm a little too enthusiastically, "He was so gentle, but forceful at the same time, it's hard to explain, but the way he touched my face, and then he put his hands in my hair, and he tasted like spearmint..."

She gushed on and on and Anna found herself wishing she could feel like that about someone, anyone. Jenna criticized her sister for flitting from one guy to the next, but Anna honestly loved that about her, she was even a little envious. To experience those feelings of excitement over and over, there was magic in that. Someday she was fairly certain Jess would settle down, but right now she was young, so why rush it? It's not as if she was sleeping with these guys, and how long did you have where you could just kiss your partners without it leading to something further?

Jenna walked over, her expression stating an acute desire to slap her sister and Anna put up a hand to stop the acid words before they came. Jenna sighed, snorted, and then grudgingly smiled. It was only Jess that made her react like that, if any of the rest of them were crushing on someone she would find it amusing. Not that Anna didn't get it. She loved Jess dearly but the girl had a tendency towards mood swings and she harbored no illusions about how difficult they would be to live with.

Austin made his way over to them and handed her a beer. "So what are we pow-wowing about? Wouldn't have anything to do with my buddy over there, hmm?"

Jess pounced on him immediately, "What did he say? Did he tell you about it? Does he like me?"

Austin chuckled, "Easy there cowgirl, yes, he's definitely into you. But he's Nate, not particularly demonstrative in that way."

"Demon-what?" Jess wrinkled her forehead.

Anna laughed loudly at her expression. "He means that he's not the type to talk seriously about it or come over and start quoting love poems to you."

"O-kaaay, so what did he say?"

Austin took several gulps of his beer then smiled at her patiently. "I believe his exact words were, 'Damn that girl is fii-iine'."

By the look on his face Anna knew he had edited that a bit.

Jess smiled broadly. "So what should I do? Should I go over there, or wait for him to come to me?"

"Oh come on Jess, you know it's always better to make them come to you." Holly said as she joined them, getting the gist immediately.

"Yeah but I'm not patient," Jess pouted making them all laugh.

There was a loud chorus of "It's Party Time!!" shouted from the top of the deck stairs and they looked up to see about twenty or so kids making their way down.

"Well, I think it's time to get this party started," Austin stated.

He set about organizing the games and shouted over the noise, "I have two lists for balls and pong, if you wanna play, getcha' names on them!"

"This is gonna be a total blow out," Macey stated as she grabbed Anna's arm and dragged her towards the dock.

"What are we doing!" Anna shouted over the music which had just been turned up.

"We're going on the first boat ride, I formed a list for that earlier!"

"Oh, good thinking!"

She had a decent sized speedboat, it fit ten people comfortably and could get up to 60 mph, which in an open boat was really zipping along.

"I'm driving," Macey announced to the group that had formed.

There were no arguments and they clambered in, Anna making her way up to her favorite seat at the front. She loved the wind hitting her in the face as they skimmed the surface of the water.

Her friend Geordy flopped down next to her smiling widely. "Hey Bo-nana, how's it goin'? Awesome party!"

"Great, and yeah I know!" There were a couple more hours of daylight, and there was already about forty people on the beach. As they pulled away from the hoist she stood and waved to the shore dramatically shouting "Bon Voyage, We'll miss you!"

Geordy grabbed her arm and pulled her down, "You're gonna fall over the side!"

"Nah, I always stand up!"

"And you haven't gone in the drink? *You,* the world's biggest klutz?"

She slapped at him, "Stop teasing me! Why does everyone say that, I'm not that bad...anymore," she amended.

"Yeah, uh huh, keep telling yourself that."

"I really like the goatee," she said, smoothly changing the subject. He had started growing it a few months ago and it definitely made him look older. Without it his boyish face had him at a perpetual fifteen.

"Thanks, it's pretty chill right?"

"Definitely."

They chatted about nothing in particular and twenty minutes later Macey turned the boat back in the direction of the hoist. Anna was in mid-sentence when she looked towards the shore and felt her heart do a stutter step.

Not now, she thought with an inner cringe, *and not here*. She closed her eyes tightly and looked again. Gone.

"You all right, you look a little pale?" Geordy leaned towards her.

She forced a laugh, "Fine, just had a little vertigo all of a sudden, weird."

Geordy was studying her, eyes narrowed doubtfully.

God what had she looked like? She smiled wider, "Seriously G, I just got a little dizzy for a sec."

"Kay, if you're sure."

She stood as the boat slowed and drew in a deep breath letting it out in a rush before plastering her face with a smile. She kept the smile fixed as she scanned the shoreline for more signs of them. The shadow men. Trying not to shiver with the thought, she disguised her nervousness by climbing hastily onto the dock.

"Anna, you don't have to get off," Macey yelled to her over the music, "I'm going to keep driving!"

"I want to, but you go ahead, I know you love it!" She shouted back.

Geordy linked his arm through hers and they headed up the dock together.

"Would you get me a refill?" She asked him, pushing her cup in his hand, "I need to use the Ladies'."

They had rented a port-a-potty for the night in order to keep the party out of her house. It was set up a ways down the beach and she made her way towards it greeting people as she went. Once inside she locked the door and lined the seat sitting heavily. She didn't need to use it, she just needed to clear her head.

The shadow men. She had first seen them shortly after her sixteenth birthday. If they hadn't appeared until after her mom's death she might have attributed it to a trauma induced hallucination, but that wasn't the case. Her first sighting had been at a train station about a month or so before her mother's accident. There had been two of them, and at first she'd thought her eyes were playing tricks on her. When they were still there after some vigorous rubbing she'd sat staring at them numbly as a chill made its way up her spine.

In both cases they had seemed to be tracking someone. They had no real definite shape, just fluid blackness like a person's distorted shadow. One had passed so close to her that she could feel its presence, an evil malice filled thing that made her mouth go dry and her skin crawl. She couldn't tell if it knew she was staring since there weren't any features, but the person it was following had seemed terribly agitated. He'd turned to her and said, "What are you looking at?" in such a way it had made her shrink into the bench mumbling "sorry" and "nothing."

Then more had appeared until she thought she might run screaming from the building, at which point she'd mentally shouted "NO MORE, I DON'T WANT TO SEE

THEM", and shut her eyes. That time when she'd reopened them, they were gone. From then on it was always like that. Any time she spotted them she would squeeze her eyes shut and will them away.

She hadn't told a single soul about them. She'd considered it time after time, telling her dad, telling the girls or Austin, but when she played out the conversation in her head....yeah, she sounded nuts. So she'd half convinced herself they were figments of her over-active imagination. She had *never* seen them in a group of teens before now, and them being HERE, on *her* beach was not a good sign. Not a good sign at all. The shadow men, (*demons* her mind supplied as it always did, and she shut the thought down as she always did) are growing in numbers, she thought grimly. And they were.

In the beginning she had only ever seen them when she'd been in or near a city. Recently she'd seen them in her town. And *now* they were on her *freaking beach*, THE BASTARDS!

Oh how she wished she had told her mother about them. She might have been able to make sense of it since she'd believed wholeheartedly in the supernatural. She wouldn't have thought her daughter was crazy. In fact it was the notion that her mom would have not only believed her but even had an explanation for it that kept her from feeling crazy, especially after the airport incident six months earlier.

She had been waiting for her dad to fly in from Tibet and had wandered into the airport bar when she saw him. A guy (HOLY GOD, HIS EYES ARE BLACK) wearing a professional suit, briefcase, and a charming smile, flirting with the bartender. And his eyes were *all black*, even where the whites should have been. She had turned away from him after the initial shock, praying he hadn't noticed her, and then someone had touched her shoulder and she'd nearly screamed.

Her dad had turned her around to face him and she'd hugged him tightly, mumbling how much she'd missed him into his coat sleeve. After a minute or so she'd gained courage from his presence and looked at the guy again. Brown eyes, normal, nothing strange about him. And then she had looked away and thought, "I want to see it" and just like an on and off switch they were black again. She had quickly turned it "off" and pulled her dad away.

She knew that what she had witnessed that day was a shadow man possession. What she didn't know was why. Why did she see these things? What was the point, what could she possibly do besides scare herself?

Well at least I would not be suckered into flirting with him like that bartender, she thought with a sigh. She had watched the news for days afterwards, convinced the woman's face would be on it with the headline "Serial Killer On The Loose." But it hadn't happened and she'd pushed it to the back of her mind.

Someone knocked and she realized she'd been in there awhile. She stood and pushed open the door- Geordy, crap.

"Okay seriously, what's wrong Anna, are you getting sick?"

She took the drink from him and shook her head. "I told you I just got a little dizzy, really it's nothing to worry about, I probably just need to eat something."

He followed her back to the food table, and she started getting irritated. She liked him but he was definitely interested in her a great deal more than she was him, and they didn't have the kind of friendship to impart confidences, particularly of this nature. She scanned the people for her friends, trying to find a tactful way to ditch him.

Austin came striding over. "'Sup Geordy."

"Hey man."

Anna looked from one to the other, mentally rolling her eyes at their silent pissing contest.

"Something's wrong with Anna," Geordy stated.

She shot Geordy a dirty look.

Austin's brows arched. "What do you mean?"

"She got all pale on the boat ride, looked like she'd seen a ghost, fo' real, then she just spent like ten minutes in the john."

Austin was looking closely at her now and she grabbed his arm pulling him away from Geordy. She leaned up and whispered, "I'll tell you about it later-can you help me ditch him, but nicely?" She knew the request would distract him and it worked like a charm. His chest even seemed to puff out with the "I'm the Winner" thing that guys did.

"Look man," he told Geordy, "she doesn't wanna talk about it. Don't worry, she's in good hands."

A hurt look flashed across Geordy's face.

"I said *nicely*," she whispered fiercely. She stepped away from Austin and gave Geordy a quick hug. "I appreciate your concern, but really I'm okay. Don't feel bad, I just don't want to talk about it, I'd rather party like it's 1999," she grinned reassuringly.

"That's cool. Do you wanna be my pong partner?" he asked hopefully.

Austin stepped in between them, "She already has a partner," he stated and steered her away. He looked a little pissed, probably because of the hug, but that was his fault.

"Where are you leading me?"

"Away from him like you asked, remember?"

"Oh yes, I remember the word nicely too."

"So? The guy's hot for you, do you really want him puppy dogging you all night?"

She shook her head, "No, but I don't want to make him feel bad either."

"Whatever."

"Okay, so now you're mad at me for not wanting to stomp on his poor little heart."

"I'm not mad, Christ."

"Ohhhh yeah, because you *usually* swear at me when you're not mad."

"Anna....hey look, it's your girls." They stopped in front of Marina and Jenna. "I'll find you when it's our turn for pong, okay?"

She looked up at him questioningly. He bent down and kissed her forehead, an 'everything is cool' gesture, then saluted the girls and took off in the direction of the horseballs game. She followed his progress thinking....thinking what?

"He really is good-looking isn't he." It wasn't a question, and the surprised looks on the faces of her friends told her she'd spoken aloud.

"Whoa, are you actually considering-"Jenna started.

"You and Austin?" Marina cut in.

She shook her head to clear it. "I don't know. Maybe. I don't know, bleh."

Jenna giggled and started to say something but was interrupted by Jess calling Anna's name. They turned towards her and saw her standing near the dock waving at them frantically.

"What's got her all excited?" Marina laughed.

Jenna and Anna shook their heads in unison and the three of them hurried across the beach to find out.

"Guess what?" Jess whispered excitedly when they reached her. "You are NOT going to believe what I just heard!"

"Out with it!" Anna laughed.

She leaned in, her eyes widening dramatically. "Leo is going to ask you on a date!"

Anna blinked. "What, wait, *Leo*?"

"Yeah, as in Luscious lips Leo, as in Holy Crap he is so freaking hot Leo!"

Leo Giovanni had graduated the year before her and to this day was the most gorgeous guy to ever grace the Halls of Sentinel High. She hadn't even noticed he was here but now that she did, damn. Hot, definitely hot.

"Who told you this?" She asked suspiciously.

"Carrie Wesler, she said she overheard him talking to Bob Billings and he was saying you had the most beautiful eyes he's ever seen, and he's been all over the country, and that he didn't know you well, but you seemed like a sweetheart, and *then* he said he was going to ask you to dinner and a movie!" She took a breath and clasped her hands together.

She was so excited you would think it was her that he was asking. It was a very endearing trait of hers to always be happy for the good fortune of her friends.

"Okay, he hasn't even talked to me...." Anna trailed off as she watched him coming across the beach towards her.

"Oh my God," Jess gripped her arm hard.

"Ouch!"

"Sorry, just OMG."

When he reached them he graced Anna with a very slow, very sexy smile and she briefly wondered if he practiced that expression in front of a mirror. *Has to*, she thought as she stared at him, smiling uncertainly in return.

His dark hair fell over his eyes which were golden with flecks of green on a perfectly sculpted face. He was always dressed sleek, his apparel made you think sports car, and his face made you think (angel).

"Great party Anna," he said holding out his hand in greeting.

"Th-thanks." She took his hand. *Please do NOT stammer like an idiot*, she berated herself.

"Do you play beer pong?"

"Oh, yeah, I love that game, I'm actually pretty good at it." STOP gushing, be cool!

"So...do you wanna be my partner, I'm up next."

"Sure, yeah great. Oh damn, I already told Austin...

"Aww come on, you guys are buds, I'm sure he won't mind, he can find someone else."

She found herself nodding stupidly in agreement as he took her arm to walk her up the stairs. She threw a "Holy shit" look over her shoulder to the girls who were grinning and waving at her.

Austin walked up beside Jenna just in time to see Leo drape his arm around Anna's shoulders and announce their partnership. His expression went from shock to anger, and if you knew him well enough you could see the hurt mingled in with it.

Jenna watched the facial changes and winced. "She tried to tell him she already had a partner, but he just sort of swept her away," she explained.

"Did he." He said flatly.

"She's just flattered, every single dimwit girl in school is flattered when he deigns to talk to them, myself included, something about him..." Jenna trailed off thinking she probably wasn't helping.

"Something about him, yeah, he's an arrogant asshole who treats girls like objects." A muscle ticked in his jaw and he kept his eyes on the pair as he spoke. "Did you know that from his freshmen year on he took bets in September on how many cherries he was going to pop? That's right, and then as he got older it was more specific, certain girls, the more challenging the better. Then he might keep the girl around awhile, but only until his next conquest. He's a fucking predator." He emphasized the last two words and turned to the girls, his expression dark.

Jess frowned, her previous excitement fading into worry. "So you think he's just trying to get Anna into bed? Because I heard from Carrie that he wanted to ask her out for dinner and a movie...

"Carrie? Wesler you mean?" Austin barked a laugh. "That little bitch is probably setting her up."

He spun around and took off across the beach to where Leo's friends were gathered, the girls trailing after him at a discreet distance.

"You got a bet going on boys?" Austin lit a cigarette and grinned wolfishly as he put it between his teeth.

"Bet? I don't know what you mean." Rodney tried for an innocent expression and failed miserably.

"Sure you do, come on, what's the stakes, what's the terms?"

"Why, you want in?" This from Kelley who over compensated for his girlie name with a major macho attitude.

"Hey dude, there is no bet." Rodney shot his friend a warning look.

Austin pulled a wad of money from his wallet. "Don't you like cash?" He held the money up and raised an eyebrow.

"I like cash," Kelley grinned stupidly.

"Don't be an idiot dude, don't you see who followed him over here?" Rodney pointed to where Anna's friends were gathered several yards away.

"Okay," Austin stuffed the money in his pocket and threw up his hands, "you got me. So how about you tell me what this bet is so I don't beat your asses into the ground." He dropped his arms to his sides and flexed his fingers, his eyes narrowed in hostility. He looked so menacing that every girl on the beach who happened to glance his way developed an instant crush.

Rodney snorted, "You and what army?"

They had attracted some attention at this point and Nate came hurrying over with a couple of their friends.

"What's going on here?"

"Rodney is about to learn firsthand what water boarding is if he doesn't start talking NOW, *that's* what the fuck is going on," Austin growled.

"He thinks they made a bet about Anna," Jess jumped in and pointed to where Anna and Leo were playing pong.

"I don't think it, I fucking *know* it!" He broke and rushed Rodney, taking him down to the beach as Nate and the others held Rodney's friends at bay.

Austin raised his fist, calculating his best shot.

"Okay, fuck, yeah we made a stupid bet, but I don't know why you're going after me, it's Leo that's trying to fuck her man, he thinks he can get her in bed if not by the end of tonight then the end of the week, Jesus, get off me!"

Austin climbed to his feet and turned towards the deck stairs. A number of people had crowded around them in an attempt to find out what was going on and he forced his way past them. He looked up at the second deck and locked eyes with Leo who was watching the beach intently. He started in his direction and when he reached the stairs he took them two at a time.

Anna intercepted him placing her hands on his chest, "What are you doing, what's going on?"

He ignored her, staring hard at Leo. "Leave. *Now*."

"Why?" Leo's expression was all innocence. "What did those douche bags say? Don't listen to them...

Austin picked Anna up and placed her behind him then stalked towards Leo who threw his hands in the air.

"Come on man, what's your problem?"

In a movement almost too fast to follow Austin's fist caught Leo on the jaw line with a resounding crack and sent him flying into the stairs behind him.

Leo scrambled up a few steps holding his face as Austin advanced with his arm cocked back for another shot.

"All right, shit, I'm going, I'm going!"

Austin halted with his fist in the air and Leo turned and ran up the stairs, skating a glance over his shoulder to make sure he wasn't being followed. When he reached the top he hollered for his posse before disappearing from view.

Anna, who had watched the scene unfold in startled confusion, finally recovered and turned on Austin. "Please tell me what the HELL that was about! Jealousy? So another guy can't talk to me or flirt with me because you're jealous? Do I have to warn every guy I meet that my best friend might beat them up if they stand too close?" She heard her voice rising and couldn't seem to stop even when she noted the flash of hurt in his eyes.

He didn't reply, just stared at her with an unreadable expression. He shook his head and took a breath before turning and jogging back down the stairs.

She watched as he leapt off the last couple of steps feeling a sudden wave of dizziness. She had drunk the equivalent of two beers in ten minutes and the alcohol chose that moment to dive-bomb her head. She sat on a chair trying to get a hold of her runaway emotions. *Come on light weight*, she scolded, *you've only had four beers total*. But she knew that wasn't really it.

Jenna and Marina sat down next to her. "He made a bet about you," Jenna said quietly.

She looked at her questioningly.

"Leo bet his friends he'd have you either tonight or by the end of the week, and when I say have you I mean *have you*."

Anna snorted. That would most definitely *not* have happened. As flattered as she initially was from his interest, within a few minutes of listening to him talk she knew he was not for her. Which was partially why she was upset, it was frustrating to not be able to give in to just a little bit of crushing. What would be the big deal if she made out with a guy that she knew was not in her future?

She winced, realizing she had just shouted at her knight in shining armor. "How did he find out?" she asked sheepishly.

"I guess Leo's pretty famous for making bets like that, so when he saw him with you...well he made the jackass's friends 'fess up." Jenna patted her arm then gave her an earnest look. "I know that we can't force our feelings, but seriously Anna, you might want to consider it. He looked extremely hot taking Rodney down!"

"Yeah he did," Marina agreed, "manly."

Anna smiled a little. "I know, he looked pretty hot taking out Leo too." Her smile faded and she blew out a puff of air in frustration. "I don't know what's wrong with me. It's just that we've been friends for so long and I know that if we don't make it as a couple our friendship will be over...and that really sucks."

"I hate to break it to you sweetie, but I have a feeling your friendship will end eventually no matter what," Jenna told her.

"Why?"

"He wants to be with you, and the friend thing is definitely wearing him out. So you're either going to give the relationship thing a try....or he's going to let you go. Don't ask how I know, I can just....see it."

Anna didn't question further, Jenna had an uncanny way of knowing things like that. "Okay, understood, but I can't decide right now. I want to drink some more, and have some fun. Beer pong partner?"

Jenna nodded and as they set up their cups Anna heard the sound of a motor and turned to watch Macey pull the boat into the hoist. The sun was setting and she could just make out her friend waving up to them through the glare. She waved back and scanned the beach locating Austin who was lounging in the center of a crowd of people. She could tell they were talking about the fight from his repeated slaps on the back.

She watched as a girl from her graduating class, Gina Rollins, walked up to him and looped an arm through his, leaning up to whisper in his ear. Anna stiffened as she felt her very own first taste of jealousy. Suddenly she realized it had been a long time since she'd seen him with a girl who was not among her friends. And she definitely didn't like it.

"Anna, get your head in the game!" Jenna waved a hand in front of her face and she forced her attention back to the table, but her gaze kept getting pulled back to Gina's form draped all over Austin.

They lost the game, big surprise, and she continued watching the beach. The fact that she didn't like the shallow little backstabber was not helping. "Who invited *her*," She mumbled irritably.

Jenna followed her gaze. "Smart boy."

"What?"

"You heard me. A little taste of your own medicine. Now I suggest, since the game is over..." she paused to let the double meaning sink in, "you go down there and stake your claim."

Anna hesitated, taking a deep breath, before heading down the stairs to change her life. Dramatic, yes, but that's how it felt.

She made her way over to where Austin was seated and nearly lost her nerve as she stopped in front of the campfire. The disgusting girl (pretty, yes she was pretty, but only on the outside) was in his lap and she sucked in a breath as he glanced up at her. He was extremely handsome by firelight. She mouthed "I'm sorry" and he nodded briefly before returning his attention to the kid sitting next to him. Damn, he was going to make her beg for it.

She sat down on the rocks and picked up a stick to poke at the fire. She imagined it getting nice and red and "accidentally" touching Gina's leg which was currently rubbing up and down on Austin's.

"So Anna," Gina spoke up in her fake sweet voice, "how did it feel to be the object of Leo's bet you poor thing."

Anna rolled her eyes. "Since there is no possible way he would have won that bet, despite what little faith some of my friends seem to have in me, 'poor thing' is a little much."

"Oh come on," Big Mouth pushed, "tell me you weren't eating right out of his hand before this guy," she patted Austin's leg, "saved the day."

"Hmm, let's see…halfway between 'Last week I got so drunk I fucking puked in my neighbor's bird bath' -and-'I got some wicked stuff last night, I couldn't even tie my shoes I was so zooted'- I pretty much decided his looks can only make up for so much. So, that would be a No, no hand-eating for me."

She snuck a look at Austin, who was watching her intently. Dropping the stick in the fire, she pulled herself to her feet. "Can I talk to you?" Please don't say no, please don't…

He didn't answer right away, and she felt her stomach tighten. If he humiliated her in front of Gina she was pretty sure it would be the end of them. "Austin," she said quietly. "Please."

He lightly pushed Gina, who pouted but got to her feet. "I'll keep your seat warm," she sang as he walked over to Anna.

She grabbed his hand and led him farther down the beach, past the potty, around the large bush that hung out over the lake, and stopped at the crumbling stone fort. No one at the party had discovered it yet for which she was exceedingly grateful. She let go of his hand and looked out over the water.

"So what is it?" He asked. He turned her to face him and she chewed on her lip not knowing how to proceed. He started to say something else, but she stopped him by reaching up and touching his cheek. She searched his eyes which were narrowed in temporary confusion and watched as they gradually widened in understanding.

"I…" she got no further. Austin took his opportunity and leaned down, pressing his lips on hers. She wrapped her arms around his neck pulling him closer and he backed her up into the stone wall. His tongue darted into her mouth and she tentatively touched it with her own which seemed to set off fireworks for him. Next thing she knew he was lifting her up and wrapping her legs around his waist, sandwiching her between his body and the wall. It felt amazing to be this close to him, especially since the slide of his tongue was distracting her from thinking.

"Wha-whoa, what have we got here?" Geordy. Of course.

They broke the kiss but Austin kept her where she was, like he was afraid if he let her down she'd run away. Which...her heart was racing so hard she might have done just that.

"Do you need something?" Austin cocked a brow at Geordy.

"Nah, I'm cool. So the two of you, huh? I guess everyone saw that coming." He was slurring a bit and holding a bottle of J.D.

Austin raised his brows, his expression clearly stating his irritation with the interruption, but Geordy wasn't reading facial expressions in his current state.

"Well, maybe not everyone," he slurred, "'cause, see I thought you guys would just stay buddies, you know, and like I really like her, Anna I really like you, it's true." He took a long drink from his bottle and Anna could feel Austin taking a deep breath, getting ready to put her down.

She gripped his arms. "He's really drunk, I don't want you to hurt him, he's harmless."

He rolled his eyes at her and turned to the swaying Geordy. "Look G, I'm sorry she's not interested in you that way, but we're kind of in the middle of something, so can we talk about it later?"

"Oh. Yeah, sure, I mean, who cares how I'm feeling anyway, right?" He staggered and tripped over a rock landing in the lake.

"Shit," Austin said. He put her down and strode over. He frowned down at the capsized Geordy for a second before grabbing his arm and pulling him up. Geordy yanked back landing himself right back in the water.

"Dude, I'm just helping you up."

"I don't want your help. I want her help." He pointed at Anna.

"Anna, no." Austin gave her a meaningful look and turned back to Geordy. "You're wasted numb nuts, so either you accept my help gracefully or I throw your dumb ass over my shoulder and toss you in the boathouse. Your choice." He held out a hand again and Geordy took it, grumbling under his breath.

Once on his feet he wobbled a bit but somehow managed to make it back around the bush.

"Where were we?" Austin started to pick her up again but Geordy had attracted attention and they were interrupted by a loud group.

"Hey guys, what's doin'?" Nate was among them along with Jess who was attached to his hand and giggling.

"Are we interrupting something?" Jess asked waggling her eyebrows suggestively.

"Actually..."

"No!" Anna jumped in. Austin looked down at her and gave a brief nod before striding away.

"Wait, where are you going?" She followed him making a grab for his arm.

He stopped and glared down at her, his pale green eyes narrowed, "Away from you."

"But I didn't mean it like that!"

"Then what exactly did you mean?" he demanded.

"I just didn't want to be teased, okay? It was a big moment for me, and I didn't want Jess to ruin it with..." she hand gestured in frustration, the right words eluding her.

He shook his head, folding his arms across his broad chest. "It's inevitable that the girls will tease you."

She sighed dramatically, "I know, I know, but just not right then. Can we go upstairs or something?"

The anger faded from his expression replaced with something else, something that made her stomach flutter. His eyes traveled her body and her face flamed making him laugh. He grabbed her hand and pulled her through the throng of people and up the stairs, not stopping until they'd reached her back porch.

She unlocked the door and he practically pushed her through it, lifting her and heading to the couch. She wanted to tell him to slow down, but his mouth captured her words and she forgot everything including her name when he landed her on the cushions and pinned her beneath him. She started to think he should be heavy, but lost the thought as his hand traveled up and down her thigh.

He kissed her softly for a moment before increasing the pressure and then his lips traveled down her neck sending little shock waves of pleasure down her skin. One particular spot felt so good she barely suppressed a moan. He had one hand cradling the back of her head while the other traveled from her thigh and up the side of her body, making its way under her shirt. When she felt it skim the bottom of her bra she jumped, logic breaking through the runaway hormones.

"Austin, too fast," she said in a small voice.

His hand stilled and he lifted off her to look at her face. He was breathing heavily and he closed his eyes for a minute. "Sorry, I know, you're right. It's just, I've wanted you for so long..."

"And now you have me, so we can take it slow, right?"

"Do I? Do I have you?" He searched her face.

She smiled at him and ran a finger along his jaw line. "Let's just say it wasn't easy to tell you to stop."

His expression went from earnest to teasing. "Oh no?"

"What you were doing felt good."

A purely masculine smile formed on his lips. "How good?"

"You're making me blush again."

He laughed. "Like that's hard."

She giggled and he kissed her chin then sat up and pulled her into his lap, cupping her face. "I've dreamt about this moment, I know that sounds ridiculously corny, but it's true."

She was seated sideways on his legs and she looked down at her hands.

"It's okay, I know you haven't, but tell me what changed your mind." He stroked his fingers down her cheek and she shivered a little.

"I guess...Leo kept putting his hand on my butt and it made me want to slap him..."

Austin tensed. "I should not have let him walk away," he growled.

"I'm not finished."

He nodded for her to go on with narrowed eyes.

"And then his conversation was so immature and stupid...and I just kept thinking about you, comparing him to you. And he, who is supposed to be this ideal in our tiny circle of the world, fell short. Way short."

"Then why did you react like that, when I hit him? You wanted to slap him but you yelled at me for punching him?" he raised a brow.

"Because just before you came up the stairs I realized I might want something more with you, and it was a Huge realization, and I was overwhelmed, and I didn't understand what was going on...I don't know, I'm really sorry. What you did was awesome and I love you for it, even without knowing your reasons I would have known there *was* a reason, but I was startled....and then I saw Gina hanging on you, and I actually wanted to hurt her!"

He grinned and she smacked her hand against his shoulder. "You were trying to make me jealous," she accused.

"Maybe," he agreed, still smiling.

"I'm scared though." She looked down at her hands.

"Of what?"

"Of losing you as my friend."

He frowned. "You think we won't be friends if we're dating?"

"I think that we're young. And things happen...

He grabbed her wrists. "Stop. Don't do that, don't peer into the non-existent crystal ball. We might not work out, that's true, but if we don't try then we'll never know. I know it bugs you when the girls tell you not to think so much, but seriously Anna, sometimes you just have to go with the flow instead of analyzing everything."

She looked away from him, and he swore under his breath before wrapping his arms around her and kissing her again. When she tried to pull away he gently but firmly kept her there until she gave in and kissed him back.

He broke the kiss and took hold of her arms holding her away from him. "Do you like this?"

She nodded, swallowing hard.

"Then do me a favor, and just go with it. Pretend there is no future, that every day is your potential last, and just…

"Okay," she broke in, "okay. Let's go back to the party now, because I think too much alone time with you could be hazardous."

He laughed, "Hazardous?"

She narrowed her eyes. *Live in the moment, huh?* She smiled slyly and placed her hand on his erection. "I've heard blue balls can be a very painful condition." She jumped up quickly and ran for the door.

He caught her just outside making her squeal as he whirled her up into his arms. "That was very bad little girl, I think you should be sent to your room. With me in it."

"Ha ha, nice try. Put me down."

He dropped her on her feet and wrapped his arm around her waist.

Chapter Four

For the next couple of hours he seemed to be everywhere she was, and she wasn't sure if she liked it. Two hours into their new relationship, her first relationship, and she was already confused about her feelings. On one hand she had loved kissing him, on the other she didn't like being so monopolized.

He sensed something was up and whispered "What's wrong?"

She shook her head and shrugged then downed another cup of...what was she drinking now? Oh yeah, rum and coke. "I'm getting a little drunk," she supplied in answer. Actually she was hoping the alcohol might help. "I need another," she told him, her speech slightly slurred.

"Maybe you should slow down."

She scowled up at him. "What are you my dad now?" His face darkened and she pulled away from him and strode to the table where the liquor was.

After she replaced her drink she found Macey and latched onto her arm. "All done riding, errr...driving the boat?"

"Uh huh, whew Anna, are you drunk?" Macey teased.

"I think maybe so, and I pissed Austin off again. I am turning out to be a bad girlfriend already."

"Hey Austin," Macey said over her shoulder in warning.

"Hey. Can I borrow her?"

Anna turned and rolled her eyes at him, "Shouldn't you be asking me that? Macey isn't my keeper any more than you are."

"What exactly is your problem?"

"You. You are hovering. I don't like hovering." She fell back a step, her drink sloshing in her glass.

"Great. So now you're drunk and pissy."

"I am not pissy! I am merely trying to tell you that you are overbearing me. Err, you are being overbearing."

"Okay. Right." He turned and walked off and she watched him go, wincing inwardly.

"That didn't go very well," she grumbled.

Macey laughed. "I think you are messing with that poor boy's head."

"I don't mean to!" She insisted, sloshing more of her drink. "I just...I..." she froze suddenly, the words evaporating on her tongue.

They were here again, and there were half a dozen at least.

She stumbled backward a step and squeezed her eyes shut telling them to be gone. She took a deep breath and opened them back up. They were still there. *Oh God.* She tried again and again, but they wouldn't go away. The alcohol seemed to be screwing with her "off" button.

"Anna what's wrong, are you gonna pass out?" Macey asked anxiously.

She shook her head and backed away even more. Three of the shadows passed right in front of her and the guys they were dogging started shouting across the beach. A fight broke out and Austin, Nathan, and a few of their football buddies ran into the melee to break it up.

The entire time it was happening Anna stood watching in frozen horror. It appeared as if the shadow men were *driving* the kids involved, undulating and pulsating bigger and bigger. She started shaking and even when the fight broke apart she couldn't stop. She numbly watched as Jenna ran past her down the dock and a minute later the radio was turned down. Several minutes after that Austin and the girls arranged for the problem starters to be taken home, but a few of the shadows still lingered and she could not make them disappear. Her legs finally gave way and she sank down on the dock, burying her head in her arms.

"Anna, what's wrong?" Jess hurried over. "The fight's over, they're leaving, it's okay."

She nodded without looking up, hot tears squeezing out of the corners of her eyes. Crying was extremely rare for her, but fear and revulsion had created a pressure inside her chest that required relief. "Can you get Austin for me," she mumbled to Jess.

A minute later she felt his presence and peered up at him through blurred vision. His expression changed from unreadable to alarm and she held her arms up to him like a child, making her earlier "dad" accusation seem a bit foolish. When he lifted her up she buried her face in his neck.

"I'm sorry. I don't know what's the matter with me, I'm a mess," she sniffled.

He rubbed her back gently. "Do you want me to take you upstairs?"

She nodded and he carried her away.

When they were inside the house, she asked him to turn the lights on. "All of them," she said shakily.

When he finished he sat down on the couch with her, one eyebrow raised in question.

"Your mouth is bleeding!" She started to jump up but he stopped her, wiping the back of his sleeve across his bottom lip.

"Just a little cut, nothing to worry about." He pinned her with a look. "Are you crying because you're drunk, or is something else going on?"

She took in a shaky breath. "I think I'm sobering up."

He continued to look at her, waiting for an explanation.

"I'm sorry I called you overbearing," She looked down at her hands. "You know I've never been in a relationship, and I just don't know how it's supposed to be. I think I need time to get used to it, used to us."

"Okay."

"You're mad."

"No, just trying to figure you out."

She laughed shortly. "Good luck, please clue me in when you do."

His lip curved slightly. "Is that why you were crying, because of us?"

She stared at him and thought, can I tell him? Should I? What was the worst that would happen, he would think she was crazy? Well no more PDA to worry about then.

She chewed her lip and spoke quietly. "I see shadow men."

His brows furrowed. "Huh?"

She took a fortifying breath and launched into it, telling him in vivid detail about the first time in the train station. His eyebrows were climbing higher and higher so she carefully avoided his eyes as she described the possessed guy in the airport.

"And then earlier when I was on the boat, I saw them onshore. That's why Geordy made the comment about me seeing a ghost. And just before we came up here, those kids who started the fight had shadow men with them...." She started crying again and he pulled her into him tightly. "You think I'm crazy, huh?"

"No. Not crazy."

"Over-active imagination?"

"Maybe...

She started to pull away but he held tighter and she gave him a dark look. "It's not my imagination. It would be easier to think it was, but it's not, I see them."

"Okay. Why?"

"I don't know. That's what I hate about it, I don't know why! But I swear I saw them and they were *driving* those kids who started the fight! And because of the alcohol I couldn't shut them off! And Austin, don't try and figure this out for me, okay? I will not take medication, or go to a shrink who will try and explain it away as some childhood trauma. There is nothing I can do except what I already do, which is ignore them for the most part. I told you about it because I was scared and I trust you."

He nodded taking a deep breath. "Thanks. That means a lot."

She searched his expression but found only mild concern and acceptance. She sighed and looked around, realizing the house was lit up like Christmas. "You can shut off the living room lights now."

"You sure?"

"I want to make out with you."

"Okay then."

He switched off the lamps and pulled her back into his lap, tipping her face and gripping the back of her head gently. His lips were warm and her fear faded into the background as she was overtaken by new sensations. She tugged him until he was lying on top of her.

He kept his hands from roaming too far this time and they made out for twenty minutes before getting interrupted by the girls.

"We just wanted to check and make sure you were okay, Jess said you were crying?" Jenna raised a brow in question.

"I'm fine, I was just drunk and upset over nothing." She leaned back against Austin who had pulled her into his lap and his hold on her tightened. She was relieved to find it comforting rather than restricting.

"Well, if you're sure you're okay, we'll leave you two lovebirds alone." Jenna grinned and the girls giggled as they left the room.

When Anna heard the back door bang shut she stretched and yawned. "I'm wiped out, do you want to sleep with me?"

Austin's brows shot off his forehead.

"Sleep, nothing else," she scolded.

"Yeah, sure, let's hit the hay."

They went upstairs and climbed under her covers, Austin spooning her from behind. She could feel his erection against her backside and it was a little disconcerting. *Not ready for anything like that*, she thought, *but the cuddling is nice*. She drew his arms around her more securely and drifted to sleep.

Chapter Five

The next morning Anna woke up with a start. She'd had a disturbing dream where she was running from something...she couldn't remember what but she figured it was shadow men. Austin stirred and turned over to face her.

"Morning," he smiled.

She smiled weakly back, remnants of the dream still hanging on.

He peered at her. "What is it?"

"Had a bad dream."

He put his arms around her and she snuggled into them. This was a definite benefit to the whole relationship thing, she decided, large arms for comfort.

"Coffee?" he asked after a minute, and she nodded. He got out of bed and looked at her. "On second thought..." He started to climb back in, but she shooed him away.

"Morning breath, go make coffee."

He mock pouted then grinned and strode away.

I'm his girlfriend, she thought suddenly, and shook her head in wonder. She still wasn't sure how she felt about it. *Nope, not going to dwell on it, just gonna go with it.* She pulled herself out of bed, yawned and stretched. Amazingly she didn't seem to be suffering from a hangover. She shuffled off to the bathroom to gargle some mouthwash then went downstairs.

Austin was standing in the kitchen next to the coffee pot looking seriously cute all rumpled from sleep, and she was suddenly struck by the urge to make him take off his shirt. She realized it had been nearly a year since she'd seen him shirtless and in that time his arms had grown pretty substantially causing her to wonder about the rest of his physique.

"You looking at something, friend?" His lip curved.

She smiled impishly, "Actually I *want* to look at something..."

His eyebrows went in the air. "What?"

"Would you take off your shirt?"

"Take off my shirt?" he repeated, brows still raised.

"Yeah, I wanna see your chest."

His face broke into a grin. "Tell you what, I'll show you mine if you show me yours," he waggled his eyebrows and she gave him a stern look.

"What? That's only fair."

"Not the same thing."

"Come on you're wearing a...." he looked at her chest and his mouth seemed to dry up. "No, you're not. When did that happen?"

"I can't sleep with one on."

"You weren't wearing one all night and I didn't cop a feel? I am seriously slackin'." He shook his head in mock regret.

She folded her arms across her chest. "So you won't take off your shirt for me?"

He laughed again and pulled it up over his shoulders and off. For some reason just the act of him removing it was pretty sexy. "Happy?" He asked.

She let her eyes roam over the broad expanse of bared skin in appreciation. Not an ounce of fat on his body, muscles bulging in all the right places. His skin was very lightly tanned and she knew from the past that by the end of summer he would be bronze. They had a phrase for his physique--eye candy.

He was watching her reaction and she grinned at him. "Not bad, not bad at all."

"Oh yeah? Gina said something like scrumptious...

She grabbed a dish towel and threw it at him. "Wait, when did she see you without a shirt?"

"I was kidding."

"Well...I guess I have to agree with that statement, fictitious or not." Actually she was having a tremendous urge....why not? She walked over to him and placed her hands on his pecs, then slid them down over his abdomen then back up and over his biceps. He watched her with a lazy half-smile.

"What?" She flushed at his bemused expression.

He leaned down and whispered, "My turn." He swallowed her into his embrace and ran his hands over her butt and up her back, sliding them down the sides of her breasts. A shiver coursed through her body as he tilted her head up and kissed her, there was something about the feel of his warm skin against her that made it more intimate. Suddenly she was consumed by the desire to pull her own shirt off and feel what it was like to be skin to skin, an urge she resisted, but barely.

She pulled back from his embrace and brightly said, "Coffee?" then grabbed a cup and busied herself with the menial task, trying to get her hormones under control.

She heard the girls' voices coming from the guestroom and was a little relieved. She had a feeling that spending too much time alone with him would result in her doing something she'd regret far sooner than she should. She poked her head inside the living room and saw there were other party-goers sleeping on the couches and the floor. *And I was going to take off my shirt?* She started giggling at the image of her standing half naked with him in the kitchen amidst all those people.

Austin cocked a brow, "What's funny?"

She laughed even harder and it took a few seconds for her to gasp out, "I forgot that I likely had house guests."

His brows came together, "And why is that so funny?"

She shook her head still giggling then grabbed her coffee and headed for the back door. Just before she opened it she turned her head slightly and said, "I considered taking off my shirt," letting the door shut on his reply.

God it was fun to tease him. He came out onto the patio a few seconds later, considering her.

"You're lying," he said finally.

"Nope."

"You don't have the guts."

"Ohh, now you're going to play the chicken card?"

"Yup, I'm playing the chicken card."

"What, you mean right here?" She indicated the patio.

He narrowed his eyes. "No, not here, there are people."

"Oh but you called me a chicken, so I think I better prove you wrong," she made a show of pulling her shirt up, knowing full well he would cover her before she got far. He didn't disappoint, pulling her into his arms and pinning her hands behind her back. He walked her backwards until they were going through the door of the garage then kicked it shut with his foot, letting her go at the same time. He folded his arms. "*Now* you can prove me wrong."

"Well...that's not fair. I was going to and you stopped me, so too late."

He was already shaking his head, and she knew she wouldn't get out of it that easily so she flashed him very briefly then tried to run to the other door.

He caught her and turned her around. "I believe the terms were the shirt comes off, not up."

"Terms, there were no terms, I just said I was considering it." He started to tickle her, and in seconds she was down on the cold concrete floor, laughing and crying for mercy.

The "look" came over his face again, the "I really want to have sex with you" look and her stomach did a somersault. He lowered himself on top of her and pressed his mouth on hers, coaxing her lips open and pushing his tongue inside. She met it aggressively with her own. His hands were caressing her sides one moment then under her shirt and cupping her bare breasts the next, and it felt *so good*. He made a noise in the back of his throat as he slowly ground his hips against her and she put one arm around his lower back and pressed down, causing him to make the noise again and god it was turning her on. She had a vision of him naked and moving on her and she made her own excited noise into his mouth. He broke the kiss and for a second she really wished he hadn't because she was brought back to reality and a Too Fast warning sign flashed across her mind.

"Okay, let's go back inside now," she said shakily.

He pulled her to her feet and wrapped his arms around her. "You make me so hot," he whispered.

His husky tone made her shiver. "I know that's why we're going back inside."

He chuckled and put his hand on her back as they headed back to the kitchen.

The whole house had come alive while they were necking, it seemed. Her kitchen was crowded with people, the girls among them, and she immediately herded the latter upstairs into her room.

"He slept in here with you," Marina accused, raising her brows.

"We just slept."

"Riigghtt," Macey said smiling slyly.

"No seriously, we messed around on the couch for a while, but in here we slept. Although in the garage a minute ago..." she let it hang.

"Tell us!" Jess demanded.

"It's going too fast. I've decided that's why I'm being so fickle. At the rate we're going...I really can't have sex with him!" She flopped backward onto her bed.

"Austin wouldn't pressure you for that," Holly stated.

"No?"

"*Is* he pressuring you?" Jenna demanded.

"Not exactly, it's just every time we start kissing he pushes the limits a little more, and the problem is that I like it. Or at least my body definitely does. But I'm not ready at all. At least my mind and heart aren't, achh, this is so confusing," she stated, making a face.

"I had sex with Nathan!" Jess blurted and promptly burst into tears.

All five girls turned to her in shock. "When!" "Where!" "Why?" They fired questions at her in rapid succession, and she looked more and more miserable until Holly raised a hand for silence and nodded at her to speak.

"Last night, in the boathouse," she sniffed, "just like Anna said, we were making out one minute and then it just kept going a little further, and it did feel really good...until he...and then it really, *really* hurt and I wanted him to stop, but I didn't tell him to so it isn't his fault, but it was a mistake!" She started crying in earnest.

Jenna surprised them all by sitting next to her and putting her arms around her. If there was ever a time for her tongue lashing, they would have thought it would be now but she seemed to understand the damage was done.

Marina turned towards the door, her foot tapping in angst. "Is he still here?"

Jess nodded miserably, "He was in the living room."

"Did he talk to you afterwards?" Holly demanded.

Jess shook her head, "He said he had to use the bathroom, but he didn't come back, so I just sat in there for a while then I came up to the house and climbed in bed."

"That rotten son of a bitch!" Anna exclaimed.

"How dare he do that and then lounge around the house like nothing happened!" Holly stated.

Marina snarled and started for the door.

"Where are you going?" Jess cried, "Don't please, it's embarrassing, I don't want everyone to know!"

"The only person who should be embarrassed is him," Holly said firmly.

"Hell yeah," Macey agreed.

"I know but I don't want people to know!"

"Don't worry, we will be sure to get him away from people," Anna said as she followed the rest of them out of the room.

They located him outside on the patio talking and smoking a cigarette. When he saw the five of them approaching with identical scowls he at least had the decency to look properly guilty.

"Have a minute Nate?" Anna asked sweetly. He nodded and flicked his smoke, then followed them inside.

Austin watched the five girls herding his friend inside and followed as they practically shoved Nate into the guestroom and shut the door.

"What's going on?" Austin broke the thunderous silence.

"Look girls," Nate stammered, "I know you think I'm an asshole right now, but I didn't mean for it to go that far, I was really drunk."

"So you left her in there because you were drunk?" Anna snapped.

"I wasn't thinking clearly, and I intended to talk to her, I was just waiting for people to leave."

"Really? Good, then go right upstairs to Anna's room where she is crying her eyes out. Now." Holly pointed towards the door.

He nodded. "Going."

"Is this about what I think it's about?" Austin asked quietly.

Jenna answered, her mouth trembling. "If you think your friend totally stole my sister's innocence and then left her without saying a word, then yeah, it's what you think it is." She was furious. It was the first thing she'd said and it had come out through gritted teeth. If there had been any doubt about her love for her sibling, the doubt was gone. All of them were angry but she was literally shaking with it.

Austin put a hand on her shoulder. "It's all right," he said softly, "Nate's not a bad guy, he'll fix it as much as he can."

Jenna threw his arm off violently. "And how the HELL do you suppose he'll do that? He can't take it back, it's done!" Tears came down her face and she swiped at them angrily. "Careless, thoughtless, God what is wrong with guys? You too," she pointed a finger at him accusingly, "pushing Anna too far too fast, don't guys ever think about anything but their stupid dicks?"

Anna's face flamed and she ducked her head.

Austin nodded slowly. "I'm sorry your sister was hurt Jenna."

He turned to leave the room and Anna caught his arm. He put his hand on hers and kissed her head, "Talk later," he told her quietly and left.

All eyes were on Jenna now, and Holly broke the new silence with a softly whispered question. "Jenna....did something happen to you?"

Jenna shook her head in denial, but the tears came harder and she sat down on the bed.

"Jenna?"

"I don't want to talk about it. Not. Now. Not. Ever."

"But..."

"I said I DON'T want to talk about it, so leave it!"

They stood there awkwardly for a moment then Holly beckoned them to leave the room.

"Go for a walk?" Anna suggested after the door was shut and they nodded in unison and headed out the door.

***

Jenna sat on the bed trying to get her emotions under control. After a few minutes she was once again breathing normally. *Not the same situation*, she thought, *Jess was bound to have this happen the way she's been going lately, and honestly it could have been worse than Nate.* She took a deep breath and got to her feet.

Not all men suck, she told herself. It had become a mantra for her, to remind herself that all guys weren't the same. Yes they were led around by their penises, but that was probably just as annoying for them as it was for everyone else. She felt bad that she'd yelled at Austin who was definitely one of the good guys. True he was advancing the physical situation with Anna a bit too quickly, but he loved her. He'd loved her for a long time, and he would never hurt her, in fact he was far more likely to be the one that ended up hurt. Anna cared for him, but there was only one soul mate for her and he just wasn't it. Jenna knew this the same way she knew a lot of things- about other people anyway, never about herself.

She went to the kitchen and found that it had cleared out. She could see a few kids standing around and talking on the back patio, but a glance through the living room windows showed her most of the cars were gone.

She heard a noise on the stairs and recognized Nate's voice. A moment later he and Jess appeared in the entryway to the kitchen and her sister's entire countenance had completely changed.

She was smiling brightly as she announced, "We're going to the park to take a walk."

Jenna nodded. Nate was fidgeting and she decided to give him a break, smiling slightly.

He smiled widely back. "Don't worry I won't have her out too late!"

Jess laughed like it was the funniest thing anyone had ever said and Jenna shook her head, her smile widening.

She watched her sister flounce across the driveway then decided to locate the rest of the girls.

Chapter Six

The next two weeks passed in a blur of activity. Anna spent a great deal of her time shopping with the girls for their trip and devoted most evenings to Austin who insisted on being old fashioned and taking her on dinner dates. Movies one night, bowling the next, she felt like she was packing in years' worth of missed boy/girl outings. Of course she was going to be gone for a month so she understood his desire to be with her. She had effectively pushed her misgivings of them to the back of her mind, and even found that his arm around her in public was not so terrible. She hadn't let him back in her bedroom however, and had set some definite boundaries for their make-out sessions. He still pushed a little but he wouldn't have been a guy if he didn't.

Everything was....good. Good friends, a good boyfriend, shopping malls, parks and lakes, dates and parties, all the things that made the normal average college aged kid's life in America....well perfect. Except Anna had always believed herself to be above average and she was beginning to believe she was not quite normal.

The shadow men sightings were increasing and she wasn't sure if she was just noticing more of them or if there *were* more of them. Either notion was disquieting. She couldn't quite pin down why it bothered her though, since other than the chill of malevolence she felt if they got too close there didn't seem to be anything they could do to actually harm her. She kept picturing the night of her party, and while she firmly believed the shadowy figures had somehow influenced the fight (which she later found had resulted in a knocked out tooth and a broken nose) the fact of the matter was boys fought. It was something they did with or without supernatural influence. Now if they had broken out some chain saws and started hacking people up it would have been a different story, but all and all it had been a fairly ordinary brawl.

She found it extremely odd that the shadows seemed to be little more than a slight disturbance when on some very basic level she knew they were the things of nightmares. And not just your run of the mill "a ghost is chasing me" nightmare, but the kind where a person wakes up so terrified they have to use a great deal of will to block out the image and it takes hours of daylight to feel normal again. It was distressing in a way she couldn't define, but no matter how hard she tried to make sense of it she couldn't.

At the moment she and her friends were gathered at Nate's house for their friend Tyler's "after hours" grad party. Nate's parents were out of town and since he had an Olympic sized swimming pool along with a very large hot tub, his place was where to be. And because it was the night before they left for Europe it was a going away party as well.

Jess and Nate had made it through two weeks without any big fights which was impressive considering they were with one another constantly. Generally Jess would have found a thousand things to despise about a guy by now but clearly adding the element of sex bought him a little extra time...and they were active-you did NOT want to walk in on them when they were alone. *Kudos to that*, Anna thought, though some of the other girls were critical. She personally felt that once she was ready to take that step she would be a nympho, which she stated in her friend's defense on several occasions. Not that she would be a slut, she fully intended for only one guy to receive the benefit of her sexual prowess. Whether that guy would be Austin...she still had yet to make up her mind.

She was currently standing in Nate's bathroom feeling a little naked as she checked out her new swimsuit in the full length mirror. She'd never worn a two piece before, but Jess and Jenna had convinced her to buy it when she'd tried it on at the store. Admittedly it *was* very attractive. It featured just enough cleavage to be enticing and the color complemented her eyes.

She checked once more to make sure her "cheeks" were covered and headed outdoors with her clothes draped over her arm. Austin's eyes widened as he spotted her and he hopped off the bench, whistling low as he approached.

"That is one sexy suit, a little bit too sexy actually," he told her as his eyes wandered over every inch.

Blushing she shook her head. "J&J convinced me."

"You plan on wearing that over in Europe?"

"Hey, over there they go naked, consider this ultra conservative," she stated defensively.

He frowned. "Are you trying to tell me *all* of their beaches are nude? I know they have them...you're not going to one are you?"

She patted his arm. "The last thing I wanna do is see a beach full of hairy asses and saggy boobies."

He threw back his head and laughed. "Yeah, we imagine those places are filled with hotties, but your description is a hell of a lot more likely."

She grinned and nodded, pushing him lightly towards the pool. "Ready for a swim?"

He pulled his shirt off and grabbed the clothes from her arm, tossing them over by the bench. She was about to comment on his physique when he picked her up off her feet and jumped in the water.

She came up spluttering and slapping him, "Jerk, I snorted it up my nose!"

He grinned as he grabbed her smacking hands, "Sorry babe, it was too good an opportunity to miss."

She leaned up and bit his lip.

"Ow!" He made like he was going to dunk her and she screeched in protest.

"Okay you two." Jenna came to the edge of the pool with her hands on her hips looking ridiculously scrumptious in her dark red bikini with black flowers. Her generous boobs were threatening to spill out, and Anna feared if she attempted to jump in she would lose the top completely.

"What mom, what'd we do?" Austin teased.

"I never thought Anna would become one of those girls who giggled and flirted and shrieked, but it appears you have demented her!" She was smiling as she said it, but Anna didn't doubt she was half serious.

"No, I think it's Jess's influence," Marina stated coming up to the side of the pool.

"I do not shriek!" Jess protested walking up beside her.

"Oh no?" Marina promptly pushed her over the side laughing gleefully as Jess obligingly shrieked.

That started a war. Every girl at the party was being chased and tossed in the pool with the exception of Marina who continually dodged, pointing and laughing at the rest of them. At least until Anna made a suggestion to the ever willing Austin who came out of the water and grabbed the lithe blonde around the waist. To Marina's credit not only didn't she shriek, she kicked and wrestled almost free of him.

He finally managed to pull her over the side and give her a dunk for good measure.

"Damn that girl is deceptively strong!" He exclaimed. "She may look thin, but she is wiry as hell, and those legs!"

"Oh you're checking out my legs now Aussie?" Marina's blue eyes flashed as she came after him for revenge.

She was so tenacious that he finally had to give in and let her dunk him or he would have had to watch his back for the rest of the night.

"Are you guys done, because I would really like to go lounge in the hot tub with my boyfriend." Anna was sitting on the edge of the pool by this time, a mock look of disapproval on her face. She knew the casually thrown boyfriend comment would make Austin happy and she found that despite her Sometimes Claustrophobia (which she decided was more the case than bipolar disorder) she did enjoy making him feel good.

Marina grudgingly let go of his hair which she was still holding for another dunk and Anna had to laugh at her expression. She was not one to piss off. Of their little group she and Jenna were the two you wanted to avoid confrontation with, although with Marina it was definitely more physical where Jenna could kill you with a look.

Austin climbed out of the pool and pulled her to her feet, kissing her lightly on the mouth. His eyes were crinkled, which meant he was enormously pleased by the comment as she'd figured, and he scooped her up and brought her over to the hot tub.

Nate and Jess were already in it with Holly and Tyler and as Anna and Austin settled in Anna noticed that Jess was trying to get Nate's attention without success. He was animatedly talking about the football teams he and Austin were putting together for the summer and she couldn't compete with that, a fact which was irritating her more and more by the second. As a last ditch effort she placed herself between him and Tyler.

"Excuse me, hello, your *girlfriend* is trying to talk to you, you know the one that's leaving tomorrow for a WHOLE month! Maybe you could talk to Tyler about football when I'm gone?" She was scowling, distorting her normally beautiful features.

Nate leaned back against the side of the tub and crossed his arms over his chest, glaring at her. "What do you want? What can't wait until I'm finished talking?" His voice held a note of reined in hostility, and Anna braced herself for an argument.

"I just TOLD you, I'm leaving tomorrow, I want your attention, I want you to focus on me!"

"I have done nothing BUT focus on you for two weeks straight, and now you're gonna bitch at me for talking to someone for five fucking minutes?"

"Don't swear at me!"

"Fuck, Fuck, Fuck."

Jess stood up and pointed a finger in his face. "You are being an *asshole*, and I am *leaving*."

His arms came up on either side of his head, "So GO."

She looked momentarily surprised, then splashed water in his face and climbed hastily out of the tub.

Anna watched in amusement as her friend stormed across the deck, thinking the probability of her actually leaving the premises were slim to none, and if she did, she would be back.

"Are you going after her?" Austin asked.

She shook her head snickering. "Nah, she'll be fine, she just needs to chill-ax." That was their favorite phrase to throw at her when her mood swung south. Chill-ax Jess, or as Macey would say, Chill-ax Crabby pants.

Nate resumed his conversation about football and Anna eyed him thoughtfully. He actually had a chance of holding onto her friend if that's what he wanted. It was best not to cater to Jess when she was in one of those moods, especially guys, or she wouldn't respect them.

She continued her quiet study of Nate and decided she could definitely understand her friend's attraction to the guy, there was just something about him. Aside from his all American good looks she knew that despite his preference for slang he was very intelligent. She'd had debate class with him in high school and he'd never lost an argument.

"Well, my focus is all on you, baby." Austin kissed the tip of her nose and she smiled at him fondly. He really was a sweet guy. He would make a terrific husband someday. As soon as the thought entered her mind she inwardly grimaced and claustrophobia tried to strike. She put her arms around his neck and buried her face against his chest forcing the feeling to pass. He ran his fingers lightly up and down her back, mercifully oblivious to her thoughts.

"I'm really going to miss you," he whispered against her hair.

She nodded against his smooth skin fervently wishing she could match the depth of his feelings. The only time she ever felt as strongly as he did was when they were making out. It made no sense to her, how she could be attracted to him like that but not find herself really falling for him. Holly had pointed out that it might be because he was marriage material and she was not in a place to consider it. After giving this some thought she decided there was truth in it. She could easily picture her life with him and knew he would be wonderful to her-faithful, supportive...a great dad. But she was nineteen and the idea of her whole life being set in stone was terrifying.

She wanted adventure and excitement. She wanted fireworks. That was the main source of the problem-with him it was comfortable as if they'd already been together for years and years. But comfortable wasn't a place she wanted to begin at, it was where she wanted to arrive after being with someone for a long time. Lightning first, Little League later. Much later.

Stop it, she scolded. *Give him this night and worry about the rest later.* After all, who knew what would happen in a month?

The party was still in full throttle when she asked Austin to drive her home. She would be getting on a plane early the next afternoon and she didn't want to be exhausted on her first night in a foreign country. Plus she wanted to spend some alone time with him before she left.

Her dad was still somewhere in Africa. He'd called the other day and left a message telling her that if he didn't talk to her before she departed that she could reach him by leaving messages on his cell. Also he told her he loved her and to be safe, the same things she always said to him before he left on one of his trips. It would have been nice to hear "have fun", but fun was no longer in his vocabulary. It tore at her heart when she thought about how much he missed her mom, how much his love for her had cost him. She'd once asked him if he would still have chosen to be with her mom if he'd known he would lose her so early. He had stared into space for several minutes and she'd thought he wasn't going to answer when he'd finally said, "I would suffer all the pain the world can throw at me for just one day with her." He'd smiled a little then, a ghost of his former robust grin, and told her he was certain they would be together again, he just had to endure the separation.

She had forced herself to smile back, but the comment had made her heart ache with the knowledge that nothing in this life would ever make him happy again, not even her.

When she and Austin reached her house he wasted no time pulling her to him and locking his lips on hers. There was an urgency about it that set off little trills of excitement in her belly. He picked her up sliding her body against his entire length until she wrapped her legs around his waist. As his lips found hers again she decided to break her bedroom rule. "Upstairs," she whispered against his mouth. He wasted no time obeying.

Their lips stayed locked as he carried her up the stairs and put them in her bed. She could feel his erection straining the light material of his swimsuit and it made her feel giddy. There was very little between them as she was wearing only a pair of thin jogging shorts with nothing underneath.

"I want you Anna, so badly." His voice was rough with desire and she almost felt guilty knowing his need could become painful. Most girls had no empathy when it came to a guy's anatomy but she wasn't most girls.

She ground her hips against him and the place between her thighs came alive with heat. He moaned against her neck in response and she felt herself moisten which created a whole new sensation for her.

"I'm wet," she blurted, immediately wishing she could take it back. His whole body stiffened and he lifted off her. Of course by the time he looked at her face she was flaming red, chewing her lower lip.

"You know what that means don't you? You're body's ready for me."

She continued chewing her lip, anxiety replacing desire. She shook her head. "Maybe, but my head isn't yet. I shouldn't have said that, it just slipped out, I didn't mean to get your hopes up. It just hasn't happened before and I thought out loud…

He put a hand lightly on her mouth. "It's okay, don't be nervous, I won't press you. And don't worry about me, I can handle it. I'm glad you said it, a guy likes to know when his girl is turned on." He grinned at her and she smiled back.

"Maybe the bedroom thing is a bad idea," She looked at him apologetically, and he nodded, pulling them both to their feet.

When they were back downstairs he settled them on the couch and she snuggled into his arms, her thoughts alternating between her impending trip and her confusing relationship. He clicked the television on and found a movie for them and after a while she was able to shut down her mental warring and get lost in the film.

Chapter Seven

The following morning Anna was sleeping so soundly it took the phone ringing off the hook to wake her.

She pulled herself to a sitting position on the couch and looked around, spotting a note on the coffee table.

Anna,

Had to go help my dad this morning, you looked so peaceful

I didn't want to wake you. Be back soon- Love you-

The phone started ringing again and she hurried to get it.

"Anna! You have to do something!" Jenna sounded frantic.

"Why! What's going on?"

"Jess is saying that she isn't coming, she is being absolutely ridiculous! She doesn't want to leave Nate for a month, blah blah, I swear I'm going to kill her!"

Anna took a deep breath and let it out slow. "Is she right there?"

"Yeah, but she won't take the phone. Marina is here, and neither of us can talk sense into her. I figure you can at least play the guilt card since you paid for NON-REFUNDABLE tickets..."

Anna heard mumbling in the background.

"She says she'll pay you back," Jenna stated sarcastically.

Anna considered her friend and sighed heavily. "Jenna, I'm afraid we might have to let this go."

"*What??*"

"Every time we have ever forced Jess to go somewhere we've ended up regretting it, every single time. She'll be miserable. She'll spend the entire time holed up in the rooms of the hotels texting him-which I kind of thought she would be doing anyway-though at least if she wanted to come she might have enjoyed some things. If she doesn't want to be there she'll cry every night and constantly worry about what he's doing, where he is, and who he's with. She's your sister Jenna, you know I'm right."

"I don't CARE if you're right, this is so freakin' stupid! If she doesn't go, I am not speaking to her for the rest of her life!"

Anna coughed out a laugh at that dramatic statement. She could tell Jenna was holding the phone away from her, but she could still hear what she was saying. She went upstairs to gather her things together listening to the background conversation.

"Don't talk to her like she's a baby Mar, she doesn't deserve to be coddled! Jess, you are going with us, do you hear me? No! That is not acceptable, stop crying! He will still be here in a month. Like I said, if you two are meant to be than....Oh my GOD, do you seriously think that whether or not you go will make any difference? Whatever, I'm done. Stay here, without your friends, we'll be sure to fill you in on all the fun we're having, all the cool things we see, but believe me when I say that if you call me at any point whining about him I will hang up on you!"

"Still there?"

"Yeah, I'm here," Anna pinned the phone between her shoulder and ear so she could carry the rest of her bags into the back porch.

"I've decided you're right. I'll have a better time without her anyway, the whole image of her crying and texting him non-stop makes me nauseous. I'd probably end up pushing her out the window of the Eiffel Tower."

Anna laughed. "Yup. Don't worry, we're going to have a great time. It's her loss. Of course if she was in the right frame of mind she would've been great to have with us, but like this....not so much."

"Okay, I'm getting my bags together now. Mar and I will be at your house in half an hour."

"Cool. Chow." She hung up the phone and made a face. Jess could be so short-sighted. The chances of her and Nate lasting were slim to none and she was really going to regret missing out on this. But...that was her mistake to make, she'd have to live with it and hopefully learn from it. The phone rang again and she answered half expecting it to be Jenna saying Jess had changed her mind.

"Anna?" Holly's voice sounded a little shaky.

"Holly, what's wrong?" Anna squeezed the phone tighter.

"My dad went to the hospital last night, and...there's something wrong with his heart...I'm sorry Anna, I'm not going to be able to leave today," she sniffled.

"Oh no! Will he be okay?"

"I think so, they're talking about surgery but they said it was fairly minor. Just a little scary for me, and I don't want to leave mom right now."

"Of course! We'll postpone...

"No! Please don't do that, I would hate for you guys to do that. I know the tickets are non-refundable. I'm thinking that if everything turns out okay then I can meet you guys wherever you are at the time."

Anna frowned as she considered her friend. She knew Holly really would be upset if they didn't go, but she felt guilty at the thought of leaving her. "Holly I really want us to wait. A few days or a week won't matter and you know I don't care about the money.....

"Anna, I seriously do NOT want you to. I'll be spending all my time with mom or at the hospital, please I'm asking you not to," she insisted.

Anna sighed. "Okay, but please keep us updated and when you can come I'll take care of the ticket, no arguments. Jess isn't going either, so she'll be here if you need her."

"What? Why, what happened?"

"Nothing to be alarmed about, believe me," Anna snorted. "She doesn't want to leave Nate, and you know how she gets and if we force her to go..." she trailed off, figuring she didn't need to finish.

Holly was silent for a few seconds, and Anna could picture her shaking her head.

"Well, maybe if I'm able to meet you she'll have changed her mind and she can come with me."

"That's an idea."

"Okay. Well, I'll let you get ready, and don't worry about me, I want you guys to have fun! I promise to keep you informed. As long as he comes home and everything is going well, I'll meet you, so...take lots of pictures, and would you mind telling everyone else for me?"

"Of course. We'll really miss you Holly."

"Thanks. I have to go, but I'll talk to you soon, okay?"

"Okay."

Anna pressed end and stared at the phone. From six to four in less than an hour. *Hopefully nothing else happens, or I'm going to start wondering if our plane is going down*, she thought morbidly.

Macey walked in the back door a minute later grinning from ear to ear. "Are you ready to go to Europe or what!"

She looked so deliriously happy Anna almost didn't want to fill her in.

Macey's eyes narrowed a little, noting the look on her face. "Uh oh, what's wrong?"

She told her about Holly first, for which she was properly concerned, and then about Jess.

"No! That is so stupid!"

"I know, but like I keep saying, she'll be miserable if we force her. Anyway, she can keep Holly company now, so maybe it'll work out for the best."

"True...oh well, the four of us will still have a blast! I wonder if we'll meet up with Rudolph and Julien!"

Anna smiled. "That would be fun." Rudolph and Julien were two extremely hot French exchange students who had gone to their school a couple of years before. Macey and Marina kept in contact with them via email.

Anna heard Austin's SUV pull up the driveway and her heart did a little lurch. *Where the hell did that come from?* The girls pulled up right behind him and she didn't have time to examine it. She met them in the driveway and filled them in on Holly.

"You're sure we shouldn't wait for her?" Jenna asked when she'd finished.

Anna frowned, "No I'm not sure, I wanted to but she made a huge point of saying she'd be upset if we didn't go."

"That sucks," Marina made a face, "poor Holly."

They loaded their bags into Austin's car and discussed Jess's foolishness.

"Have you talked to Nate today?" Jenna asked Austin.

"No, but I'm sure he wouldn't want Jess to miss out on this, he's not like that."

"I know, I was just wondering if he thinks she's as stupid as we do."

"Okay, enough with the Jess bashing. It occurs to me that none of us truly understands how she feels," Anna pointed out. After all, none of the rest of them had been fully intimate with a guy.

Jenna rolled her eyes but said no more.

Austin shut the hatch and turned to them. "Time to roll." He hoisted Anna up into the passenger seat and the girls climbed in back. They spent the hour long drive to the airport talking excitedly and before they knew it they were checking in their luggage.

Anna wrapped her arms around Austin and felt the little heart thing again. Whoa, was she going to cry? Yup. She choked up a little and he lifted her chin.

"Hey, don't do that." He hugged her tightly and she let a stream of silent tears get soaked up in his shirt. Her shoulders were shaking slightly, and unfortunately the girls noticed.

"Oh no, please don't tell me Anna doesn't want to leave Aussie now," Marina sounded put out.

She pulled away from him and stuck her tongue out at her friend. "Don't be a jerk I'm just going to miss him a little."

"A little, huh?" Austin raised his brows.

"Okay, maybe a little more than a little." Although what she actually thought her tears were about was something different. Like everything might have changed by the next time she saw him.

She leaned up to kiss him and froze as she caught a glimpse of black eyes over his shoulder. For a second she thought it was the same guy as the last time then noticed he was much thinner. Her mouth went dry and she tore her gaze from him, refocusing on Austin who was looking at her strangely. He didn't ask what was wrong, which told her he had guessed. She inwardly thanked him for being sensitive enough not to draw attention to it.

She drew in a breath and shut her eyes briefly "turning it off", and when she looked again the guy was normal. Or appeared that way.

Austin hugged her to his chest and whispered, "Seeing them?"

She nodded. "But he's walking away," she whispered back.

"He?"

She discreetly pointed to her eyes. He got it.

"Show me."

He wanted her to point him out. She wasn't sure if that was such a good idea, the guy (thing) might realize or at least suspect that they knew and...what? She didn't want to find out. She shook her head, "I don't want him to know I know."

"What are you guys whispering about?" Jenna cut in.

They both shook their heads, and Jenna rolled her eyes at them. "Probably don't want to know."

They nodded in unison and the girls laughed.

Anna looked around, but he'd disappeared into the crowd of people. She prayed he would not be on their flight-*that* would be a nerve wracking fifteen hours.

The girls suggested they wander around until it was time to board, so she tucked herself into Austin's side and strolled.

It felt like seconds later it was time for them to go. She and Austin shared a long kiss goodbye while the girls teased them, and then they were on the plane, in the air, watching New York disappear beneath them.

Chapter Eight

All four girls flopped on their double beds at the Regency hotel in London with an audible sigh. The past couple of weeks had been a whirlwind of events as they'd traveled from Paris to Venice to Dublin where they'd spent the majority of their time on tours and in museums.

Their days had been so filled with activity Anna had had little time to dwell on anything disturbing. The shadow men she'd seen were just a blur as she blinked them away and went on to the next place--with the tiny exception of one time in France.

They were walking through Montmarte and she'd found herself trailing behind a bit, lost in her thoughts and taking in the sights. She'd noticed an aged yet still attractive woman seated on a stone bench writing a letter, and as she'd approached she could tell the woman had been amused with whatever it was she'd been writing down. And then she'd glanced across the street and her expression had turned dark.

Following her gaze Anna had been startled to see a shadow man. She'd looked back at the woman who had already returned to her letter, her eyes filled with amusement once more.

As she'd walked past her she'd met eyes the exact same shade as Jenna's and been greeted by a wide smile and a little wave that she'd returned. For a moment she had been tempted to stop and talk to her, but then the girls had called for her to catch up and she'd decided to let it go.

They had spoken to Holly several times in the last couple of weeks and although her father had come through the surgery without complications she'd decided to stay with her mom and help with the recovery process.

Anna had assured her that she would have no qualms about returning to Europe the following summer, though they were all sad she wouldn't make it this year. Jess on the other hand had been nearly impossible to get a hold of. They knew from Holly that she had no intentions of changing her mind so it appeared it would remain the four of them for the rest of the vacation

Anna picked up their travel guide and lay back on the bed reading out loud. "According to many sources the capital is seething with after-hours drinking and dancing dens of all shapes and sizes. From the pulsating dance floors of major nightclubs to the chilled intimacy of smaller DJ bars, London has something to offer both the hardcore party animals and those looking for a quiet drink and some good conversation." She put the brochure down and grinned. "I'm pretty damn sure we will fall into both of those categories before this trip is over, whatcha think?"

"Hell yeah, but right now I'm leaning towards the hardcore," Marina stated.

"You know it," Macey gave her a high five.

"I love art and all, but sheesh my brain is exhausted. I couldn't look at another painting without going into mental overload," Jenna sat up and crossed her eyes and Anna laughed as she nodded.

Marina turned on the hotel supplied radio and Werewolves of London blared from the speakers. "Oh yeah, good song!" They all howled in unison than dissolved in gales of laughter.

Anna's phone beeped announcing a new text message and she pulled it from her purse.

"Austin?" Jenna guessed.

"Uh huh. He says if we're going out-Yah, *IF-*"Anna rolled her eyes, "be sure to stay in main clubs and not go to any raves. Oh and he sent an attachment. It's an article, apparently some girls went to an underground rave and had some drugs slipped in their drink....and ended up being raped. Nice. Smart. Okay, so if we do go to any raves we follow a few simple rules--watch each other's backs, stick to bottled beer and be sure to watch them being opened. Accept no drinks from strangers and keep drink in hand at all times."

"What's a rave?" Marina asked.

Macey giggled and Jenna explained. "It's like an underground party. You have to be invited and then you have to stay until morning. Lots of drugs and in some cases people having sex right out in the open."

"Oh, no thanks, I think we'll pass on the orgy," Marina made a face.

None of them were into that kind of scene, but...

"Oh I don't know," Jenna said, "If we follow what Anna said it might be interesting to check one out, they're not always that hardcore."

Anna was nodding. "Well, we'll see. Let's get ready and head downtown."

Since it was a Wednesday night the clubs weren't very crowded and they passed by several as they walked down the strip. It was fun just to be walking the streets of London commenting on the different people they saw. There were a large number of weirdoes covered in tattoos and piercings, but there were also kids dressed mostly like they were, as well as...well suffice to say the people were varied and eclectic.

There was one thing they all had in common, something Anna had noticed in other parts of Europe as well-everybody smoked. Rudolph and Julien both had and all but Macey had ended up trying a few cigarettes, especially when they were drinking.

Anna felt like having one now and said so. They located a small convenience and bought a pack.

"I don't want to get addicted to these things," Anna commented, "but I think it's fun to have one once in a while. Austin only smokes if he's drinking so I'm guessing it's possible to be part-time."

"Definitely, you just have to make up your mind about it," Jenna looked by far the sexiest when she drew it in, as if a cigarette was meant to be between her fingers.

They rounded a corner and saw a group of girls headed around the back of a building. They were all holding something and there was an air of electric excitement about them.

"Let's check it out," Anna suggested.

They hurried up to the last few people disappearing around the bricks. "Hey, what's going on?" Marina asked a freckle faced girl.

"We're going to invoke our inner powers under the light of the full moon," the girl replied in hushed tones. She was holding a bag that appeared to have different colored candles.

The foursome raised their brows at that. "You're witches?" Marina asked.

"No, we're Goddesses of Power."

"Can we come?"

"I don't know, you'll have to ask the Mistress." She pointed to the front where a fortyish woman with long blonde hair was facing the gathering.

"I'll go ask," Anna stated and made her way up to the front where she waited for the attractive older woman to notice her.

"May I help you?" She asked in a melodic baritone.

"My girlfriends and I were wondering if we might join you."

"Certainly, all women are welcome." She reached inside of her oversized purse and pulled out bags containing candles. "How many of you?"

"Four."

She handed Anna the bags. "Just follow us, I'll instruct everyone in what they are to do."

Anna walked back to her friends and handed them each a bag, a small smile on her face. Personally she thought these things were ridiculous. Not that there wasn't magic in the world, but groups like these were generally made up of wannabe's. Wanna be what? Wanna be a part of something.

"Okay guys, no matter what *no* outbursts of laughter, seriously, that would be very rude when we were so graciously invited." She tried to look stern but ended up giggling, and knew that with Macey and Marina it was a hopeless request.

The group started moving again and they found themselves in the middle of a large abandoned parking lot.

The "Mistress" addressed the gathering, her smoky voice carrying easily across the empty lot. "You may all sit down, be sure and leave some space between you and the person beside you."

After the group was seated she spoke again. "If you look inside your bags you'll find a small piece of chalk. I would like you to draw a circle around yourselves. Not too small, you will need room to place your candles."

"Oo-kay," Jenna grinned, "We have officially entered strange zone." But they followed the instructions and waited for more.

The Mistress was wearing a blousy white dress and when she lifted her arms Anna thought she must have intended to appear as an Angel since her sleeves hung down in wings. She began to speak and her voice grew louder, but the words were foreign.

She brought her arms back down and addressed them in English. "I have called upon the Goddesses of old and asked them to be with us this night! All of you sit here today surrounded by a circle which represents the universe. We are all our own unique stars in the vast expanse of space!"

Marina started to titter and Jenna shushed her with a look.

"Some of you may be unaware of the powers that lie within you. You must open up your hearts and minds and embrace the uniqueness of your true selves!"

Anna looked around as the Mistress continued in the same vein and noted there were definitely other skeptics but there were also girls who seemed almost reverent.

"Now, I want you to remove the book of matches from your bag along with your white candle!"

As she pulled out the items Anna made the error of looking at Macey whose face was red from restrained laughter. She felt a giggle building and had to bite down hard on her lip to keep it from erupting.

She drew in a deep breath and let it out slow, holding matches and candle in hand. It was a tea candle with a little aluminum casing. *How convenient*, she thought, *no mess*. That almost did her in, she had to squeeze her eyes shut and force the hilarity back down with an intense concentration of will.

"This white candle represents the powers of healing and long life! We all have these abilities lying dormant within our minds, the ability to heal mental, emotional, and physical ailments, in others and in ourselves. If we can just tap into this power we might live many years beyond what is expected! Light this candle and place it in front of you, meditating on the truth of your own inner power."

The desire to laugh faded as Anna lit her candle and stared at the flame considering. The woman might be a flake, but was she wrong? She'd always wondered about things like that. They had been created with such complexity was it impossible to imagine that they'd also been given the ability to heal themselves and others? Her father firmly believed the human body was far stronger than people gave it credit for and that the mind was a powerful tool when it came to things like sickness and pain.

"Now I want you to remove the red candle! This one represents the ability to see events that have not yet come to pass, even if is just in the form of an intuition. Though some truly have the ability to foretell, all have the ability to discern if they just listen to their inner voices! Light this candle and place it to the left of the white."

Anna looked at Jenna and winked. The voluptuous beauty definitely had that intuition. Macey and Marina were also looking at her, their faces split by shit eating grins. Jenna wrinkled her nose at them and lifted the candle high in the air, then swept it down dramatically, lighting it in the process. They all giggled and followed suit.

"Now the black candle! As all of you know, black is associated with Evil, and Goddesses I can assure you that there is evil in this world! The power we invoke with this candle is the power to truly see it, to discern its presence, that we might fight it in a world that is darkening every day! Light this candle and place it to the right of the white."

Anna shivered, all remnants of humor dissipating, as she lit the candle and considered the shadow men.

"The very last candle in our bag is gold and silver. This represents all other supernatural things in our world that dwell just beyond our limited senses. Some are good and some are evil, some are both, but they are there! We invoke the power to see, to have our eyes truly opened to all that is within our realm! Light this candle and place it beside the red."

Anna chewed her lip for a minute. She didn't really buy this. She could already see evil. Even if there were other things out there the odds that this silly ceremony would "open her eyes" to them were pretty slim. Still she hesitated. She felt someone's gaze on her and turned to see Jenna looking at her questioningly. She smiled and lit the candle. "I was daydreaming," she whispered and Jenna laughed quietly.

"Now that all the candles are lit we are going to call forth the spirits of the ancient Goddesses to invoke the powers within us. Please repeat after me...."

She began speaking in another language again, but slowly, and when it came time to echo her Anna swallowed tightly. *Words don't actually hold power, not in this way*, she thought uneasily. She briefly considered staying quiet but for some reason felt compelled to follow suit. *Magic is illusion*, her mind insisted as she spoke.

Later she would recall thinking that and mock her own naivety.

When they finished the chant, the mistress instructed them to blow out the candles and close their eyes. She continued speaking in foreign words and Anna felt distinctly strange. She had a tingling feeling in her feet and it traveled the length of her body centering somewhere in her skull. It wasn't unpleasant, in fact it felt like she was in a full body massage chair. Then abruptly a white light exploded behind her eyes and she doubled over.

The pain lasted less than a second but it was intense, and when she opened her eyes again her girlfriends were staring at her. She smiled weakly and managed to wink pretending she had done it on purpose. She noticed Jenna looked a little pale and wondered if she had felt something too.

"Now my beautiful Goddesses, we will reconvene at the KilKant and talk about our experience." She waved one blousy arm for them to follow.

"No way, we're not going with them, that was sooo retarded!" Macey stated as they gathered up the candles and dropped them back in their baggies.

"Definitely, let's go hit some bars," Jenna suggested.

Anna was shaken but didn't want it to show. She piped in with, "So we haven't been recruited by the G.O.P.'s then?"

"G.O.P.'s?" Marina laughed loudly. "We're down with G.O.P's yeah you know me!"

They all dissolved into laughter but Anna's was a touch forced. The strangeness she'd felt was still lingering.

Chapter Nine

They stopped for a drink at the first bar they came to but after ten minutes in the place they decided the music was too mellow and headed out to find a more upbeat club.

As they walked Marina entertained them with an exaggerated impression of the Mistress. They were all giggling and Anna had just begun to feel normal again when she saw something that could not be real. She froze completely. The girls kept walking but she couldn't move.

It took them a couple of steps to realize she wasn't with them and they looked back at her questioningly.

She squeezed her eyes shut. *Not real*, she told her pounding heart. What she thought she just saw... She opened her eyes and looked fearfully towards the group of approaching guys.

Normal teeth, normal eyes. *Oh God, get a grip Anna, you are seriously freaking yourself out*. She took a deep breath and let it out on a laugh.

"Anna?" Jenna looked concerned.

"Sorry, I don't know what happened, I just...yeah I let those freakazoids mess with my overactive imagination, don't worry," she laughed airily, "it's nothing."

The guys slowed as they neared. "Hey girls, where are you headed?"

Anna's heart picked up again and her throat closed. The good looking blonde who posed the question was one of the ones that had appeared to be....*nope, not going there, totally ridiculous*, she chewed her lip.

"Not sure yet, just wandering around," Marina told him.

"Really? You should come with us then."

Anna saw it again and was seriously glad her instinct was to freeze in place, because if she had screamed or in any way brought attention to herself at that moment, and he really was what he couldn't possibly be, then he would know that she saw him......*shit, shit, shit*, she thought. He had fangs. He had fangs and his eyes were...were not right. They seemed to have some kind of illumination in their depths that was throwing off shimmery beams of light.

She heard the girls agreeing and her freeze frame unlocked.

"No!" She said loudly, startling everyone. She coughed, "Err...I'm sorry, I just meant that I want to go up that way," she pointed in the direction they had been heading, "and you know maybe you can tell us where you'll be and we'll meet up with you." She forced herself to look at them and once again they appeared normal.

"Why?" Marina asked, "What's up that way?"

Jenna's eyes were narrowed on her a little as she spoke, "Actually, that's a good idea, why don't we do that?"

The guys gave the name of their destination and expressed a desire to see them there, then to Anna's immense relief they walked away.

When they'd put a little distance between them and the group, Jenna stopped, forcing all of them to do the same. "Okay Anna, what gives?"

Her hands were shaking and if it weren't for her desperate need not to appear crazy she would be running like mad. Shadow men, now this? No, no, no, she had imagined it. She looked at Jenna with a forced smile while she hurriedly thought of some logical excuse. It came to her.

"I think maybe the candles had something in them, you know like incense that affected me," she couldn't keep the tremor out of her voice.

Jenna noticed and was instantly concerned. "Affected you how?"

She paused. No way was she telling them about fangs, No. Freaking. Way. She ducked her head and gave her best sheepish expression. "I felt like evil was coming off of them."

"*What??*" Macey exclaimed.

"Seriously, whoa Anna I didn't think you were that easily duped!" Marina laughed.

Jenna studied her for a moment saying nothing. She glanced across the street and Anna watched her face abruptly drain of color and followed her gaze. Her own eyes widened in disbelief as they landed on the object of Jenna's sudden fear. A shadow man.

"Jenna?" She whispered.

"I uh, shit, I think you're right, there *was* something in the candles," she stammered.

"Whoa, what's going on here you two?" Marina stopped smiling.

The fear in Jenna's expression intensified as her eyes landed on another one.

"Oh my God," Anna whispered, "you see them."

Jenna looked back at Anna, her face ashen, "You too?"

"See who? What's going on?" Marina demanded.

Anna strode forward and linked her arm through Jenna's then turned to Macey and Marina. "I'm sorry but I can't explain right this minute, Jenna and I are going to go for a little walk...

"I don't think so, not without us!" Marina insisted.

"Please, guys, I promise I'll explain later, but right now you two really need to go find us a bar to hang out in while we sort this out." She gave them a pleading look while her mind desperately attempted to grasp the implications of Jenna's newfound ability. She was amazed and somewhat proud of herself for continuing to speak coherently.

Macey looked flabbergasted but when Marina tried to protest again she stopped her. "Let them go, they'll tell us later."

Marina reluctantly ceded and Anna pulled Jenna away, striding back the way they'd come. Jenna's whole body was trembling and she stumbled a little so Anna slowed the rapid pace. They went around a corner and she spotted an empty bench outside a coffee house and led her quivering friend to it.

"Do...do you think that meeting was for real?" Jenna's voice was several octaves higher than normal and tinged with panic.

Anna swallowed thickly. Instead of answering she asked her own question. "What you saw, did they look like shadow people?"

Jenna nodded slowly and stared at Anna.

Anna stared back. For the past three years she'd half believed she was nuts. Jenna's confirmation of their existence was fucking huge. HUGE.

"So what do you think they are?" Jenna whispered nervously, "are we hallucinating?"

Anna refocused on her friend and bit her lip. "No. In fact this is the first time in three years that I can actually say with a measure of confidence that those things are *not* a hallucination."

"*What?*" Jenna drew back in shock.

She took a deep breath and looked away. "I was sixteen the first time I saw one," she explained quietly. "And I've been seeing them ever since. Then just before we came on this trip I told Austin about them after several of the creepy apparitions turned up at our party. Remember the fight?"

Jenna nodded, her eyes abnormally wide.

"A group of them were there, that's why I freaked out, and when Austin took me upstairs I told him everything. Of course he's not quite sure what to make of it but at least he doesn't think I'm crazy."

Jenna was shaking her head in denial. "You've been seeing them for three *years*? What *are* they?"

"I don't know," Anna frowned in exasperation. "It's been something of an issue for me, seeing these things and not knowing what they are. I'll tell you what I do know. I know that they don't touch. They may have some seriously bad juju coming off them but from what I can tell they can't do anything to physically harm you. And furthermore I learned how to turn them off so to speak."

"Off?" Her friend continued staring incredulously.

"Yup. I close my eyes and sort of focus, you know like getting rid of the hiccups, you concentrate them away, and when you open your eyes, voila, they're gone."

Jenna took in a shaky breath. "I can't believe you've been seeing them for that long and never told anyone."

Anna gave her a look. "Who would I tell besides a psychotherapist who would prescribe me drugs I don't need? Tell me you wouldn't have thought they were hallucinations if you didn't see them for yourself?"

"Actually, my mind is still insisting that they are."

"Yeah, see."

Jenna took another deep breath but she seemed to be getting a grip. Then her eyes narrowed and she looked at Anna sharply. "Why did you freeze when you saw those guys? I didn't see any shadow thingies with that group."

Anna bit her lip. She really didn't want to start talking fangs because that truly did seem crazy. And yet it wasn't, was it? Until this moment the shadow men had been figments of her imagination. Yes she'd believed they were real, but now she had not only another person, but a close friend who could see them too. Which made them absolutely real. So why couldn't vampires be real? And for that matter....shit.

She frowned, thinking that she'd been doing a lot of head swearing lately. Her mom had once told her that curse words were for people incapable of intelligent conversation and she'd agreed with that until recently. Now she believed certain words were for lack of a better word. And no matter how educated you were there were times there was a definite lack. Words like shit and fuck encompassed a feeling that could not be conveyed any other way, not in English at least.

Jenna cleared her throat bringing Anna back to her question. Instead of getting into it, she stood. "I think we should go visit that Mistress Goddess lady at the Kilkant. She might be able to shed some light on the subject and believe me when I say I would *really* like to learn something, *anything* about those shadows."

Jenna nodded and stood with her, pulling her phone from her purse. She called Macey and told her they would be a bit longer while Anna went in the coffee shop to get directions.

As they walked towards the bar it occurred to Jenna that Anna hadn't answered her last question and she pointed it out.

"I know, I avoided it because I can't quite make myself believe what I saw," she laughed shortly. "Strange how I can totally accept the shadow men but anything new I want to automatically reject."

"Don't leave me in suspense!"

"Fine. Vampires, okay? I saw fangs and weird eyes, and when I say weird…it was like they had lights somewhere inside of them, not quite like they were glowing, more like there were penlights somewhere in their depths throwing off beams. But mostly it was the fangs that screamed vampire."

Jenna stared at her.

"I know, nuts, but that's what I saw."

Jenna said nothing just faced forward shaking her head. Shadow men, vampires, she had to be dreaming. When they'd arrived at the hotel they'd all been pretty tired, maybe they had never gotten around to going out, maybe they'd decided to sleep and do the club thing the following day.

Anna saw the doubts shadowing across Jenna's face and understood completely since she was wrestling with her own feelings of mild hysteria. She was used to the shadow men--and they didn't talk. They couldn't touch. But vampires? She'd watched all the movies pertaining to them and until recently they'd never been painted as anything but evil predators tearing out throats or changing people into monsters.

She shivered and Jenna's hold on her arm tightened.

They saw the KilKant up ahead and Anna sped up the pace. If the mistress was for real….all of a sudden she was flooded with an excitement that nearly drowned out her anxiety. She might finally get some answers!

Chapter Ten

They entered the bar and spotted the group of "Goddesses" sitting at some tables and chatting. They walked over but Anna didn't see the mistress among them. She cleared her throat and a curly haired blond looked up.

"Uh, do you know where we can find the mistress?"

The girl jacked her finger in the direction of the bar and Anna saw the woman seated on a stool between two girls. She and Jenna headed over and listened in for a minute.

"Yeah!" A perky redhead was exclaiming, "I just know there were ghosts in that house!"

"Well at least your ghosts didn't throw things around," a plain faced bespectacled girl put in, "the house I lived in had a genuine Poltergeist. We brought in a medium and everything and she said she could feel the vibrations and there was definitely something there and it wasn't happy!"

"Mm," the mistress said, "how fascinating girls. Would you excuse me for a moment?"

She glided off the bar stool, drink in hand, and Anna hopped off her seat.

"We really need to speak with you."

The mistress had a polite smile fastened on her face. "Certainly but first I must use the ladies' room."

She made her way towards the restrooms and Anna pulled Jenna along behind her. They followed the woman inside and waited until she'd re-emerged from the stall.

She smiled blandly at them as she went to the sink and turned on the faucet.

Anna cleared her throat. "Tell me about the shadow men."

The woman turned, surprise flickering across her elegant face. "Shadow men?" she asked cautiously.

"Yes. What are they?"

"When did you see these...shadow men?"

Anna met the woman's shrewd gaze unflinchingly. "I myself have been seeing them for the past three years and now, after participating in your ritual, my friend can see them too."

The woman narrowed her eyes doubtfully on Jenna. "Really? That would be unusual."

"Would it? Why?"

"There are few who ever gain enough sight to physically see the spirits and far fewer who can see them naturally. It would be highly unusual if two such people knew one another."

"Well I can assure you that I've never told her about them before tonight. Then we leave your gathering and...she's not faking it."

The woman gave them an assessing look. "Tell me more."

Anna started from the beginning of her own sightings then told her about the paralyzing flash of light during the ceremony.

Jenna's eyes widened, "That happened to me too!"

"And there's more. I think...err, I'm not sure about this, but I could've sworn I saw....maybe not. Maybe my mind is working overtime now," she said uncertainly. She didn't want this woman to think she was a fake now that she seemed to believe her.

"What? What did you see?" The mistress leaned forward staring at her intently.

She took a breath and blurted, "Vampires. Or at least that's what they appeared to be, with fangs and strangely lit up eyes."

"Oh my," the woman breathed, "it's been a long while since I've encountered anyone with a real gift. Not even I possess it." She pulled a long chain up from the place between her breasts producing a strangely shaped medallion decorated with colorful stones. "This is how I "see". It's been passed down through the generations of my family. Come, let's go sit at a table and talk some more."

She exited the bathroom and the girls followed.

Once seated several girls came over and the woman adeptly and politely dismissed them for her "private conference."

She sat back and lit up a long slender cigarette smelling of cloves. She took a drag and blew it out, her gaze turning inward. Fingering her necklace she began. "My great grandmother was the last one in my family before myself that this worked for. For reasons no one fully understands, the stones are attracted to certain people and will only lend their powers to them. When I was a little girl Nanna told me this medallion was given as a gift to one of our ancestors by someone who had had natural sight, and that this ancestor fought in a great battle against the dark spirits and what she referred to as "the fanged ones." Nanna also told me it was rumored there were other "fanged ones" who were not in league with the dark forces and that they had come to the aid of my ancestor's village and were the reason they were successful in battle."

Anna mulled this over. "Have you seen them?"

"Yes, I can see them. But I have never approached one. It is impossible to determine their allegiances and far too dangerous to expose oneself." She gave Anna a warning glance. "The reason I began these meetings five years ago, was because I had noticed a dramatic increase in the number of dark spirits out and about. An increase that seems to have tripled over the past few months alone."

Anna frowned. "I've noticed that too. Do *you* fight them?"

The mistress sighed and leaned back against her chair again. "No. I'm afraid that although my ancestor managed it, the details on how this was accomplished have been lost. For most of my life I have done as you have and ignored them. When I was young they frightened me and the only reason I kept the necklace was because the idea of not knowing where they were frightened me more. It wasn't until I was much older that I began to seek answers pertaining to them in the books my Nanna had left me when she died."

"Is that where the ritual came from, the books?"

"Yes. I did some thorough research on the content of the old volumes and eventually determined which words and ceremonies held true power. If a person harbors latent abilities my ceremony can bring them out, though most of the time it will manifest subtly. A person might sense the evil rather than see it or simply find that their intuition is something to pay attention to and trust."

"You said it had been a long time since you had met someone with a true gift?"

"Ah yes. There was a young woman during the second year of my gatherings that could "see" as I do once she'd been through the ritual. She had always been able to sense things but her eyes were opened as well. Unfortunately we lost touch." She leaned back in her chair taking a sip of the golden liquid in her glass.

"I must warn you, pertaining to the fanged ones, they have the ability to...well for lack of a better term, disguise themselves. That is why no one else could see the fangs when you could. But they can even go so far as to make themselves completely invisible to people if they wish. However it won't work with you as it doesn't with me. So you need to watch for a kind of static electricity in your vicinity. If you sense this DO NOT acknowledge the presence of the one it surrounds or they will suspect that you have the sight."

Anna swallowed thickly. Static electricity, right, got it.

"I'm afraid there isn't much more I can tell you. But I will give you my card and you can feel free to contact me with any further questions which I'll do my best to answer." She dug around in her handbag and pulled out a card that contained her name, Contessa De'LaCoeur, and her phone number.

"Thank you," Anna said, "will you take my number as well, that way if you come across anything that might be helpful to me..."

"Of course, I would be delighted."

Anna took out a scrap of paper and jotted her info on it.

"Do you have any idea why I have this ability?" She asked hopefully, as she slid the paper across the table.

"Well, there are many possible reasons. Perhaps you will call me when you're at home and I can give you the names of some books or places on line that may be helpful to you."

"Okay that would be great, thank you." Anna stood and Jenna stood with her. They exchanged farewells and parted ways.

When they were outside the bar Anna sighed and stared at the sidewalk for a moment. Other than further confirmation of her sanity the woman hadn't given her a lot to go on.

Jenna pulled out her phone and frowned at it. "What are we telling the girls?"

Anna looked up and studied her for a moment as she thought about it. "I don't think we can tell them the truth. They'll think we're crazy or they'll be freaked out, either way…. I think we should say that once we got to the Kilkant a girl told us there was some sort of hallucinogen in some of the candles. What do you think?"

Jenna nodded. "Yeah, that's good. We'll tell them that." She called Macey and learned they were waiting in a club several blocks over.

As they walked towards it Anna explained in greater detail how she was able to block out the shadow men. "Although recently there have been so many of them I find it easier to ignore them instead."

Jenna nodded slowly. "So what about the vampires? My God, there are actually vampires. Vampires exist. I keep thinking that I'm going to wake up any minute now."

"I know. I've been dealing with the shadow men for years and I still feel like tonight is some sort of insane dream."

Jenna looked thoughtful. "What else might be real I wonder. If there are demons and vampires…it seems like the possibilities are endless. Ghosts, monsters, werewolves, Bigfoot….from now on I won't be so quick to scoff at the possibilities."

Anna laughed feeling a little lighter. "True. You know what? We're about to meet up with M and M and since we've decided to keep this to ourselves I think it might be best to try and forget about it for the night. I really, and I mean *really* want to drink and party."

"Amen to that, show me the booze."

They stopped in front of the Frat House where Macey and Marina were waiting expectantly.

"Okay, what gives, spill it," Marina demanded.

Anna told them that they had gone to the Kilkant to talk to the mistress and while they were waiting one of the girls told them that some of the candles contained hallucinogens in order to "open their minds."

"Oh my God, what a bitch!" Marina exclaimed. "She just wants people to think she's not a fraud! Did you say anything to her?"

Anna and Jenna shook their heads simultaneously, exchanging glances. "No," Anna shrugged, "we decided it wasn't worth it. We're just gonna ignore things out of the ordinary until it wears off. Come on let's go in, we seriously need to forget about it."

They went inside the club and Anna made a beeline for the bar. She was in desperate need of a buzz right now. Jenna came up beside her and they decided to order a couple of shots to jump start. Jenna took hers and went back to join the others but Anna stayed put, ordering a beer and glancing nervously around the room.

Four shots and three beers later she slid off the stool and ran smack into a guy's chest.

"Oh God, I'm so sorry, I wasn't paying attention!" She heard laughter and looked up into one of the most handsome faces she'd ever seen, with a dimpled smile that was utterly disarming. He was about six foot two, well built, and she could feel a blush climbing her neck as she ogled him.

"No harm done. Except I think you lost your drink. Here, let me buy you another."

"Oh no, it was totally my fault...

"Either way I'd like to buy you another. Jake,"he said, extending his hand.

She took it and smiled self-consciously, "Anna, and I really am sorry."

He smiled wider and gently tugged her in the direction of the bar. He hopped on a stool and indicated for her to do the same.

"American, huh?"

"Yup."

"What state?"

"New York."

"Really? You don't sound it."

She laughed. "Not from the city, from upstate. Pastures and cows...waterfalls too," she added, feeling like a moron.

"Oh yeah? So how do you like London?"

"So far it's great. I've only been here for a day."

"Well, then you haven't had time to form an opinion." He stirred his drink, which was some kind of liquor. "So who are you here with?"

"My girlfriends. We went to Paris, Venice, and Dublin, now we're staying here for the next couple of weeks."

"Oh, that sounds like a great time."

Anna kept stealing glances at him, crushing hard. He was breathtaking, just something about the shape of his face, and perfectly formed features. His eyes were bluish grey with a silvery ring around the iris that made her wonder if they were contacts.

Blue Oyster Cult came over the speakers and Anna could have predicted that Jenna would turn up.

"Hey, nice song huh?" Jenna looked at her meaningfully.

Anna grinned. "Don't fear the reaper, baby take my hand," she sang, then realized Jake was watching her and blushed. " Jake-Jenna," she introduced.

Jake took her hand. "Nice to meet you. Can I buy you a drink?"

"Um, yeah sure," Jenna shot Anna a "Holy Cow" look and she smiled in commiseration.

Marina and Macey wandered over. "Come on guys, we want to head down the street," Marina announced.

"Why, what's down the street that isn't here?" Jake cocked his head, one beautiful brow raised in question.

Anna introduced them and before long they were all engaged in lively banter. She'd been flattered by Jake's initial attention but as he spoke she got the feeling he was a player, and an excellent one at that. It was uncanny how he picked up on their individual vibes so quickly. She started to get a little nagging feeling in the pit of her stomach and tried to shush it, telling herself he was just gifted at reading people. Guys like him had a string of girlfriends for that very reason. So what if he was a ladies' man? That didn't make him supernatural.

"You're awful quiet all of a sudden," he was looking at her intently and the rest of the girls chimed in.

"That's just Anna, she's a daydreamer. If you don't have her undivided attention she'll go off to la la land," Marina teased.

"Hey, no giving away my deep dark secrets to strangers," Anna chided.

Jake smiled, "If that's your deep dark secret you are a very pure individual."

"Ah, but you don't know what she daydreams about, aarroo," Macey made a suggestive face and laughed obnoxiously.

"Thanks. Thanks guys, I appreciate this, really."

"Aw, come on, we're only teasing you," Macey made a kissy face and Anna rolled her eyes.

The whole time this was going on she could feel Jake observing them, studying them. *Probably just trying to decide which one of us he has the best chance of taking home tonight,* she thought.

"Girls, girls, this is the place to be on a Wednesday night. Take it from me, there's nothing going on that's better than here. Now on Friday there's a place across town called Legend and if you're going out, you'll want to go there, but tonight? That place is here."

This was said with such confidence Anna found it difficult to doubt him.

"Are you here with friends?" she asked suddenly.

He turned to her with hooded eyes, a sexy half smile playing on his lips. "You want to meet my friends? I thought there was a connection here." He gave her a look of mock hurt.

She raised an eyebrow. "With which one of us?"

He tilted his head to the side and eyed her in a way that made her shift uncomfortably. He looked as though he was disappointed, and for some reason it bothered her. He managed to avoid her question and make her feel foolish at the same time. He was so good.

"Well," Macey said standing up. "I'm sure this probably *is* the best place to be tonight, but I heard there was a jazz band at a place called Fresno's and I really want to check it out." The other girls stood because it was Macey and her mind was made up.

"Why don't you come with us?" Anna suggested to Jake as she slid her purse onto her shoulder.

"Why don't you stay here with me?" He directed the question at only her and she was really tempted to do just that.

"Because we don't separate, that's our rule," Jenna told him.

"Well then, maybe I'll see you at Legend on Friday."

"Definitely," Marina piped in, "anyplace called Legend has my vote."

As they left the club Anna looked back to where they'd been sitting but he'd already disappeared, likely on to his next potential victim. She frowned at her choice of words as images of fangs popped into her head. She was being paranoid. It wasn't as if there'd been anything overtly disturbing about him, he just had a fine-tuned charm.

"Yoo hoo, where are you?" Macey was tapping her as they walked and she realized she'd been staring intensely at the ground.

She forced a laugh, "I don't know."

"I think you liiiked him," she teased. "Poor Austin."

"Hey, low blow. Okay, he was definitely cute, no need to throw guilt pie in my face."

Macey grinned, "I bet you'll be looking for him on Friday."

She rolled her eyes but knew that was absolutely true.

Chapter Eleven

They entered Fresno's and she was immediately glad they'd come. The music was so upbeat it was like walking into a crowded park on a sunny day. There was even a smoked food smell that made her think of barbecued chicken and corn on the cob. She smiled with enthusiasm for the first time since the witchy meeting.

There were plenty of people inside, but it wasn't crowded and they were able to find a table. After ordering some drinks, she took a look around and noted there were few shadow men here. Not really surprising since they probably didn't get off on the happy, jazzy vibe, and likely the people they dogged didn't either.

Unfortunately the place shut down a mere hour later but by then she was feeling much lighter, ready to brave less wholesome places. They ended up at a club right across the street from the Frat House, and Anna couldn't help but wonder if Jake was still there.

They weren't there for long when they met a trio of guys with whom Anna's friends clicked, leaving her to contemplate sneaking away. She didn't know why she felt so compelled to see him considering the doubt she had about his character, but maybe it was just curiosity. *Yeah, and you know what curiosity did to the cat*, she chided herself.

She danced for a while, getting lost in the music, until some guy started grinding her from behind. With a pointed goatee and grotesque tattoos, he looked diabolical. She threw him a scathing look and went to find her friends who were engaged in some grinding of their own.

Once again she was looking at the exit. Her friends were so involved she knew they wouldn't miss her for a few minutes...*Okay, I'm going*, she decided.

The Frat House had drastically increased in numbers since they'd left. She practically had to carve her way through the gyrating crowd, and she decided that coming was a stupid idea. She didn't even know how she'd find him in here.

She got trapped in the midst of three couples who were engaged in some serious liplocks and was in the middle of trying to find a way to ease around them when she saw the blood and froze. *He's biting her neck*, her mind supplied helpfully as her stomach seized with panic. She looked around wildly, but no one seemed to notice. Then she saw another couple engaged in the exact same way. And then another. *Oh God*, she thought, *no one can see this, they're doing it right out in the open and no one knows!*

She forced herself to get a grip and started pushing and shoving her way towards the bar. She broke through the writhing bodies and ran up the steps onto the deck where the bar was located and managed to squeeze into an opening. She gripped the mahogany counter tightly and took deep breaths.

After her heart rate had slowed she turned and looked out onto the dance floor. She was about ten steps up giving her a pretty clear view and she located the offending neck biters and saw that only one was still sucking away. The others were just dancing as if nothing strange had occurred, and not one person in the place seemed a bit disconcerted.

And then she saw him. Jake. And his mouth was on the neck of a scantily clad leggy brunette. Her eyes were closed, head tilted back, mouth parted like Anna imagined a person would look if they were nearing climax. And she might have convinced herself that he was just sucking, if only his eyes weren't throwing off shimmery golden light. She forced herself to look away and scanned the place for the easiest and quickest route to the exit. She spotted a relatively clear path to the far left and took off in that direction.

Once she was in the path she fought the urge to run. *Don't draw attention*, she coached, forcing even steps until she was back on the sidewalk. She stopped by the curb and fumbled in her purse for her cigarettes. Lighting one up she understood why people used them as a way to relax. It forced your mind to focus on something else, the whole process from lighting it, to inhaling, to exhaling. And it made you look like you had a purpose for just standing on a sidewalk. And she desperately needed to just stand there for a minute.

The club her friends were in was nearly as crowded as this one and right now she was feeling claustrophobic. Besides, it wasn't as if she could tell them what she'd just seen since the only one who wouldn't think she was crazy was Jenna and she didn't want to spoil her friend's night. She took another long drag of her cigarette and blew it out, trying to decide what to do next.

Someone came up and stood beside her and Anna jerked as she realized it was the girl that Jake had been devouring. The brunette lit a cigarette and glanced at her.

"Do I know you?" The woman narrowed her eyes and Anna realized she was gaping.

"Um, no, sorry, it's just...how do you know Jake?" she blurted.

The woman snorted. "Everyone knows Jake, at least everyone who lives around here. You're American and I've never seen you before, so how do *you* know Jake?"

Anna noted that she sounded exactly like the actress Elizabeth Hurley, even looked a little like her. "I met him earlier," she said weakly.

"Ahhh." "Elizabeth" took a long drag and rolled the smoke off her tongue. "I'm sure he laid it on nice and thick. He likes American girls, especially the young and naive ones."

Anna knew she'd just been insulted, but she was way too freaked out to care. "Are you dating him?"

The woman snorted louder this time. "Nobody dates Jake. They get seduced by him and then either live with a one night stand or continue fucking him if they don't mind sharing. I am the latter."

Anna decided to take a chance. She wasn't sure if she'd have another opportunity to ask questions, or if she even wanted another opportunity. "So it doesn't hurt when he bites you?"

"Excuse me?" The woman looked genuinely surprised and confused.

"Well, I saw you guys and it looked like he was biting you...."

"Biting me?" She laughed out loud, "If you mean nibbling on my neck, of course that doesn't hurt. You really are naive, my God, I think you are out past curfew infant." She dropped her smoke and put it out with her black heel. "You should really leave Jake to the big girls, you aren't ready for him."

She went back inside leaving Anna to question her sanity for even broaching the subject. Especially since there hadn't been any marks on her neck. If it wasn't for the Mistress woman confirming the existence of vampires she would not be certain of what she was seeing. She wrinkled her forehead.

The Elizabeth look alike didn't know he'd been drinking her blood-that much was clear. Whether or not he had actually been drinking it, well....how couldn't the woman know? Especially since she'd implied she was intimate with him often. She chewed on her lip trying to work through it.

In most legends a vampire bite turned its recipient into a vampire, which was apparently false. *If* she were sane of course and this was actually real. So if the bite didn't change a person, or even harm them in any way, the woman certainly hadn't appeared to be harmed, then that begged another question. Was Jake evil? Or was he one of the supposed good guys? And how or why would there be good vampires?

She had also noticed there weren't many shadow men in the Frat House. Across the road there'd been a great deal more of them, though no blood sucking going on that she'd seen. Was there something to that? God she had so many questions and no answers, it was frustrating.

The gold and silver candle, she narrowed her eyes. She should've listened to her intuition. She recalled the words of the mistress during the ceremony—"This is for perceiving other supernatural forces that dwell with us..." *supernatural but not necessarily evil*, she reminded herself. She mulled this over. Yes, seeing someone sink their teeth into a person and drink their blood was alien, but people always feared things that were foreign to them, things they didn't understand. That put a new slant on the situation.

The shadow men were only scary because of the dark feelings emanating from them, if not for that they were almost just a part of the scenery. Except for the ones that were inside of humans, those disturbed her on a level she chose not to explore. But vampires, they were only scary because of the way they'd been portrayed in books and movies.

She pictured Jake, she had known something was different about him. But evil? She wondered if she should just go inside and ask him. "Hey, I know what you are, can you tell me about your kind? I'm not judging, I'm just curious." *Okay that sounds stupid, you are definitely not going to say that*, she scolded. But...she could take him aside and talk to him about it. He could answer so many questions for her, maybe he knew about the shadow men, maybe there was a whole realm of things the average person knew nothing about and he could.....

WHOA ANNA, you haven't even decided if what you saw was real, remember? Despite their confirmed existence. And yeah it's fun to romanticize, but HELLO, he could still be a very, very bad man vampire thing. Better safe than sorry, ever heard that phrase dumbass? She blew air threw her nose and realized the only thing she was going to do tonight was go back to her friends, go back to the hotel, and possibly, if Jenna wasn't too inebriated, discuss it with her.

She took a step and a hand gripped her arm nearly giving her a heart attack.

The timbre of his voice when he said her name sent chills straight through her, though of the excited or frightened variety she wasn't sure. She forced a smile on her face when she turned to face him.

"Jake, hey, I had been hoping to find you in there...." he was looking at her strangely and she trailed off.

"From what I heard you did...find me."

The pause was subtle. The orbs of light that appeared in the depths of his eyes and grew? Not so subtle. The actress look alike must have told him what she'd said. Shit, how couldn't she have thought of that? All of Anna's doubts about what he was slid away, and she was faced with the choice to either own up or play dumb. *No one else can see this*, she thought, *he's testing me*. The trouble was she didn't know if passing was actually failing.

"Cat got your tongue," he purred.

She bit her lip and made a decision. "Guess your girlfriend told you that we met."

He cocked his head to the side a little and smirked. "Lena was rather amused by your question. I myself was…intrigued."

"Intrigued? Come on, I may be naïve but I know how silly I sounded." She smiled wider, "I've had a bit too much to drink tonight and I'm afraid alcohol brings out the blonde in me. I better round up the girls and get myself to bed. But I'm glad we met even if you are a player, and I might still see you on Friday."

She tried to step away but he caught her wrists and forced her to look up at him. It took everything she had to appear innocent and unassuming because inside she was coming apart.

He narrowed his eyes a little.

He's not sure, she thought. Not sure is good. Very good. Then her phone started buzzing and he reluctantly let go. She pulled it from her purse-Jenna.

"Hi, I'm on the sidewalk across the street talking to Jake."

"Okay, we're coming out."

She flipped it closed and smiled at Jake who was watching her intently.

"They met a few guys and hit it off," she said airily. *Good girl*, she commended herself, *keep talking like he's just a guy*. "That's kind of why I came to find you, this creepy guy with a goatee kept trying to rub himself all over me, and well I wanted to dance with someone I actually found appealing. But then you were busy." She lifted one shoulder in a "that's the brakes" kind of way, continuing to smile at him.

He didn't get a chance to reply. The girls and their new friends were already calling to her and crossing the street.

They were all smiling and joking around and Anna suddenly felt like an outsider. *She* should be enjoying herself like that without a care in the world, instead of standing on the sidewalk with a vampire, knowing he's a vampire, knowing that strange things existed. It was like a chasm had formed between herself and her friends over the past few hours. Well maybe not Jenna, she had a bridge. But...something inside of her was changing, she was losing another piece of her blissful childhood ignorance and it made her feel off center.

"The guys want us to go back to their hotel, whaddaya think?" Jenna stumbled a little then let off a burst of wind chimes. "Oops, I think I'm a wee bit buzzed."

"Yeah, sure, why not?"

"Am I invited?" Jake asked the group.

Anna winced as the girls nodded with enthusiasm.

"Of course!" Jenna exclaimed, "The more the merrier!"

There were cabs sitting alongside the curb up and down the street and Anna grabbed Macey pulling her towards one. She hoped the guy Macey was with would follow and Jake would be left to fend for himself. No dice, Jake followed them in.

"Oh, I better go ride with Brent or he'll be stuck by himself," Macey announced.

Anna watched her climb out, resisting the urge to grab her again. Shit, shit, shit. *He's staring at me, and I am not going to be able to keep this up.* And now they were practically alone, what good was one measly cab driver against a vampire?

"Do I make you nervous?" He was doing that purring thing again.

She forced a bright smile as she answered. "Of course you do, you're a charming smooth talker who apparently doesn't date, just has lots of casual sex. Which I don't hold against you, I mean you're a guy and that's what most guys wish their lives were like. But I'm not a casual sex type of girl, so we're not well suited. And I have a boyfriend," she added.

He was giving her that insect under a microscope look again. She could almost see him weighing the odds that she was just a bit of a ditz who happened to use the word bite in reference to him as a mere coincidence.

"Why did you think I was biting Lena?"

And there it was. "I meant nibbling," she said too quickly.

"Hmm. Anyone would wonder if hurt to be nibbled." He had one eyebrow raised slightly and Anna looked at the driver.

He followed her gaze and his lip curved. "He's a cabdriver in London, you can't imagine the strange things he's seen and heard."

She drew in a breath and let it out slowly, "I don't know what you're talking about."

"I think you do. Answer my question Anna."

She studied her hands. "I don't know why I thought that."

"Anna."

"Are you going to hurt me?" she asked in a small voice, still concentrating on her lap.

"Why would I do that?"

She glanced at him and saw his expression had changed back to the disarming guy she'd met.

She thought it over and decided to direct the conversation. She lost the "airhead" look and took a deep breath. "Tell me what the shadow men are."

His brows flew up in surprise and he stared at her for a moment before responding. "You see them?"

"Yes."

He grew very quiet before shaking his head slowly, carefully. "They're demons. My kind destroys them, it's what we were created to do."

It was Anna's turn to be surprised. "Vampires were made to kill demons? How? I mean how do you kill them?"

"Kill isn't the right word. We end their existence, it's difficult to explain."

"Are you old?"

He smiled in amusement. "That's a relative thing, age. Your idea of old and mine are not the same."

"Are you immortal?"

"In a sense."

Her brows drew together at the vagueness of his answers. "I've never seen your kind before tonight."

His gaze sharpened. "Never? And yet you don't question your sanity?"

"Actually I did think I might be hallucinating, except I've seen the shadow men, err demons, since I was sixteen so I'm somewhat accustomed to the supernatural."

He smiled again and it both chilled and warmed her at the same time. A loud sound came tearing out of his jacket and she leapt back.

"My phone," he chuckled, before answering.

He spoke in a foreign language, so all she got out of the conversation was that he was bothered by something.

"Anna. I'm afraid I have to go, but I really want to see you again and continue this conversation. I'm sure you have more questions for me which I'll be glad to answer. Could I have your number?" He held out his phone to her and she paused briefly before taking it and punching her digits in his contact list.

He told the driver to pull over and handed him some money. He leaned down and kissed her lightly on the forehead. "I'll call you."

She nodded and watched him leave feeling a wave of disappointment mixed with relief. He was a source of answers, and for that she was excited, but she couldn't help being nervous about someone who was not quite human. She leaned back against the seat and realized she was exhausted. After a quick call to the girls she changed her driver's route so she could go back to the hotel and get some sleep.

Chapter Twelve

The next day Anna waited in anticipation for his call. She received several texts from Austin, a call from her father who checked in with her about once a week, but nothing from Jake. She kicked herself for not asking for his number, patience was not a virtue she possessed.

Her friends slept the day away after getting into the room sometime late morning, so she was alone with her thoughts for most of the afternoon. It occurred to her that if any myths about vampires were true then he could be sleeping in a coffin somewhere. Well...she doubted the coffin part, but it was possible he couldn't go out in the sun.

Then again he might have given her some thought and decided she was of small consequence. Someone who blurts out "Does it hurt when he bites?" is not particularly formidable in either the ally or the enemy camp.

She decided against telling Jenna about it for now. She needed to talk to him some more and she had a feeling her friend wouldn't let her go off alone with him if she knew. Not that she would isolate herself, she fully intended to meet him in a public place. Still, he had some kind of unnatural ability to disguise things from the general populace, and who knew how deep that went. Could he kidnap her in the middle of a crowded room and make it appear she was willing? Quite possibly. But at this point her need to understand overrode her caution sensors. Sometimes you had to take a risk.

The guys her friends had spent the night partying with came to their room in the evening and ordered pizza, opting to rent a couple of videos on demand while they recuperated from their previous night's excess. Anna pushed her thoughts aside and let the movies give her a brief escape.

On Friday they went with the guys, Brent, Kip, and Les, on a tour of London. All day Anna was filled with a sense of anxiety and anticipation. They were going out to Legend that night, and since Jake had been the one to recommend the place there was at least some chance he'd be there. Jenna was too preoccupied to notice Anna's state of mind so she was spared the grill.

They arrived at the club at just after 10pm, and it was already packed. It had three stories and two sections per floor, and Anna soon realized the chances of happening upon him were pretty slim.

The night wore on and she put on a good face- laughing at her friends and their escorts, sipping on beers, dancing, and going through the motions. By three am she had to accept that she wasn't going to see him. He had obviously decided to ditch her. Either that or something had happened to him....she recalled that he was edgy during his phone conversation. And he had said he fought demons.

She spun a tale in her mind that involved him being badly injured in a supernatural battle, painting him the big hero. She searched the place for signs of other vampires, but if they were there she didn't see them. By the time they left for the hotel she was enormously disheartened.

The next night they went to yet another club, and it was more of the same. Anna couldn't enjoy herself. She tried, really tried, but found herself on constant alert for signs of strange activity. She was beginning to think she had imagined it all, that she really had ingested some kind of hallucinogen at that meeting.

By Sunday evening she was almost convinced that was the case.

Her friends' male counterparts were with them constantly, so on top of feeling like she had briefly lost her mind, she was also feeling a little left out. It wasn't their fault, they did their best to include her, and she knew if she wasn't so messed in the head over the events of Wednesday she probably would have been fine. As it was she frequently lapsed into silence and there was no "Austin" to pull her out of it.

When Wednesday rolled around again she talked them all into going to the Frat House. Lena, the Elizabeth Hurley look alike, had said that everyone from around there knew Jake. Anna decided she would ask the bartenders about him, and if they couldn't help her she'd have them point out some of the regulars. It was the first time all week that she'd felt enthusiastic about anything, and by the time they reached the strip she was giddy with excitement. Even the girls noticed her drastic mood change.

"You want to see Jake, don't you?" Marina teased.

"Oooh, yeah, that's why she's so bouncy today!" Macey laughed and waggled her eyebrows.

"You should've given him your number," Jenna told her, "instead of pining for him all week long, maybe he could have hung out with all of us."

She bit her tongue. She had told them he'd received an urgent phone call from a friend and had to get out of the cab, but left out the fact that she *did* give him her number. Which was probably a good thing, they would have just insisted he was a bum who wasn't worth her time.

"Yeah, but I felt guilty doing that," she lied, "because of Austin."

"Yet you were hoping to see him on Friday and are hoping to see him tonight," Jenna pointed out.

"I know, I know."

Their guy friends met them at the front of the club and Anna immediately put her plan in action. She made her way up to the bar, scanning the place as she went.

The bartender acknowledged her with a slight lift of his head.

"Porter draft," she told him.

He brought the drink over and quoted the price.

"I was hoping you could help me find someone," she smiled sweetly as she handed him her money.

"Who would that be?"

"His name is Jake, he's about 6'2", brown hair, hazel eyes, he comes in here a lot. He has a friend named Lena...

The guy was nodding so she stopped. "Yeah, I know him, haven't seen him tonight, but it's still early."

"Can you tell me his last name by any chance, or point me to someone who might know more? It's important." She put on an earnest face figuring with her pixie looks she would come across harmless.

"I don't know his last name, I only know who you mean because you mentioned Lena. Haven't seen her yet either." He looked around the bar and pointed to a couple of women standing at the left corner of it. "Might try them, friends of Lena's."

She thanked him and gave him a big tip. He acknowledged it and added, "If I see him I'll let you know."

She started in the direction of the women, then slowed a bit and studied them. They were wearing a great deal of make-up and sporting bad hair dye jobs, one bleached blonde, one strawberry. They were in their mid-twenties and dressed like street walkers. Lena had definitely been classier despite her skimpy clothing.

"Excuse me," she said as she approached, "I was wondering if you could help me."

The women looked her up and down. "With what?" The bleached blonde asked.

She repeated the questions she'd ask the bartender, adding that he'd pointed her their way.

Strawberry spoke. "I know Jake, but he doesn't do last names. In fact when a girl he wants to shag is the type who needs a last name, he makes one up. All his buddies are like that. Great lay though, have you done him?"

Anna blushed and shook her head.

"Oh, you're one of those innocent types he likes. It's some kind of game for him to seduce girls like you." She smiled and flashed a set of crooked teeth. "Haven't seen him around tonight, but if I do I'll be sure to say you're looking for him."

"What about Lena?"

"What about her?"

"Have you seen her around?"

The woman snorted. "Even if I had, the chances she'd know where he is are pretty slim. She likes to pretend she's tight with those guys, but she doesn't know last names or addresses any more than the rest of us. So unless she's just seen him, I'm afraid you're S.O.L."

Anna thanked them and walked away, her heart sinking in defeat. She had been so certain she would find out something useful. Damn it! She only had six more days before they were on their way back to the states. She couldn't stand the thought that she would go home without answers, without knowing for certain what she'd seen was real.

Jenna tapped her shoulder. "Find him?"

Anna shook her head.

"Were you asking those girls about him?"

She nodded, "The bartender said they might know him."

"And?"

"They do, but not where he is, or his last name, or where he lives, so yeah, they know him about as well as I do....aside from the fact that they've apparently slept with him." She winced, immediately wishing she could take that last back.

Jenna wrinkled her nose. "Ugh, Anna, I'm thinking that maybe it's a good thing you're not finding him. Those bimbos look like disease on legs."

"It's not like I was going to have sex with him!"

"I know...look, I don't want to crush you, but I'm thinking he might've bailed on you because he knew he wasn't getting laid. I liked him and everything, he was definitely handsome and charming, but face it, he's a player, and he must've decided that with you he'd lose."

Anna blew out air in frustration.

"What was that?" Jenna raised an eyebrow.

"I'm sorry, I just...well you have a guy to hang out with, and please don't think I'm trying to make you feel guilty because I'm really *glad* that you do, it's just.....

Jenna looked at her sympathetically, "I understand. So why not try and meet someone else tonight, we still have six more days."

"Austin," Anna mumbled.

"Forget him."

Anna jerked in surprise.

"No, I don't mean *forget him*, I just mean don't let him stop you from having a good time when he's not even here. You guys aren't married. In fact the only real obligation you have is to tell him if you've fallen for someone else. And if that happens, it does. So just take a look around and see if there's anyone that interests you, then go talk to them. Usually you're the one giving the "Don't worry be happy" speeches, come on Anna, relax and have fun."

She nodded and smiled at her friend. "Okay, I'll do that, but first I have to pee." She took off towards the ladies room letting her smile slip. If only it really was about any of that, oh what a carefree life she'd have. She was once again struck by a feeling of alone-ness. Not loneliness, just alone-ness.

She stood in the middle of the restroom and made a decision to take Jenna's advice, at the very least it would provide a distraction.

Over the next few hours she met a few cool guys and had a small amount of fun. She even gave one of them, Andy, her number. He was cute and nice and at least if she invited him along on their excursions she'd feel less out of place.

For the next few days she explored London thoroughly-sometimes with just the girls, mostly with the guys plus Andy-resigned to the idea that once again she had questions without answers.

Lucky for her Andy was not the aggressive type. It would've sucked to hurt his feelings by shooting him down if he tried anything. She decided he would make a good face-book buddy and found herself missing Austin a little. Oh well, at least she had nothing to feel guilty about.

Chapter Thirteen

It was two days before they were supposed to return home when she saw them again. Not Jake, but others like him. She was walking down the sidewalk near the Frat House with her friends when they walked by, flashing their fangs and strange eyes.

She grabbed onto Andy's arm, startling him.

"Did you trip?" he smiled.

"Um, yeah, clumsy me." She took a breath and looked over her shoulder and one of them looked back and met her eyes.

"Uhh, do you know that guy?" Andy asked.

She tore her gaze away. "Um, I thought I recognized him. I was wrong." She smiled benignly, and they resumed walking down the street in the opposite direction.

They went into Fresno's and had just ordered a pitcher of beer and nachos when her phone rang, the number coming up unlisted. She stared at it for a minute, then excused herself and went outside to answer it.

"Hello?" her voice quavered.

"Anna."

Oh God. When it rains it pours.

"Sorry I haven't called before now, I've been preoccupied. I heard you were looking for me the other night." His voice had a light-hearted casual tone to it, and she remembered her image of him as a super-hero.

"Uh, yeah I guess I was." Intelligent Anna, smooth, Jesus.

"You're supposed to leave in two days right?"

She blinked. Oh yeah, when they met she'd told him when her trip would end. "That's right."

"Unfortunately I'm still tied up in some things, but I'd really like to see you again. It's not every day a human can see through the "dimming" and I feel drawn to you. Have you told any of your friends about me?"

She snorted. "That would be a no, I'm pretty sure they would think I was nuts." Well except for Jenna.

He laughed. "Yeah, people tend to only believe what they see, sometimes they even question that. So what would you say if I offered to buy you a ticket home for later next week?"

What?? "Why?"

"Well, like I said, I'm still tied up with some things but I want to see you. I'll understand if you can't, but if you say yes I'll buy the ticket and send it to your email so you can print it out. It will be for next Saturday. I'm not sure exactly when I will get free to see you, but it *will* be before then, I promise."

He sounded so normal, so reasonable, so friendly and disarming. She could picture him leaning casually up against a wall, smiling into the phone. Peter Parker from the Spider Man movies, only not so geeky.

"Is there anyone you've met whom you might be able to hang out with until I can get away?"

She chewed her lip. Of course the money for a return trip was not a problem for her, but she had to admit the idea of him buying the ticket did make it appear above board.

But the girls...she could tell them she just wasn't ready to go home yet. But then Jenna and Marina might want to stay too. Though unlikely they'd ask her to buy them new tickets, they definitely wouldn't understand why she'd want to stay alone…. She stared at the sidewalk for a moment before a plan began to form.

"Okay," she told him, "buy the ticket."

"Excellent! I'll call you tomorrow to be sure you received it."

She gave him her email address and hung up.

She went back inside and tapped Jenna on the shoulder. "Will you take a walk with me, we need to talk."

Jenna nodded and stood.

"Where are you going?" Marina asked, starting to rise.

"No, hang out here, we're just going for a walk, don't worry we won't be long."

Marina frowned slightly but sank back in her chair.

Once outside they walked slowly down the sidewalk and she could feel Jenna's eyes boring a hole into the side of her head as she worked out exactly what she was going to say.

Jenna put a hand on her arm forcing her to stop. "So, what's going on?"

Anna took a breath and spoke carefully. "There's something I didn't tell you." She pulled out the now rumpled pack of cigarettes. Two left not bad, she mused as she handed one to Jenna.

She lit hers and passed the lighter, taking a long drag and letting it out slowly before speaking. "Jake can see the shadow men. He knows what they are."

Jenna reared back. "*What?* And you didn't tell me this *why*?"

Anna bit her lip and launched into the lie full speed ahead. "Because he asked me not to, even though I told him you could see them as well. I described the ceremony to him, and he wasn't certain that your abilities would even last. Whereas with me I could see already...anyway, there's like an underground network of people who can see things like that, and they know things. They fight them Jenna. That's why he left that night, it had nothing to do with sexual exploits." She took a deep breath, weaving the story in her brain. "I have been living with this for three years, and I have so many questions I need answered. He can answer them."

"So that was him on the phone?"

"Yup."

"So when will you see him?"

"That's what I needed to talk to you about. He's tied up in something and he can't get away until later this week. He offered to buy me a new ticket home, for Saturday, he's sending it to my email right now."

"Whoa, wait, you're going to stay here?"

"Just for a few more days."

Jenna leaned away from her and frowned. "Well, I want to stay with you then. I haven't lost the ability I've just been ignoring it, *believe* me I still see them."

Anna shook her head and looked down. "The underground society is extremely secretive. Jenna, he could get in trouble if he brings someone in without their permission. Apparently he made a case for me, so what I will do is get the information…and then once I'm in I can bring you in if that's what you want."

"Of course I do! I don't see why he can't make a case for both of us," she insisted.

"Please, Jenna! I'm asking you as my friend to trust me and let me do this first. I've been living with this for years, you've only had to think about it for a couple of weeks and at least you had me to let you know you weren't crazy! If you stay with me, he won't do it. Please, I need this."

"Okay, okay, I see your point. But how do you know you can trust him? I mean, this underground society could be some sort of cult, he could totally be lying to you.

Maybe not about seeing them....how did you find out that he could see them by the way?"

"He saw me watching a couple of them rather intently, and asked what I was looking at. I laughed and said "the shadow men", thinking he would consider it a joke. Instead he looked as if I'd just slapped him in the face. "Describe them", he'd said, and I did....the rest is history." Anna took a breath. Wow the lies were coming easier and easier.

Jenna nodded, but frowned. "Still, it could be a cult."

"You know what? You're absolutely right. He could be a Satanist. His underground network could be a psycho group of devil worshippers. But I have to take a chance, sometimes you just have to risk it. Because I think I will go mad if I continue seeing things that I can't understand or do anything about. Did you forget about the blood suckers Jenna, because I still see them too. I need to know, and he's the only link to information that I have and potentially will ever have. Look, if anything weird happens, you at least have some information. And if it makes you feel better, if it turns out he is a Satanist, I will totally play along until I can get my ass out of there and home. Okay? I won't point my finger at him and say "The power of Christ compels you", I will keep my mouth shut and pretend that I am on his side, and then I will get my booty on a plane and come home."

Jenna smiled a little at that. "All right. So I guess we tell the girls that you are starting to have feelings for Andy and you need to see where they're leading? Although you haven't exactly made a case for that, and I'm not sure what you'll tell Austin....actually, do me a favor and tell Austin what you told me. He knows what you see, I can confirm that what you see is real, and at least I won't have to worry alone."

Anna started to protest, but reconsidered. What else would she tell him? He would be extremely hurt that she chose not to come home, even if the girls didn't say anything about her alleged crush. Which of course they wouldn't, she trusted them. But it might make her feel less out of it if he at least knew something...even if it was mostly bullshit.

"Okay. I'll write him an email explaining it the best I can, and when you get there you can talk to him about it. He'll worry like crazy, but I'll keep you both apprised of my general well-being." She thought about it some more. "Another thing. I have an access card to one of my main accounts in my underwear drawer. And I think you should take my license with you, I have my passport so I don't need it. That way you'll have money and my identification in case you need to fly back here and bail me out of something. I DON'T want my dad involved under ANY circumstances, promise me."

Jenna stared at her before nodding. "I'll make sure the situation is dire before I even consider it."

"Okay. Good. Let's not tell the girls until tomorrow night. That way they won't have time to analyze the way I behave around Andy."

"Deal. Let's go back."

That night Anna sat at her laptop frowning. She'd just written Austin a very brief rundown of events and an abbreviation of the discussion she had with Jenna. She hadn't wanted to go into serious detail but she knew as soon as he got it he would be calling to let her know how he felt about it. And it wouldn't be a pleasant conversation.

She could avoid his phone calls and allow Jenna to better explain when she got there. Or she could try and face the music. She pushed send and sighed. It would be about 8pm there and since his phone alerted him to new emails, she knew she didn't have long.

A half an hour later her phone played doomsday music, (she had set it to Austin's ring tone as a way of amusing herself). She could pretend to be asleep, after all it was nearly two am here. She let it go to voicemail the first time, but he wasn't having it. The third time through she picked up making her voice sound groggy.

"Hello."

"No fucking way. No way. You get on that plane tomorrow Anna, or I'll be on the next one to come and get you."

"Look, I probably didn't explain myself well enough....

"Oh I think you did, and I can fill in the blanks. I don't need Jenna to tell me anything. I don't care what she sees now, in fact I'll go as far as to say that I believe you. I believe you see those things, and she does too. Okay? I don't think you're crazy, at least not about that, but this? Some strange guy and his underground cult? You can't be that stupid, I know you, I have known you for years, and I know that you're an intelligent girl....

Anna held the phone away from her ear as he continued on his rant about her lack of common sense and yada yada. It made no difference to her what he said, her mind was made up.

"Hey, are you listening to me?"

"Of course I am. But I knew everything you were going to say before you said it. I didn't tell you my plans to get your approval or consent, I told you out of consideration for you. Because I care about you, about us, and I didn't want you to make up some other scenario for my extra stay...like for instance a romantic interest, especially since that's what we're letting M&M think it is.

I'm doing this Austin. And don't bother with the I'll Get On A Plane And Drag You Home bit, you won't find me. If you were actually foolish enough to try, it would be an enormous waste of your time. I will be home Saturday night, if you want to pick me up my flight arrives via Conway in Syracuse at 8:35 p.m. There's nothing you can say, nothing you can do. You don't understand what it's like to be me, to live with this and not know why. I have a chance to get some answers and I'm taking it. Period."

She could hear his uneven breathing through the phone and she knew he was really upset. She felt a little bad, but there was nothing she could do.

"If anything happens to you....you can't know how devastated I will be. Jesus Anna, I've never felt this kind of fear before." His voice was strained and she felt her heart tug a little.

"You're wrong," she said softly, "I can put myself in your shoes, and I know that I would feel just like you, helpless and scared. With my imagination I would drive myself crazy with the possibilities. And I am so sorry that you have to go through it. Maybe I shouldn't have told you, maybe it was selfish to involve you."

"God Anna, don't say that. I would hate to think you wouldn't tell me things like this." He sighed. "Call me every day. Please. Just let me know everything's okay. And I'll see you Saturday night. Get some sleep." He paused. "I love you, you know."

"I know. I love you too."

"Goodnight."

She hung up the phone and sighed. Well, that could've been worse.

The moment she laid her head on the pillow she was out.

Chapter Fourteen

Jake's call didn't call until Friday, and she had to bite her tongue against some seriously sharp words. The past few days she'd been wandering the streets of London aimlessly, waiting for her phone to ring. Of course it did ring, Austin called constantly and so did Jenna, but not him. Sure he was immortal and time probably didn't pass the same for him as it did for her, but he mingled with humans, he had to know she was waiting impatiently for him to call.

"You're still at the Regency, right?" he asked as soon as she pushed talk.

"Yeah, still here."

"Okay, I'll pick you up out front in an hour."

He hung up without saying anything else and she stared at the phone shaking her head. *Finally*, she thought on one hand, and *Shit* on the other. She called Jenna.

"He's picking me up in an hour."

"I don't know Anna, I have a bad feeling about this. He didn't call you all week, don't you think that's strange? And now he's just going to show up on your last night there...I mean how much can you learn in one night from these people?"

"Admittedly I'm having doubts of my own."

"Then don't meet him. Just stay in your room and get on a plane tomorrow. I promise that I will help you in your quest to learn more about this, I will research with you, okay? Let's do that."

"Tempting." She rolled her shoulders and ran her hand through her silky hair. "No, it's gonna be fine. What could he possibly gain from hurting me? And why give me such ample opportunity to back out if that was really his intention? Everything is always worse in your imagination, in people's I mean. It'll be fine."

She repeated that in her head like a mantra, but a feeling of dread had curdled her stomach. She had to wonder if that feeling was the perception the Mistress had been talking about. Perceiving evil. Yet she couldn't back out now. Why hadn't he just called her a couple of times, just to tell her he was busy but thinking about her? At least she would feel comfy as she headed to her doom.

"Anna?"

"Still here. Look, I'm gonna go...

"I thought you were going to meet him someplace public, what happened to that idea?"

"I don't know, he just called me and said he would pick me up in an hour then hung up. I didn't get a chance to make suggestions."

"Not good Anna, I think he did that intentionally. He probably knew you would be willing to go with him since you've been waiting on pins and needles for days. He's very intelligent, he could have predicted your plan was to meet him somewhere safe and thwarted it. I don't like this."

"I'll have my phone on me."

"Yeah, as if that will matter if he holds a gun to your head and takes it away."

"Not helping." *If she only knew what he really was....she'd kill me for even considering this.*

"Don't go."

"I have to."

"No, you don't."

"Jenna, please. I do. I'll be fine. I love you, call Austin for me, okay, can't deal with round two of this conversation."

"No way, *you* call him, maybe round two will change your mind."

"I'll call you later," Anna hung up the phone and took a deep breath, then let it out slow. She got ready, than on impulse tucked a credit card along with her passport down between the box spring and the bed frame underneath the headboard.

Her phone rang startling her. She really needed to take a chill pill.

Austin of course. She pushed ignore and texted him. "Can't talk right now, on my way out, I'll call you later, love you."

She took the elevator to the lobby and walked slowly through it, the acidic taste of anxiety filling her mouth. Her hands trembled as she pushed open the glass door and walked onto the sidewalk where she stood shifting her weight from foot to foot nervously. *Please God, let me be okay, let this not be a mistake.*

A few minutes later he pulled up to the curb in a sleek blue sports car and rolled down the window. He was smiling broadly and did not appear evil in any way. He just looked like a cute guy in a cool car.

"Hop in," he leaned across the seat and opened the door.

She climbed in and smiled nervously. "Where are we going?"

"To the first day of the rest of your life," he smiled wider and gave her shoulder a reassuring squeeze.

He turned the music up loud as he raced down the streets. She could feel the bass reverberating in her chest, the vibration making it difficult to think. Where ever they were headed, it was taking a while to get there.

He finally pulled to the side of the road in front of a large building. It didn't look like an operational business, but the amount of cars parked up and down the street suggested otherwise and made her feel more comfortable--safety in numbers and all that jazz.

"Have you ever been to a rave?" he asked as he switched off the ignition.

The sudden silence was deafening and it took her a moment to understand what he'd asked. When it sunk in her eyes widened. "That's where we are? Why?"

"Well, because this is where a number of my kind come to party. Don't worry, it's not an orgy or anything you may have heard, it's just a place where people are a little more lax about the rules."

She stared at him blankly for a moment as she absorbed this, then felt a sudden rush of anger and narrowed her eyes. "Don't *worry*? I don't want to be here Jake, I just wanted you to answer some of the questions I have and I was thinking more along the lines of a pub where we could sit in a corner booth and talk. I'm supposed to leave tomorrow, you never called, and now you're taking me to a party where it will be too loud to hear anything, and the *rules are lax*. Not what I had in mind. Look, if you don't want to fill me in, that's fine, I'll call a cab and we'll part ways." She reached for the door handle and he put a hand on her knee.

"Anna, look at me."

She stared at his hand and considered ignoring the quietly compelling command. She would open the door, leap from the car and dial a cab service...she heaved in a sigh facing the fact that she would do no such thing. Her curiosity was still greater than her fear.

She turned towards him, meeting his earnest expression.

"I won't let anyone hurt you. I promise I will not let anything happen to you. There are just some things I need to show you in order for you to understand. Words aren't always enough. You know how you can't quite describe the shadow men?"

She nodded slightly.

"It's like that."

She bit her lip. "Couldn't we at least talk about some things first, and *then* you could show me?"

He sighed. "Anna, you're going to have to trust me on this. What could I possibly gain from hurting you or allowing you to be hurt?"

"I have no idea."

"If I wanted to hurt you I've had plenty of time to do it," he frowned, narrowing his eyes thoughtfully. "Look, just walk over there with me," he pointed towards an alley, "and I'll show you something. We'll talk a little, and if you still want to leave then you can go. Okay?"

She nodded reluctantly and her stomach knotted as they got out of the car.

They turned down the alley and she hesitated.

"You watch too many movies," he laughed. Then he grabbed her hand and Ran? Whizzed? down the path. A millisecond later they were behind the building and his arms went around her waist as he leapt into the air, landing on the black tarred roof. She had no time to process this before he jumped down into a parking lot, landing between two cars.

"Back up," he instructed.

She did so a bit jerkily and leaned against another car for balance as she watched him disappear underneath a rusty old blue Buick. A moment later he hoisted it over his head and stood there grinning at her before setting it back down.

Wuhh, she thought, her eyes blinking rapidly.

He approached her still wearing the grin and put his hands on her shoulders his eyes holding hers. "I move faster than your eyes can process, I can leap onto buildings and hoist cars over my head...believe me Anna, if I had wanted to hurt you, there's nothing you could have done about it. So will you please relax and go inside with me?"

She nodded mutely. What could she say? She was still trying to process what she'd just experienced.

He took her hand and they "whizzed" back to the entrance of the alley. He caught her arms as she nearly tripped.

"That makes me dizzy."

He laughed and tugged her into the building. They walked down a corridor and she could feel the bump of the music on her feet from down below. He led her down a wide stair case into an enormous dark room filled with people.

The strobe lights were overkill, the pulsating effect of them disorienting, and Anna experienced a sudden case of vertigo to add to the warning bells chiming in the back of her mind. He still had a hold of her hand and was pulling her through the distorted dancers, and she blinked her eyes rapidly in an attempt to get her bearings. The flashing lights made the expressions of the people around her appear somehow malevolent and the dark tone of the music added to her unease.

Jake moved behind her and slid his arms around her waist, propelling her forward. His warm breath brushed her ear and she had the fleeting thought that it should have been chilly. Like he said, too many movies, highly inaccurate. He pulled her into him and she felt the steady beat of his heart- another myth busted- and a hardness pressing into the small of her back that made her own heart speed up. She recalled what Lena and the other woman had said about his sexual prowess and shivered.

"Relax little one, you're safe with me," he spoke softly in her ear. He whirled her around to face him and graced her with the most knee weakening smile she had ever witnessed then pulled her into his arms. As they danced she wondered what exactly it was he wanted her to see here. It was too loud to ask him anything, despite the fact that his voice seemed to cut right through the noise as if it wasn't there.

After a few minutes he whispered, "Come on, let's get a drink," and half carried her as he danced them through the crowd to the long steel counter that served as a bar.

"She'll have a Tequila Sunrise."

She immediately shook her head. "I just want a beer," she shouted over the music, "in a bottle!"

He frowned but nodded his assent to the bartender who flashed a set of fangs at her, causing her to stumble backwards.

Jake caught her. "Careful," he whispered, "you'll give yourself away."

The barkeep had eggshell white hair and eyes the color of a robin's egg. If a person was into the metro sexual look he could have been called cute, but to her he was a bit freaky. She watched as he popped the cap off her bottle then held her hand out for it. She wasn't taking any chances of being drugged.

She drank half of it down then covered her mouth as she burped, her stomach feeling a tiny bit better.

"Do a shot with me," Jake suggested.

"No thanks, no liquor for me, the lights are making me dizzy enough. I can pace myself with beer."

"You're kind of a prude aren't you?"

Her brows drew in at the slight and she frowned at her beer. "I'm just not comfortable here."

"I've already told you that you're safe. With me as a bodyguard you can't get any safer." He lifted his brows at her.

She frowned. "I thought you had something to show me."

"I do. Later. Now, I want you to have a few drinks to relax, there's so much anxiety flowing from your pores I can smell it."

She drank the rest of her beer. "I'll take another one of these, don't worry, if I keep drinking this fast I'll have no problem relaxing."

He stared at her for a moment then shrugged. "I saw someone I need to speak to. In the mean time you might consider why you bothered getting involved with me if you were going to continually doubt my motives."

He disappeared into the throng of people and she watched him go with a mixture of confusion and irritation. *Trying to goad me into drunkenness? Not that easily pressured bloodsucker*, she thought.

She turned away and made accidental eye contact with the bartender who was staring at her intently. A little chill made its way up her spine. The message his strange eyes were conveying made her think "Anna-it's what's for dinner."

She broke eye contact and took a long pull from her beer, wondering if some vampires could disguise their nature's better than others. Or maybe they were like people and some of them were just plain weirdoes. God she wondered a lot of things, it was frustrating not to KNOW anything. Why *had* she come here if not to get answers? And how would she accomplish that sitting alone sipping a beer?

"Hello," someone said to the right of her, breaking into her thoughts. She turned to look and saw the flash in his eyes. Yet another, and this one was startlingly handsome. He had raven black hair that hung loosely around his face, and his eyes were the deep blue of the ocean. His skin had an olive tone, *Italian*, she thought, *or maybe Greek*.

He extended his large, long fingered hand and said, "Paulo, and you must be Aphrodite."

His line caught her off guard and she laughed.

"No? Than perhaps Luna, the Goddess of the moon." He took her hand and raised it to his lips.

As corny as the line was, with his accent and delivery it came across sexy. She stared at him without replying and he leaned in, his expression conspiratorial.

"A delicate angel such as you would look far better holding a glass with a cherry in it. Let me buy you a drink that will titillate your senses." He caught hold of her beer and slid it out of reach on the bar, getting the attention of the white haired freak.

She tried to protest and reach for her bottle, but he gently and firmly stopped both her hand and her words. "Trust me," he whispered.

He said a few words in a foreign language to white hair and in seconds he was pushing something towards her that smelled like strawberries and cherries. Its fragrance was so strong she thought it might intoxicate her with just its fumes.

"Go ahead," he coaxed, "try it and tell me it isn't divine."

He lightly brushed her arm with his knuckles and the effect of his touch was disconcerting. She took a deep breath and closed her eyes. *Get a grip Preston*, she scolded, *danger here, fangs, might bite you...*

He put his hand on her cheek and she jumped a little.

"Easy little Luna, you've nothing to fear from me."

My ass, she thought and found her voice, raising it to be heard, though she had a feeling it wasn't necessary. "I'm sorry Paulo, I'm sure the drink is delicious, but I have an allergy to liquor."

He drew back, his blue eyes widening in mock surprise. "Surely not! I've never heard of such a thing."

"No, it's true, something about the sulfites...it makes me violently ill. Just beer for me I'm afraid."

His eyes narrowed a bit, his expression conveying disbelief. Then a hand came down on her shoulder and a familiar voice said, "Paulo."

"Jake."

They exchanged a few words in Italian or Latin and Paulo stood up, clasping her hand to his lips once more. "Until we meet again little Luna."

Jake sat down where Paulo had been and Anna decided he was far less intimidating.

"So you're allergic to liquor now?" he sounded amused and a little pleased. Presumably since Paulo had done no better convincing her. It seemed no matter the species all males were alike in matters of pride.

She shrugged. "I didn't think he'd take no for an answer."

"You're right about that, he has skills in persuasion that even I have yet to master." He considered her for a moment, "But he didn't persuade you. I take back what I said earlier, you're not a prude you just possess a strong will." He picked up the drink that was meant for her and downed it in three swallows, licking his lips. "That was delicious, are you sure you don't want one?"

She was glowing a bit from his compliment and felt her resolve weaken. Not that the drink couldn't have been drugged, he could be immune for all she knew. But then she remembered that aside from not wanting to be drugged she also preferred to stay relatively sober until he'd "shown" her some things.

"Look, I'm relaxing now, I promise. I just don't have any tolerance for liquor and I'd rather not start stumbling."

"Fair enough." He slid her beer back down the bar and handed it to her.

She tipped it back nearly emptying it. "I can handle beer," she told him as she set it down.

He was looking at her strangely, a small smile playing on his lips. "Can you?" he asked softly.

She started to nod and nearly doubled over from a crushing wave of dizziness. She put her head in her hands. *Never lose sight of your drink*, she thought miserably.

Jake took her by the elbow and murmured something in her ear, but her brain was too jumbled to understand.

"Ladies room," she managed to squeak. He helped her up and led her through the club and it felt like she was floating. She tried to glance around her and winced, pressing her face against Jake's side. In that brief surveillance she had seen fangs and lit eyes EVERYWHERE.

He opened a door for her and she stumbled over the threshold, struggling to keep her mind from cracking apart. She grabbed the edge of a sink...at least she thought it was a sink... Oh God, why did it have to be dark in here too? She desperately needed light to get her bearings. Her vision was spinning crazily as she fumbled for the knobs on the faucet. She heard water, but her sense of touch seemed to be on hiatus. *Shit, oh shit, WHAT THE HELL did they put in my fucking beer!* She felt a wave of anger crash over her and welcomed it greedily. *That's it Anna, get pissed, you can fight this!*

She needed to get outside, needed air, but how when Jake was standing on the other side of the door waiting for her? *Damn it!* Wait, did he do this to her, or was it that other guy? *Luna, Luna*, oh shit, her mind was fraying. Paulo. Paulo had white hair do it maybe. Maybe Jake's still a good guy. *Oh please let him be.* She felt hysterical laughter bubbling and bit down hard on her lip. If she started with that, she would be lost.

She made her way out of the bathroom straight into Jake's waiting arms. She lifted her unfocused gaze to his and said with all the venom and strength she could muster "Get me out of here, now!"

"Okay, just relax," he soothed, "let's go."

"You put something in my beer," she slurred, "Why'd you do that?"

"No, I wouldn't do that."

"Then freaky bartender did, or th'other one, I don't know," she stumbled and he picked her up.

"I told you I would take care of you, and I will," he breathed in her ear, "you're special Anna, you're different."

She struggled to comprehend his words through the thick fog of her thoughts. Was he calling her special? Was he acting weird or were her crazy thoughts making it appear that way?

She vaguely realized he was weaving her back through the gyrating masses. *He's taking me out of here*, she thought, *Oh thank God*.

She saw the stairs they'd come down, but he passed them by.

She pointed as if he missed them on accident, and he stroked her hair, turning them down a hallway. He walked her inside yet another dark room and sat her down on a couch of some sort. She could make out other shapes, but barely.

"Why is everywhere so freaking dark?" she mumbled, "I don't like it, I want to go outside, want to get out of here."

He pulled her up on his lap. "It's all right, you just need to rest a bit, let the drug work its way out of your system."

Her throat was really dry and when she swallowed it felt like sandpaper. "I'm so thirsty," she told him.

"Okay, I'll get you something. Just sit and rest."

He disappeared and she fought to stay conscious. He reappeared a minute later and put a cold glass to her lips.

"What is it?" she managed.

"It's a special kind of wine, it will help you feel better. Trust me."

She was really getting sick of that phrase and shook her head violently. She'd suffer with a dry throat.

He pulled her back into his lap again and she tried to struggle. It was futile.

"You're strong," he told her in a conversational tone that did not fit the atmosphere. "You have no idea how easy this usually is. I've never seen a girl fight this hard to keep her mind intact after ingesting S E C. Usually they've passed out or are babbling incoherently by now. Not you though, you're determined. That's very good, I really believe you'll make it through the transition."

"The...what?"

He put his hand on her jaw and forced her to open her mouth, pouring the cool, thick liquid onto her tongue. She gagged, ejecting it back onto his shirt. It tasted like...flowers smell.

"Don't fight me anymore. You can't win, and if you don't drink this, you'll die."

Die? Don't want to die! She felt tears forming in the corner of her eyes and her shoulders started to shake.

"No, don't do that, just drink and everything will be fine."

She felt the cup pressing against her lips again and *knew,* even in her fragmented mind she understood that she had two choices. Drink it and become...become a monster. Or refuse it and die. One way or another, she was going to die.

She parted her lips and he smiled.

"Fuck you," she managed, then pressed her lips tight.

The hand that had been gently massaging her shoulder stilled. He laughed, a dark and chilling sound, right out of a horror flick.

"Oh yeah, you'll make it," he gripped her face and tilted it back then forced her mouth open and plugged her nose. This time her throat convulsed and it went down. There was a sensation at her neck...BITING ME, she thought wildly. A feeling of euphoria overwhelmed her senses and all thought scattered like debris in the wind.

Chapter Fifteen

Jared strode into a seedy club on the outskirts of London, a tangible anger rolling off him. Even veteran bar brawlers cringed away as he passed, the alcoholic haze that comprised their lives momentarily penetrated by an ancient instinct to fear a dangerous predator.

Every man in the place fought the urge to flee while the women struggled with the desire to throw themselves into his arms. None would have hesitated if he crooked a finger their way, such masculinity was not seen in this century of weak men. The blatant dominance exuding from him served as both a warning and a mating call.

An age worn, yet still attractive redhead whispered to the woman sitting next to her. "Even a proper young virgin would throw 'erself beneath him and spread 'er legs wide." Her companion nodded in wide eyed agreement as the bartender shook his head and wondered what made dangerous men so bloody attractive to the fairer sex.

Jared slid into a stool. Even seated he dwarfed the men in the room. "Langyard Scotch, just bring the bottle." The low timbre of his voice resonated like the strum of a perfect note on a bass guitar, sending shivers of pleasure through every female present.

The bottle was placed in front of him and he tipped it back, reveling in the slight burn. It was the most potent brand of alcohol made on the planet, and the only one that could calm his temper and settle his nerves.

Her face. He growled deep in his throat and startled the barkeep who hastily retreated to the far end of the worn and severely scuffed wooden counter.

Her face haunting him.

Throughout the ages he had seen females who had resembled her and given him pause, but not in the past fifty years since he woke from his last hyberstasis". Until the dying human girl in the Godforsaken gaming dungeon. Her eyes had been the same shade of brilliant turquoise, a shade that could never decide between blue and green.

A sharp pain lanced through his psyche and he squeezed his eyes shut, attempting to dispel the images that caused it. His thoughts turned to the males of his acquaintance and his lips curved into a sneer of disgust.

Generally he was unconcerned with the depraved activities they labeled entertainment, but earlier that night he'd learned a vial of his own blood had been used in their deviant practices and the information had turned his vision red. For some reason the idea of any part of him being any part of that made his skin crawl. They'd apparently believed it might aid in successful transformation. The fucking fools.

He grabbed the bottle and tipped it straight up, opening his throat, willing himself to blessed intoxication.

It had been more than a century since she had been so vivid in his mind. The memory of her voice and laugh, which time had faded and eventually taken from him, had returned and left him feeling desolate. He slammed the bottle down on the bar and half of the patrons jumped.

He glanced around and thought what he always thought. Weak. Pathetic. Unworthy. That last drew out in his mind. Humankind and their proclivities for shallow and meaningless pursuits. Treacherous and petty minds filled with unwarranted pride and hopeless vanity. He'd once devoted his life to the service of protecting them, of saving them from their own ignorance and self-destructive behavior. Until they had repaid him by taking *everything* that had offered joy in his battle weary life.

For a long time his hatred had been a living thing, as was his resentment for the One who had made him. But time had a way of dulling strong emotions, and centuries later he was mostly indifferent.

He caught a whiff of cheap perfume as a woman slid into the bar stool next to him. She daringly placed her hand on his thigh and wet her lips, the smell of her desire dark rum in his olfactory. He despised her even as he knew he would use her. His need for release had turned his prick to fortified iron and it kicked painfully as she brushed an ample breast across his arm.

Burying himself between the thighs of a female was the only source of pleasure he had left, the only reprieve he had from the stretching emptiness. With human women it was brief with little intensity, but the females of his own kind came with a price. Those who still lived were little more than demons in corporeal form.

He finished off the bottle and stood, inclining his head towards the door.

She placed a hand on his arm as they exited and spoke in a voice husky from too many cigarettes and long nights of drinking. "My car or yours?"

"Yours." He hadn't brought a car. He rarely used one, preferring his species unique method of travel loosely translated as "blurring". Moving faster than the human eye could see he could cover miles in seconds.

She drove and he avoided conversation by turning the radio up as loud as the cheap stock speakers could manage. Fifteen minutes later they pulled up in front of a crumbling old apartment building that had once been beautiful, much like the woman it housed.

Once inside he allowed for no small talk, shoving her up against the wall and thrusting his tongue inside her mouth. She attempted to protest and he pulled back, leveling a gaze at her that caused her mouth to clamp shut. He kept eye contact as he stretched her arms over her head and pinned them there with one hand. With the other he ripped off her blouse and bra, then leaned down and drew the nipple of her large tit inside his mouth. She gasped and ground her hips into him.

He palmed her other breast, squeezing hard, and she moaned as he ripped off her pants and pressed his cock against her entrance. He recaptured her mouth, catching the inevitable cry as he thrust the enormity of himself deep inside her womb, he ground himself against her and she came viciously.

Gripping her soft ass in his large palms he moved her to the couch and spun her around, bending her over the arm and driving into her from behind. He grabbed a handful of her fiery hair and pulled, causing her to shout with a mixture of pleasure and pain. He thrust into her hard and fast, her inner muscles contracting around him as one orgasm followed another. He finally felt his own release building and shouted in a forgotten language as he pumped his fluid into her. For the briefest of moments he felt warm again.

When he was finished he slid out and pulled his pants back on and without a single word he blurred into the night.

Chapter Sixteen

Austin and Jenna sat in a diner just outside their hometown, pushing food around on their plates. It was Wednesday, and the past five nights had taken a toll on both of them, emotional and physical exhaustion was evident in their drawn expressions and bruised eyes.

On Saturday, the day Anna was supposed to have returned, they had taken turns calling her every half an hour, but it went straight to voice mail every time. They had driven to the airport together in virtual silence and sat in the terminal without much hope. By Monday they'd been frantic with worry and they'd gone together to the local police station and filed a missing person's report. They'd given as thorough an account as possible without mentioning the shadow men, instead implying that it seemed as if Jake was part of some kind of cult.

The following day they learned that the Investigations unit in London had interviewed everyone at the Frat House, but no one knew Jake's last name, where he lived, or had seen him in over a week. In addition to that the woman Anna had seen with him-Lena-had overdosed on Heroine ten days earlier.

So far they'd kept her disappearance a secret from the rest of the girls, figuring it was pointless to worry them until they had no choice. They had tried to reach Anna's father however, but no one seemed to know how to contact him besides her.

"I think we should go," Austin said finally. "Maybe no one at the clubs are talking to the police, but that doesn't mean they won't talk to us. People don't trust cops."

Jenna nodded. "Yeah, I was thinking the same thing. Besides, it would be better than just sitting around and waiting. I hate this..." her voice broke and Austin reached across the table to squeeze her hand.

His own eyes were bright though he'd refused to give in to tears. He felt if he did it would be like giving up.

Jenna took a deep breath and pulled Anna's credit card out of her purse. She dialed information, called the airline, and booked a flight to London for the following morning. It would leave at 7:40 am their time and arrive in London at 11:30 pm.

That being settled they paid their bill and went outside.

"I'm going to tell the girls tonight," Jenna stated. "Not everything...just that she was supposed to come home and we haven't heard from her...I'll wait until we're on our way before I let them know we're flying there, otherwise they might want to come."

Austin nodded.

They had driven separate cars since Jenna was borrowing Anna's. Initially she had been so angry at her for not contacting them she figured she was entitled. Now she gleaned a kind of comfort from being surrounded by Anna's apple scented body spray and listening to her music.

Austin leaned in to hug her and she let him, returning it with one arm. She wasn't much of a hugger usually, but when she felt the tremor in his chest she wrapped her other arm around him and swallowed hard. They parted with plans to meet and stay at Anna's for the night so they could get up and go early the next morning.

Once on the road she called the girls, all but Holly who was in North Carolina, and told them to meet her at Anna's around dinner time. She had several hours to kill and found herself driving aimlessly, finally ending up at Logan Point. She sat in the car staring out at the lake.

She shouldn't have let Anna stay in London. She'd known something wasn't right and she never bet against her intuition. Her friend had been determined but she still found herself thinking of all the ways she could have prevented this.

Please God, let her be all right, she petitioned for the thousandth time since Friday. She had called Les and asked if he, Kip, and Brent could scour the area, particularly the clubs and bars. They'd come up with nothing.

Though she was normally not one to let emotion get the best of her, she had been a complete wreck for days, crying one second, burning with anger the next, and otherwise filled with anxiety. She would stare at her phone and just will it to ring with Anna's musical little voice on the other end.

She tried to take a leaf from Anna's book and imagine she was fighting demons side by side with Jake, so caught up in that other world that she'd lost track of time. But it didn't stick, it always ended up with a vision of her dying on the floor of some abandoned warehouse. The image was so strong she had to force it away and tell herself it was not a *true* vision. Just because she'd always had a bit of sight did not mean she was clairvoyant. *It's just what you're afraid happened and you're making yourself believe it's more vivid than it actually is,* she thought adamantly. She stared at the water trying desperately to convince herself of that. *At least you don't see her dead*, a small voice whispered, *dying, but not dead.*

She got out of the car and paced around the park, willing the hours to slip by. She desperately wanted on that plane, needed to be in London. It was the sitting around on her hands that was driving her batty, she was an action kind of person.

She finally got back in the car and drove to Anna's house, deciding she could keep herself busy by making one last attempt to find a number for Martin Preston. It really bothered her that the guy didn't provide a way for people to reach him, that his daughter had been missing for days and he had no idea. She knew he generally checked in with Anna once a week, but the last time had been Friday so he wouldn't know anything was wrong for at least two more days.

She searched high and low, in every drawer and cabinet, but aside from numbers they'd already tried she came up empty.

She spent most of the time trying to figure out exactly what she'd tell the girls, but when she heard them pull up the driveway she had an overwhelming urge to spill it all. If it wasn't for Austin she already would have.

They came through the door talking and laughing. She was happy to see Jess could pull herself away from Nate for a few minutes....*stop that!* She commanded. She'd been working on thinking more generous thoughts about her sister lately. She had come to realize life was too short to waste on negativity. Something she now understood Anna had learned from her mother's death.

Jess put a halt to their bantering as she looked closely at her sister. "Jenna, what's wrong? You look terrible!"

She took a deep breath and pushed out the words. "Anna's missing."

Saying it out loud, and to them in particular, made it more of a reality. She felt the tears coming and tried to get a grip but ended up breaking down instead.

They all became animated, the questions firing at her.

"What do you mean, missing?" Jess's voice went up an octave. The sight of her stoic sister unraveling sent a wave of panic through her body.

Macey and Marina started talking at the same time but Jess shushed them, indicating they wait until Jenna got it together.

"She was supposed to fly home on Saturday, I know I told you that she'd changed her mind, but I lied. I haven't h..h...hheard from her since Friday."

"Oh my God, we have to call the police!" Marina exclaimed.

"Already did," she sniffed, "Austin and I filed a missing person's report on Monday m..morning."

There was a moment of shocked silence. Jess broke it, her concern giving way to anger.

"Why didn't you tell us! I hate that you always think you need to deal with things by yourself! You didn't want to worry us, right? God Jenna, you look like you haven't slept in days! We could've been in this together!"

"I know! And I'm telling you now, okay? You don't understand....she...it's," she faltered not knowing how to continue without telling them more of the truth.

"She what?" Macey asked quietly her dark eyes narrowing a little.

Jenna took a deep breath and let it out slowly. *They'll think I'm nuts*. But what choice did she have?

So she told them, slowly and carefully, beginning with the whole Goddess meeting, moving on to her new ability to see demons and Anna's already established one. When she was finished their reactions were varied.

"You really see demons?" Jess whispered.

"There is no such thing as demons!" Marina stated.

Macey just shook her head, her eyes wide.

Jess turned on Marina, "So what are you saying, Jenna's making this up? Or that she's crazy? Which one?"

"I don't know, maybe they think they're seeing things...

"Oh bullshit, just because you don't see it doesn't mean it doesn't exist!"

Marina rolled her eyes, "We're not going to have another God conversation are we?"

"Oh okay, like Jenna really beats you over the head with things like that!"

"No, she doesn't, but you have."

"But this isn't about me...

"Stop it, both of you!" Jenna turned to Marina, "Regardless of whether or not you believe these things exist, Anna went off with a guy who led her to believe he was some sort of demon fighter, and now she is MISSING, for the past *five fucking days*!"

Marina closed her mouth as that sunk in.

Macey finally spoke up. "You're going to London, aren't you?"

Jenna was startled by that deduction. "Austin and I."

"When?"

"Tomorrow morning."

"I want to go!" Jess demanded.

"You didn't even go in the first place..."

"Oh, so now you're going to hold that against me? You're the one who kept this from all of us and LET her stay knowing the guy could be a cultist, and you're condemning *me*?"

The tears returned immediately, "You're right, it's my fault, which is why I'm going."

Jess shook her head, her own eyes tearing. "I'm sorry, I didn't mean that. It's not your fault." She wrapped her arms around her sister, and Marina started pacing.

"So what are you going to do there?" Macey asked.

Jenna gently pushed her sister's arms away and got a hold of her fluctuating emotions. "We're going to visit all the bars, talk to people...we're hoping that since we aren't cops someone might talk to us."

"I could help," Jess insisted.

"I know. I probably should have given you the option. But Austin and I got the last two tickets for that flight, so even if you do go it can't be with us." A small lie, but she really didn't want her sister anywhere near danger.

Jess sighed. "How long will you be there?"

"I don't know. It depends."

"But what if something happens to you....

"Austin will be with me, we won't separate for any reason or do anything stupid."

The room grew quiet then as they all began to wonder if they were about to meet with tragedy, and through all their differing thoughts there was one common plea. *Please let her be okay.*

Chapter Seventeen

Anna woke up starving. Her whole body was shouting for food, and for a moment the shout was so loud she forgot where she was. She slowly focused her eyes and realized she was curled up under a stairwell, the musty smell of mildew and stagnant water clogging her nose.

Images accosted her, glimpses from the horror show of....when was it? Panic flooded her as she fully acknowledged where she still was. She strained her ears for the sound of voices but aside from the dripping of a pipe it was silent.

She forced herself to crawl out of the space then carefully stood up. Peeking through the doorway she found the place deserted and her relief was immense. But on the heels of that relief were two distinct desires....to eat and to flee.

There was a delicious smell coming from inside the basement and as she struggled to place it she found her body moving towards it. She had the sense that it was dark, but her eyes seemed to make their own light as she walked. Her addled brain refused to explore that further.

Stopping in the middle of a large room, she located the scent on the floor at her feet. As her mind registered just exactly what had drawn her she turned and fled up the stairs, through one corridor after another, until she found a door with light pouring through it. She yanked it open and leapt out onto the sidewalk, the sun momentarily blinding her.

The sun. She stood frozen in place, some part of her mind expecting to go up in flames. But nothing happened and she let out her breath in a whoosh.

She sat down on the cold cement and tried to sort things out. The street was deserted and of course she had no idea where she was. She skipped through things, not willing to face everything just yet. The hunger was nearly unbearable and it *really* fucking hurt. What she was hungry for....she shut her mind down on for the time being. *Okay, just take it one step at a time Anna. You have to get back to your hotel.*

She got up and started walking toward the nearest street sign, straining for the sound of cars. She could hear traffic to the north and though she was incredibly weak she began running in that direction, needing to put as much distance between herself and That Place as possible. She turned down several empty streets before she spied an intersection. She sprinted toward it, startling a woman waiting to cross.

The woman wrinkled her nose and moved a few steps away making her aware of her haggard appearance along with an unpleasant smell emanating from her clothing.

Nothing in the world sounded as good to her right then as a shower. A hot steamy shower to wash away all of the filth, both physically and emotionally.

She spotted a taxi driving in her direction then realized she didn't have any money. *Oh well the driver won't know that*, she thought, and she could hopefully take care of him once she got to the hotel. She mentally praised herself for having stowed away her credit card and passport since her purse was long gone, along with her phone. She flagged down the cab hoping he wouldn't demand to see money first considering her appearance.

"Where you headed?" he asked as she climbed in, eyeing her in the mirror.

"The Regency Hotel in London Square."

He looked surprised. "You're American," he stated.

She nodded.

"Looks like you had a rough night."

She nodded again and breathed an inner sigh of relief as he pulled away from the curb. She settled back against the seat and started to smile but it fractured as she became aware of a drumming sound. Her focus zeroed in on the driver's neck where a vein was pulsing and she abruptly realized the drumming was the beating of the man's heart. *Oh shit*, she thought, *not good.* Her hunger intensified and her mouth began to feel strange, fuller. She clapped a hand over it and squeezed her eyes shut.

"You going to be sick miss? I'll pull over, I don't want no regurgitation in my cab."

She shook her head and spoke through her hand, "I'm not going to puke. My mouth hurts, I have a toothache." She could've laughed at that statement if she wasn't envisioning sinking those aching teeth into the man's neck.

He looked at her doubtfully, but mercifully kept going.

She kept her eyes shut tightly and tried to gain control by conjuring up an image of her mom. Her voice, her smell, her laugh. The way she always had of seeing the bright side of everything. *It's all a matter of perception*, she coaxed herself. *I perceive that I am lusting for blood, but that I still love my mom. And my dad. And my friends. I am still Anna Preston.* She focused on these thoughts and felt her...teeth- she couldn't bring herself to think the other word- return to normal.

Twenty minutes later they pulled in front of the hotel.

"That'll be twenty-two euros," the driver told her.

She bit her lip, "Look, I'm really sorry, but I have to go inside to get money. My purse was stolen, but I have a credit card in my room and there's an ATM in the lobby."

He frowned slightly, "Fine, but I'll have to charge you for the wait."

"No problem."

She entered the building wishing she had her hotel key. She really didn't want to approach the desk, but there was little choice in the matter.

"Excuse me, I'm sorry, but I'm in room 305 and I've misplaced my key."

The lady at the desk looked startled. "Miss Preston?"

Anna's turn to be startled, "Um, yes..."

"Oh my, the police have been looking for you. You are a missing person, did you know that?"

She shook her head slowly and realized she didn't know what day it was. She asked.

The woman looked surprised again, then concerned. "It's Thursday hon, they've been looking since Monday. Why don't you have a seat...

"No," she said quickly, "I have to go to my room, the cab driver's waiting to be paid and my credit card is in there...

The lady was shaking her head. "There's nothing in that room, the police searched it. It appeared as if you checked out without letting us know."

Anna stared at her. "Nothing? My clothes are gone?"

"I'm afraid so," she said sympathetically.

They'd gone to her room? Who had? Jake...? She shook her head, it didn't matter, "Well I actually hid my passport and card, so they might still be there. Could you just take me up so I can look?"

"Well, okay."

The woman called a bellhop over and he took her up to the room. She mentally crossed her fingers as she went into the bedroom, and sent up a silent prayer as she reached down inside the frame. She pulled out her things and smiled, relief crashing through her.

She mumbled "thanks" to the waiting bellhop and hurried out into the hall. There was an ATM on each floor and she located one, extracted some cash, then took the elevator to a side exit. She hurried around the building and got back in the cab.

The driver told her the fee and she handed it to him along with a large tip.

"Could you take me to the nearest airport?" She asked, climbing back in.

"Oh, I thought you were...he stopped at her shaking head. "Okay then."

She needed a shower badly, but there was no way she was talking to any cops and she was sure the lady at the desk would call them. The hunger was like a beating drum in the back of her head, it took most of her focus to ignore it.

Luckily the airport wasn't far and she thanked the driver generously.

Once inside she made a beeline for the nearest clothing shop. One very nice thing about large airports, they were equipped like mini malls. She bought an outfit then found a drugstore and bought some toiletries. She made a final stop at a burger joint hoping like hell the food would help. She took a bite half expecting it to taste bad, but it still tasted like a hamburger. She gulped down the ice water which felt really good going down her throat, soothing, and when she was finished she did feel a bit better. Not a lot, but a bit.

She found a handicapped restroom and locked the door, leaning against it for a moment as a bout of dizziness struck her.

Got to get home, she thought.

She gave herself a thorough sponge bath at the sink and when she put her head under the faucet she nearly moaned in pleasure as the grime poured down the drain. When she was finished she pulled on the khaki shorts and light blue t-shirt she'd purchased and apprised herself in the mirror. Better. Much better.

At the ticket counter she managed to find a flight that departed for home in one hour. The benefit of being able to pay for first class was that you rarely had to wait.

She flopped down on a bench and was struck by a thought that managed to break through the ever increasing need in her body-*she was a missing person.* Which meant Austin or Jenna or both had filed a report, *Oh God they must be out of their minds with fear*, she thought. And what about her father, had they contacted him too? She stood up shakily and headed for the pay phones.

When she reached them she just stared for a moment. Who first? *Dad,* she decided. There was at least some chance he wasn't aware of her disappearance since no one knew how to get a hold of him besides her. As long as he hadn't tried to call her too many days ago she would be safe.

She dialed the number and held her breath.

"Hello?"

"Dad..." she said carefully.

"Hi honey. Where are you calling from?"

No alarm or concern, he didn't know, *Thank God.*

"I'm at the airport in London, on my way home."

"Really? Oh I thought you were leaving last weekend."

"My plans changed and I lost my phone. I didn't want you to worry if you couldn't get a hold of me."

"Oh, okay. Listen honey, I'm going to Haiti next week, I'll probably be there for a while, unless you needed me to come home for anything...

"No. No, that's okay, I'm fine." *Fine?* God she was *so Not* Fine.

"All right. I'll call you when I'm settled. My battery's dying, but I love you, and hope everything is well."

"Yeah, good, fine. I love you too."

She hung up the phone and felt tears stinging the back of her lids. A part of her wanted to call him back and cry "Daddy please come home, I'm scared!" But she couldn't do that, she couldn't….God she couldn't think that way right now, she had to pretend everything was normal or she'd fall apart. She dialed Austin's number and got his voice mail.

"It's me. I'm...I'm coming home. My flight gets in at 9:30. I..." she trailed off and hung up. What else could she say? She would need to be in person for this conversation and even then...."I'm sorry, I lied to you, the guy was a vampire and he turned me into one too, so how do you feel about dating a bloodsucker? And by the way, your vein looks really good tonight." A slightly hysterical laugh bubbled up and she pressed her lips together tightly to contain it.

It was the first time she'd fully acknowledged her condition, and as the thought of his vein stuck in her head, the crippling hunger hit her again. She sank down on the floor and willed her mind in a different direction. It took longer to push the feeling back this time, and she was beginning to fear she would end up attacking someone. She went over to a bench and sat down wearily, waiting to board what would likely be the longest flight of her life.

Chapter Eighteen

Jenna and Austin woke up the next morning to find that sometime during the night the power had gone out and in their rush to make the flight on time, Austin forgot to turn his phone back on. They pulled into the airport at 7:25 am and ran full tilt to the check-in. They were rushed through the baggage check and made it on the plane without a minute to spare.

They would be flying to the International airport in Virginia first, arrival time-one hour, than wait for two hours to get on the flight to England.

Once they were in their seats, Jenna texted her sister whom she'd promised to keep in constant contact with and Austin took out his own phone and turned it on. When it was loaded an electronic voice informed him he had one new voice mail. It was from an international number and he sat forward with his heart in his throat as he loaded the message.

"What is it?" Jenna asked.

He glanced at her as the message came on, "Hi...it's me...

"Holy shit, oh shit! It was her, damn it I had my phone off, she called like an hour ago...she's on her way home!"

Jenna's eyes widened and her heart slammed in her chest. "All of a sudden," she said breathlessly, "I'm really happy about the layover."

Austin laughed, relief washing over him as he realized just how hopeless he had thought it was.

Jenna was smiling so broadly she thought her face would crack. "Oh my God, I have never been happier about anything in my entire life!" She started to laugh, all of the tension that had built over the past week flowing out of her in great whooping bursts. Austin joined her, eliciting strange looks from all over the plane.

When they finally settled down, Jenna realized there was still the tiny issue of her being MIA for nearly a week. She asked Austin to play the message again.

"Do you think she got cut off?"

"No, it sounded more like she trailed off," Austin frowned, "You know I needed to let go of all that tension, but the fact of the matter is...something happened. We should be prepared to nurse her back to mental health. Either that or she is the most self-centered, thoughtless person I have ever known and I'm going to strangle her."

Jenna shook her head, "She wouldn't have just neglected to call, or at least text. Even if she thought what she was doing wasn't something we'd approve of, she would've let us know she was safe."

"I know. I was just saying."

"So what do you think?"

"I have no idea. There's no point in speculating, we'll just have to wait until we see her. Speaking of which, you should call the airline and book us a flight back from Virginia."

***

Anna spent the first few hours of the flight desperately trying to ignore her ever increasing need. Aside from the fact that it was like a mantra pounding in her head, she felt weak, sick, and the fire had come back. Nowhere near as bad as it had been the previous night, but it was there. She felt eyes on her and turned to see a guy around her age checking her out. He was nice-looking, his skin color suggesting mixed races. She forced her gaze away as a thought entered her mind. No, not so much a thought, but an image of her leading him to the bathroom….

NO! She thought adamantly. But she glanced back at him and he smiled, and God she was soo thirsty, she just needed….her thoughts began to fray and she stood up and headed toward the bathroom. As she passed his seat she paused and smiled before continuing down the aisle.

What the hell am I doing? She thought desperately, but deep down she knew and was not surprised when he followed her, his expression shouting "Mile High Club here I come." The moment the door to the restroom was shut she put her hands in his hair and started kissing him frantically. He emitted an excited noise in the back of his throat and she vaguely noted the sound of a zipper. She broke the kiss and licked his neck, her hunger flaring unbearably, and she pushed his face against her shoulder as her fangs dropped. She sank them into his pulsing vein and pulled hard, at which point all thoughts fled.

"Oh God baby, that's good, keep doing that," the guy urged. He moaned and panted and began struggling to undo her pants, but she pressed him against the wall and slid her hand down his pants instead. After only two strokes she felt warm liquid flowing over her fingers as he groaned. With an enormous effort she forced her fangs to contract. She was shaking all over. Her body was screaming for more and it was only the image of him dying in her arms that gave her the willpower to do it. She stared at the trickle of blood on his skin then darted her tongue out and licked it away. Her eyes widened as she watched the punctures close and disappear.

That's how they do it, she thought, remembering that Lena hadn't had any marks. Must be something in the saliva…*God this was so incredibly out there beyond anything she'd ever dreamed up.* She washed her hands and backed away from the guy as he cleaned himself up. This was *so* not a situation in which she could have ever seen herself. But the excellent news was she hadn't hurt anyone, in fact she highly doubted "hurt" would be the way he'd describe it.

He looked at her and grinned. "Man, whatever you were doing to my neck, it drove me crazy. I'm sorry I didn't take care of you...

"No," she cut in hastily, "that's okay, this was a bet, my friend bet I wouldn't do something like this, she thinks I'm a prude, and anyway I wouldn't have wanted it to go any further because I am a little well, prudish, so anyway, yeah. Thanks." She started to back out the door, her face flaming red with embarrassment, and he caught her wrist.

"Hey, don't be like that I'll be ready again in just a few minutes."

Her hunger flared. "Oh no. No, once is enough, I have to go back to my seat now."

He pouted. "All right, well if you change your mind, we still have hours left to go."

"Yeah, okay, I'll let you know."

She hurried back to her seat and hastily put on the courtesy headphones, her heart beating frantically. *Ready again in a few minutes*...Jesus, the offer was almost too tempting to refuse. Though the fire in her blood had diminished, it was still hissing and crackling. Tears blurred her vision and she choked them back. Thoughts were racing through her mind at a million miles per second, overwhelming her to the point of panic. She turned the headphones as loud as they would go and focused on the movie screen mounted in the front. It leapt towards her and she pressed backwards into the seat, hearing a loud crack. She froze.

"Um, miss, I think your chair is broken," someone screamed into her ear.

She spun around and the source of the voice looked startled. "Are you all right?" He roared. She blinked at him. Other voices accosted her and she spun around again. Everywhere people were yelling, and above all of that was the sound of explosions, and metal scraping on metal.

Oh God, she forced her head into her lap, covering it with her arms. She gulped in air.

Someone tapped her on the shoulder and she shook her head violently, refusing to look up.

"Miss," a woman's voice shouted, "it's all right, it's just an anxiety attack. Here drink some water."

She shook her head again. OFF, she yelled inwardly, TURN OFF!

Silence descended immediately.

Okay, she thought shakily, *okay. Get a grip. The blood must have done something, just calm down, your senses have been heightened, that's all it is.* Oh yeah, that's all it is no biggie, righhhtt. She felt tears burn the back of her eyelids and clenched her hands into fists. She felt the tapping again and put up a hand in a universal "hold on" gesture.

She took some deep breaths and began to calm down. It was still completely silent as if she'd pressed a mute button. Which was nice, but not practical. She worked on the problem for several minutes and discovered what seemed to be a volume control inside her head. She was able to turn the noise back up very slowly. *To human levels*, she thought and a crazy giggle escaped her lips. *Stop that!* She commanded, *No hysteria!*

She lifted her head up slowly and met the concerned gaze of a flight attendant who was standing next to her, holding a glass of water. Anna reached for it and drank it down greedily.

"I'm okay now," she told the woman. She looked around, and though people were sneaking looks at her, their expressions were mild. She must not have done anything too freaky, thank God. Her gaze landed on the bathroom guy and he started to get up. She shook her head slightly and he stopped, sinking back down.

"Your seat appears to be broken," the flight attendant informed her gently.

She nodded. Luckily the seat beside her was empty. She felt a giggle building again but stomped it down. She moved over and nodded once more, the action making her feel grounded somehow. "I'm okay," she repeated.

"Okay hon, but if you feel another attack coming on just push the button on the armrest."

"I will."

She watched the attendant move down the aisle and leaned back against her seat, closing her eyes. Tentatively she sought out the "volume" in her head and started playing with it.

She learned that in addition to the ability to mute everything, or turn it up and down, she could also be specific. If she focused on one particular voice she could hear everything they said as if they were sitting next to her. *Holy shit, I'm eavesdropper extraordinaire.* The thought made her smile a little. She opened her eyes and snuck a look at the bathroom guy and was relieved to see he appeared to be sleeping.

Remembering what had started her "panic attack" caused her thoughts to turn to her sight. The television had appeared to leap at her. *Huh*, she thought as she glanced around. Unlike her hearing, nothing seemed out of the ordinary. She frowned, that didn't make sense. She turned towards the window and scooted over into the broken chair. *The chair that you broke*, her mind butted in. She pushed the thought away. One thing at a time.

She looked out the small circular pane and at first all she could see were clouds and sky. But when she focused harder she was startled to find she now had a "zoom lens" on her eyes. That must have been why the screen had appeared to leap at her, she'd zeroed in on it in an attempt to block out her thoughts. The harder she focused, the faster the landscape rushed up at her. She closed her eyes to let the feeling of dizziness pass and tried again. After a while she figured out how to slow it down.

We're flying over tobacco farms, she mused.

She leaned away from the window and studied her other senses. They were all more acute, though none as drastically altered as her hearing and sight...and possibly her strength, though she couldn't test that theory right now.

Since she hadn't noticed a difference until after she'd taken in blood, she decided it must be linked to nourishment. Taken in blood. Drank blood out of somebody's neck. She shook the thought away and forced herself to continue being as logical as possible under the circumstances....okay nourishment, so how long could she go without it before she started feeling weak and sick, and especially before the pain hit?

At least she'd found she could control it. She shuddered to think she might have gone too far and hurt someone. Since she hadn't planned it out she was damn lucky that was the case. She wondered if all vampires instinctually knew when to stop so they wouldn't cause harm to the...source.

She had an inspiration and flagged down the flight attendant. "Do you have any notebooks and pens?"

"Certainly." The woman left and came back with a black marbled composition notebook, the kind you used in grade school for English.

Perfect, she thought. She chewed on the bottom of the pen trying to decide where to start. Finally she put the pen down on the paper and let it decide for her.

I have fangs. I drink blood, though I don't harm the person I drink from. In fact, they don't know what it is I'm doing, and....it feels good to them. It's somehow tied to sexual desire. Meaning? I am a vampire. Not sure if they are different species, and if so does that mean I'm only half? Or once you change do you change all the way? I can go out in sunlight, either myth is busted or I'm different. I still feel like me in matters of the mind and heart. So I'm not like the ones who made me this way. Also, every other person I witnessed change turned into a monster or died. Does *that* mean I'm different? Or they just couldn't control themselves?

Maybe most people are like that to begin with, then with help they learn to control it. Which would mean that I possess a strong will. Or maybe vamps are whole other species and humans don't always change right. But if that's true, why me?

She hazily recalled Jake calling her different and special as well as mentioning her strong will. The memory of that monster holding her and crooning made her stomach queasy, but what had he meant? And if he really thought that, then why had he brought her to that place? *Don't bother Preston, you couldn't possibly understand a mind as evil and warped as his. Besides he's dead.* That brought to mind an image of the Greek god who had killed him.

Do vampires have human like emotions? (Besides me) Obviously not the ones I've seen. Except..maybe Greek god guy, at least at some point.

What is my life expectancy? Am I immortal? Jake said..."Something like that". Have to do a little experimenting, see if I heal fast. Also need to test out strength and speed.

She tapped her pen against the paper. What else? Well, she couldn't read minds as far she could tell, and she really hoped there were no mind control aspects, she definitely wouldn't want that kind of power. She had to wonder about the whole "created to kill demons" thing. Since it had come from Jake it was probably bullshit, he'd just wanted her to think of him as a superhero so she would...well do what she did.

Can they destroy the shadow men/demons? Was there any truth to them being created to fight them? And how can I get answers to these questions?

She sighed and shut the book. She would wait until she at least figured out what she could on her own-such as strength, speed, agility, and healing, and go from there.

Superhero. Well obviously Jake had been a super villain, but there was a definite appeal in thinking she had super powers. *I'm not a monster*, she told herself. *Different, yes. But I love, and monsters don't know the meaning of the word*. Besides, she could still feel a sense of goodness in her being, whatever else had changed, the essence of her remained the same. And somehow it all seemed fated, why else would she be able to see the shadow men and then become what she was now?

She chewed her lip and stared out the window. As usual she had way more questions than answers and she felt a tension headache coming on. She decided to just lay back and think happy thoughts.

Surviving the past week, mind, body, and soul intact was a happy thought. Seeing her house again was a happy thought. Seeing the girls again, happy. Seeing Austin...she winced as she thought about her little bathroom rendezvous. Was that cheating? She hadn't been in a right state of mind, and she'd done what she did to prevent anything further from happening....What the *hell* was she thinking? As if *that* was the greatest obstacle? She was a *vampire*.

Happy thoughts slipped away as the enormity of what that meant slowly sunk in. If she was immortal, or at least disease and age proof, she would be living a long, long time. In this body, looking like this. All of a sudden she felt dizzy.

A scene played out in her mind of the life she might have had. She and Austin were married, then having children, then going to little league and soccer games, plays, and dance recitals. They had Christmas dinners and Easter egg hunts, and on Halloween he dressed up like the Boogie man and chased her and the children around......

As the scene faded she felt tears pushing at the back of her eyelids. Maybe this was why she had been afraid to be with him, maybe deep down she had known she could never have those things. She was reminded of a scene in the Lord of the Rings where the king Elf had shown his daughter a vision of her future. She had watched her true love grow old and die, condemned to walk the earth alone through all of the ages thereafter.

She was now the elf. She would lose everyone she had ever known, ever loved. Once again she saw the face of the "Vampire of Fury", and began to grasp the despair in his eyes. Had it been like that for him? Did her face remind him of someone he had loved and lost? She forced her thoughts to stop. What good could did it do to dwell on it? She didn't even know for sure she was going to live on like that, did she? No.

So much for happy thoughts, her head was splitting from the pressure of the emotion she was attempting to suppress. She closed her eyes again and concentrated on the here and now. After all she had time to deal with these things. She didn't have to face it all at once. Or all alone.

***

When the plane touched down in NY Anna braced herself for a long night. She had left Austin a message so she knew he would be waiting for her, probably with Jenna and the rest of the girls too.

You spent all this time thinking about so many different things, you think you could have worked out how you were going to explain any of this, she berated herself. She felt anxiety in the pit of her stomach which increased tenfold when she noticed the bathroom rendezvous guy looking over at her.

He squeezed in behind her as they exited. "I guess I fell asleep, my name's Jonathan by the way."

She glanced back at him nervously, "Uh, Krissy."

"So you live around here Krissy?"

"No, I'm just visiting."

"Think we can get together during your stay?"

"Um, I don't...." They were walking through the gate and into the terminal and she had to get rid of him. "Look, I'm sorry, but I told you it was just a bet thing." She spotted Austin first and then the girls and fast walked in their direction.

"Those your friends? Which one made the bet, I can confirm you won...

She whirled on him. "Please, no! Just I have to go, I'm sorry, please don't keep following me."

She turned around- smack into Austin's chest. He was looking past her at Jonathan.... he'd heard, *damn it*.

"'Sup man." Jonathan fucking persisted, why wouldn't he just go?

"Who's this guy?" Austin's voice was all edge.

"No one, just a guy on the plane, can we get going, I really need to go."

"Don't be like that Krissy, is this your boyfriend or something?"

"Yes, it is, and we're leaving, now."

But her friends were standing there waiting to be greeted, making it impossible to hurry away. Shit, like she needed this on top of everything! *Please Jonathan, please don't say anything just go*, she attempted to plead with her eyes.

"Krissy?" Austin was looking at her now, his brows drawn.

Jonathan snorted, "Not her name? I guess when you do dirty things with a random stranger you like to keep it anonymous, huh? S' all good, you'll live on in my memory as hand job girl."

Her heart sank and she gave him a pained look as he saluted her and strode off.

She turned to see her friends gaping at her in variations of shock and reproach and she wanted to just...disappear. If only she hadn't made that call to Austin she could have seen them when she was ready, and certainly not like this.

Austin broke the silence. "What the *fuck,* Anna? Do I even know you? You disappear for a *fucking week*, leaving Jenna and I to imagine the worst...we were on a *fucking plane to London* when you called! Christ, I was dying inside these past few days..." his voice faded into pain and Anna couldn't look up from the floor.

"Say something!" He demanded.

"Can we please go," she asked quietly. She was on the verge of a total meltdown, and all she could think about was getting home.

"Maybe you should find another ride, I don't know if I can stand to be near you."

The disgust in his voice struck her like a hammer blow and she lost it completely. Great heaving sobs tore from her chest and she sunk down to her knees.

Jess knelt down next to her instantly, putting an arm around her shoulders. "Come on," she said, "we're going home, let's get your bags."

Anna shook her head, unable to speak.

"No, it's okay, I'm sure you can explain everything, even that guy, come on get up."

She let Jess help her to her feet and folded her arms tightly across her stomach, taking in shuddering breaths.

"I d..d...don't have any bags. Everything's g..gone." She stared at the floor, biting her trembling lip.

"What do you mean everything's gone?" Marina came over and grabbed her chin, pushing it up to meet her eyes.

"I guess Jake took it all and I don't know....I don't know what happened." She shook her head back and forth.

Jenna took charge. "Okay, let's get her home. Now."

They led her through the glass doors and when they reached the cars, Austin stepped up beside her.

"Look," he spoke in a strained voice, "I guess I'm sorry. I don't know what's going on and I'm exhausted. I'll drive you and maybe you can just....explain a little?"

She looked up at his face and the pain and confusion she saw there made the tears start again. She turned to her girls, looking mostly at Jenna and her voice was thin and shaky when she addressed them. "I know you've been through a lot this week because of me. I'm sorry for that, I'm sorry that I didn't listen to you. And I will talk to you. But for tonight, I just want to be with Austin. I can't handle anything more. I hope you understand."

They nodded reluctantly and Jenna spoke up. "Okay, then we'll call you tomorrow." Her facial expression suggested she was struggling against demanding more.

Anna cast her an apologetic look as she walked around to the passenger side and climbed in the SUV. She leaned back against the seat and closed her eyes as he started the engine, waiting for him to speak. He didn't, not until they were on the interstate.

"Anna?"

"Can this wait until we're home?" she asked softly.

"Yeah but....you didn't really do something with that asshole...did you?"

Her responding laugh was more like a sob. He didn't ask again, and after a minute he turned on the radio.

Chapter Nineteen

When they pulled in her driveway she felt her heart lift a bit. Home. She was home. Against all odds, she reminded herself.

She climbed out of the car and walked in the house, flipping on the lights as she went. She'd had enough darkness to last a lifetime. Austin followed and his presence was a conflicting thing for her. She didn't want to be alone, but the thought of telling him everything, reliving everything....and of his reaction...What if he was completely repulsed? What if he just couldn't handle it at all, confirming her fear that she was forever an outcast?

She sat on the couch and he sat down next to her, waiting patiently for her to speak. He was a very patient guy.

"I lied to you," she whispered. "You and Jenna. Jake wasn't...he...." she felt her voice waver as the image of his head being thrown against the wall flashed in her mind.

"Wasn't what?" His voice was all edge again.

"Human."

That wasn't what he expected. He blinked and waited for her to continue. When she didn't he sighed and made a harsh sound in his throat. "What does that mean? Come on Anna, I need more. I don't mean to push you, but please, please help me understand what's going on. Where were you all week?"

"Hell."

He reared back. "Stop it! Not human; hell; demons...Anna *stop*. Make sense to me for a minute."

She looked at him wondering if she should just let him have it. It wouldn't take much. If she just concentrated on the vein pulsing in his neck, he would see what she was in a hurry.

NO! She commanded. She *could* explain it in a way that he would understand....*So do it then idiot*! But she kept hitting a wall when she tried to form the words.

She forced herself to speak. "Okay. It's just, I'm having a hard time deciding..."

"Start with why you didn't get on the plane," he interrupted.

"I was drugged," she answered immediately, "Friday night. I tried not to let it happen, I ordered a bottled beer and refused all other drinks, but I put it down for a minute and that's all it took."

He nodded slowly. "Who drugged you? Jake?"

She nodded.

He swallowed hard and his voice was very quiet. "Did he rape you?"

She shook her head and once again, not what he expected.

"Then why would he drug you?"

"Because he is, or he was a vampire, and he wanted to get me to drink, what I think must have been blood. Not that he couldn't have just forced me to begin with...I don't know what all of his reasons or motivations were since he was ultimately a sociopath who is now dead."

Austin stood abruptly and strode across the room. He stopped at the fireplace and folded his arms across his chest, a muscle ticking in his jaw. "I think maybe they did slip you psychotropic drugs at that witches meeting you went to. And now you've been given more so your mind is unraveling. Or maybe you're still tripping. Maybe the shadow men are not even related, but I believe if your blood was tested right now it would turn up some LSD or PCP."

And that's why this was an impossible conversation. But she could still tell him everything before she showed him, then at least he would know she was still herself in a way.

"Austin, I know how crazy it sounds. I can show you something that will force you to believe me, but I wanted to talk to you before you ran screaming from me." Tears again.

He crossed the room and sat down putting his arm around her. "No matter what Anna, I will never abandon you. Whatever this is, I'll help you. I love you so much, and I'm scared, but not *of* you Anna, *for* you."

She smiled sadly. "You say that now."

"Anna."

"Will you let me finish my crazy story? Please?"

He sighed and sat back.

So she told him. Everything. About drinking the blood and being out for days. About waking up and what she saw. In graphic detail she described her transition and the rabid animal transitions of the others. Jake's death, and the male who killed him. Crawling under the stairs and waking up, catching a cab, the hotel and all of her things gone...and there she stopped.

He was staring at her with a mixture of deep concern and blatant disbelief. She knew the time had come to show him. Without evidence he would go on arguing the hallucinogenic induced nightmare theory, and who could blame him? No sane person who had not experienced serious paranormal happenings could accept such a story.

She expressed this last thought to him before saying, "I know I have to show you now, but I'm still afraid of the running and screaming."

"Anna...

"He turned me into *one of them* Austin. I don't know everything that means yet, but I'm not quite human anymore and I'm really, *really* scared. So please tell me that after I show you, you won't think I'm a monster, okay? I still feel like me inside, I still love you, and the girls and my dad. I still miss my mom..." Her voice broke.

He said nothing, just stared at her.

She took a deep breath and thought about the blood running through his veins. She felt a stirring, but it was slight. She moved closer to him and watched the little pulse on his throat and imagined drinking from it while he climaxed...that did it. She felt her eyes begin to flash and her teeth elongating. She opened her mouth so he could watch it happen.

His eyes widened until they were unnaturally big and she could hear his heart speeding up as his breath came out in little whooshes.

She vaguely thought that this would be a good time to turn it off, but it wasn't that easy. She wanted him. Then she remembered she hadn't explained that the bite didn't do any damage to the recipient and she squeezed her eyes shut, willing herself to revert. When she was normal again she opened her eyes and regarded him warily. His eyes were still round with shock and every muscle in his body had tensed.

"I forgot to tell you that the biting process is not like in the horror movies," she said quietly. "It doesn't change the person. In fact they don't even know what's happening except that it feels really good." She looked down at her hands, waiting for him to say something.

He drew in a deep breath and let it out very slowly. Then he stood up and turned towards the back of the room putting his hands behind his head and stretching his neck. She guessed he could probably understand her fear of him screaming and running now.

He turned and looked at her, then away again.

Rationally she knew it would take him time to process, but she felt herself growing anxious as he remained silent. Maybe because he was rarely at a loss for words, or maybe because she desperately needed his acceptance. Either way she felt her emotional tightrope fraying again, and when he looked at her and away once more it snapped. The tears came and choked her. "I need you!" she cried. "Austin please, I need you, I can't face this without you, I can't do this alone," she pleaded with him as the tears came harder and blurred her vision. "Please tell me it's gonna be okay."

And then he was there, his arms engulfing her, bringing her into his lap, rocking her and murmuring in her hair as she cried like a small child. Sobbed the way she had after her mom died, with her heart breaking apart and her shoulders shaking.

After a while it passed and they continued to sit there. She looked up at him and saw that his face was wet as well.

"We'll figure this out," he told her in a rough voice. "I'm here, I'm not going anywhere, I promise."

He stretched them out on the couch and pulled the throw blanket down on top of them. He wrapped his arms around her and stroked her forearm until she fell asleep.

***

The next morning she got up and carefully extracted herself from the still sleeping Austin. She climbed the stairs quickly and proceeded to take her long overdue hot shower.

When she was finished she dried off and stretched in front of the mirror noticing that her body looked different somehow. She did a closer inspection and realized she was not sporting an ounce of body fat. Of course she hadn't eaten anything for days, but in that case she should have looked slightly emaciated. Instead she looked as if she'd been hitting the gym.

She stretched again and this time she noticed how incredibly good she felt. Energized was the best she could come up with, but it was more than that.

She tiptoed down the stairs and into the kitchen, peering around the door to the living room to peek at Austin. He was still breathing deeply so she decided now would be a good time to go experiment with a couple of things.

She walked out onto her back patio and looked around her. She was fascinated by how much detail she could see, it was like trading a regular television for a High Definition. She could see every vein on every leaf of the large elm tree in the back corner of her yard. There was an opening in the trees to the back field and when she focused on it she could bring the field toward her and look right into the woods well over four hundred yards away.

She fiddled with the "volume" in her ears, and she heard Mrs. Kuwicky from down the street talking on the phone to her sister about a grape festival.

Yup, she thought with a sudden grin. *I'm eavesdropper extraordinaire, all right.*

She decided it was time to find out about some other things. She looked at the roof of her garage, crouched and jumped...a whole five inches. She frowned and backed up, this time taking a running leap...about two feet that time. Maybe this wasn't something she could do.

But....she imagined she was being chased by someone and had to get away. Concentrating everything she had on it, she ran and leapt once more. She hit the side of the metal roof off balance and started falling backward. Her arms pin wheeled and she managed to throw her body forward, and then she was sliding down the smooth surface and falling over the side. She landed rather less gracefully than she would've liked. Although she did hit feet first, the momentum carried her backwards and she skinned up her elbows when she fell.

She studied the bloodied scrapes and in seconds they faded and were gone.

Oo-kay...she thought her eyes wide, *what have I learned? I can leap high, just need some practice. And I can be hurt, but I heal wicked fast.* She felt a smile growing on her face and she heard the screen door open.

She looked up from her butt on the patio and grinned foolishly at Austin who was regarding her warily.

"What are you doing?"

"Well," she said still grinning, "I was testing out my new abilities. I just leapt onto the roof! Granted it took a few tries and I fell off...but I did it! And I scraped myself," she held up her unmarked elbows and his brows came together.

"Yeah, I know, nothing there, I watched it heal! Austin I have super powers, I am like...Bat Woman!" She busted out laughing at the cliche then abruptly stopped. "Oh. I really hope that the whole bat thing is a myth, I don't like the idea of that." She wrinkled her nose.

He smiled a little uncertainly. "That's...I don't know what to say. This whole thing, wow. I'm glad you're feeling better about it." He laughed a little. "Leave it to you to find the bright side so quickly."

She nodded, still smiling, and got to her feet. "I don't know Austin, I feel great! The whole undead thing is definitely not true...well obviously since I'm still breathing and my heart still beats...but what I mean is, I feel more alive than I ever have! The transition was horrible...no horrible is too mild, it was a fucking nightmare. But it's over and I have to go forward now. Do you know I can hear Mrs. Kuwicki on the phone down the street?" She nodded as he raised his eyebrows. "And I can see into the woods in the back of the field as if I were standing right in front of it! I had to practice with that stuff on the plane, adjusting my sight like it was a pair of binoculars, my hearing like a volume control, and obviously I have to work on the physical stuff....God, it makes me think of that movie I used to love when I was a kid, you know the one about the teenage super hero academy?" She grinned.

He was finally smiling for real, her excitement infectious. He shook his head and chuckled. "Well super woman, what else do you got?" he quirked an eyebrow at her in challenge. She loved him so much in that moment.

"Hmm. Come with me up to the field, I wanna check out my speed."

They walked up the patio steps to the backyard and crossed it. At the edge of the field she stopped, zoning in on the woods. She put all of her focus at the tree line and added the element of being chased again as she took off.

She started out at a normal run but the more she concentrated the faster she went, the wind hitting her in the face, until she was standing right in front of a large elm. She looked behind her and watched Austin sprinting towards her. She realized she wasn't even out of breath, and judging by the look on his face she had definitely moved pretty quickly.

He put his hands on his thighs breathing hard, staring at her. "You would kick ass in the Olympics."

She threw her head back and laughed before responding. "How fast do you think I ran it?"

He shook his head. "I'd say twenty seconds. You ran four hundred yards in twenty seconds."

She grinned again. "I'm not even winded."

"I see that." He cocked his head up, hands still on his knees, and smiled at her, shaking his head. After a moment he straightened up. "So what's next?"

She gave him a wicked smile and came toward him. Grabbing him around the middle she hoisted and he popped off his feet, falling forward over her tiny shoulder. His body was so large his feet only came a few inches off the ground in that position. She had to secure him there by holding tightly to his calves.

"Okay," he said from behind her in a voice filled with awe, "you can put me...

She lunged forward and ran with him back to her yard. When she got there she let him go and he staggered back a few feet.

When he was steady his eyes narrowed on her. "Don't do that again."

Her smile fractured and she bit her bottom lip. "Sorry."

He came forward and picked her up, wrapping her legs around his middle. "This is more like it. I carry you, not the other way around." He smiled.

"I am man, hear me roar?" She teased.

He chuckled and nodded. "Yeah, it is a little emasculating to be manhandled by a tiny elf."

The elf comment struck her sideways, bringing the Hobbit movie back to her mind. She leaned forward and wrapped her arms around his shoulders hiding the change in her expression. Don't Anna, her inner voice warned, there's no point in dwelling on that kind of stuff right now. She mentally shook it off then kissed him lightly on the neck....which was a huge mistake. Her body immediately went into vampire mode and she stiffened against it.

He felt her do it and froze. "Anna?"

"It's okay, I got a handle on it."

He forced her to look at him and studied her for a minute. "It's something you need, isn't it?"

She sighed. "Yeah. In fact I think I might be able to go without regular food, but not that."

"You said it doesn't hurt, doesn't affect the other person?"

She shook her head. "Not in my limited experience, anyway."

He carried her inside the house and up to her room, sitting them on the bed.

"Take it from me Anna."

She started to shake her head and he stopped her. "I want you to. Please."

He pulled her up on his lap and she kissed him. His eager response excited her and she could feel her mouth changing. She pulled away and went straight to his neck, sinking her teeth in deep. He made a noise and she felt him harden between her thighs.

On impulse she slid her hand inside his pants and gripped him hard, stroking as she sucked. He moaned loudly and she pulled harder and faster in both places. His breathing grew rapid and he gripped her hair.

"I'm gonna come," he groaned in her ear and she felt his fluids spilling over her hand as he moaned.

She kept up the motion until he stopped jerking, then broke away from his neck and licked it clean watching the marks fade. When she turned back to his face he was staring at her strangely and seemed upset, so she jumped up worrying that she'd hurt him.

"I won't do it again, I'm sorry, I thought it would be okay...

"Anna stop, it's not that. It felt good, all the way around." He took a breath. "That guy from the plane.....you did this with him."

His voice was a little flat, and she absorbed the fact that he was not upset about what they'd done, he was angry and hurt by what *she'd* done.

She picked up a shirt from the floor and wiped off her hand then handed it to him before sinking down on her knees. She looked up at him, her eyes beseeching. "It wasn't the same thing. I would never have done it, but I was weak and sick and in pain. Every five minutes I was hiding my face in my lap forcing my features back to normal and it was getting harder. He was there, silently flirting with me, I went to the bathroom and he followed, and I just...I was overwhelmed with the need like a person starving on a deserted island. He had more in mind, Austin, I did the other thing to prevent worse from happening." Her eyes pleaded for his understanding.

He refused to look at her and she thought, *of all the things he's had to accept about me in the last twenty-four hours he's the most distraught over this*. Men were funny creatures.

He finally looked at her, his eyes narrowed. "Never again. If you even feel the slightest urge for that, you come to me, I don't care what I'm doing at the time. I don't want you doing that with anyone else."

"Okay," she said in a small voice.

He pulled her up in his lap and stroked her hair. "Don't be upset, I know it's not your fault. Everything you've been through, you don't need a guilt trip from me. I just, I don't like to think about anyone near you in that way."

She cupped his cheeks and kissed him firmly. "Don't worry, I don't like to think of myself near anyone else in that way either. I hated what I did. It made me feel cheap and dirty on top of everything else I was feeling."

He nodded. "All right, let's drop it."

She spent the next several hours working on her physical skills in the backyard. Just like with anything else she got better with practice, and soon she was leaping onto the roof of the house and landing agilely, then jumping from there to the garage to a tree branch. It was absolutely exhilarating.

Austin coached her and cheered her on, watching in equal amazement as some of the injuries she sustained in the beginning faded before both of their eyes. He started calling her the Indestructible Fairy and they argued over her insistence on being called Bat Girl.

"You wear pastels and love the color pink, sorry but your Fairy Girl."

"That is too Disney, I want to be Marvel."

"You'll have to change your wardrobe...though I can't say the idea of you in black leather is unappealing."

She laughed and smacked him playfully.

The sun was going down when Jenna called and she told her to get the girls together and come over. She turned on the outside lights and paced around the patio nervously, letting Austin soothe her with positive affirmations.

"They love you, maybe as much as I do, they'll accept you no matter what. They're loyal and trustworthy, you did really well in the friend choosing department. Besides, I have a way of making people comfortable, and I'm here to help with the dealing."

She nodded but continued pacing.

When they pulled up her stomach instantly knotted. "I think I'm gonna be sick," she said.

"Come on," he pulled her into his arms, "it'll be fine."

The girls climbed out of the vehicle and gathered around. She turned her face into Austin's chest.

"You tell them," she said, her voice muffled in his shirt.

"Okay, I'll start for you," he whispered.

She kept her head buried in his shirt and he spoke over her head.

"Something rather difficult to understand happened to Anna over the past week," he began, then with sudden inspiration he leaned down and whispered, "Leap up on the house, jump to the garage and then land right in front of them smiling like you were at me this morning. We'll go from there."

She laughed shakily. "It sounds like I'm performing a circus act," she whispered back.

"Exactly. You don't want them to be scared of you, so awe them instead."

She nodded and stepped away from him. She took two running steps and lunged, landing perfectly on the peak of her house, then ran forward and leapt onto the garage. She could hear the girls' exclamations as she turned and leapt down, landing right in front of Jenna who was gaping at her.

"Whoa," Jess gasped, "How are you doing that?"

She smiled widely. "As it turns out, after a horrifying ordeal, I am now super human."

She waited for the questions, concentrating on Jenna who was searching her expression and moved closer to her. "Remember what I saw," she said quietly, "Jake was one of them."

Her eyes widened into saucers.

"Hey what are you saying to Jenna, we want to know too," Jess demanded.

Macey and Marina were staring at her in wide-eyed question and Jenna looked over at Austin. He smiled reassuringly, putting his hands on Anna's shoulders.

"There are things we've read about and seen in movies that we've been led to believe was fiction, but as it turns out there is a whole lot more to this world and life then we understand. More than most people will ever know about. I know some of us were skeptical about the whole shadow men thing," he looked specifically at Marina who nodded. "But we were wrong."

He paused to search for the right words.

"The little we do know of the supernatural world is completely skewed, by Hollywood especially. Vampires, for example, are portrayed as evil monsters that prey on people and sleep in coffins during the day. Of course they're also portrayed as fiction, but it turns out they do exist. Just not the way we imagined them." He looked at each one of them meaningfully.

Jenna stared at Anna who nodded slightly. The others still had no idea what he was getting at and were waiting for the punch line. She decided to take over.

"Thanks Austin, for that enthusiastic speech."

He laughed. "Yeah, I guess that was a speech."

"Uh huh." Anna rolled her eyes and smiled at him affectionately.

She focused on her friends who were still waiting, with the exception of Jenna whose face had gone pale. She might need to hear the confirmation, but she knew where this was headed.

She sighed, turning serious. "Look guys, what I went through this past week ...changed me. You saw what I did and that's just the tip of the iceberg. I can also hear....."

She cocked her head and concentrated on Macey's parents down the street. "Right now Macey, your mom and dad are talking about your older brother Tony and his fiancée, and whether or not Ally's parents will have a formal engagement dinner. Your mom thinks they will and in that case they need to start making plans to go to California."

Macey's eyes widened as she spoke.

"If you don't believe me you can call and ask...

"No, I...I was just there and they were talking about the wedding. I didn't tell you they were getting married!"

She smiled, but her gaze landed on Jenna and her smile slipped. Unlike the others, she wasn't excited. There was fear and denial in her dark blue eyes. Anna looked down at her hands which were suddenly fidgeting. It was all well and good to tell them about her "super powers", but fangs and blood drinking?

She sucked in a breath.

"Anna?" Jenna prompted softly.

She looked up. "I'm sorry Jenna," she whispered. "I lied to you." Tears filled her eyes and Austin wrapped his arm around her shoulders, giving her a comforting squeeze.

"You knew what Jake was." Jenna's voice held reproach.

She nodded.

"What was Jake?" Jess asked, looking back and forth between them.

Anna looked at the four of them and swallowed hard. "A vampire," she said quietly. "Jake was a vampire."

Marina's brows shot off her head and Macey took an unconscious step backwards.

"But..." Jess frowned, "are you saying that he...you..." She shook her head.

Jenna moved forward until she was directly in front of her. "Why did you stay?"

"He said vampires were created to fight demons," she whispered. "He said he would answer my questions." She bit her lip, knowing how lame and foolish that sounded.

"But he lied?"

Anna shook her head. "I don't know. Probably. *He* didn't fight them, I know that much."

Jenna looked away.

"Hey," Austin touched Jenna's arm. "She made a mistake, and yes she lied to us. But trust me when I say she *paid* for it."

Jenna stared at him, her expression unreadable.

"You're not going to try and bite any of us, are you?" Jess piped in.

Her abruptness startled a laugh from Anna. "No."

"But you are a vampire?" Macey asked. "You have fangs?"

She nodded.

"Whoa, wait a minute, this is a joke right?" Marina looked around. "Come on, this has to be a joke! Anna can't be…"she blinked and shook her head.

Anna looked at the willowy blonde, realizing she was going to be her hardest sell. Not about what she was, that would just take showing her concrete evidence. But accepting it, accepting her?

She didn't pause to think, just ran at Marina and grabbed her. When she was securely in her arms she jumped, barely acknowledging her startled cry. She bounded straight off the roof onto a tree branch, then another and another until they were at the highest point around for miles.

It was full dark by then and the sky was glittering with stars. She set her friend down on a thick branch which she immediately clutched, her expression conveying a mixture of fear and awe.

Anna looked up. "I've often stared at the sky at night wondering if there was more to this life than what we've been taught or what we can see," she said softly. "So many stars, so many possibilities. We are a tiny planet within a small galaxy within a vast universe. To me it always stood to reason that there was something else out there, I just didn't know until three years ago that there was something more right here. And even then it was just a small glimpse. Now, standing here on a tree branch that I just leapt onto like a mountain lion, I am certain that what I do know is nothing compared to what I don't."

At this point her friend was staring up at her, struggling to bend her mind. Out of all of Anna's friends, Marina was definitely the most tied to the earth. An animal lover, someone most at home in the middle of the woods, she had this way about her that made Anna think she'd been born in the wrong century. It seemed she would have been happiest and most comfortable during the little house on the prairie era. And there was absolutely nothing wrong with that. In an age where people had long forgotten about the simple pleasures in life, like the first scent of flowers in spring or the beauty of the first snowfall, Marina was a breath of fresh air. She *did* see and glory in those things.

"You're really a vampire?" she finally asked, looking up at Anna with eyes that...well once they accepted what they saw there would be no shaking it.

"I have fangs and today I sank them into Austin's neck and drank his blood." She looked down at her to gauge her reaction.

"Did it hurt him?"

"No. I guess it felt good."

"Will he become a vampire now too?"

Anna shook her head. "No. It doesn't work that way."

"Oh."

They lapsed into silence looking at the glittering expanse of sky for a long while.

"You're still you, right?" she finally asked.

Anna nodded, "Still me."

"Then I'm okay with it."

Anna let out the breath she'd been holding. In a strained voice she said, "You have no idea what that means to me."

"Yeah I do. If it were me, I'd hope my friends would feel that way."

"You know they would," Anna smiled.

"Does this mean you'll live forever?"

Anna's stomach clenched and she opened her mouth to answer then shut it again. "Wanna go back?" she finally managed.

"Okay."

She put her arm around her friend's waist and they jumped together, retracing her steps until they were back on the patio. When she let go Marina was grinning.

"That was fun, a little like flying!"

Jess's brows winged into the air. "*Can* you fly?"

"I don't think so."

"Austin told us a little of what you went through," Jenna interjected, giving Anna a look that said she wanted more details.

"Yeah, we should go inside so you can tell us the whole story," Macey stated.

"You're not afraid to be around me?" Anna asked.

All of them shook their heads in unison.

"We love you Anna, and we trust you," Jess told her.

Anna smiled at her gratefully before her expression clouded again. "The problem is, I don't know very much about...what I am. I'm sort of on my own in this since I don't have a clue how to find out, and there's no way I'd try and ask any of the sociopaths from London."

"Not on your own," Marina stated. "We'll help you, right guys?"

They emphatically agreed and Anna couldn't believe how lucky she was to have friends like them.

Chapter Twenty

Jenna fell to her knees, suffocating in sorrow. It was as if the innermost part of her was being compacted and crushed together, the smoke so thick in the air it seemed to have texture, choking her.

Oh God, she cried silently, don't let this happen. She tried to block out the sound of the screams as she pulled herself to her feet.

This time it would be different. This time she would change the outcome. But her hand passed through the axe and a feeling of hopelessness brought her back to her knees. She fell forward and put her head in her hands.

She couldn't help them, she never could. The screams began to ebb, until finally there was only silence.

Jenna sat straight up in bed, sweat pouring down her face, her heart pounding.

She'd been plagued with vivid dreams ever since the "Goddess" meeting in London. Most of her nightly visions involved people she knew and by the time she wiped sleep from her eyes they would fade and fragment, leaving her with a sense of urgency to recall them. She couldn't shake the feeling that they were real somehow, showing her things to come. This last one, however, was not a premonition. It was a scene from a long ago past and she remembered every detail with vivid clarity. It was a continuation of another dream she'd had on several other occasions, one in which the people were still alive and well. Men, women, and children joyfully interacting in this small village of the past. Except they weren't exactly human, in fact she was fairly certain they were vampires.

The females had a gift. A few nights ago she had watched from a hillside as an entourage came through the gates of their little community carrying sick and injured humans and the "women" of the village had laid hands on them and healed them.

In every one of the dreams there was a little boy that caught her eye. He was about ten years old with light blonde hair and bright green eyes. He was constantly pretending to fight, using sticks to stab invisible fiends, whirling and jumping until a woman, presumably his mother, came and hugged her to him. She would then take his hand and lead him into one of the small wooden houses.

The dreams would start out so picturesque and then the scenery would swirl and change, darkness closing in, and that's when she would see the fire and run down the hillside to help them. Which of course she couldn't. Sometimes, right before she woke up, she would catch a glimpse of a terrifying male landing on one of the houses next to the burning structure. Whether he was the cause of the mayhem or someone trying to help she didn't know because she always woke up at that point.

She shook her head and frowned, wondering why she would dream these things. For Anna? Was there a message in there for her? Perhaps that vampires were not evil? It was irritating to be given just a tiny piece of something important and not know what it was.

The past several weeks had been the most interesting of her entire life. Anna had developed her abilities at an amazing rate. She really *was* like a super hero. All of the girls watched in awe as she leapt into trees or raced across the field and back in seconds flat. They had also entertained themselves with Anna's ability to eavesdrop on all the neighbors, Macey stating that she wished she'd had the ability in high school.

Macey. She would be leaving for college in two weeks. It was only three hours away, but it would change things. Initially she and Marina had intended to go as well, not to the university, but the community college in the area. They were supposed to have gone there to search for jobs and an apartment, but Anna had changed things. Not intentionally of course, she tried to insist they go not wanting to hold up their lives, but at this point it seemed a hell of a lot more important to help her figure things out. They could always go for the spring semester instead.

She, Austin, and Marina practically lived with Anna these days, going home only occasionally. It was as if they felt they needed to cocoon her with normality. She rarely left her street, sticking to the beach and the woods and her house. At first Jenna had thought it was so she could get a handle on the changes in her body, but now she'd begun to wonder if it had something to do with the shadow men. Anna had mentioned in passing that she wondered if they would sense she was different now. Since Jake had told Anna that vampires were created to destroy them- although he was a liar so chances are he had made it up- she knew it was in the back of Anna's mind and she probably feared they could interact with her now.

Jenna had spent the previous night at her own house. Her parents were out of town so she'd come the day before for some much needed alone time. Jess had stayed at Nate's, as usual, though she was under strict instructions not to tell him about Anna. She'd tried to argue the point, but Austin had been firm in his resolve. "No one besides us, Jess, so don't do it because you'll look like a fool when the rest of us deny it," he'd warned. Jenna had adamantly agreed. Most people were far too narrow-minded. Anna would become a freak show and have to move away.

She pulled herself out of bed and wandered into the den, flipping the switch on the computer and watching it load. She started to click on the email icon, but a news headline caught her eye and she froze when she noticed the pictures beneath the story. They were of two guys in their early to mid-twenties...and she'd dreamt of them a couple of nights ago.

They were both good-looking, one was blonde and smirking at the camera, the other had brown hair with a serious and pained expression. She racked her brains to remember what the dream had been about, but it wasn't forthcoming, all she knew was that they were definitely in it.

She read the story and her eyes widened. Apparently they were being tried for a murder they'd committed in New York City and were suspected of several more. They were currently being held in Schenectady county jail outside Albany. William and Joshua McClaron. They were brothers. She googled their names to find out more, and found another story that had labeled them vigilantes. They were caught stabbing a man through his heart in a darkened corner of Central Park, and the police believed they were responsible for several more unsolved murders in the past several years. All of their alleged victims had been taken out in the exact same fashion and each of them was linked with heinous crimes ranging from rape to torture and murder.

She sat back and stared at their pictures, wondering why she would have dreamt of them. She had a vague sense that they were not villains but heroes and thought of Anna, though it was highly doubtful they were vampires or they wouldn't have been caught by human cops.

She gathered a few things and headed back to Anna's, her mind spinning with possibilities.

***

Anna stared at the computer screen and re-read the article.

Austin was leaning against the table frowning. "You dreamt of them?" He asked.

Jenna glanced at him. "Yes, I told you, just a couple nights ago."

"But you don't remember what the dreams were about?" His voice held an edge of doubt.

"No, okay? Sorry my visions aren't more helpful."

"Hey, don't get mad, I just don't understand what they have to do with Anna."

"I'm not saying they have anything to do with her. I don't know."

Anna clicked on some related articles then decided to do a search on the potential victims. Pictures of both men and women of varying ages, ethnicity, and class came up on the screen. She scanned their faces and her heart lurched as her gaze landed on the face of a man she'd seen before, a man who wasn't quite a man.

Jenna noticed her reaction. "What is it?"

Anna cleared her throat and pointed at the guy. "I've seen him before. He's the guy from the bar in the airport, the guy with black eyes." She shuddered, remembering that she'd expected to see that bartender on the news as a victim of a violent murder.

"Whoa. So these brothers are what? Hunting the demon possessed?" Jenna asked.

"If I had to guess...

"Wait a minute," Austin interjected, "it could be a coincidence."

The girls looked at him doubtfully.

"Maybe they hunt down and kill people connected to violent crimes and this possessed guy was one of them."

"And I, who can also see shadow men, am dreaming of them why?" Jenna cocked a brow.

Austin shook his head, "I don't know, but what exactly do you plan to do? These guys are locked up for murder...

Anna stood. "I'm going to talk to them."

"No!"

"Why not? They're in jail, it's not like they can hurt me," she rolled her eyes, "as if they could anyway."

"I just don't like it, Jesus Anna haven't you learned your lesson about strange and dangerous men?"

Anna cast him an injured look and he tried to put a hand on her shoulder but she shook it off. "It's not the same anymore, what exactly can they do to me, what exactly can anyone do? I hate to break it to you, but I'm the dangerous one now. And if these guys are demon hunters, or whatever, than they might know things, things that can help me understand more about what I am."

"Yeah, if. Or they might just be fanatics...

"You're right," she cut in, "they might be. But I'd say the fact that Jenna is dreaming about them gives me a reason to look into it. Sorry, but if I have a chance to find out anything, I'm taking it. And spare me the "That's what you did last time" speech, I'm hardly the same vulnerable girl."

It was his turn to look injured and she winced. She knew he was struggling with what she had become, worrying about the future of their relationship and trying to still see her as his Anna.

She put her arms around his waist. "I know you're afraid for so many reasons, and so am I," she said softly. "But we can't keep pretending that everything is normal, or avoiding the larger issues like...Will I Age." She felt him stiffen and squeezed him, looking up at his face which held a tightly guarded expression.

"I love you," she told him. "But I have to figure these things out." And she did love him, though she always felt that her love was missing something. That no matter how wonderful he was, he was not her soul mate. They still hadn't progressed past the stage of her jerking him off while sucking on his neck. He had tried to do the same to her, tried slipping his hands underneath her waist band, but she resisted. She had this crazy feeling sometimes like she was cheating on someone she hadn't even met. The idea of sex seemed wrong to her, she just couldn't bring herself to that place. Even when she was aroused there was a block in her mind.

She let go of him and went back to the computer, jotting down the address of the jail and its visiting hours. If they were what she thought-she would get them out. With the amount of money she had, she didn't see a problem, and if money didn't work, well...she'd been working on a new ability she'd discovered.

It seemed she could make herself invisible to people by concentrating on the area around her as a force field. She wasn't sure of the mechanism, but like everything else she used her imagination to enhance it.

The first time had been an accident. She was walking down the nature path by her house when she'd heard people coming from the other direction. She had been so lost in thought she hadn't noticed them before that. Usually she would stretch out her hearing to make sure there was no one around, this time she'd forgotten. She'd turned to race back the other way, but then heard people coming from that direction as well. She looked into the woods, but the trees were spaced too far apart and they might see her running off.

It wouldn't have mattered so much except she'd recognized both of their voices as former schoolmates and knew they would stop to talk to her, which she'd had no desire to do at that moment. She'd reluctantly started walking again wishing hard she could disappear.

And then they were walking past her without even glancing her way. She'd stared after them noticing the area around her body was slightly static. That's when she'd recalled the Mistress warning her about static electricity and how the vampires she'd seen in London had been able to conceal themselves from the people around them.

After that she'd practiced it on her friends and like all of her new abilities there seemed to be degrees and she was figuring out how to control them.

She turned to Jenna and Austin. "There's visiting hours tonight from 7 to 9. I plan on being there, so are you coming with me, or do I go alone?"

"Definitely coming," Jenna stated and Austin nodded.

Chapter Twenty-One

They pulled into the jailhouse parking lot at 6:30. She'd called ahead to see what the requirements were, and since the inmates could only have one visitor at a time she was going in alone. She'd decided to talk to William first, since he was the older of the two, although, she conceded, that might make him more difficult to derive information from-especially if he had the basic big brother instinct to protect his younger sibling. She had a backup plan though. If she couldn't get either of them to talk she intended to use her dimming ability to slide in later on and hopefully find something out that way. She refrained from expressing that out loud however, since Austin would definitely balk.

Once inside she was led into a room with windows and little phones, just like on TV. William was already seated on the opposite side as she sat down. His eyes indicated surprise and his gaze turned curious as he picked up the phone. The guards moved out of earshot and she decided to go with a direct approach.

"Tell me about the Shadow Men."

His eyes widened slightly before resuming their quizzical expression. He studied her thoughtfully for a moment. "What do you know about them?" he asked finally.

"Not much," she admitted. "I can see them." She watched him carefully but his expression didn't change. When he didn't comment she continued. "Look, I just need to know if you and your brother are doing what I think you're doing. Because if you are then I want to help you."

"What do you think we're doing?"

"I think you're hunting them. The ones that take over people."

He looked startled. "Who are you?"

"I'm...no one really. Just a girl who has been able to see these things for a few years, with a whole lot of questions and no answers."

"So you're what, about nineteen?"

She nodded.

He shook his head a little studying her. "What made you come to that conclusion, that that's what we're doing?"

"Well...my friend dreamt about you, although she doesn't remember the details, and I also saw one of your alleged victims in an airport once and his eyes were black. It was the first time I'd ever seen one inside a person."

He drew in a sharp breath. "There hasn't been any female seers in over a century. If you're telling the truth....then the line didn't end after all."

She wrinkled her forehead. "The line? Is that what I am, a Seer?"

He laughed shortly. "You really don't know anything."

She shook her head.

"So how could you help exactly?"

"I have a lot of money. You must have a bail bond."

His skepticism turned to interest. "Our bonds are set at two hundred fifty G's apiece."

"That's not a problem."

He stared at her, his lip curving. "You're gonna shell out half a million on a hunch? What if I'm playing you?"

She studied him and chewed on her lip considering. "Do you plan to see the trial through?"

He shook his head, "Not if we can help it." He leaned back and waited her out.

He has intelligent eyes, she thought, if he wanted to take advantage of her it would make more sense for him to convince her she would get her money back. Instead he'd outright said they weren't sticking around. This was an honorable guy, she could sense it. A little voice in her head tried to dispute her...*you trusted Jake too, look where that got you*. But she ignored it because she hadn't really trusted Jake. She'd felt the whole time that something was off, she had just been so desperate to learn something that she'd ignored her instincts. "I want to talk to your brother first," she told him.

He nodded and stood up. "Nice talking to you..."

"Anna."

"Nice talking to you Anna." He hung up the phone and she got the distinct impression he didn't believe she would end up rescuing them.

She spoke to the guards who had been chatting away in the far corner, and one got up to retrieve Josh.

When he was brought in she was struck by a kinship that she couldn't explain. It was something in his eyes as he sat down and stared at her, pain and fear mixed with weariness.

"Hi, I'm Anna," she said simply when he picked up the phone, "I just spoke to your brother."

He nodded, waiting.

"Can you tell me something about Seers?"

His brows lifted and he stared at her for a moment. "What do you want to know?"

"Anything at all. I am one I guess, I didn't have a term for it until William said it, but I've been able to see the shadow men, or demons, for the last three years."

"Will talked about seers?" he looked surprised.

"Yeah. He said he thought the female line was extinct."

He nodded. "There hasn't been a girl seer in over a century."

"So he said." That collaboration went a long way to fading any doubts she had left about what they were.

"Look Josh, I want to help you guys. If you are what you seem to be, then I don't want you in here, I don't want to see you end up with a life sentence...or a death sentence for that matter. I need answers and you need out."

"Did he tell you what our bail is set at?"

She nodded. "Yeah and he also told me you wouldn't stick around which means I wouldn't be getting it back. He could have lied about that, but he didn't." She spoke quietly, the same as Will had, though the guards seemed preoccupied and disinterested in their conversation.

Josh just looked at her. What could he say, the ball was definitely in her court.

"Just tell me something about what we are, something that will concrete it for me if you can."

He looked down, then back up at her, his eyes filled with emotion. "The line we come from is called Faerian. It's widely believed by other members of our race that the original Faerians were not from this world, but they mated with humans and produced a line of seers. We live to be about 150 years old and are impervious to disease. We can see the supernatural, more so when it's invoked. In fact some people can have these abilities lying dormant their entire lives and never even know it. I would've been like that if it weren't for my dad and brother. I can give you the name and number to a close family friend, he's a seer and a hunter as well. You might want to talk to him before making up your mind about us."

She nodded, a feeling of excitement growing inside of her. Finally answers! Faerian, she was Faerian! She pulled out a pen and paper from her purse.

"Richard. 288-088-0988. Tell him Josh gave you the number and say the words "Dämonischer Jäger."

She furrowed her brow.

"It's demon hunter in Latin," he explained.

She repeated the phrase a couple of times, then looked up at him.

"I'll call him first. But as long as I have no reason to disbelieve what you're telling me, I'm going to get you out of here."

He smiled a little then, a dimple creasing his right cheek. "We'd definitely appreciate it."

She gave him a little wave as she left.

She climbed into Austin's SUV and recounted everything to them. When she got to the part about dormant abilities she looked meaningfully at Jenna.

"So you think I'm from this Faerian line too?" she was excited about the new info, unlike Austin who just looked skeptical.

"I would say it stands to reason."

"But...what about Jess? Do you think she could have dormant abilities?"

Anna hadn't thought of that. "I guess so, I mean she wasn't with us at that ceremony. Although I'm not entirely sure Jess would want the ability."

Jenna nodded, "True, it freaks her out just knowing about it."

"So what now?" Austin put in.

"I'm gonna call this Richard guy."

She dialed the number and a gruff male voice with a slight southern accent answered on the third ring.

"Hello?"

"Richard?"

"Who's this?"

She took a breath. "Josh gave me your number and said to say Dämonischer Jäger."

There was a moment of silence. "You've seen Josh?"

"I'm at the jail."

"I see. What can I do for you Miss...?"

"Anna. Um, I'm not sure exactly." She told him about her conversations with the two boys. When she was greeted with more silence she added, "I guess Josh thought that if I talked to you I might be more comfortable with the decision to spend a half a million dollars on their...escape."

"I'm not sure what I could tell you that would make that any easier except to confirm what you believe. Those they kill are not human anymore. They've given themselves over to a demon, and there's no going back from there. They're not only dangerous because of the evil in them, or the fact that they live to deal out pain and misery, they're also able to sway others that are on the fence. You've seen the shadow men as you put it, how they seem to be attached to a person. Well eventually they get inside their minds enough to persuade their hosts to "share" themselves. It's not really sharing though, the demon takes over once the person gives them permission to enter."

"Why? What's their purpose?"

His laugh was humorless. "To have a corporeal form. Without humans giving over their wills they can do nothing but influence them on a subconscious and very minor level. They want the ability to, well live for lack of a better word I guess. There's a lot more to it, of course, but it would take a much longer face to face for that...Look Miss Anna, us seers have been fighting the war against their possession since a time before time. Unfortunately our numbers have dwindled and it seems that the demon numbers are increasing, as well as the amount of people they are able to persuade. Will and Josh are crusaders, unrecognized heroes. I myself don't have the kind of resources to get them out of this particular fix, nor does their father. In fact our people as a whole tend to get by on rather little. If you have the ability to help them you can rest assured it is money well spent."

She smiled into the phone. "Thank you for talking to me Richard, I think I'd already made up my mind beforehand, but every little bit helps."

"No problem. Oh, and by the way, have you ever healed somebody?"

Anna frowned. "Healed someone?"

"I take that as a no. Doesn't mean you don't have the ability though, generally female seers do in different capacities. You might try it out, we could sure use a healer on our side."

"Okay, I'll do that."

"Hope to meet you sometime Anna."

"Yes, I'd like that."

She hung up the phone and saw that Jenna looked as convinced as she felt, though Austin was still chewing on doubt.

"You know if you bail them out and they run, which they're going to do, then you could be held accountable if the authorities have reason to believe you knew they would-

Anna held up her hand. "First of all, I think our justice system sucks. I always have. Second of all, how do you propose they catch me if I don't want to be caught?"

"You wouldn't be able to go home." He pointed out.

She nodded. "I know, which is why I'm thinking that maybe I could break them out instead of bailing them."

"*What*? How....oh, but you haven't perfected that skill! And you're talking about getting by everyone and snatching keys or something, and then how exactly would you explain it to your new friends without letting them know what you are? Or more importantly, how do they waltz out without getting caught, your ability didn't extend to any of us when you tried it."

She sighed. "I know, but it seems like it would be worth a try. I could get into their cells and they could plan their escape. Maybe I could take the guards guns or something."

"And you get caught in the act when your dimmer "fizzles" out." He laughed a little. "Besides they have you on camera from tonight's visit, you'd be implicated in the escape, still presenting yourself with the problem of going home."

"Okay, but with this plan I keep the money in my pocket, which I'm not even sure how to go about getting in the first place." She thought about her dry financial manager and wrinkled her nose.

They decided to continue their debate down the road at a restaurant. Anna continued to eat real food, although she still wondered whether or not she had to since the only hunger pains she ever felt were in association to blood.

She wiped her mouth with the scratchy napkin after she'd downed a chicken sandwich and some fries, still waffling on which way she wanted to go with the boy's rescue.

Jenna finally put in her two cents, making the decision for her. "I say you attempt to get into their cells. You can just tell them you have the ability to make people not take notice of you, and then go from there."

Austin frowned hard at Jenna.

"Sorry but what good are the things Anna can do if she doesn't put them to use? And besides...I see you coming out of the jail without getting caught." Her blue-violet eyes went far away for a second then she blinked and nodded.

"Right. So at midnight you guys drop me off down the road then go park somewhere you can watch for us." Anna nibbled her lip hoping she was doing the right thing.

"This is insane, you know that right? The chances of it working are slim to none." Austin scowled tossing his napkin on the table.

Anna sighed gustily. "Don't be so hasty to bet against Jenna's intuition. Besides, if it doesn't work I'll just move to plan B and pay the bail."

"Uh huh, that will be easy when you're wanted for attempting to break out two murder suspects."

She smiled sweetly, "Well that's where my friends would come in then, isn't it?"

Chapter Twenty-Two

At precisely midnight Anna slunk across the parking lot with her heart in her throat. Imagining doing something and actually doing it, two distinctly different things, she decided. She concentrated every part of herself on being invisible as she walked through the front doors. She had removed anything that might have caused the metal detector to go off and she made it through the archway without a problem. Once inside however, all the doors that led anywhere were locked, controlled by a woman behind a wall of bulletproof glass. It would be a waiting game. She'd have to slip by the next person who came in or out.

Fortunately it was only about fifteen minutes later when two guards came through the door she'd been taken through earlier. She caught the door with her foot, slipping through it as gently as possible. So far so good, no one could see her.

She made her way down the hallway and came upon a guard sitting behind a large desk surrounded by monitors. The screens sported all different areas of the jail, and a couple of them were devoted to the cells, blinking through each one. She caught a glimpse of the brothers who were in separate cells, though at least it didn't appear they had cell mates.

The room she was in had another electronically operated door, so unless the guy got up she was stuck. She moved silently around the desk and saw there was a circuit board with numbered buttons and wondered if they operated the cell doors. She'd been thinking keys, but she realized in this modern age only backwoods facilities were likely to still use them.

The guard was playing Solitaire on the computer she assumed must have the information she required.

It was completely unnerving to be standing there practically on top of him, she kept thinking he would look up and see her, but the static around her body assured her she was still covered. She located the button that operated the door and wished she could press it without him noticing, then realized she would also have to find a way of keeping the door from shutting all the way so they could get back out. She chewed on that one for a moment before pulling off her shoes and socks replacing her shoes.

I'm going to orchestrate a break out with ankle socks, she grinned.

After over an hour the guard finally stood. He seemed to look at her for a second, causing her heart to pound thunderously. Then he looked away and moved around the desk. He went down a short hall that depicted restrooms and Anna hurried into the cubicle. She minimized the Solitaire screen and saw folders on the main window. One was conveniently labeled Prisoner Information. She clicked on it and quickly scanned, finding Will's info, continued to scan...Bingo! Cell number 213. She found Josh's next, 215, then glanced up nervously praying the guard was doing number two. She pulled Solitaire back up and took a deep breath hoping the locks wouldn't make too much noise when they disengaged. She pressed the button for the inner door first, heard a click and saw a light above it turn green.

She hurried over to the door and opened it a little wedging her socks in at the bottom. It held, so she hurried back once more and pressed both cell numbers at the same time. There was a buzzing sound as she rushed back to the door and she froze, expecting the guard to come running out. He didn't. *Must be number two*, she thought, silently thanking the man's bowels.

She eased through the door and secured her socks, hoping they'd go unnoticed. As long as he didn't walk over to it, she'd be okay. Otherwise...she shook her head and hurried down the hall.

When she got to their cells they were both standing up and staring at the bars in confusion. Obviously they'd heard the lock disengage. Will's brows shot up as she approached. She put her finger to her lips and opened the door slipping in.

"Okay, not much time," she whispered speaking rapidly, "I have the outer door propped open with my socks, there's only one guard in that room and he's unsuspecting at the moment, so here's the plan," she drew in a breath, "he can't see me, I'll explain that later, but for now I thought I could distract him while you get through the other door, maybe grab something of his and throw it over by the restroom while I buzz you out, and then we just have to run for it, I have friends waiting for us outside."

She finished breathlessly and to his immense credit he didn't remain dumbstruck, he seemed to be considering.

"The rush being that he might notice the socks?" He raised a brow and smirked, obviously trying to picture her makeshift prop.

She nodded vigorously.

He moved to walk out and she followed. Josh was standing at his cell door and looked astounded when Will slid it open.

He motioned for them to follow him and they crept along the wall until they were just outside the door.

"Okay, this is the plan," Will whispered, "There's another door down a different corridor that leads to the back of the building, and it isn't electronically operated, so we just have to get there unnoticed. There's an exit that we should be able to leave through without an issue, so..." he depressed his lip with his tongue, eyeing Anna. "Do you think you can get the guard out of the room? Otherwise it would make more sense for Josh and I to overtake him. If he sees us run the entire place will be on top of us in minutes."

She frowned a little as she thought about what she could do, than indicated for them to wait while she inched the door open and slid through it. The guard was sitting at his desk eating a TV dinner and flipping electronic cards.

The dinner offered inspiration and she crept up to the desk and slid around it then flipped his tray of food along with a fountain soda into his lap.

He jerked backwards and stared at the contents of his dinner, his eyes blinking rapidly. "Well that just fuckin' figures!" he said aloud. He brushed the fried chicken and fake potatoes into the waste bin by his feet then stood up and strode towards the restroom. As soon as the door closed behind him she motioned the guys in. Josh retrieved her socks and they ran for it.

Will led them down a series of empty hallways and they found the exit that led to the back parking lot which was nearly deserted, just a few cruisers parked here and there.

"My friends are supposed to be sitting somewhere looking out for us," she whispered.

They made their way carefully through the lot, keeping to the shadows, than circled around through a grove of trees on the far lawn. Anna came out onto the sidewalk motioning for the brothers to stay back. She walked into the middle of the street and let her "dimmer" go for a few seconds and headlights immediately popped on down the road. She walked back to the sidewalk and waited.

Austin's SUV came slowly down the road and when he reached her she motioned for the guys. She opened the back door and they all piled in, shutting it quickly, then Austin continued down the road and turned as quickly as possible.

"Are we being chased?" he asked looking at Anna in the rearview.

"I don't think so. Pretty sure no one knows we left."

"Oh my God that's awesome!" Jenna exclaimed leaning through the middle from the passenger seat, grinning widely. "I can't believe you did it, despite my good feeling I half expected the alarms to go off and a swat team to show up!"

"Okay," Will interjected, his eyes on Anna. "Can you explain to me about the invisibility thing?"

She looked at the two guys and chewed on her lip. "Umm, well it's complicated. Could you see me the whole time?"

They both nodded. Then Josh spoke up. "There's only one thing I know of that has that ability. I didn't think humans were capable of it."

"Well, you learn something new every day, right?" Austin's tone was sharp and filled with warning. He didn't want Anna to fess up just yet.

"Did you talk to Richard?" Josh asked and Will swung his gaze at him.

"You gave her Richard's number?" His tone held serious disapproval.

"Yeah, what's the harm?"

"Yes I did talk to him," Anna put in before Will could continue. "He seems like a really good guy and he's very fond of you two."

Will shook his head, and Josh shrugged a little at him. "It obviously worked out for the best, right?" he defended.

Will cleared his throat. "All right, so where are we headed?"

"I thought we could get a hotel," Austin answered, "Anna can ask you her questions there and you guys can be on your way."

Anna gave Austin a look and turned towards the brothers. "What would you say to heading to my house?"

Austin glanced at her sharply, "What? No way."

He was really starting to wear on her nerves.

"If you're tired I can drive from here," Jenna offered.

"It's not that, I just don't think we should bring two strangers back to where we live. I know you're both convinced they're fighters for truth, justice, and the human race, but I still think we should err on the side of caution."

"Where do you live?" Josh asked.

"In Olin Falls about three hours from here."

Austin made a disgusted sound and she glared at him.

"I'm game for whatever," Will voiced, "We need to lie low for a bit then get away from NY." He looked at Anna, "Look, no matter what we can't thank you enough. Even if they couldn't make all the charges stick they had us for that guy in the park. I'm glad you didn't have to shell out all that dough to accomplish this though."

"I would have if there was no other choice, and really there's no need to thank me, it was the right thing to do," she shot a pointed look at Austin. "I guess we could get a hotel tonight and decide what to do tomorrow."

Chapter Twenty-Three

Anna switched seats with Jenna and stared out the window as they drove, her head buzzing from the night's events. She still couldn't believe she'd pulled off the break-out. It was beginning to feel like her life had split into two parts, "Before Europe" and "After Europe". Before Europe she would have given the situation serious thought before even bailing them out. After Europe? Forget bailing them out when she could just sneak in and bust them out!

She laughed and Austin glanced at her, eyebrow raised. She shook her head pressing a hand to her mouth to conceal the smile of bemusement that was stuck there. Looking out the window once more she decided her altered thinking process might have something to do with her new energy levels. Well that and all of her new talents which made her feel less like she was in the real world and more like she was in a sci-fi action thriller.

They drove for nearly an hour before deciding it was safe to stop somewhere. Jenna and Austin went in to the office to get two rooms then they filed into the McClaron's room to talk. Anna sat down between Austin and Jenna on one bed and the brothers sank down on the other. When they were situated Anna started.

"Tell me about the Faerians."

Will spoke up, "Alright, where should I start. I guess with the story we were told, huh?" He looked at Josh who nodded. He cleared his throat. "It's been passed down through the generations of our family, though we've found there are variations depending on who you talk to. Everyone has their own take I guess. Long, long ago," he grinned briefly then continued, "the Faerians lived on a secluded Island somewhere off the coast of Spain in the

Atlantic Ocean. Many believe that this Island is actually Atlantis, though it can hardly be proven. The way my grandfather told it was they were believed to have come here from another world, whether by physical transportation or some sort of dimensional porthole is up for debate. Anyway they lived on this Island for an indeterminate length of time until at some point a portion of the Faerian men began looking at each other instead of their women to get some lovin'." He flashed another grin and his brother raised his eyes to the ceiling, shaking his head.

"So two groups of women left the island, and when they reached land they went separate ways. One group came upon a village and because of their great beauty they were instantly taken as wives. It was discovered they had the gift of healing, something they were initially revered for, though eventually and over time there were some that considered it witchcraft...but that's a whole other story." He leaned back and stretched, gathering his thoughts before continuing. "They also lived a great deal longer than the average person, something like 3 to 4 centuries. The mixing of the blood created offspring who lived about half as long, which is still true to this day. The gift of healing was passed down to the females while the males were gifted with strength and speed, both lines with the ability to see the supernatural, which is how they became known as Seers."

He paused for a moment and Anna piped in. "What about the other group?"

"Ahh, the other group. Well they also came upon a village, but those who occupied it were not human. They were what we know of as the Vampire."

Anna exchanged startled looks with Austin and Jenna, and Will narrowed his eyes a little taking note.

"There *are* vampires," Josh added, "but once upon a time they were supposedly good."

Will nodded. "In fact our legend declares that vampires were once a race of only males who were created for the sole purpose of destroying demons and protecting humanity. They were considered warrior angels by those who knew of them. Then the Faerians entered their lives and changed everything. A vampire by the name of LeSauronde'dachielle fell head over heels in love with a young Faerian woman, and because of their faithful service to the Creator in the protection of his beloved humans he granted the vampire race the ability to breed, under the condition that they would die when their mates did. Eventually the entire line of vampire males took their mates and a whole new line began. Because of the dominance of the vampire DNA, every one of the children were born vampire. And there were females of their kind for the first time. This is where the story gets a little hazy, because some believe that all female vampires were born evil, while others contend that it happened over time due to jealousy." At their questioning glances Josh jumped in to explain.

"Supposedly the vampire females were far more aggressive and dominant than they're Faerian mothers, and though the males of their race could and did breed with them, they rarely fell in love or bonded with them, preferring the gentler natures of the Faerians. So, out of jealousy, the vampire females banded together and sought the help of demons to get rid of the Faerian women."

"But wait," Jenna cut in, "If all their children were vampires than where were they finding these Faerian women they're shunning their own kind for?"

"Good question, keep in mind we're talking many generations later, so the assumption is they found the Faerian humans, our ancestors if you will." Will sat back and thought for a moment. "That of course is all based on legend. What we definitely know is there are lines of Faerians that pass down the ability to "See" as well as prolonged life, and the females are all supposed to have the gift of healing." He looked quizzically at Anna.

"I don't know I've never tried, Richard mentioned it too, but..." she shrugged.

"Anyway, that's definitely making a long story short. In our family the men have been fighting demons for generations. Our father tried to turn his back on the lifestyle when he met my mom, not wanting to put her in danger, unfortunately danger found her anyway. A demon with a vendetta against our grandfather possessed a man in our town and killed our mother and infant sister." He waved a hand to stop their expressions of sympathy. "It was a long time ago, and the bastard's dead, so it's good."

"Anna lost her mom too," Jenna spoke up, "though not like that."

"Something in common then, well besides the obvious," Will chuckled and Josh shot him a scolding look.

"Actually Jenna can see them as well." Anna jumped in. She went on to describe the Goddess meeting and what had occurred afterwards, leaving out the vampires for the time being.

"So you were a dormant. Wow, two Faerian women who just happen to be friends, what are the odds of something like that? Especially when they were thought to be no more." Will cocked his head and looked at them, his eyes unreadable.

"Actually," Josh said looking apologetic, "and I'm not saying that it's a sure thing, but unless either of you are healers, then you may not necessarily be Faerian. In fact it's supposed to be the identifying trait, otherwise you may just be humans who happen to be able to see demons. It happens."

Will nodded, his gaze pinned on Jenna. "And you don't fit the physical description. All Faerian women are supposed to be smallish in size, like her," he shifted his gaze to Anna. "And fair-haired," he added.

Jenna shrugged. "I'm okay with that. Anna's the one who's been dealing with it for years, and with no one to guide her. At least when I started seeing them she was there to tell me I wasn't crazy."

Will looked at Austin. "By any chance do you have a pocket knife?"

Austin stiffened, "What for?"

"A little experiment. Don't worry, I'll be using it on myself."

"You want to see if we can heal you," Anna stated. He nodded.

"That's a little over the top," Austin shook his head.

Anna looked at Austin and silently pleaded. She wanted to know and she was pretty sure the demon fighter could handle a little cut.

"Damn, this whole thing is just out there," he said, but he reached down in his right pocket and drew out a knife.

Will took it and in a swift movement he sliced the back of his arm.

Anna's reaction to the blood was instantaneous, she felt her fangs elongating and dove into Austin's chest. *Stupid, stupid*, she thought, *didn't think about that, did you?* Austin's arms went around her protectively.

"What's with her? She squeamish?" Will cocked a brow, his eyes narrowed slightly.

Jenna and Austin laughed nervously. "Yeah, a little."

When she got it under control she carefully looked back at Will who was studying her in a way that made her nervous. *Intelligent eyes*, she thought, *they don't miss anything*. She wondered if he might have had dual motives for his action.

She swallowed her fear and met his eyes directly. She could do this. She got up and sat next to him. He held his arm out and she put her fingers on the wound. As with all of her other abilities she concentrated everything she had on her task. She closed her eyes and pictured the cut sealing up and disappearing. She felt an electrical current, different than the static of dimming, more powerful and concentrated, travel from the center of her and then down her arm into her hand. She winced, feeling a bit of a sting on her own arm. She opened her eyes and found the cut had vanished and they were all staring at her in awe. Healed. Whoa, that was just...incredible.

"Well I guess that answers the question for you," he turned to Jenna, "Your turn?"

She shrugged and he sliced his arm again. This time Anna was prepared and easily contained her reaction. Jenna put her hand on it and looked like she was concentrating hard, but nothing happened. After a few minutes she shook her head. Anna touched the wound again and it disappeared more quickly than before.

"Well she's good to have around, huh?" Will grinned. "I could have used that trick a time or two."

"R'ight?" Josh grinned. "That's wicked awesome."

Austin stood up abruptly. "All right everyone, I think we've learned enough for one night, unless there was something more you needed to know right now?" He raised his brows at Anna.

She shook her head. What she wanted was to sate her need and get some sleep. She hadn't drank for a couple of days and though she didn't feel sick yet, she was starting to daydream about it, particularly after Will's little teaser.

"We'll be next door if you need us," Austin steered Anna out of the room with Jenna in tow.

She felt a little weird about the idea of drinking in front of her friend and started to pull Austin into the bathroom.

"No, don't guys, I actually want to take a nice long hot shower, so you know, do what you need to do." She brushed past them and they headed to the bed instead.

She followed the same routine every time, kissing first, then moving to his neck, then her hand inside his pants, then clean up. Although sometimes they stretched it out a little more, starting with a heavier make out session, but she didn't want Jenna to bust in on them so they made it quick. The entire time she was drinking she had her ears trained on the room next door. Will had gone into the shower so there wasn't anything to hear for a minute.

By the time she and Austin were finished Josh had just entered the bathroom, so she took the opportunity to talk to Austin before the eavesdropping session began.

"I guess I'll concede that they're legitimate," Austin spoke first and grudgingly. He seemed a bit more relaxed, probably from what they'd just done. "It's highly doubtful they just pulled that story out of their asses."

Anna nodded. "It was nice to hear that vampires were originally good, even if they have defected to the other side since then."

"You don't know that they all have," he reminded her gently.

"Yeah, I know."

Jenna came out and the three of them discussed everything they'd heard in detail, particularly Anna's newfound ability.

She heard Josh exit the bathroom and shushed them.

Will spoke up first. "They're hiding something."

"Huh? Like what?"

"I'm not sure, it's just a feeling, but it's something to do with Anna and the invisibility thing."

"Come on Will, you can't seriously think that she's a...

"I said I'm not sure, but I've never heard of anything else that could do that."

There was a sigh. "Yeah well, like her boyfriend said, we learn something new every day. I mean how can we of all people not be open minded?"

"I know, but it's more than that. It's the tone her man had when he made that statement, and the way she reacted to my blood, did you see that? She panicked."

"People react that way to blood."

"I don't know."

"Okay, how could she be? She doesn't fit the bill, in fact her friend Jenna is far more the profile, even her eyes are nearly purple."

"Actually, I was wondering if maybe both of them, hell even all three..."

"I don't think so. If that were the case how wouldn't they already know the things we were telling them?"

"You're right. It's just...I don't know."

"Okay, what if you're right? They're obviously on our side. I know how dad feels about non-humans, but dad isn't the end all be all. He could be wrong."

227

"Maybe. Oh well, let's hit the hay and worry about it in the morning."

"Yeah, actually the daylight would be pretty telling."

"Not really, there are still some that can go out in it."

"Yeah, which we both have agreed in the past likely means the difference between the bad and the good."

"True....'night bro, glad we're back on this side of the wall."

"Me too, no matter what they are, they did this for us."

When Anna was sure the conversation was over she related the details to Jenna and Austin.

"He's no fool, I'll give him that," Austin commented on Will's deduction.

"Look, now that you believe they are what they say, there's no reason why they can't come back with us."

"Actually there is, the police will be looking for them and they most likely have your visit on tape."

"But I didn't use my real name or show any ID."

"Doesn't matter, with the technology they have today...not to mention you were a missing person not too long ago, the file could still be there."

She had gone to the local PD to clear that up a few days after she'd returned home stating she'd left a message on Austin's phone about her change of plans, but he'd never gotten it. They hadn't bought it, but it wasn't as if she'd committed any crimes so it didn't matter what they thought of her failure to check in.

"Fine," she conceded, "but they can't prove anything."

"No they can't, but that doesn't mean they won't come looking, so Will and Josh would be a whole lot better off hiding somewhere else."

She could hardly argue that point. She sighed heavily. They decided that the following day she would buy a car for the boys and give them some cash. She also intended to get them cell phones so she had a way of reaching them, because she definitely saw them in her future.

Chapter Twenty-Four

The next morning she knocked on the brothers' door and Josh opened it with a genuine smile. There was something about him that she really liked. Not that she didn't like Will, but Josh made her feel like they could become fast friends.

"We're going car shopping," she told him. "For you."

"For us? No, you don't have to..."

"Yes I do," she cut in.

"Actually my brother is plotting a way of getting his car out of impound. He loves the thing, it's his baby."

"Where is it?"

"A lot in New York City. It's not registered to either of us so it was picked up as an abandoned vehicle."

"Oh. Well how can I help? Do you think I could get it?"

He smiled that dimpled smile again. "I guess with your unique ability that would certainly be a possibility. In fact I'm pretty sure my brother intended to recruit you."

She knew Austin would not like that plan. "Okay. Look, my guy uh, well he probably won't like the idea. So, I'm going to have to...okay how about this, I buy a car which I say is for you, put it in my name and then we can meet somewhere in a few days for operation "rescue Will's baby."

Josh laughed. "That'd work I guess."

"What would work?" Will walked out of the bathroom toweling off his hair. He had that sexy guy out of the shower look and Anna couldn't help but appreciate it.

Anna told him the plan and he considered it and nodded. "Yeah, sounds good. I'm definitely getting the jealous boyfriend vibe, pretty sure we're not winning him over anytime soon. So we'll hole up in a seedy hotel and call you in a few days, see what's up?"

"Actually I'll grab you guys a couple of pre-paid phones so we can keep in touch. Plus I'll give you some cash..."

He waved his hand, "Nah, we just gotta get back to the city, we've got money stashed."

"So you're going to play Mr. Too Prideful to Take Your Money, yet you have no problem using me to rescue your car? Which of these things do you think requires more effort and strain on my life? 'Cause Austin and I are going to have a fight about me going anywhere pertaining to you, or I'm going to go without telling him which means we'll have a fight later....."

He threw up his hands half smiling, "Hey, you don't have to, I can get it myself."

"Oh yeah, that was the point I was making." She rolled her eyes and put her hands on her hips.

"We'll gladly accept your money Anna, we really appreciate it as well everything else you've done," Josh shot his brother a look.

"Sure thing," Will shrugged, "if your handin' out cash who am I to argue?"

There was a light knock and Austin and Jenna entered. "So, we ready?"

"Yeah."

"There's a dealership right down the road." Austin's demeanor had not improved. Usually he was a friendly guy, but as Will noted, he was not thawing towards them.

"Right, so let's go."

An hour later they said their goodbyes. Anna didn't hide the phone purchases from Austin and she could feel his disapproval making her wish she had. They needed to have a serious conversation about this.

She privately asked Jenna if she would listen to her mp3 player so she could talk to Austin on the ride home, and she didn't wait until they were far down the road before starting.

"You were a complete ass to them, just thought you should know."

Austin went on the defensive, "Hey, I can't help it if I'm cautious and protective, we don't know those guys, even if they are Seers or whatever. That doesn't make them saints."

"You know what, that's not what your problem was. If it was anyone but me involved you probably would've been friends by this morning."

"Hence the protective part."

"So you admit it?"

"Freely."

She stared at him, anger mounting. "You are not, and I repeat NOT my father. Or my husband last time I checked, so this possessive thing you're doing, I don't like it."

He glared at her. "Why is it that whenever you get irritated you aim right below the belt? This cruel hurtful person just springs right out of you."

Anna opened her mouth then shut it again. Was she being cruel? She looked over at him and bit her lip. His eyes were on the road but a muscle was ticking in his jaw indicating his distress.

She took a breath and let it slip through her lips slowly. Before they'd left to meet the McClaron's she'd made a comment about them having to stop pretending everything was normal. If she boiled it all down his negative reactions of the past couple days were probably stemming from that, from the fact that somewhere deep inside he was waiting for the inevitable heartbreak of her leaving him.

Her life was changing, had changed the minute she'd been turned into this....this thing. Yet she was still only nineteen years old and it would be some time before it became readily apparent that she was different. She pictured herself twenty years from now, still the exact same. Then she pictured Austin. A forty-year old man, though still undoubtedly handsome he would have grey in his potentially thinning hair and wrinkles around his eyes, and then how about twenty years from that? At sixty, no matter how well he maintained himself, he would be entering the winter years of his life. And she would still be...this. She could continue telling herself that she didn't know it to be true, but it was a lie. She felt different inside, all of the normal aches and pains that came with being human were absent, she felt the way she imagined she must have felt at six or seven with the added element of inexhaustible energy.

She turned and looked out the window, watching the scenery race by. Time was like that when you were human and there was a finite limit on life. At their age it wasn't something they thought about much, the years seeming to stretch out ahead of them endlessly, but she knew better. And she knew that Austin did too. She wished he had never felt so strongly for her. If only he'd been able to look at her as just a friend, then she could be in his life in the same capacity she would be in the girls' lives. But he had to go and be in love with her, and for him fate would be cruel in that department. Not that at nineteen he wouldn't get over it and meet someone else, but just like she knew it had to end, she also knew that if things had been different they could very well have ended up together.

They spent the rest of the drive in silence. Jenna fell asleep listening to her music while she and Austin stayed lost in their own thoughts.

Chapter Twenty-Five

When they reached home the girls were waiting for them. They'd been apprised only briefly on what was transpiring and they were definitely interested in the details and the outcome.

Anna let Jenna fill them in and when she was finished they all looked at Anna for her input.

She smiled widely, "I performed a movie style jailbreak, what can I say except it was about time I put my superpowers into action!"

They laughed and chatted excitedly and Anna walked over to Austin wrapping her arms around his waist. She rested her head against his chest for a moment then pulled back turning towards the girls. "I think we should plan another party, you know have an end of the year summer bash."

"Oh yeah definitely!" Marina exclaimed.

"How about Saturday night?" Jess suggested.

"We should get fireworks," Macey put in, "The Pennsylvania border is only an hour and a half away. We missed fourth of July this year," she added.

"Yeah, we can drive up there tomorrow," Jenna stated. The girls wandered out onto the porch and Anna hung back with Austin.

"So what brought that on?" Austin raised a brow.

"I don't know I just feel like we all need something....fun and distracting. You start classes in two weeks, you must want to have some fun before you hit the grind, right?" She cocked her head, "Or do you figure you'll be involved in all those 'girls gone wild' college parties....

He laughed and grabbed her wrists, pulling her to him. "Those won't start until I hit the university next year," he teased. He was completing a two year Associates for drafting at the local community college, then going on to a university for his architectural degree.

"Yeah, I hear those SUNY guys are off the hook," she poked him in the ribs. They continued bantering back and forth and she felt the tension ease between them.

***

The next day Anna made a secretive call to the McClaron's explaining that she couldn't get away until after the weekend to which they replied "no worries". She spent the rest of the week in the company of the girls savoring every minute and of course she spent time with Austin. Their escapade with the McClaron's had vastly diminished her fear of the world outside Olin Falls, so they resumed the dating they'd done before her trip to Europe.

She'd come to a concrete decision during the moments she spent alone. Sunday would be her last night at home, for a long time anyway. She was going on the road with the McClaron's. Once the decision was made she pushed it aside not wanting to dwell on the idea of goodbye until she absolutely had to.

On Saturday the girls gathered at her house and spent the early afternoon setting things up for the party. There were six kids on the blacklist- the boys who'd been dogged by shadow men and started the fight at her last party. The fight was a good enough reason to be banned so no one questioned it and Anna crossed her fingers that A: they wouldn't crash it, and B: no one else would show up with one in tow. She'd only seen a few of the malevolent entities since she'd returned from London and still didn't know if they would sense the change in her. She really didn't want to end up going all Buffy the Demon slayer in her hometown.

She called her dad to apprise him of her plans and as usual his response was neutral. He was too preoccupied with the happenings in Third World Haiti to be overly concerned about some teenagers drinking beer. After their brief discourse she found herself wondering if his reaction might have been different had she said "Dad, in Europe I was kidnapped and turned into a vampire, and I believe my new role in life might be to hunt and slay demons." She shook her head, smiling a little. It wasn't likely he would've taken that seriously, the best she could have hoped for was him returning home because he was concerned about her mental state.

Once the beach was set up she ushered the girls up to her room. Austin was working until five so she had a little time with just them before things started. They all flopped onto her bed.

"This is going to be so much fun!" Jess gushed. "I love parties!"

Macey laughed and smacked Jess on the butt.

Anna smiled a little, but couldn't hold onto it. All week she'd persistently pushed thoughts of the future away but in the back of her mind she kept thinking This Is It.

"Uh oh, what's wrong with you?" Marina asked, cocking her head to the side.

She shook her head and bit her lip, trying to force back the Sweeping Tide of Change, as she'd dubbed the feelings that kept trying to erupt. "I was planning on waiting until tomorrow before I..." her voice broke off on a sudden sob and she struggled to keep it together.

"Anna! What's going on?" Jess scrambled across the bed and put her arms around her.

She sighed and figured she may as well explain. "The real reason for the party is for us to have one last hoorah before our lives change. Tonight I plan on focusing most of my attention on Austin, making him feel special. I'm not sure if it's a good plan, maybe it's selfish and I'm just making things harder in the long run, but I want him to feel how I feel..." She made a face finding it hard to articulate. She tried again. "What I mean is that he's this amazing, wonderful guy who I adore, who deserves to be idolized, never mind appreciated, and I'm about..."she stuttered as the tears tried to come, "about to shatter his heart into a million pieces.." she started sobbing in earnest then, shudders wracking through her body as she bent over her knees. He had been there for her when she'd needed him and she was going to hurt him unmercifully in payment. He'd called her cruel, and he was so right.

"You're gonna break up with him?" Jess asked with a frown.

Anna couldn't stop crying to respond so it was fortunate that Jenna understood. "She has no choice," she stated. "She's a vampire. For us this is not as much of a problem, but for a relationship? She might be *immortal*, do you guys understand what that means? Because I've been trying to wrap my mind around the idea and it isn't easy. But what I do get is that while we all age and eventually end up crippled old crones in rocking chairs, she will still look like she does right now."

There was a few beats of silence while the girls contemplated the things that Anna's own thoughts had been more and more consumed by.

"Poor Austin," Jess said quietly, and that really said it all.

She got herself together and went to the mirror, Jess helping her fix the make-up she'd ruined with tears. "I'm going to go on the road with Will and Josh," she stated, still looking in the mirror.

There was a chorus of "Whens?" though none of them seemed surprised.

"Soon. After I tell Austin...." she trailed off, "I can't be around here after that, not for a while."

She was greeted by silence again and in the mirror she could see them looking at her sadly.

She shook herself. "Okay, enough crappy sad stuff, that's why I wanted to wait. Sorry about that guys, it just bubbled out of me. Tonight we are not going to worry about it, tonight we're going to have fun and pretend the future doesn't exist! Tonight is our last day on earth, okay?"

"Yeah!"

"Definitely!"

"Let's parrrttttyy!"

On that note they headed down to the beach.

Chapter Twenty-Six

They decided to go on a boat ride and Macey went up to the stereo on the deck and turned on the music so people could begin the party without them if they didn't get back in time. They rode down past Logan point then headed across the lake and by the time they turned for home the sun was setting. The sky was painted pink and purple and Anna soaked it in thinking there were few places in the world that she'd seen with sunsets as glorious as the ones over Seneca Lake.

They could hear the music cranked over the sound of the motor as they pulled into the hoist and Anna spotted Austin standing at the end of the dock with Nathan. She hopped out of the boat and beamed a smile at him then swayed her hips provocatively as she made her way down the dock. The song ended just as she reached him and she threw her arms around his shoulders pulling her body up to wrap around his waist.

"Hey...

She halted his words with a steamy kiss that she continued through most of the next song, putting her hands inside his hair and holding him firmly. She was vaguely aware of the shouts and lewd comments thrown their way, especially when Austin's hands wandered over her backside. She felt him smile against her mouth and returned it.

"Yo Valence, you lucky bastard, how do you feel about sharing?"

Austin turned towards the obnoxious entity of Tim Wheelin. "Sorry Wheelin, I'm pretty fucking selfish." He kissed Anna again to punctuate it.

Anna pulled him under the pavilion and they danced for a couple of hours before joining in on some beer pong.

They made an excellent team beating one pair after another, but still drank their share of missed shots and Anna felt her buzz growing. Fortunately the effect only served to make her giggly, and she found she was thoroughly enjoying herself.

Around two a.m. the crowd began to thin and Macey told her she'd done a general head count around midnight and there'd been over a hundred and fifty people. *Not a bad turnout Preston*, she thought, a farewell party to remember. And she *would* remember it, she'd made a point throughout the night to capture faces in her mind. Mostly though, she'd focused on her nearest and dearest.

She filled her cup with the dark ale she favored and went over to where Austin was seated by the bonfire talking to Nate. Jess was sitting on the stones between Nate's legs talking to Macey who was giggling as usual and Anna smiled at the scene.

She seated herself in Austin's lap and he wrapped an arm around her waist, continuing his conversation about Texas Hold'em.

"I have an idea guys," she interrupted, "do you have your guitars?"

"In my trunk," Austin nodded.

"Yeah me too," Nate arched a brow and grinned at her, "sing along time?"

"That's my idea."

Austin and Nate headed up to get their instruments and Anna joined Jess and Macey's conversation. Marina plopped herself down next to Macey and when the guys came back the twenty or so people who were left gathered around, pulling up chairs and logs and putting in requests.

"This is the perfect way to end it," Marina said, and she nodded. It sure was.

***

The following day they all slept in, then eventually made their way to the lake for the cleanup, which was surprisingly less daunting than Anna had expected. Some kind souls had taken it upon themselves to gather up most of the cups and other party debris.

Once they'd finished she suggested they rent some videos and veg. They ordered pizza and watched movies, Nate and Jess curled up on one recliner, Jenna on the other, M and M stretched out on the floor, she and Austin tangled on the couch. It was a truly cozy scene. The party had been fun, but this was the life she was really going to miss.

"Are you petting me?" Austin asked with a smile in his voice.

She had been absently stroking him, first his hair, then his arms as she snuggled in lower, then his chest, "Yeah, I think I am."

"It's nice."

She continued it, her chest tightening up at yet another "last" moment. She felt the tears trying to well and squashed them. *Still not ready for this to end*, she thought. But it had to be tomorrow. She'd called Will and Josh the day before and told them she'd be ready to meet them in a day or two. Josh had joked that it was a good thing since Will was tempted to bail his "baby" out on his own. They were currently on the outskirts of Manhattan and Anna had expressed concern over them getting caught. "Nah," Josh had assured her, "we know how to disguise ourselves and blend in with the surroundings. Besides they don't expect to find us around here, they figure we're long gone."

Tomorrow. Her breath hitched and she curled herself into Austin, pressing her face in the crook of his arm. "Tired?" he asked and she nodded slightly. The idea of just drifting off and letting go of her tomorrow whoa's was appealing, but she had to drink. She peeked up at him, and he caught her expression.

"Come on," he said.

"It's okay, finish the movie."

"Nah, not that interested, let's go upstairs."

Once in her room she put on some mood music and joined him on the bed. She kissed him long and slow, savoring what would be their last time in any kind of intimacy. Her stomach clenched with guilt and she held him tighter. She broke away from him and whispered, "I want to be naked with you."

He drew in a sharp breath as she stood and slowly took off her clothes. His eyes traveled her body greedily and she could smell his arousal. When she was fully unclothed he said what she knew he would say.

"You are so beautiful."

He stood and undressed himself and she returned the sentiment, taking in his muscle-toned body and finally dropping her eyes to his jutting erection. She felt her face heat and he pulled her closer to him stroking his hands slowly down her neck and finally stopping on her breasts. He massaged them, gently running his thumbs over the tips. She kept eye contact with him as she explored his body, bringing her hands between his legs and gently massaging the hard length. He kissed her softly and tugged her towards the bed.

They lay facing one another, skin to skin and she placed gentle kisses down his face and neck, her teeth elongated and throbbing by the time she pierced his vein. She started to caress him with her hand but he stopped her, rubbing his erection up and down on the curls between her legs instead. She started to pull back but he pressed down on her head and whispered, "It's okay, I'm not trying to go in." She relaxed and let him rub against her, a strange tingly feeling building in her lower stomach and traveling down her thighs. She felt wetness at her core, and his groan said he did too.

He continued stroking up and down and she felt him getting thicker and harder which she knew meant he was about to come. He shouted and she could tell his release was powerful from the way his body jerked against her, warm liquid shooting onto her stomach and chest. She pulled back and laid her head over his heart which was beating hard.

"That was incredible," he whispered. "Indescribable."

She kissed his pec. "I'm glad."

He leaned over and grabbed something to clean them off with, then pulled the blankets over them. She lay awake for a long time after he'd slipped off to dreamland, just listening to the sound of his heart, praying that it would recover from the blow she was about to deal it.

The next morning she woke to him caressing her. His hands were stroking up and down her arms and the first thought she had was 'It's tomorrow'.

"You awake?" he breathed into her hair. She nodded slightly. "You hungry?" She shook her head. "Coffee?" Another shake. "Just wanna lie here then?"

She sighed and turned away from him then sat up to retrieve their clothes from the floor. She dressed, feeling his eyes on her back. She continued to look across the room after she was done and she heard him pulling on his own clothes. She couldn't turn and face him. She could feel the sorrow pooling in her eyes.

He chuckled, "It's safe to turn around now."

He thought she was being shy. She felt a sob welling up and choked a little.

"Anna?" Concern and alarm in his voice now, she turned into him, wrapping her arms around his chest. She broke down completely, something she'd been doing a lot of lately it seemed, and he pulled her tightly against him as she cried.

He rocked her murmuring in a soothing tone and she kept thinking *I can't do this, I can't do this*. But she knew she had to, so she slowly pulled herself together.

"What is it?" he asked when she stopped shuddering. "Come on talk to me."

She looked up at him then, hot tears still leaking from her eyes. "I want you to know, that you are the greatest person I've ever known. That I love you and I always will." The guarded look that came over his face made her lose her momentum and she looked down.

"Anna, what are you doing?" His voice was strained and fearful.

"I'm so sorry," she breathed, "I wish it could be different. I wish it so much."

"Anna, look at me."

She forced herself to meet his eyes which were filling with pain.

"There's no reason for you to do this, we can figure this out, we...." he stopped as she shook her head. "Why now? Why this moment?"

"Because I have to. Because it won't get any easier." Her voice was shaky but her tone held a resolve that he heard.

"Did you plan this?" He searched her eyes and got his answer. He put her off him onto the bed and stood, looking around like he was lost.

His voice, God his voice sounded so broken when he spoke. "So you thought we would have one last night huh? Wanted to make it perfect? Did you think it would soften the blow?"

"I don't know," she whispered, "I just wanted to be near you."

"So it was about you. Of course," he started shaking his head and just kept at it like he could deny what was happening.

She tried to go to him, but he warded her off with his hands, the look in his eyes making her want to scream.

"I know deep down you know this can't be. You have to know, Austin," she pleaded with him to understand, but his expression was turning hard.

She felt anger bubbling up, not at him but at fate and the world and everything in general. "You're going to grow old and I'm not, *don't you get that*? Don't you understand that I'm TRAPPED in this *place*, that I'm FROZEN in time! It's not fair, I didn't ask for it! I *saw* us getting married and having children. Taking them to baseball games and out for ice cream, and all the holidays, and growing old together, I saw it so clearly *and I can't have that*! Not with you, not with anyone!" She sunk down on the floor and buried her head in her arms. She was shaking out of fear and anger and sadness, and she wondered if she would be condemned to this kind of recurring misery.

She thought he might just leave the room, she heard him head in that direction. If he did she wouldn't stop him, if he needed to hate her she would let him.

But then he halted. After an endless moment he crossed the room and sat down beside her. He put a hand on her shoulder and she heard him take a shaky breath, and then another, and she knew that he was crying. She turned to him and he pulled her in to his body and hugged her tightly. Her chest hurt so bad she could barely breathe as they cried together. After a bit he pulled away wiping his face across his sleeve.

"Christ, I haven't cried since I was a kid," his voice sounded terrible. He looked at her, and his eyes held sorrow and pain, but also an acceptance that made her feel a little better. "You're going to uh..." he looked away, then back, "the McClaron brothers," he finished.

She nodded. "I have nowhere else to go."

He drew in a shaky breath. "You were right. I did know this was coming. That's why I hated them so much. I knew that it would happen that much sooner because of them." He closed his eyes tightly then opened them and sighed. "When are you leaving?"

"I need to go soon. I can't bear this, it hurts too much," she broke into another sob and he put an arm around her pulling her close.

"I'll miss you like crazy," he told her in a shattered voice kissing her hair.

She looked up at him. "I don't know what I would've done without you."

He smiled weakly. "You would have been fine. You're strong Anna. You will be fine." He took in a deep breath and let it out. "Look, for a little while I think it would be easier for me if we don't communicate. Just for a while. When I can handle it, I'll call you. And I *will* handle it eventually." He attempted another smile. "I know down the road I'll want to hear all about your adventures in demon slaying."

She smiled a little at that. He stood up and pulled her to her feet, wrapping his arms around her in what she knew was goodbye. He kissed her head and then gripped her face gently. "Take care of yourself."

She nodded, the tears coming again so she couldn't speak. She grabbed his hand and kissed it, rubbing it against her face, then let it go and went to her bed where she curled into a ball. Hugging her pillow against her chest she listened to the sound of his footsteps all the way out to his car.

Chapter Twenty-Seven

Anna played with the car radio, snorting in frustration. Nothing but static, wasn't there any radio towers? She would think so since she was only about ninety minutes from the fringes of the Big Apple. She finally landed on a station playing tolerable soft rock.

Her mind was in a hyperactive state. She kept jumping from one thing to the next, thinking about what her new future held, wondering if the brothers would let her tag along with them, especially wondering if they'd accept her once they knew what she was.

She'd packed only one suitcase full of clothes and a bag with necessities figuring she could always pick up what she needed along the way. Not for the first time it occurred to her that it was convenient to have an abundance of money.

Her thoughts drifted to the girls, picturing them waving to her as she left. After the gut wrenching emotional break up with Austin she'd been far too drained for another weepy goodbye so she'd opted for the see ya later alligator version. It wasn't like she was leaving them forever anyway, not the same as the split with Austin.

She marveled at how well she was now coping with the change. This morning she'd felt like she was being ripped apart and her world was coming to an end but right now she was feeling antsy and chipper. Moody, some people would call that. Or bipolar like she sometimes felt she was.

Actually, she preferred to think that it was inner strength. Austin had called her strong and at that moment she would've begged to differ, but the truth was she did have strength. She had dealt with tragedy in her life. Her mother's death had been sudden and terrible, especially because they'd been so close. Yet she had been able to go on and after a bit she'd been back to her normal, enthusiastic, cup half full self.

Her life was in upheaval, once again, and honestly there was no place for a lingering depression over the fact. It wouldn't do any good, wouldn't change anything, just leave her feeling hollow like she'd felt for the couple of hours after she'd said her morning farewell.

Her mind wandered back to Will and Josh. Apparently Will had tired of waiting for her to appear, or rather disappear for him and his "baby", which she'd learned was a black 1973 Plymouth Barracuda. Late last night they'd successfully broken into the impound lot and rescued it and right now it was parked in a dark corner of a car garage. She was a little disappointed, she had relied on her rescue of his car to further endear herself to them, but at least they hadn't told her to "shit in her hat" since they didn't need her anymore. Of course at this point they thought her intention was just to learn more about herself, not tag along.

She saw her exit up ahead and felt her heart kick-she was almost there. She was going back and forth on the subject of her true identity, wondering if she should tell them outright or wait until they'd gotten to know her a bit. If she was even given the chance. She imagined that with her abilities they would see the potential asset she could be, so if dishing was her only choice, so be it.

I have no place to go if they turn me away, she thought, *so I better convince them one way or another.*

She turned onto the ramp and hung a left, spotting the motel sign up ahead. The start of a new life, she thought, for better or worse.

She knocked on their room door and heard movement inside. Will swung the door open wide and then stepped to the side to let her in. He seemed to watch her movements with interest. It made her think about the whole 'vampires can't come in unless invited', but if that wasn't a myth then it didn't apply to her.

Josh smiled warmly. "Nice to see you again."

"You too," she smiled back and turned to Will. "Sorry I didn't get here sooner to help with your car."

"No worries, I took care of it." He walked over to a drawer and pulled out a stack of papers then turned and held them out to her. "Josh and I photocopied a bunch of stuff for you. It's sort of a Faerian basic history, most of it has been passed down through the generations of our family, some we've added along the way. I thought you could hang out here and look it over while we go shoot some pool. Just jot down questions as they come. Of course you won't get through it all in a day, but we can answer some things now and down the road you can always give us a call."

She frowned and Josh looked at her sympathetically. "Will's in a rush to get going now that his car's back in action. Not a whole lot we can do in this area now that we're fugitives."

She nodded deciding she might as well do as they were asking for the moment. She could talk to them more when they got back. She figured she might find out some things about her own kind....God that sounded weird, and anyway she was still nervous about her proposal.

"All right so we'll see you in a few hours." Josh smiled at her warmly and she watched the door fall shut before settling back in the armchair with the papers.

Two hours later she rubbed her eyes and set the stack aside. It was interesting stuff, a lot of it written as if it were a diary. She'd learned the brothers' line came from Ireland, though she'd guessed that from their name, and their family had immigrated around the time of the civil war. She'd also found out the "seeing" trait was passed either daughter to daughter or father to son, so of course in their case it was on the paternal side all the way down through. Which meant that in her family it came from her mom....she wondered if her mother had been able to "see" and mentally kicked herself for not confiding in her before she died.

Their father was around eighty if she figured the dates correctly, and the two of them were in their early thirties. They looked no more than twenty-three to twenty-five, but then they had already told her Faerians lived for about a hundred and fifty years. She wondered if their father looked anywhere near his age. Their mother had been run of the mill human and only thirty when she and their sister were murdered. The boys had only been six and three and Anna felt a pang of sympathy for them and their dad. That could not have been easy times.

She'd found a few notes about vampires but it was mostly what they'd already told her. The only thing of interest she'd learned was that vampires were in America, but only those that enjoyed the Vegas, Orleans type of scene. Apparently they weren't overtly dangerous to people but at the same time they no longer fought the good fight. Seemed it was only in Europe that they were completely warped.

She wondered if the brothers had ever met a vampire and leaned towards No so since she'd read the things they'd added and they hadn't mentioned it. That might make things harder. Or easier maybe, at least it would mean they had no bad personal experiences. Their dad on the other hand, some of the things she gathered from what he'd written made it pretty obvious he held a great disdain for all non-humans. *Don't want to meet him anytime soon*, she thought, *or for him to know what I am at least.*

She *was* learning a vast amount of useful info pertaining to the shadow men. They referred to the ones they dealt with the most often as the Jinn. They also made reference a few times about possible "Dantalion" which she was able to deduce was some sort of demon class distinction, the Jinn being lower on the totem pole. In retrospect she might have deduced some of this information on her own if she'd only faced them instead of shutting them out every chance she got. She berated herself a bit for that then filed it away as another lesson learned.

Had she studied them she might have noticed that there was a difference in the distances they were from a person they shadowed. Apparently this said everything about how much influence they had. For instance if they were trailing several feet behind that meant their influence was minimal, the person might be allowing a slightly negative slant to be put on their perspective-or just having a bad day. At that point they could literally shake the demon off by simply making a decision to see the glass half full. Seers didn't concern themselves with cases like those since more often than not the demons would move onto someone else. It was when the shadow was close enough to be touching that it became a concern. This generally meant they'd been with the person awhile and were making some headway. She remembered times where it had appeared they were riding piggyback, apparently that was when the individual was allowing them to influence some large decisions on a subconscious level.

Finally there was the cloaking effect, where they seemed to surround a person. A "cloaked" individual could actually hear a voice directing them to do things, and once they acknowledged this voice it was only one small step to possession. They needed only to say "Yes I know you're there" and give permission for them to "share" control. She had started to wonder why a person would do such a thing when she found the answer. In a nutshell, the kind of person who would allow a demon so much access was generally selfish and lacking much in the way of a conscience. And the demon was deception and manipulation. It would seduce its hosts with visions of wealth and power. Once the person invited it in consciously, it was game over, no going back. And the sharing thing was a laugh. The demon absorbed the person, consumed them, became them.

The movies had it all wrong. The only exorcism that could be performed was death once the demon took over. At the levels beforehand there was a potential of turning back, and in that sense exorcism worked in a way. But only if the person desired it. No priest could come along and force it with prayer, the will of the person had to be involved in the process. It all made sense, she was a firm believer in the idea that if one wants to change their circumstance they must only change their mind about it.

She heard footsteps and the door swung open, Will sauntering inside with a smug look on his face, Josh trailing behind looking perturbed.

"I still say that was a damn lucky shot, no way you meant to pocket four balls on the break."

Will cupped a hand to his ear and made a smart ass face, "Who won?"

Josh shook his head in irritation.

Still cupping his ear Will squinted and leaned forward, "I didn't hear you."

"Oh shut your face, I paid up."

Will shook his head, "Uh uh, you have yet to pay in full, not until I hear the words Will you are The Billiard Master and I am but your lowly apprentice."

Josh smirked, "In your dreams."

"Sore loser."

"Ass face."

Anna watched the exchange in growing amusement. She felt an enormous amount of affection for the brothers even though she barely knew them. That they spent their lives taking on the darkness and still managed to have moments like this? Worthy of serious admiration and respect.

They finally focused on her. "So, whatcha got for us?" Will asked.

Questions. Right. "Uh, well let's see. It's very detailed and likely whatever questions I do have will be cleared up once I read it through more thoroughly."

"Oh? So you don't have any questions?"

"Well...I do. Just not about Faerians and demons."

"What about then?"

She looked down at her hands. "Vampires," she said softly.

Will quirked and eyebrow and glanced at Josh who cocked his head and frowned. "What do you want to know?"

"Whatever you can tell me beyond what you said the other day."

Will, still looking at her in his shrewd way, obliged. "Well, let's see. Like I said, vamps were created to take out demons, so once upon a time they did what we do, only a helluva lot better because they can take 'em out in their shadow forms."

Anna bit her lip. "How? Do you mean they're solid?" She did not like that idea.

Will frowned a little, looking at her strangely. "Well, a vamp makes them solid with their touch and then they rip them apart with their fangs and bare hands. This actually destroys them, whereas what we do just sends them back to hell, and we can't do anything about them in shadow form."

"You said "once upon a time," do you mean they no longer do it, not any of them?"

"Not sure really, definitely not the ones who reside in this country. They prefer to hang out in places like Vegas and debaucherize. Which, hey it's not my place to judge as long as they don't hurt anyone, to each their own."

Anna digested all of this, not sure what else to ask. It didn't appear they were aware of the whole underground scene going on in London, and she wondered if they would have reason to know if it was going on in America. Jake had brought her to that place after setting up the circumstances in such a way that her friends wouldn't know where she was or where to look. Obviously they kept their activities well hidden.

"Are their seers who do what you do in London?" she asked finally.

They both nodded. Which meant it *was* possible the vamps here were exactly like the ones there and they didn't know it. Jake had certainly come across as someone who just "debaucherized". Which left her where, exactly?

"All right, gotta ask, why so interested in vampires?" Will pulled a chair up, turned it around backwards and sat, folding his arms over the back. Josh remained standing with his arms folded over his chest, both of them wore expressions of curiosity and suspicion.

Well, she thought, what choice do I have? "I told you about my trip to Europe, how my girlfriends and I went to the Goddess meeting and Jenna started seeing the shadow men. What I didn't tell you is that I saw vampires, and witnessed them biting people in the middle of a dance floor though no one else seemed to notice." She stopped and chewed on her lip, trying to decide how to proceed.

"That's not unusual," Josh offered, "we see past their dimming abilities too. You must have opened yourself up to the rest of your power."

Will spoke up. "*You* can dim yourself, and I gotta say I've never come across another seer with that ability. Or even heard of one that has it."

She nodded slightly. "I am about to tell you how that came to be, it's just a little hard for me."

They wore Go On expressions and she obliged. Like with Austin she left nothing out, though this time she didn't cry, just got a little shaky in places. When she came to the part where she was getting on the plane for home she stopped and gauged their reactions. They looked astounded and she had a feeling it took a lot to surprise these two.

"You survived the transition," Will murmured. It was a statement rather than a question. They seemed to be finding it difficult to comprehend and Josh voiced the sentiment.

"How is that possible?"

She shook her head slowly. "I don't know," she said quietly, "I don't know anything. Other than I *am* a vampire, or at least half, not sure how that works obviously since I don't know anything. But I have fangs and desire blood. And I can dim myself and run like the wind, and leap onto my house, and throw my friends over my shoulder, and then there's my super enhanced vision and hearing...." she let that hang in the air and waited for them.

"Holy shit!" Will grinned. "That's just...it's definitely a new one for me. Jesus, you must be one hell of a chick to make it through that! And your friends, the two we met, how did they take it?"

Josh was still staring at her wide eyed. She felt her eyes water a little as she thought about Austin, how amazing he had been, how understanding.

"They were incredibly accepting. Not just Jenna and..."she swallowed thickly, "but also three of my other girlfriends. If it wasn't for them I don't know what I would've done."

Josh lost his wide-eyed stare, his expression changing to sympathy. "You must have been terrified, not just during the ordeal, but on your way home."

"You have no idea." She smiled a little as she remembered Austin's grand speech in front of the girls. "Austin made it...well he helped me look at it like I was a superhero." She laughed, "We argued about what to call me, I wanted to go with Bat Girl but he kept insisting on something pertaining to fairies, the Indestructible Fairy was one."

Both boys laughed with her.

She lost her smile and took a deep breath. "So here's the thing. I want to throw in with you, and before you say anything I need you to understand that I can't go home and I have no place else to go."

"Why can't you go home?" Will raised a brow.

She felt tears welling. "Austin and I were together and I had to stop pretending it would work. I just can't be there, I don't fit anymore, I have no purpose. I don't fit anywhere, but at least with you two I could have a purpose. I could help you."

Josh smiled at her. "Well I for one don't have a problem with it."

She looked at him gratefully, but Will jumped in, "Whoa, whoa, all right look, we need to talk about this a little before making hasty, potentially life altering decisions." He turned his sharp gaze to Anna and her defeated expression made him chuckle a little. "You are way too damned cute, do you know that? You remind me of that cat with the boots on Shrek, with the eyes...I'm not saying no, I just need for us to make sure it's the right thing."

He raised his eyes heavenward then looked back at her, "What about the whole fangs needing blood thing, how have you been doing it?"

"Austin."

"Austin? Are you serious?"

"It doesn't hurt, I didn't hurt him, I wouldn't hurt someone, not ever," the way he was looking at her made her feel guilty and defensive, "the first time I did it I was so sick and weak and the hunger physically hurt, it felt like my blood was burning, a lot like when I was changing except not as intense."

"You're not supposed to drink from humans," Will stated.

She furrowed her brows in confusion.

"Actually, how do you know that?" Josh asked his brother then turned to her, "does it affect your abilities, do they decrease during the day?"

She shook her head.

"What about after, do you feel like you're high from it?"

She shook her head again, confused by the questions.

He turned to Will, "Since she was human to begin with, it might be different for her. After all, vampires drink from one another."

Will made a "that's plausible" face and shrugged. "You are an anomaly all the way around Anna Preston."

"So they drink from each other then?"

"Well that and animals."

"Oh." It hadn't even occurred to her to try animals. How would that work, would she have to hunt them and bring them down? She shuddered a little picturing it.

"Hey, don't sweat it. If it didn't affect you negatively, than for you it must be all right." Will's expression changed to a sly smile. "What'd your boyfriend say it felt like?"

She blushed, warmth climbing up her neck into her cheeks.

"That good huh? Feelin' hungry now?"

She blushed harder and looked away. She'd known she would have to drink from them, but the idea made her uncomfortable, the whole association was too sexual.

"Well?" he persisted.

"Leave her alone Will, you're embarrassing her."

She looked at Josh gratefully thinking she wouldn't mind so much with him, she'd just keep the sexual stuff out of it.

But Will wasn't letting her off the hook, the persistent pain in the ass.

"I need you to do this so I can see if it's something we can deal with on a regular basis. I know you're preferring Josh for the task right now, but little girl I'm afraid it's me you have to convince."

She knew she wasn't getting out of it, but since she wasn't hungry at the moment her fangs seemed to be suffering from cold feet. "I can wait until tomorrow, or maybe the next day," she attempted hopefully.

"Nice try."

"But I'm not sure I can do it right now since I'm not feeling the need."

"You can."

"Hey Will, give her a break, how do you know she can?"

"I just know." He stared at her unrelentingly.

She sighed. "Fine. Let's sit on the bed." She stood up and he joined her. When they were side by side she bit her lip. "Austin and I were somewhat intimate, and we made it a part of that. You know like we started kissing first and then I moved over to his neck."

He leaned in and she reared back. "No! I didn't mean I wanted you too, I was just explaining how this could be awkward for me."

"So do what makes you comfortable."

She darted a look at Josh and he nodded in understanding—she didn't want an audience. "I'll just go down the street and order some pizza."

When he left she relaxed a little, this whole thing was definitely a one on one type experience, at least for her. Will leaned in for a kiss and this time she let him, but only briefly before she broke off and brushed her lips lightly on his pulse. She listened to the rhythmic beat and opened her senses to the smell of him. She felt her teeth elongate then he startled her by leaning back.

He stared at her fangs in fascination. "You sure this isn't gonna hurt? I'd like to be prepared."

"Yes, I think there might be a numbing agent involved, or maybe they're just so sharp...."

He nodded and leaned forward. She kissed him where his pulse was strongest and then sunk her teeth in and sucked. She could hear him making sounds of enjoyment, but she was *not* going to touch him. The last thing she needed was any weird sexual tension if they were going to work together. When she was finished she backed off gently. His eyes were closed and he opened them slowly like he was waking up from a nap.

"You're right, it felt good. Really good."

She saw him shift a bit and knew the male part of him was alive and ready for action. Not gonna happen, she thought.

"So you said you and Austin were somewhat intimate? What does that mean exactly?"

She blushed, again. "I told you he was my boyfriend."

"Uh huh." He raised a brow waiting for more.

"I'm a....I haven't you know....with anyone, so we were," she stumbled over the words, "We didn't have sex, okay?" She blurted. "But we did some other stuff, and that's all I'm going to say since it really isn't your business." She stood up and crossed the room, turning to face him with her arms folded protectively around herself.

All signs of smartass had disappeared from his face. "I'm sorry Anna, I didn't mean.....Jesus you're so young and innocent, it makes me wonder what the Big Guy is up to with this whole thing." He shook his head looking slightly bewildered. "A sweet little virgin vampire, unbelievable, I thought I'd heard it all, but apparently not."

Josh walked in, his expression amused. "Interesting conversation," he put the pizza down. "So I hope this means you're gonna ease up on her."

"Are you kidding? I feel like I'm about to adopt a kid sister." He shook his head and crossed the room to grab a slice.

Anna stared at them. "Does this mean I can stay with you?"

Will chewed, staring back at her. He swallowed and smiled, his eyes twinkling with amusement. "Yeah, yeah, but if you're joining our team I've got some rules."

She felt giddy, not realizing until that moment how important this was. She grinned, "Go ahead."

"You do what I say, when I say it. First we're gonna go somewhere and you can show us what you can do, you know pull some weight up, do some sprinting, that kind of stuff, then we can test out your hearing, do some eavesdropping, which reminds me," he looked pointedly at Josh, "gonna have to keep in mind she can hear everything we say so talking about her when she's not in the room ain't gonna work." He looked back at her and folded his arms. "You heard us in the hotel that night."

She nodded.

"Shit." He grinned. "All right, so you're gonna need a crash course in the things we do. For now I don't want you trying to vamp out on the shadows since we don't know enough about it. Just tag along and observe until I think you're ready for other things. It might be damn hard to kill you but it's not impossible, so you know, let's not push the limits right away." He stopped to shove some more pizza in his mouth so she jumped in smiling widely.

"Thanks you guys! I promise to do whatever you say."

Josh came over and sat beside her draping an arm around her shoulder. "I have a good feeling about this," he said, and with that they began discussing their plans.

Chapter Twenty-Eight

Jared sat in one of the local vampire hangouts, his feet up on a bar stool, cigarette in one hand and scotch in the other. The large flat screen was tuned into the local news and he watched it with a mixture of mild irritation and wry amusement.

When he'd come out of his last hyberstasis, a voluntary hibernation for vampires who needed a break from living, the world had changed immensely. He'd been intrigued for the first time in centuries, with the invention of automobiles and airplanes, the telephone and the television.

Since shortly after his mother's murder and consequently his father's death he'd been taking fifty to one hundred year sabbaticals. Unfortunately the limit for hyberstasis was a century and the catch was that you had to remain in the land of the living for the exact amount of time you'd "slept". This last time he'd gone under for the full term and still had another fifty years to go before he could do it again. But at least the constantly evolving technology kept it slightly interesting.

There were a number of others in the bar shooting pool and bragging about their latest exploits. Once in a while they glanced warily in his direction. Ever since the night he'd put a gruesome end to one of their buddies, they tread softly when he was near.

A couple of human males came in the door and headed to the bar. They were young and definitely not local- this he knew because the locals tended to steer clear of this place. He listened to their dialogue and as usual they had nothing of value to say.

Humans, he thought with disdain. They were responsible for destroying everything and everyone he'd ever loved. His mind touched briefly on Ceri, the female he would have mated. A human mob had slaughtered her village because they had deemed them to be witches and sorcerers and monsters. Such short existences men lived, how could they possibly think they understood anything, let alone come to the conclusion they had some unholy right to pass judgment? And yet they did, over and over, throughout the ages, human ego never changed.

Once upon a time he had viewed them as ignorant and helpless children in need of his protection. He'd had an affection for them similar to that of a parent towards unruly offspring. He'd believed they were mostly good despite their ridiculously short-sighted concepts, that it was only their lack of time to gain wisdom through experience that led them to frivolous and often destructive pursuits. There had even been a time when he'd called some men his friends, men who had fought beside him in battles against the common enemy of the shadow demons. But such humans were rare even back then and had long since disappeared.

Now he just saw them as selfish, parasitic brats, lower than the lowliest of animals. Because unlike the other beasts of the world they had the ability to understand the effect of the choices they made, but continued to make them regardless. Which was why he generally didn't care what his fallen brethren did with them, except that they proved to be similar in nature. The newest generation of vampire cared about the same things as the human populace did- sex and drugs, money and power, and above all mindless entertainment, the more gruesome and shocking, the better. He was reasonably sure that the practice of drinking from and especially draining humans of their life essence changed something fundamental in their make-up.

Long ago, when vampires had first taken this path it was said they were damned. They could no longer withstand the sun and it was related to another son by members of his race who still held the old ways. For his own part he didn't know. He had never tasted human blood, the very thought of it repulsed him. But he still felt a bit of lingering resentment that humans could be forgiven for all manner of heinous sins and a vampire could commit one and be irredeemable. He understood that to harm or take the life of another being for nothing more than selfish desire was the very definition of evil. But as far he was concerned the whole of humanity fell into that category.

He took another sip of scotch and glanced at the other patrons. There were a few of his kind who mingled in this pub that had yet to make the final leap into the abyss. He knew this from the conversations he'd overheard along the way. He was also aware of small factions of his race that continued to perform the duties they were created for, and he had, on occasion, watched from a long distance away as some of these hunters tore into a group of unsuspecting demons. He'd had no desire to jump into the fray. These days he was content with the malevolent shadows keeping their distance. They could sense he was no one to fuck with the same way everyone else could.

He looked out of the corner of his eye as a couple of males approached him.

"Terrence was wondering if you wanted to join us tonight under The LeRoux," the shorter one conveyed nervously.

He eyed the jumpy male and gave a slow and emphasized shake of his head.

"Oh. Okay, but uh..it's gonna be off the hook, the girls they hired are into you know, everything and anything, plus we have some pills that actually work for us...." he trailed off noting Jared's growing irritation. "Sorry to bother you, we just thought we'd ask." His pal who had been standing further back turned tail and they both hurried away.

For the years he'd been coming here he'd had many offers like this one. As if he wouldn't just show up if he was so inclined, he did not require invitation. He knew they were referring to a rave, he'd been to many in various locations. He'd lost interest after the first dozen or so. If he wanted human girls to perform for him all he needed to do was walk into a club and beckon. They followed him out like the pied piper.

Fifty more years, he thought, *and I can sleep again.* He lit another cigarette and returned his attention to the television.

Chapter Twenty-Nine

Will held up a twenty dollar bill and looked around at the men gathered by the pool tables. "Who wants to play?"

A burly hillbilly leaning against the far wall scratched his beard and eyed the brothers. "Not you," he said after a moment's consideration, "but I'll play your buddy for forty." He pointed his cue at Josh and walked up to the table.

Will stood back to watch his brother go to work.

Anna watched the scene with fascination. She had wondered how they made money since they weren't paid for their real job, and soon discovered they were a couple of hustlers. Not a surprise really. And it was perfect, something they could do in every town in America.

The art of hustling was not what she'd imagined it to be. She'd always thought that it meant tricking people and ripping them off, but the brothers didn't play like that, they didn't pretend to be terrible until the real money was laid down. They simply offered anywhere from five to fifty dollars for people to play, and most men were game for a little gambling. They could walk out of a place with up to three hundred bucks for just a few hours of shooting balls, and for the most part no one chased after them shouting and cursing.

Josh wiped the floor with Sir Beer Gut then offered to buy him a drink which the man grudgingly accepted. He was one of "those", the sore loser kind, but there was still no yelling or fist raising, just some grumbling about lucky shots. After Sir Beer Gut polished off his drink he suggested they go double or nothing.

Josh decided not to spank the guy too hard, missing a couple of shots his companions knew were purposeful.

Beer gut looked like the type who *could* potentially start something if his ego was crushed too hard, and the boys liked to avoid pointless confrontations.

Josh won again and the guy pushed four twenties towards him with a scowl. "I think you boys should head on down the road before I decide you piss me off."

"Aw come on Randall," an older guy missing a few teeth goaded, "that boy won it fair and square, you got no business fuckin' wid em."

Randall turned to the gap tooth and glared at him. "Maybe I should fuck with you instead."

Will inclined his head toward the door and they walked out onto the sidewalk.

Josh held the cash out and Will snatched it from his hand. "Am I ever gonna get to play a game, asshole?"

Josh laughed. "They never cease to be fooled by my boyish charm."

"I think it's the dimples," Anna teased, "no one with dimples can kick ass at bar games."

Josh grinned showing off said dimples and Will pinched his cheek.

"Hey cut that shit out!" He flipped Will's hat off his head.

Anna giggled as they climbed in Will's car, the boys still bickering like children. She slid into the backseat and Will roared away from the curb, his classic rock drowning out Josh's last retort.

They were currently in "small hick town" Virginia. They'd had a lead on some strange activity in the next town over but it turned out to be nothing. Well, nothing that concerned them anyway, just some juvenile delinquents causing trouble.

In the meantime Will had called some of his contacts to see if he could pull any more useful info on vampires. He'd learned that a vampire could both touch *and* communicate with demons. The general consensus was that a demon on its own was no contest for a vamp, but if there were enough of them they could do some damage, though not physically. It was their psychological powers that made them something to be wary of. Apparently vampires could be tainted by the demons they destroyed and they'd have to do some serious R&R to expel the effects, but all of Will's sources were of the mind that there were few, if any, that bothered anymore.

They'd also learned there was another speed besides Olympic by which a vampire could travel. Faster than the eye could see, it was loosely translated into Blurring. Anna had tried to figure out how to accomplish it, but so far no dice.

The only other piece of information that all the sources agreed on was there were few female vampires left, and they could no longer breed. They hadn't been able to in well over a century. Some believed what Will and Josh had been told, that all females were evil to begin with, however two of their sources had heard an entirely different story. They attested that though many of the females were born with more aggressive and masculine traits, there were also a number who were born more like their mothers, gentle healers, and then somewhere along the way some bad ass vampiress was scorned and became a vengeful evil bitch. She, along with others she'd convinced, took out the gentler of their species, hunting them to extinction.

Anna was once again frustrated by the lack of anything truly concrete. Legends were just hearsay, holding grains of truth but normally wrong about many things.

She was mulling this over as they pulled into the parking lot of yet another dingy motel. A couple of times she'd convinced them to stay somewhere nicer on her nickel, but they seemed to have a thing against using her money. Men.

Josh's phone went off with an odd sounding ring as they were getting settled in their room.

"Dad?" he answered.

"Hey boy, where are you two?"

Anna loved her ability to hear both ends of the conversation.

"Virginia, some little town east of bumfuck."

"Really? That's great, I'm driving through the bottom of Pennsylvania so let's meet up tomorrow."

Josh gave him the location details and hung up.

"Dad's coming huh?" Will was smiling genuinely at the news. In the two weeks she'd been with the duo, she'd learned that their feelings about their dad differed pretty greatly. They both loved him, of that there was no doubt, but Will was definitely closer to him. Josh seemed to harbor some resentment for their childhood, or lack thereof, and at the moment he looked decidedly un-enthused about a reunion.

"You could at least pretend to be glad to see him," Will said, picking up on the vibe.

"Don't start."

"He's not so bad."

"You're right, he's wonderful. I'm ecstatic." He plastered a fake smile on his face and Will shook his head then turned his attention on Anna.

"Did he say how long he was going to hang?" Will asked Josh, still looking at her.

"Uh, no. He didn't. Does he ever?" He rolled his eyes.

"So, I guess we just tell him Anna's a healer and traveling with us for a bit then, huh?"

"No Will, I think we should tell our intolerant father that she's a bloodsucker." Josh smirked.

"Sarcasm doesn't become you."

Anna chewed her lip nervously, she was seriously hoping she didn't do anything to give herself away. The picture she had in her mind of Jack was of a great big bear of a man with a bushy grey beard and hands the size of baseball mitts. Not that either of the boys had ever described his physical appearance, it was just the larger than life way they viewed him that gave her that particular mental image. Even Josh who wasn't in love with the guy talked about him like he was a god.

Josh sat down next to her and Will flipped on the television. "Don't worry about it," he said softly, "there's nothing about you in general to suggest what you are. Just act the way you do when you're out in public."

She nodded.

"You might want to take my vein tonight, so you can go a couple of days without." He suggested.

She'd found that three days was the magic number, after that she started feeling sick and light headed. She'd just drank yesterday, but it definitely didn't hurt to stock up. She alternated between the boys, it somehow kept it from being as personal or turning sexual. Although it didn't seem to have the same effect on Josh as it did Will. In fact the last time she'd drank from Will he'd picked a girl up at the bar across from where they were staying and went home with her.

For the most part the brothers treated her like a kid sister and she figured that in Will's case it was the virgin thing. He was what her friends, whom she'd kept in pretty constant contact with via texting, affectionately called a horndog. Yeah, he was definitely that, so with her it had to be the intact cherry. His taste in women tended to be of the more experienced and worldly variety, a love 'em and leave 'em kinda guy who at least had the decency to pick those that didn't mind.

Will lounged on a worn armchair, leg draped over the arm as Anna drank from Josh on the bed. She was amazed at how nonchalant they'd become about it in such a short time. Sinking her fangs in their neck was just business as usual. Being no strangers to the strange apparently made it easier. And she no longer cared if they were both in the room, it was too inconvenient to always send one of them away.

She finished and was surprised to find she was tired. It had been a long day but normally it gave her a boost when she drank.

"I'm gonna get some sleep," she announced. Josh was still sitting next to her and he started to get up but she put a hand on his arm. "You know if it's more comfortable for you to sleep next to me, I don't mind, I'm much tinier than your brother."

Generally they only got one room with two beds and the guys had been sleeping together. She had thought about making this offer several times, but was concerned that it would lead to something. Lately however, with the brotherly way they treated her she was feeling pretty safe, especially with Josh.

He seemed to consider, then shrugged. "You sure?"
"Definitely."
"A'ight."

Will glanced over. "What's this, you ditchin' me bro? Who am I gonna cuddle with now?" He turned his lip into a pout.

Josh grinned, "Just think, now you won't need the bathroom for your midnight wanker yanking."

"Shit, I don't need it anyway, just face the other way and I'm good to go."

Josh grimaced as Will waggled his eyebrows.

Anna laughed and was proud to find she wasn't blushing. With these two the locker room talk ran rampant and she was becoming desensitized to it.

She climbed under the covers and Josh got in with her, stretching out his big body. "Ahh, so much more room, so much more comfy."

Will hopped into his bed and sprawled out, "Not as much room as I've got."

Anna laughed. "Is everything a competition with you two?"

"YUP," they said in unison.

Anna smiled. God she was falling in love them. She closed her eyes and snuggled closer to Josh's warmth.

***

Jenna sat on Anna's dock staring at her phone. Maybe if she kept on staring it would ring, she thought, blowing hair out of her face in frustration. Anna had been good about sending texts, but she needed to actually *speak* to her. She'd called and left three messages saying as much and she'd yet to hear anything.

Lately she'd been dreaming of the vampires more and more often.

She'd learned it was a group of fanatical humans who were responsible for the mass murder that always left her feeling helpless and angry when she woke. A few nights ago she had entered the dream just in time to watch in horror as a crowd of leering people set fire to the structure which she thought might have been some kind of community center from the olden days. It was made of both wood and stone and large enough to hold about a hundred people. She'd seen a few women fighting their way out of it only to be stabbed through the heart or beheaded by a waiting fanatic.

In the dream she'd had last night she'd come into it when the fire was in full blaze and those inside were screaming, but this time she'd woken up for a few minutes and then slid back to sleep and dreamt about a young female who'd looked a bit like Anna. She was a daughter of one of the female healers, and Jenna guessed her age to be about seventeen.

Although none of the women looked over the age of twenty-five, which appeared to be the magic time when they stopped aging all together, you could still tell which ones were older by their movements or their eyes. And in the case of the Anna look alike she could tell it was mother and daughter by the way they interacted.

The girl had been sitting in the grass just outside the wall that surrounded the village, stripping flowers of their petals and dropping them in a bucket. She had a wistful look on her face, a small smile tugging at the corner of her lips and Jenna could almost hear her mooning over someone. She was obviously a girl with a crush.

The mother had come through the gate in the wall and said something that made the girl look up and furrow her brows in distaste. Then the older woman had put a hand on her hip and spoke in a sharper tone and the girl picked up the bucket and reluctantly followed her back through the gate.

Jenna had been drawing her own conclusions such as the girl and her mom were Anna's ancestors, but that made no real sense if only vampires were born of vampires. And those females had died in the fire so that would have put an effective end to the line anyway. Then again the original Faerians had split into two groups and there was a good chance they had been related.

She put her head in her hands, her brain starting to hurt from straining to understand. Why was she dreaming this? And why could she remember this dream about the past so clearly and she couldn't remember the ones about the present and future except in little increments? What good was a gift like that?

She snorted in irritation and stood up, looking out over the lake. The water was so calm it looked like a sheet of glass, not even a ripple disturbed its flat surface.

She eyed a leaf floating a few feet out in front of her and envied it. *It* didn't have to make decisions. *It* didn't have a care in the world. It was the picture of peace which was something she did not have in her life right now. In fact she was lost. She'd intended to go to college in Buffalo for the spring semester but now she no longer saw the point. She no longer saw the same future.

Future. She didn't see hers at all, and if she were honest with herself she'd admit she never had, and not just in the clairvoyant sense.

She had spent weeks thinking and worrying about Anna, wanting to make her friend feel okay about the turn her life had taken. Now Anna was off on some kind of crusade or adventure, or... well whatever it was she was living her life despite its difficulties. She might have jumped onto the good ship What the Fuck, but at least she was going somewhere.

What do I do, what is my purpose, what step do I take? Questions that just went round and round in her mind with no answers. The only thing she really knew was that she had to do *something*. She started for the deck stairs debating on what that something would be.

She kept coming back to Will's take on her not being Faerian and a bubble of anger welled up in her. What the hell did he know? *So I can't heal people*, she thought, *but I have visions. And I see the Shadow Men. There is something different about me, and there must be some reason for these things.*

She thought about her family. Her mom and dad definitely didn't see things like this, her aunts and uncles, no she really couldn't...wait a minute. She stopped cold on the steps. Great Aunt Harriet. Her dad called her crazy Aunt Harry and she'd met her a few times when she was young. She vaguely recalled something about the woman refusing to take her medication anymore and the whole family basically shunning her for it. She wasn't clear on the details, it had been years since she'd even heard mention of her....she came out of freeze frame and ran up the stairs to the house.

She went inside and stood in the hallway thinking. If she wanted to ask her parents about it she'd have to do it face to face and have a good story as to why she wanted to know about her and particularly why she wanted to visit her...yeah right. Okay, she thought, I have to go around them. She mentally scanned her list of potential sources and landed on her Aunt Rona. She called her parent's house and spoke to her mom who gave her the number, asking a few questions about nothing in particular. She hung up beginning to feel a small stirring of excitement as she immediately dialed Rona. Voicemail picked up, of course, so she left a message for her to call.

And now it was back to the waiting game, but at least this time she had somewhere to go.

Chapter Thirty

The 'Cuda rolled to a stop beside the curb and Will leapt out yelling over his shoulder, "Stay here, make sure he doesn't come around the building!" He raced around the side of the abandoned structure and disappeared behind it.

"I got the son of a bitch!" He shouted, but Anna and Josh were already coming around the corner.

"She heard you tackle him from the car," Josh explained.

"Man," Will grinned as he wrapped the writhing form's arms up with a cross linked chain, "that super hearing is the shit!"

He rolled the guy onto his back and lifted a dagger in the air, chanting in Latin.

The possessed man screeched and spit in a language they didn't understand, then switched to English and hissed, "You won't win, it's too late, there's two few of you *faeries* left."

"Well fuckhead, the outcome won't matter much to you where you're going," Will replied as he raised his dagger and buried it in the former human's heart. Black liquid poured out and turned to vapor swirling up into the air. It crackled and hissed for a moment before it seemed to suction out of the atmosphere.

Anna's eyes followed the smoke, wondering about its destination. She had recently learned that "hell" was not a singular place. There were four different dimensions through which the shadow demons could potentially emerge, though it was only at rare points in history that any beyond the Jinn made it into their world. It was generally accepted that the other three dimensions housed more twisted up and powerful varieties of demons, so if they *did* make it into the world their level of influence would be scary. The one they'd just caught was suspected of being Dantalion which was cause for serious concern.

Anna looked at the dead man, a lick of sadness rising within her. He couldn't have been over twenty-five and had an all American boyish appearance now that his features were no longer contorted. She blinked several times, moisture building under her lids.

"You okay?" Josh eyed her with concern as he pulled a tarp from the backpack slung over his shoulder.

She swiped her eyes and nodded.

"We couldn't save him," Will put in quietly.

"I know that, it's just, why would he do it?"

"Although I'm told that demons can be pretty persuasive, I tend to think you've gotta be pretty twisted inside for it to get this far."

Anna nodded slightly as Josh slipped something in the guy's shirt before rolling him up in the tarp. He and Will each grabbed an end and dropped him against the building.

"What did you put in his shirt?" Anna asked.

"Oh, just a helpful little list of his recent activities so the idiot cops have it all spelled out for them."

"We're done here," Will announced and they headed back to the car looking up and down the still empty street.

They climbed in the cuda and started down the road, Josh calling his dad with an update. She still had yet to meet the man as their plans had changed several days ago when Will received a call from a hunter named Bentley. He'd been tracking the now dead guy only to discover he'd jumped a plane to North Carolina.

Bentley was currently on the west coast tracking three other humans-gone-demon, a woman and two more men, and things were getting odder by the second. First, the guy they'd just bagged was a former lawyer in California who had been instrumental in the possessions of the other three-the woman a D.A., the two men attorneys from the same firm. Secondly they seemed to have banded together in a specifically designed internet campaign, though each of them were working different angles.

The dead guy, one Lucian Handler, had set up a page with a survey that popped up on computers all across the state of California. He had craftily designed the pop up so that it froze the page until the questions were answered and submitted. Even unplugging your desktop wouldn't get rid of it, as soon as you turned it back on it would reappear.

The questions were as follows:
1) Do you believe in Love?
2) Do you believe in Heaven and Hell?
3) Do you attend church?
4) Where do you go when you die?
5) Do you believe Homosexuality is wrong?
6) What is your purpose in this life?

Eight people were killed in the exact same fashion. Every major artery was severed, and the knives that did the slicing had a broken cross carved into each of the handles and were left protruding from the victims' sternum. California officials were calling it a serial murder, but they had yet to find the victim connection. Bentley was the one who'd discovered the pattern.

All eight had filled out and submitted the survey, and all eight had answered questions one, five, and six in basically the same way. 1) Yes, they believed in love. 4) Where you go when you die is determined by what's in your heart-and 6) To love the creator, yourself, and your fellow man, or variations on this theme.

Aside from being a hunter, Bentley was also a genius hacker which is what had led him to Lucian. The dead man's objective, it seemed, had been committing a hate crime against love.

The two possessed attorneys were focusing their attention on an entirely different set of answers, compiling lists of those that readily condemned people to hell verses those who didn't believe in anything. And the D.A. was sticking to the ones whose answers were nonsense. What they had planned for the people on the lists was unknown, and Bentley was of the mind that it could stay unknown if he could just get to the bastards before they did any damage.

Not as easy as it sounded. The possessed seemed to be aware of the hunter attention they'd attracted and were sticking to public places and otherwise lying low.

Bentley had enlisted the aid of two more hunters currently in his vicinity and promised to keep the brothers informed. Otherwise they weren't needed beyond what they'd done tonight. This left them with zero to do for the moment except finally meet up with their old man who was waiting for them sixty miles north of their current location.

Josh turned to look over the seat at Anna and noticed her face was drawn, her coloring on the pale side. They hadn't had much sleep having been wrapped up in the pursuit of Lucian, and it was catching up to all of them. But lack of nourishment pushed Anna a bit further.

"Pull over Will, I've gotta get in back."

Will quirked an eyebrow and glanced in the rearview. Realization dawned and he eased the car to the side of the road.

Josh climbed in next to her, a scolding expression on his face. "You should've spoken up, you know we're meeting dad."

She nodded apologetically. He pulled her into his lap and she latched on.

A few minutes later her coloring had returned to normal and she felt loads better. His lap was so comfortable that she stayed put and he stroked her hair absently, his attention elsewhere.

Will broke the comfortable silence in his typical smartass way, eyeing them in the mirror. "You two look so sweet. Especially a couple of minutes ago when she was nursing you, it would've made a great hallmark card for vampires. I can see the illustration, little droplets of blood shaped hearts trickling down the card."

"Careful brother, green is not your color," Josh countered, tightening his arm around Anna to keep her from moving off him.

"True, but then how often do I get to be jealous of you, since I'm so much better at everything." He waggled his eyebrows and Josh snorted.

Anna shook her head with a faint smile. *Always competing*, she thought. She snuggled in closer to Josh. God he was comfortable. His big warm body would give pillow-top mattresses a run for their money.

She drifted off to sleep and didn't wake until Josh whispered in her ear, "We're here."

She yawned and stretched as she followed him out of the car.

"Here" turned out to be the kind of hole in the wall bar they favored and when they walked through the doors one of the most handsome men she had ever seen stood up from his chair, a slow smile coming over his face. She stopped behind the boys and just stared. Far from Grizzly

Adams, Jack McClaron looked to be no older than his mid-thirties, with a full and beautiful head of chocolate colored hair. His face was covered very lightly with a short and maintained beard- no beard wasn't the right word, it was more like a three day shadow that looked purposeful. And he had the most vivid green eyes she'd ever seen. The boys had green eyes as well, but a much lighter and less "leap out at you" shade. He was about the same height as Josh, who stood six feet two inches, with a similar lanky physique only Jack's muscles were more apparent. Especially in his forearms. *Wuhh...* she thought, *they could have prepared me!*

"So mission accomplished," he said clapping his boys on the back. "Nice work. I spoke to Bentley, he thinks he's found a way to get to the bitch demon."

"Good to know," Will poured himself a beer from his dad's pitcher. "So what do you make of it, them teaming up that way? Not their usual M.O."

Jack shook his head, his smile slipping. "Definitely Dantalion we're dealing with. The Jinn are generally more self-absorbed, caring only for their own personal agendas. They use a body to indulge themselves with everything they've been missing out on, mainly fucking and fighting, until it becomes too old or infirmed. That's when they usually jump to killing as you know-when they have nothing left to lose. Since they can't inhabit a new body until they're invited into it, they use each one to the max first. But this group is not following protocol."

Anna spoke up, her tongue finally coming unglued. "But I thought they helped other demons in the persuasion of human hosts?"

Jack focused on her for the first time and cocked his head to the side, his eyes conveying that he was seeing something distasteful.

Josh answered her. "They do, that's what makes them the most dangerous. See they have a pact, a sort of "scratch my back and I'll scratch yours" thing. Then down the line when they're forced to abandon their current body they have some potential inroads for another one. But that's as far as the Jinn will go in working together."

Anna nodded and fiddled with her hands nervously, the feel of Jack's eyes still on her.

"So you aided in the rescue of my boys I hear, pretty good stunt you and your friends pulled getting them out of lockup."

She said nothing. She knew Will and Josh had invented a story involving several people taking over the jail since they couldn't exactly tell him about her invisibility trick. She'd questioned whether or not he'd buy it since the news had painted a different portrait of them busting themselves out and attacking the guard. Of course since that version wasn't true either, it did stand to reason that the news was full of shit and Jack McClaron knew this.

She forced herself to meet his penetrating gaze.

"Thanks," she responded, kicking herself mentally.

"So you're a healer?"

She nodded.

He shifted his focus to his sons. "And you boys think that it's a good idea to tote around this child in case you find yourselves in need of some medical magic?"

He definitely did not approve. In fact his expression said something along the lines of "Idiots".

She made the error of jumping to her own defense. "I'm not a burden, I have my own money and I can help....." she stopped as Will gave a firm and pointed shake of his head.

"She knows her way around a computer," Will took over, "plus for the more harmless information gathering tasks her sweet innocent appearance doesn't hurt."

Josh was nodding, standing protectively close to her. Jack ignored his sons keeping his unnerving gaze pinned on her. "Not a burden, huh? So down the line when you get your cute little ass in some kind of trouble my boys won't risk their necks to extract you from it?"

Cute little ass? Anna felt her temper rising. "Exactly what kind of trouble do you imagine me in?"

"Do you have the slightest idea of the kind of danger hunters continuously face? And I'm talking about *men* who are trained to deal with it. I didn't cut my boys loose of my apron strings until they'd been hunting with me for a decade. How old are you exactly? What experience do you have in the things that we do?"

She bit her lip.

"Dad...." Will tried but was shut down with a severe look.

"You need to put Annie's fanny on a plane back home. She can only slow you down or get you killed. Especially now that the demons are organizing in corporeal form. The fucks in California are not the only ones, there are rumors of it going on in different cities throughout this country and abroad. All you need is for this little teeny bopper to get picked up and used against you." He folded his arms across his chest.

She looked at the boys who were aggravatingly silent. But what could they say? If she wasn't a vampire there was no way they would have taken her with them. And since they couldn't tell him that?

"Right dad, understood. She's just hanging with us for a little bit, learning what she can, and then she's back to NY," Will answered finally.

"Define a little bit."

"I don't know, a week or so I guess."

"Hasn't it been more than that already?"

"I meant a week or so more."

"Uh huh. I'm gonna hold you to that." He gave her one more penetrating look before walking over to the pool table.

For the rest of the night he ran between ignoring her presence completely or making insulting remarks about her size and age. Gorgeous or not, the guy was an ASSHOLE.

Anna ended up sitting at a table outside drinking alone until Josh noticed she was missing.

He sat down beside her. "Don't take it personally, he's just worried about us *and* you."

She raised a brow, "Me? No, I'm pretty sure he's just worried about you, which is understandable since he's your father. But his age is definitely showing with the whole Girls are Helpless idea. It may be true that without my abilities this would be a dangerous life to live, but it wouldn't be impossible. I *could* actually do the things you implied I was doing, computer stuff, batting my eyes at people while I asked them pertinent questions. And I'm not a moron, I wouldn't put myself in a position to get kidnapped."

Josh was half smiling at her, which made her stiffen.

"No, don't take it that way, I'm smiling because I can picture that. And you're absolutely right. I personally think having a healer on our team is beneficial, extra abilities or not." He sounded so diplomatic she had a feeling he was placating her. "Don't worry, my dad never sticks around long, he'll be gone before the week is out and we'll only have to deal with his disapproval over the phone. Much less intimidating."

"Right."

He changed the subject, asking about her friends, and they fell into a comfortable conversation about her life before the "summer of change".

***

Jack stayed with them for the next four days and Anna had never wanted to hurt anyone as badly in her whole life. He was damn lucky that she adored his sons because "little orphan Annie" would have definitely kicked his self-righteous, egotistical, condescending *ass* otherwise.

On the third day Josh caught her smiling wickedly and asked what was up. She told him she was currently fantasizing about picking Jack up and tossing him over the bar. "Can you imagine the look on his face if I did that? Bet he wouldn't think li'l orphan Annie was so helpless then." She smiled wider and Josh couldn't help but smile back.

"That would be damn funny. Too bad you can't do that." He added the last with just a hint of warning in case she was actually considering it.

She pouted, "Don't spoil my happy fantasy, party pooper."

On the fourth day Jack got a call from a couple of "hunting" buddies just back from Russia and announced that he was hitting the road. Anna literally went into the bathroom and danced a jig when she heard the news.

His parting remark to her was "I expect you to be flying away in three days little girl so it's doubtful we'll meet again."

She'd actually managed to get a classy dig in on that one answering, "Not meeting you again makes the thought of that most appealing I assure you."

But he'd only grinned at her and saluted as he walked out to his car. Infuriating bastard.

Secretly though, she found herself craving his approval and understood exactly what it was about him that made his boys treat him with such deference. And it was largely because of him that she made the stupidest decision of her life to that point, and considering what she was and how she came to be it...that was saying something.

It was a couple of nights later when she found herself walking down the street without her constant companions. Will was shacked up with a girl and Josh had gone to bed having spent the previous night doing research until the sun came up. She'd tried to aid him by using her laptop to look up various things, but found that with all of the questions she needed to ask she was more of a hindrance than a help. This in turn made her feel somewhat useless, and she started thinking that maybe Jack had a point.

No, she had chided firmly, *that's bullshit*. Sure if she really was just a girl without all of her kickass abilities there might have been some truth to it, but she wasn't just a girl.

So she set out with something to prove, a natural recipe for disaster.

She was following a guy being dogged by a shadow man for several blocks when he turned a corner off the main strip and away from people. She paused briefly, looking back over her shoulder at the comfort of the street lights and well lit shops, but then steeled herself. 'Don't be such a pansy', she thought, 'if you manage to take out this shadow then the guy will be free, it will be your first real act as a superhero'. She continued along this line of thought as she started after them, but then the shadow did something odd. It stopped and let its host move on. It turned towards her, and for the first time she saw features inside the smoky darkness. Alien eyes in a warped and haggard face regarded her with a mixture of what she thought was fear and curiosity. And then it spoke and she could only stare at the misshapen mouth, the language foreign to her. It seemed to realize this after a moment and fell silent.

And there they stood facing off, and she realized if she were going to make a move she'd better do it before she lost her nerve and fled. Which in retrospect would have been the wiser choice, but as old timers are fond of saying, you live, you learn.

In one graceful leap she was on it and it *was* solid. She didn't allow herself to register exactly how it felt before she sank her teeth in where she supposed its neck would be and began to tear........

And the world was darkness. A vast an empty void of black so thick it had texture.

And somewhere in the endless black hole of her new existence there were noises. Crunching, squishing, spitting, keening, surrounding her, engulfing her. She tried to shout but her features were frozen.

And then she heard voices. Muttering in low tones and eerie whispers, the sounds of her deepest nightmares, now her reality. She tried to move but she was made of stone, a stone without substance. She felt nothing.

And then the whispers grew louder and they began to chant, forming words and the words were reciting every sin she'd ever committed, every lie she'd ever told, every hurt she'd ever caused. They did not cease, they grew louder, still in whispers, overlapping, never ending.

She was in hell.

'Here in the dark, here in this empty void we remain for all time….'the words filled her mind and horror seized her as she realized she'd died and the myths were true, vampires were condemned and she was damned. Yessss, the voices agreed, Damned for all eternity, forever and ever and ever……..

Time was passing, flowing and ebbing and yet it was also still. It was endless infinity, time without time and she would spend it right here in this black hole where monsters moved all around her, always keening, whispering, accusing.

She could feel the beckoning to madness and it was relief, relief to lose her mind and not know where she was or who she was, and she began to slip away...

No. No. No. No. No. The word began beating at her brain like a drum, and at first she could not comprehend it….and then she saw a face. A hazy image in the otherwise unending darkness, but she knew its features. And then there was another and then another. She knew them. And she loved them.

She loved them.

She loved.

Her senses rushed in at her, coming alive, and she had a body again and a voice and she was shouting at the things surrounding her, telling them that she did not belong in this world of darkness because she *loved*....

She sat up fighting for breath and opened her eyes, light hitting her retinas and causing pain that she welcomed and refused to blink away. She heard voices and felt arms around her, holding her, and she sank into them weeping soundlessly, tears blurring her vision, and still she refused to blink.

Something pressed against her eyes and she pawed it away in horror.

"It's okay, you're okay, it's all right Anna come on, talk to us. Can you hear us?" She tipped her head up slowly and stared at the familiar features, one of the images that she loved. His mouth was moving but her brain was having difficulty unscrambling the sounds.

"I'm going to call an ambulance," said an unfamiliar voice and the garbled sounds made her afraid. She slowly turned her head in its direction and cringed away from him. He spoke again, his words drifting down a long tunnel and she shook her head violently, seeking the eyes of the one holding on to her. "Will?" she whispered.

He smiled, relief flooding his features. "Yeah, it's me."

"Josh?" she whispered again.

"Right here." He crouched down next to her.

"Home." She spoke the word and it echoed in her mind sounding strange and foreign. She began to shiver and Will's arms tightened around her.

Josh stood and spoke to the stranger and he backed off, the rest of the people disbursing now that the drama was ending. All of these things she registered in some place in her head that vaguely grasped this world she was once a part of.

"Can you stand?" Will asked her softly.

She slowly moved her gaze from his face to her legs and stared at them. She felt his arms around her waist, pulling her up and supporting her. She turned her head slowly and saw the place where the creature had stood....and it all came back to her, her mind coming back together in a rush. She was in the alley where she'd attempted to kill the demon. And he'd taken her to hell. No, that wasn't right. She hadn't gone to hell, she wouldn't be here. It was all in her mind.

She recalled being told of the psychological powers a demon could wield and she had not understood. She shuttered and stumbled and Will lifted her up into his arms and carried her down the street.

When they were back in the hotel room Josh tried to get her to drink from him but all she could see was the neck of the creature she had bitten and recoiled in revulsion. He settled for ordering tea from the lobby.

She let the warm liquid slide down her throat and felt the boys' eyes on her.

"I'm not strong," she whispered in a broken voice and started to cry.

They were next to her instantly. "Like hell you're not strong," Will said firmly, cutting off Josh's more sympathetic version. "You took out a fucking demon!"

She shook her head in denial but he stopped her. "That mofo is dead, believe me, I saw the mess of it in a pool of black liquid several feet away from you."

She looked down at herself and saw her clothing was covered in black smears and streaks and felt bile rising up in her throat. Josh picked her up and carried her to the bathroom, turning the water on in the tub. When it was full he stood there awkwardly, obviously trying to decide whether he should help her remove her clothes. She was sitting on the floor digging for the will to do it herself, then gave up and lifted her arms straight up like a little kid. He pulled off the offensive shirt, then helped her to her feet and unbuttoned her pants. He looked uncertainly at her undergarments.

"I can do it," she whispered shakily, "but don't leave me in here alone."

He turned around so she could finish undressing then turned back once she was settled in the water, the curtain partially closed. Will was hovering near the door and he grabbed a couple of chairs so they could sit with her.

She somehow managed to scrub every inch of her body and when she was finished she was exhausted. Not even when she'd been lying on the cement floor during her transition while her body was on fire and people were dying all around her had she felt this bleak.

In a way, she thought, I *was* in hell. *Because I didn't feel love there*. No, that was wrong, because she had. At the end she had felt love inside of her like a great shining light, bringing her what she needed to break the spell.

She looked up at two of the faces she had seen in the darkness and smiled weakly.

"How did you find me?" she asked quietly.

"I came out of an apartment down the street and saw a group of people gathering in front of the alley. I ran up to see what was doin' and overheard someone say 'She's unconscious.' And someone else made mention of black inky stuff and yeah, I knew it was you, so I shoved everyone outta my way. Fuck, you scared the shit out of me!"

"Then he called me," Josh continued, "when I got there he was cleaning you up and telling people that you must have slipped in some oil...and then you started writhing and mumbling something about love."

She absorbed their words slowly. "Is it still the same day?"

They looked at her strangely.

"Yes," Josh said slowly, "it's almost midnight."

She frowned. Only an hour, she had only been lying there...for *less* than an hour. She couldn't comprehend that and it made her feel shaky and quivery in the center of her soul.

"So can you tell us what happened now?"

"Don't push her Will."

"I'm askin' not pushing."

She carefully put it in words to the best of her ability but it didn't capture the feeling of it, and that was what she was still dealing with, what she felt she would be dealing with for a long time to come.

"We told you they had psychological power," Will was frowning down at her and she nodded miserably.

"What made you do it, was the demon cloaking someone?" Josh sounded less admonishing, and she wished she could say that was the case, that she'd rescued someone from imminent possession. But lying didn't feel like a good idea right now. So she humbly told them what transpired prior to the demon head fuck, including her insanely foolish desire to prove something to herself.

To her immense relief neither one took the stand she would've expected, that their dad had been right and they were sending her home. Instead Will went and gathered her clothes and once she was toweled and dressed they rented a comedy to help rid her of the heebie jeebie feelings she couldn't shake. The movie turned out to be idiotic, but the company she was in, that helped. Sandwiched between them she could feel their warmth and she knew that love was with her.

Chapter Thirty-One

Jenna swore at the computer in frustration. Not a Harriet Le'Roche anywhere on the planet it seemed. It had been the most irritating day she'd had in a very long while, starting with the returned phone call from her Aunt Rona.

Rona had first wanted to know why she was trying to find Aunt Harri. Jenna had been prepared for that, telling her she felt sorry for the woman and thought as a good Christian she should see to her well being. Her aunt had feigned hearty agreement and informed her that although she didn't personally know how to reach Harriet she would find out.

For the rest of the day she was pummeled with phone calls from every single member of her aggravating and seriously opinionated family. And the end result? Nada. No one had an address or phone number for the woman. Her grandmother haughtily informed her "misguided granddaughter" that her sister had stopped talking to everyone over a decade ago and had since moved away leaving no forwarding address. When Jenna pointed out that it was the family who quit talking to her there was a great deal of harumphing, followed by a lecture on the ignorance of youth.

Reading between the lines of her various gossiping relatives she gathered they believed Harriet was possessed by demons and that sweet little Jenna would do well to give up her foolish notion.

Possessed by demons, huh? Well if she could just *find* the lady she could determine the truth of that pretty quickly. Her intuition told her their conclusion was horseshit and she was more determined than ever to find her.

She leaned back on the chair. *I need a private investigator*, she thought. That was how people went about finding the hard to find, wasn't it? Of course that required money, which she didn't have. She flipped open her phone and called Anna for the tenth time that day. No answer. It was beginning to make her angry.

Suddenly a fluttery feeling hit her in the stomach. What the....? Anna was in trouble, something was *wrong*. She felt the flutter again and dialed Anna again. No answer, *shit*.

She spent the next hour on pins and needles and although the panicky feeling subsided relatively quickly, she still had a hard time sleeping. It was well into the wee hours of morning before she finally drifted off.

She was startled awake by her phone and the ring tone was... "Anna?" she answered quickly.

"Yeah, it's me."

"Are you okay?"

There was a pause. "I think so. I will be."

"What happened? God I got this awful feeling about you last night, I couldn't sleep because of it!"

"I'm sorry, I....I don't want to talk about it, I just wanted to hear your voice."

"Okay. I've been calling you all day."

"You have? Oh, I didn't have my phone on me and then....but sorry about that. So, uh, what'd you need?"

Can you lend me some money? Yeah, that was what you asked a friend who sounded the way Anna did right now.

"Jenna?"

"Yeah. Well I remembered that I had this aunt that my whole family deemed crazy and I started thinking that maybe she's like me. So yesterday I tried to find a way to contact her, but it seems she's dropped off the face of the earth. Anyway, I just wanted to talk to you." She made a face at herself.

"Do you need money?"

"What? No, of course not, I wouldn't ask you that...

"Jenna there's a visa card in my dresser drawer, whatever you need, please take it. Please, I want you to. I know you aren't the type to ask, I know you feel funny, but you shouldn't. I'm actually kind of sick of people being weird about it, it's just money, it means nothing. Do you know what means something? Friendship. People that you love who love you. That means everything."

Jenna shrugged, how could she argue with that? "Okay. I really appreciate it."

"I know. I love you."

"I love you too."

"Call me if you find her, let me know how it turns out, okay?"

"You know I will."

"Later 'gator."

"While 'dile."

Jenna hung up and grinned, she couldn't help it. *Harriet Le'Roche I'm hunting you down.*

Chapter Thirty-Two

Six days later Jenna found herself standing in front of a small cottage in New Jersey. Ross Cantwell, the super sleuth she'd hired, had done well. With the info he gathered there was no doubt the woman inside was her aunt.

She lived alone, well unless you counted two Great Danes and a cat, but she wasn't a hermit. In fact Cantwell had told her she was quite social. She attended a book club, spent evenings with friends at classy bars, and had casual relationships with different men. And the pictures he'd taken-she looked so much like Jenna, she could be her mother. And that was the other thing, the woman was about eighty years old and she didn't look a day over forty, and an attractive forty at that. *Not Faerian my ass*, she thought.

Now that she was here nervousness mingled with the excitement. She had learned over the past week that a group of her family members had ganged up on the woman almost fifteen years ago, and it was Jenna's own father along with an uncle who had first claimed she was possessed. Before that she'd been labeled schizophrenic. Jenna's great grandparents had taken her to doctors when she was a teenager and at the time shock treatment was in fashion. Then she was put on medications like lithium, until one day, and no one seemed to know exactly why, she flushed her pills down the toilet and told her family that she wasn't crazy. This was not the reason they disowned her however, that part came later when they found that she was "dabbling" in the occult and spending time with "witches." Right. Well now she would get the real story.

She knocked on the door and held her breath. She heard movement inside and the door swung open, crazy Aunt Harri in the flesh. And she was *ravishing*. Wearing a red dress cut low on the bosom, accentuating a narrow waist and generous hips, she had dark hair very lightly sprinkled with silver lying in loose waves halfway down her back. Her blue violet eyes were decorated tastefully with silver shadow and dark eyeliner.

She looked Jenna up and down then broke into a wide smile.

"I've been expecting you," she said, with a smoky voice. "Come in." She turned and swept into the living room.

Jenna stared after her, dumbfounded. "Expecting me?" she managed as she followed her inside.

"Oh come now child, you have the gift, you must assume that I do as well." Harriet indicated for her to sit down and took the chair opposite, crossing her legs and lighting a cigarette. "You have questions, and I have answers," she told her wide eyed niece. "Aren't you the fortunate one, to have discovered me so young. If I had had a me, how different my life would have been. But there's no point in dwelling on what might've been, you learn from the past and live in the present, hoping the best for the future, that's a motto worth committing to memory honey."

Jenna was completely thrown. It hadn't even occurred to her that her aunt might have seen this coming. Her whole opening speech no longer necessary she couldn't figure out what to say.

Her aunt sat with a look of anticipation. "You look so much like me when I was your age. Beautiful, absolutely stunning." She drew on her cigarette and Jenna watched the smoke curl into the air. Everything about this was surreal and for a moment she worried she was dreaming. After all, her dreams could be pretty vivid.

"You're not dreaming child," Harri told her, then waved her hand at Jenna's ever widening eyes, "No, no I can't read minds, you just have that look about you where you're not sure if what you're seeing is real. I should know that look pretty damn well, I wore it most of my life." She narrowed her eyes a bit. "I hope you were wise enough to keep your abilities to yourself, I can only imagine what that father of yours would do if he knew."

Jenna found her voice. "Actually, yes and no. Out of the family only my sister knows, but all my friends are aware of it and they don't think I'm crazy."

"Well aren't you the blessed one," Harriet smiled. "So how is it that they're so open-minded?"

Jenna took a breath. "Do you want the long version or the short version?"

Her aunt's smile widened. "Found your tongue and ready to use it, well of course I want the long version, I have all the time in the world."

So Jenna began it, telling this amazing woman all about London and the meeting that had brought her gifts out, and though she'd originally planned to leave Anna out of it, she found herself spilling the story in its entirety.

When she was finished her Aunt shook her head, her own eyes wide. "A human turned vampire. I'll be damned, that's a new one! A human Faerian vampire." She smiled that big smile again and clapped a hand on her leg. "Well, you told me something new, now it's my turn." She leaned back against the cushions and raised one brow, a corner of her lips curving upward. "The lines that sprung from the Faerian women of long ago are not the lines we come from. But we *are* Faerian."

Jenna furrowed her brow over that puzzle.

"I'm going to order us some food, and then do I have a story for you."

Chapter Thirty-Three

It was a week from the demon incident and Anna was finally feeling like herself again. A little older and wiser perhaps, but her gaiety had returned. The previous night she had still been in a funk- much better than she'd been to begin with, but she still felt like there was a shadow hovering over her world which was a fitting way to see it considering the source. The guys had definitely been feeling her lack of enthusiasm and they put an end to it once and for all.

She had been lying on a motel bed-a nicer one than usual since her ordeal had caused the boys to be more concerned about her comfort than their pride- reading a book about a middle aged man who had walked the Appalachian Trail. It was amusing and very well written, but her angst was making it hard to appreciate. She was staring blankly at a page when the door burst open and in came the brothers clad only in the most ridiculous matching pants she had ever seen in her life. They were silk and covered with brightly colored cartoons depicting bugs bunny and his crew, and they ballooned at the thighs tapering in at the ankles. To top it off they had neon-colored fanny packs tied around their waists and there was a cartoony sounding song blaring from the speakers of an eighties style radio which Will was carrying on his shoulder.

I walk on down the street with my boom box on my shoulder

And everyone I meet, tells me I look sweet

with my ultra cool, rules the school, boom box on my shoulder!

And I get a lot of girls with my boom box on my shoulder

And they tell me I look fine and that I can make them mine

with my super fly oh me oh my boom box on my shoulder!

The vocalist sounded like he'd sucked down some helium, all the while Will and Josh were dancing and swaying their hips, crouching down and twirling and by the time the song ended Anna was laughing so hard tears were pouring down her face and she could barely breathe. She hadn't laughed like that in eons. Even now, just picturing it had her giggling again.

Whoever said that laughter was the best medicine had known what the hell they were talking about.

After she'd stopped hiccupping they'd allowed her to take a bunch of pictures of them with her phone and at the moment she was setting her favorite amongst them as her background.

It rang, startling a laugh from her, and she pushed talk, "Hellooo," she sang brightly.

"Wow, you sound good!" Jenna exclaimed.

"Hey! Yeah, I'm great, so tell me what happened, you met her?"

"Yup, I met her. Anna she's fantastic. Right now we're getting ready to go out on a boat with her friends who are also fantastic! I was hoping that I could get you to fly out here at some point and meet her yourself. I have so much to tell you! And she really, really wants to meet you, please don't be mad but I told her about you, but don't worry, I promise she's cool."

Jenna had spoken in a rush and Anna laughed as she answered. "No worries, I trust your judgment completely! I'm ecstatic it turned out well and I definitely want to meet her at some point. How long are you going to stay with her?"

"I have to go back home and get some things, but at this point I plan to live with her for a while. She invited me and I definitely have nothing better to do. So whenever you can come here...but I hope it's soon, I really want you to meet her," she repeated.

"That's awesome! What about Jess, are you gonna tell her?"

"Yes, that's part of what I'll have to do at home. Actually Harri wants to meet her, she's had some... well "feelings" about her and she's been in a few of her dreams. She seems to believe that Jess has latent abilities."

"Don't sound so worried."

"I know, I know, but Jess isn't like us Anna, she's afraid of her own shadow."

Anna smiled at that ironic statement. "I don't think you give her enough credit honestly. I know how she can be, but I also know she's been incredibly insightful at different points."

"You're right! And you know what, I'm not actually as worried or uptight about it as I normally would be. Well, I gotta get going, but I'll call you later."

"Chow."

Anna hung up the phone and grinned. It was nice when everything was on the upswing. She decided now would be a good time to check in with her dad. They still did the weekly calls, Marty currently believed her to be traveling around the country with a group of musicians. He didn't question it and she had the distinct impression that he was relieved she wasn't hanging around the house, thus alleviating any guilt he had in rarely being there.

She dialed him and their conversation was short and sweet. He apprised her of his location, which was now Ecuador, and she made up some silly stories of her travels for his comfort and amusement. They exchanged love and she hung up thinking that someday she would be faced with either telling him the truth or disappearing from his life. But she still had years before it became necessary so no point in worrying about it now.

The guys had taken off earlier to get in some practice on the table and she tried to think of something she could do by herself. *We're in Lanford North Carolina*, she thought, *Holly goes to college somewhere in this state*. She turned on her computer and map-quested the location. It turned out her friend was about sixty miles south and she was just about to call her when Will burst into the room.

"We've gotta get our shit together, Josh spotted a motherfucker in a greyhound bus window. He's trailing the dirty bastard in a cab."

The "dirty bastard" was a possessed man in an aging body which made it a serious threat. It was generally in the last stage of life when the demon would do something particularly heinous since it would soon have to leave its current form in search of a new host. They tended to go horrific and grandiose, like a killing spree or a bombing before they departed.

They checked out of their room and threw their stuff in the trunk, heading out in the direction Josh was going. He had a twenty minute head start, so Will pushed the limits as far as he could without attracting uniformed attention, grumbling about traffic statutes. In the last couple of weeks he had educated Anna on the difference between laws and statutes, a God's law versus Man's law ideal that had drastically changed her perception of the things around her. She'd never given much thought to how oppressive it was in their supposedly free society, but after listening to Will's diatribes she now understood that the notion of Big Brother was not a far off fictional concept. He was alive and thriving in modern America. Of course now that she was no longer quite human it didn't really affect her, which in the grand scheme of things made it easier to see and deal with. She'd like to meet the cop who could arrest her without her cooperation or permission. Not frickin' likely.

The destination turned out to be fifty miles south of them in a town called Ashlyn and Josh arrived about ten minutes ahead of them. He was following the abomination on foot and just as they were nearing the turn that would bring them to where he was he let out a string of expletives that would have made a trucker cringe.

"What??" Will demanded.

"He pulled a fucking switch on me, I lost him."

"Shit! He's an old fart on foot, how the fuck did you do that?!"

The phone went dead as Josh ran up to the car and climbed in, snapping at his brother. "Don't, all right, he pulled a fuckin' Houdini-you would've lost him too!"

"Like Hell!"

They drove around for a while trying to spot him, but it was like looking for a needle in a haystack. Ashlyn was a pretty big place, on top of which the weather was beautiful so throngs of people were out and about. Will finally gave up and pulled into a diner.

They ordered food and tried to come up with a plan of action. With nothing to go on but a physical description finding It would not be easy.

Anna's phone rang and she answered it to the sound of Jenna's fearful and anxious voice.

"Where are you right now?" She demanded.

"North Carolina, why what's wrong?"

"It's Holly! My Aunt had a vision of a mall blowing sky high and she saw a face really clearly, she asked to see pictures of my friends and she said it was Holly! She's going to be in a mall that gets blown to pieces! I've tried calling her but her phone keeps going right to voice mail!"

Anna related this to the guys as a feeling of panic rose in her chest. They exchanged looks that said "One hell of a coincidence."

They checked to see how close they were to Holly's college and found it was in the next town over. They then proceeded to get the locations of every shopping mall in their vicinity.

"Ask her aunt if there's anything about the mall that we can use as an identifier. We've got a total of six possibilities in the surrounding areas, so see if she can narrow it down." Will instructed.

She relayed this to Jenna and waited impatiently.

"She says there's a Golden Torch restaurant in the parking lot. She's trying to recall something else but nothing's coming."

They found two that fit the description, one in Ashlyn where they currently were and one a couple of towns over.

"We have to split up." Anna stood.

"Does she know when it's supposed to happen?" Will said throwing money on the table.

"She thinks today, but not sure of exact time."

"All right, I'll take the one closest, you and Josh grab a cab and head to the other."

They hailed a cab and she sent a picture of Holly to Will's phone. Josh turned to Will as they got in. "It's gotta be our guy."

"No shit."

Anna called Holly's phone continuously but it was either off or dead. When they reached their destination Anna suggested they call in the threat.

"Too risky," Josh said shaking his head, "If he sees the place start to evacuate he might decide to do it right then. If we can just find the fucker we might be able to take him out and prevent it from happening."

"Assuming he's the bomber."

"He is."

Chapter Thirty-Four

They decided to take opposite entrances and work their way towards each other.

Twenty minutes later Anna spotted Holly walking into a shoe store. She was instantly flooded with relief followed by a jolt of fear as she realized this was definitely the place and they had no idea of the when. She ran towards her friend, surprising the hell out of her as they collided.

"Anna??!!"

"No time, we have to go now!" She grabbed Holly's hand and started running for an exit, fumbling with her phone and calling Josh. "Holly's here, this is the place!"

"Okay, get her out and I'll call security with a description of the fuck and get them to evacuate."

"You get out too!"

The line went dead.

She started yelling as they ran, "There's a bomb in the mall, you need to get out! Get out now, the place is going to blow!!"

People sprang into action and Anna pushed through the doors with a group of others in tow.

A few steps into the parking lot she heard the explosions and grabbed Holly around the waist. She leapt covering fifty yards before landing. She tucked her terrified friend between two cars at the far side of the parking lot and called Josh. No answer. "I'll be back," she told her stunned friend, then took off across the parking lot, leaping over cars and attracting serious attention.

Her phone chirped. "Josh!"

"Yeah, I'm all right! I couldn't find the bastard...oh shit I see you, and Anna people are staring, stop the leaping thing!"

She spotted him and ran into his arms, her heart racing.

"Will's on his way, let's get your friend and bail."

They raced back to where Holly was still crouched and wide eyed.

Anna grabbed her hand, "Come on, you need to come with us."

She blinked a couple of times but let Anna pull her up and the three of them ran up to the road just as Will was rolling to a stop. They barely had time for a glance at the rubble in the center of the parking lot before they jumped in.

"Get us out of here, Anna was practicing Spiderman acrobatics and she was definitely noticed."

They drove until they saw signs for a beach and decided to pull in there. Holly was in a state of shock, shaking and not responding to them.

"Holly *look* at me!" Anna commanded once they were parked.

Her friend slowly focused. "Wh...whu...what happened?"

Anna bit her lip wondering where exactly to begin. Holly didn't know *anything*, she hadn't gone to Europe and she was already in North Carolina when Anna had returned. She didn't even know about the shadow men, let alone what Anna was.

Will turned the radio to the local station and it was reporting the bombing.

"We're on sight at the Crawfield Shopping Center and it's a nightmare. Rescue teams are pulling people out of the rubble and we just learned that the threat was reported mere minutes before the bombs went off. An anonymous source gave a description of a man in his seventies, officials have nothing else to go on at this time. There's some sketchy reports of a teenage girl who apparently started screaming about the bomb mere minutes before the explosions started. And this is strange folks, but a number of people are insisting that they saw this same girl flying through the air carrying someone to safety."

Anna cringed, "Whoops."

The reporter continued, saying the death toll was likely in the hundreds, and Will and Josh both swore a blue streak.

"My fault," Josh said miserably, "If I hadn't lost him..."

"Don't do that bro," Will grabbed his arm, "*Not* your fault, some things can't be helped. Besides you called in the evac, lives were saved because of you."

The radio was still rattling on and they quieted when the newscaster announced "This just in, in addition to the teenage girl there was also a young man on the opposite end of the mall shouting warnings and witnesses say they saw the two of them running from the parking lot together."

The microphone was given to an excitable woman. "I saw the whole thing! The girl, she flew across the parking lot with someone in her arms and then she must have put them down because suddenly she was alone and leaping over cars, right into some guys arms! Then they both ran across the parking lot and I couldn't see them after that, but I'm telling you that girl was flying!"

There were several similar reports by other excitable witnesses before the newscaster took over. "Local authorities are currently searching for the young couple who are needed for questioning in today's events."

Will shut off the radio, and raised his brows, "Best put some distance between us and this place."

Josh still looked forlorn so Will shook his shoulder, "Knock it off bro, you know we win some and lose some. You heard the radio, between the shouting and the evac you did your best. Dwell on the lives you saved, feel me?"

Josh nodded still frowning.

Holly's eyes darted between them, her expression more focused but still a bit wild. "Anna, you *did* fly, you were carrying me and we were in the air! Please tell me what is going on. How did you know about the bomb, and how did you know I was there, and *how can you fly*?"

"I didn't fly."

Holly stared at her.

"No really, I just jumped really far."

Holly's brows lifted waiting for further explanation.

"I better call Jenna and let her know you're all right." Anna dialed the number and briefly outlined what happened.

Apparently Jenna had felt things were okay, her intuition was getting stronger by the day. "So how is Holly?"

"Umm, well right now she's staring at me like I have two heads and she's getting pretty annoyed with my lack of explanation."

"So...what are you going to tell her?"

"Not sure yet, but I guess I better tell her something."

She hung up the phone and sighed, avoiding Holly's questioning look.

"Hate to put a rush on things, but we really need to get on the highway in case they decide to throw up road blocks." Will met her eyes in the rearview and she nodded.

She looked at her friend. "Is there any way you can ditch classes for a day or two? If you want me to explain things you'll have to ride along. But don't worry I'll fly you back from where ever we end up."

Holly's brows shot through the ceiling and Anna realized what she'd said and laughed loudly. The boys were chuckling as well and Holly seemed to really notice them for the first time.

"Who are these guys?" she asked.

"Will and Josh, my partners in crime-fighting," she said still giggling.

"Okay. I don't understand *any* of this but if I have to go with you in order *to* understand then at least tell me how you knew I was at the mall."

"Have you ever heard of Jenna's crazy Aunt Harriet?"

Holly cocked her head to the side. "I don't think so, I mean Jenna's whole extended family is a little out there so maybe."

"No, this is different, the family disowned her saying she was deranged and possibly possessed."

Holly shook her head.

"Well it turns out the woman is not crazy, she just has some gifts. One of which is the ability to see future events. Long story short, she had a vision of the mall blowing up and you were in it."

Will pulled out of the parking lot and headed towards I 95.

Holly acknowledged they were on the move with a sigh of resignation. "Okay, when did you find out about the vision?"

"Let's see, probably thirty minutes before I found you."

Holly's eyes widened. "How did you get there so fast?"

"I was in Ashlyn when she called, and all they had to go on was a shopping mall with a Golden Torch at the edge of the parking lot. We found two malls fitting the description and Will went to the other one. I tried to call you but your phone was off."

"Yeah, the battery died...." she made a face and shook her head. "Why were you in Ashlyn in the first place?"

Now the questions would get harder to answer.

"We were following the guy we believe is responsible for the bombing."

Holly's brows drew together. "I don't get it. You were in Ashlyn because you *knew* about the bombing?"

Anna shook her head and sighed. "Not exactly...look there's a whole lot of things that have happened over the past few months and I can't really answer your questions without explaining it from the beginning."

Holly sat back and folded her arms, one eyebrow raised. "I'm riding in the back of a muscle car after being rescued by my friend who has somehow transformed into Super Woman, from a bomb that otherwise would have blown me to bits...and apparently this occurred because Jenna's aunt is psychic. Anna, there is no way you are getting rid of me until you tell me everything."

Put like that it was difficult to argue. She got comfortable and took a deep breath. "It really began when I was sixteen years old and started seeing the shadow men...

Holly didn't interrupt once, her eyes widening until they couldn't get any rounder. When Anna got to the point where she was going through the transition at the warehouse her friend's face drained of color but she still kept silent.

She brought her all the way to the scene at the mall then sat back feeling drained. "So now you know basically everything. I'm a blood sucking freak who fights demons and can leap long distances." She laughed a little and attempted to joke, "I hope we can still be friends."

Holly opened and closed her mouth a few times. "This cannot be real," she finally said in a thin voice. "I don't even believe in ghosts."

Will spoke up. "Actually there aren't any ghosts."

Both Anna and Holly glanced at him in surprise.

"Really?" Anna asked, "How can you be sure?"

"Do you see them?"

"Well, no, but maybe that's one thing we can't see."

He shrugged. "The generations of my family have investigated all kinds of supposed ghost sightings, interactions, etcetera, and every time it was either bogus or related to demons, vampires, or the occasional Angel. When our bodies die our souls go somewhere else, they don't stick around."

Anna thought it over and shrugged. "Doesn't matter I guess. Actually the fact that we rarely ever see Angels is more troubling to me."

Will shook his head, "The Big Man is not big on interfering. General consensus is that he keeps his presence in the world through people. Angels are basically a last resort kind of measure."

"What do you mean?"

"Well, they're not like us, they don't have free will. They are messengers who are occasionally brought in to fight the forces of evil. Period."

"Oh."

"If you want to be technical, the real warrior and guardian Angels of old were Vampires. They're the ones who were specifically put here to fight demons and protect humans. And I guess you could say that most of the ones around now are what we'd call Fallen Angels."

"I thought demons were."

"Yeah well, that's up for debate."

Anna looked at Holly who was struggling to take everything in. Her eyes were slightly glazed and she continued to periodically shake her head. Up until now the only thing she'd sort of believed in was God.

"I keep thinking that I'm going to wake up any minute," she stated, her voice dazed. She focused on Anna her head cocked to the side. "Can I see your..." she used both hands and pointed to the sides of her own mouth.

It wouldn't be hard to spring them since she was climbing up on day three but the thought of Holly recoiling in horror made her pause. "I don't want you to be afraid of me."

Holly swallowed. "It won't be real unless you show me."

Which was not exactly reassuring, but it was too late now. If she hadn't wanted Holly to know than she shouldn't have told her, or she should've made something up. Her teeth extracted and she could feel the change in her eyes.

Holly stared at her in awe. "No way. I really have to be dreaming. You can't be a vampire. There can't be vampires. There can't be...," She put her head down between her knees and began to hyperventilate.

Anna wasn't sure what to do. On impulse she placed a hand lightly on her friend's back and concentrated on calming her. After a moment Holly's breathing slowed. She leaned back up slowly and looked at Anna nervously, then at the guys in the front seat. She was badly frightened and Anna wanted to take it all back.

"Holly, I know this is overwhelming and scary, but please know that I'm not evil, I'm still me. And Will and Josh are two of the best people I have ever met."

Holly nodded slowly. "You saved my life," she said in a small voice. "I know you're not..not evil. I just, I can't wrap my mind around all of this. I don't think it's real. I just don't. It has to be a dream."

Anna nodded and spoke quietly, "I wish you were there when the girls found out, it might have been easier for you to accept."

"Maybe....I could call Jenna," Holly said, mostly to herself.

Anna handed her the phone and watched her friend's shaky hand press the numbers.

"Hey!" Jenna answered.

"Jenna?"

"Holly! Are you okay?"

"I don't....I don't know. I can't shake the belief that this is a dream." Holly's eyes watered.

"I can understand that."

"Everything Anna told me, what she is....how can this be real?"

"Hmm. Well I guess one way to look at it would be that a few hundred years ago people believed the world was flat. Imagine if we persisted in the beliefs we had centuries ago...Holly you can bend your mind to this, I know you can. Because it *is* real, and even though it's difficult, you must know it's not a dream."

Holly took a deep breath and let it out slowly. "Okay." She gingerly extended the phone out to Anna.

"It's me, I'll call you later," Anna said and hung up.

Holly was still pale and staring at her. Anna felt a little pain in her chest thinking this might be the time she found out what it felt like not to be accepted.

Then Holly's mouth twitched a little. She started giggling and Anna smiled cautiously hoping she wasn't going into hysterics. It did appear that way after a minute when the giggles became uncontrollable, but then she started blurting things out and Anna started giggling herself.

"I can jus...just see you in a tight leather outfit and the little hat with the ears, Bat girl to the rescue!" Tears were squeezing out of the corner of her eyes, and it took time before she got it under control. She grinned and Anna returned it, once again struck by how fortunate she was in her friendships.

"So, where are we going?" Holly asked, turning her attention to the guys.

Will spoke up, "Not sure yet, we're just headed north."

She sat forward through the seats and began asking Josh and Will questions about their lives. Both boys responded well to her, in fact the three of them were completely at ease within minutes of talking. Something about it struck Anna as odd. Not in a bad way, but in a way she couldn't quite put her finger on. Maybe Holly's acceptance had caused the ease but.....she shrugged and let it go. Suddenly feeling tired, she leaned back against the seat.

They drove all the way to Maryland before finally stopping at a bed and breakfast. It was late but a woman answered the door and was happy to put them up. They got two rooms, one for the boys, one for the girls, and all of them were exhausted as they climbed into their beds.

When they were settled Anna eavesdropped on the boys' conversation in the next room.

"I like Holly," Josh stated, "there's something about her that makes me...I don't know comfortable I guess.

"Yeah, weird, I was thinking the same thing."

Anna looked at Holly as she came out of the bathroom. "So what do you think of the guys?"

Holly smiled, her eyes taking on a faraway look. "I like them. It's strange but I feel like I already know them." She blinked and shook her head, "Sometimes it's like that right? There's just certain people you click with and feel like you've known them for a long time."

Anna nodded. "Yeah. I definitely felt that way about Josh pretty quickly. Will kept a distance at first but I've only known them a few weeks and I love them both like brothers, so yeah."

Holly seemed mostly satisfied, but she still had an odd look in her eyes.

They climbed under the covers and said goodnight. Anna lay awake for a while and sensed that Holly did too, but neither of them said anything. She was curious about what the connection between her friend and the boys might be. But it was one of those things that remained to be seen.

Chapter Thirty-Five

The following day the four of them headed into Annapolis, the brothers announcing that it was the place of their birth. They couldn't actually call it their childhood home since they had moved around so much when they were young, but they lived here for the first six years of Will's life and there was a wistfulness about him as he pointed out the things that had changed.

They took a drive out of the city into a more suburban area and Anna was struck by how beautiful the scenery was. Fall was just beginning to peek its head around summer, and the air had that crispness to it, even though it was still relatively warm.

They pulled in front of a pretty little house up on a hill. "That's where we lived," Will said as he stared up at the place with a shadowed look in his eyes.

Josh appeared to be trying to recall it, having only been three when they'd left.

"It's hard to imagine us living here with dad, all the other places we lived were not something you could put on a postcard," he stated.

"He was a different person when mom was alive."

"I wish I could remember that. I guess three years makes a difference at that age."

Will glanced at him and nodded.

Anna listened to the brothers as she took in the breathtaking landscape. Surrounding the house were different varieties of trees and a perfectly manicured lawn that swept down to the street. There was an assortment of smaller trees and bushes she knew would be full of flowers in spring.

She glanced at Holly then peered more closely at the odd expression on her face.

"What is it?" she whispered.

Holly shook her head slowly. "I have the strangest sense of De je vu," she whispered back. "I've never been to Maryland, but I swear I've been on this road before." Her expression was filled with wonder, and Anna's arms broke into gooseflesh.

Anna leaned forward through the seats. "You said there are no ghosts, what about past lives? Have we lived before?"

Will and Josh both shook their heads. "You get one shot at this place," Will spoke up. "Then it's on to the next."

"How do you know?"

"Okay I guess I can't be certain, all I do know is that every time we've encountered someone who claimed a past life it turned out to be bullshit. Although I suppose it is possible that you aren't meant to remember and that's why we don't."

Holly was paying attention to their conversation and chewing on her lip a little. "Yeah, I don't believe that either," she said, "I think once we reach the afterlife we'll have no desire to come back here."

Anna raised an eyebrow at her friend. "So what do you think de je vu is?"

"Dreams." Will and Josh said in unison.

Josh continued. "See we don't remember most of what we dream about, but dreams come from the places in our brain that we don't generally use. Probably because most people would blow a cork if they did. It's where telepathy and psychic abilities live, and some people are able to bring it into the waking life a bit, but for the most part it's only when we sleep that it can work. This way we can chalk it up to "imagination" and keep from blowing fuses. Although once in awhile, and for some more than others, we can bring these things into focus. Honestly I don't know exactly how it works, probably because my mind won't stretch that far, but I do know it's where de je vu comes from."

Holly nodded a little at first and then more vigorously. "I did dream this. I did! I remember it now, or just a little bit. I was walking down the road," she pointed forward, "from that direction and I passed this house and stopped. There was a woman on that porch," she indicated the boys' old house," and she was holding a baby and staring out towards the woods with a worried expression on her face. And that's all I remember. Wow, how weird is that? Why would I dream about that?"

Both boys were staring at her now, and Anna felt the gooseflesh pop again.

"Do you...remember what the woman looked like?" Will's voice was a little strained.

"Hmm. She had long brown hair like mine only fuller and a little darker. She was wearing a sun dress with little purple flowers on it." She scrunched her face in concentration. "That's it."

Will's face drained of color and he swallowed hard. Josh looked at his brother, "Mom had hair like that, huh?"

Will was trying to speak but having some difficulty. He cleared his throat loudly. "She was wearing a dress like that the day she died."

The whole car fell silent.

Will put it in drive and coasted slowly down the road, darting looks at Holly in the rear view. "Do you think you've dreamt anything else about it, or was it just the one dream?"

"I don't know. I kind of feel like I've dreamt something else, but it's not coming to me."

"Before you leave I want to give you my number, in case you remember anything else."

She nodded. "Of course."

There was a whole lot of silence for the rest of the day. They ate together in a restaurant in Annapolis making small talk then strolled down the streets of the small city's downtown. Anna had the feeling that Holly was straining to recall something further. She commented to Anna at one point that the dream seemed pointless. It hadn't told her anything useful, she felt there had to be more. Will and Josh obviously wanted there to be more and seemed to be waiting for her to have another light bulb go on.

In the evening Holly announced that it would be best for her to head back to school. She had a couple of tests the day after next and wanted to be prepared. Anna booked her a flight for the morning and they went back to the bed and breakfast for one more night.

As they pulled into the long driveway Anna surveyed the place, something she'd been too tired and distracted to do the previous night. It was a very attractive English Tudor style home located on the Chesapeake Bay. They'd barely set foot in the door when they were greeted by the woman who owned it, and after some lively conversation she generously offered them the use of one of her boats.

Anna felt a thrill as Will pulled away from the dock. She missed being out on the water and experienced a brief moment of homesickness which her phone abruptly yanked her from. She dug around in her purse and glanced at the number. Jenna.

"How's Holly?" she asked right away.

"She's dealing pretty well, she started laughing after she got off the phone with you."

"Oh good. I was wondering...."

"What's up?"

"Have you given any thought to coming for a visit?"

"I thought there was no rush?"

"There's not, but if you weren't doing anything I just thought...I really want my aunt to tell you the story of the other Faerians."

"Other Faerians?" her brows raised. Josh overheard and raised his own brow in question.

"Have I sparked your interest?" Jenna teased.

"Uh huh. Look we're out on a boat, but when we get back to shore I'll talk to the guys."

"Okay, call me later."

It was a beautiful night and once they were back at the bed and breakfast they decided to lounge on the deck overlooking the bay. Anna told them what Jenna had said and the brothers exchanged looks and shrugged.

"We've got nothing else going on and I'm curious about that aunt of hers," Will stated. "Other Faerians, huh? Do they mean a group of us hanging out somewhere?"

"I don't think so...actually remember how you seemed certain she wasn't one of us because she doesn't possess the gift of healing?"

They both nodded.

"Well she may not have power to heal, but she has visions. Even when she was younger trusting Jenna's intuition has always been a thing with us, right Holl?"

Holly inclined her head in agreement.

"And then there's her aunt, who's actually her great aunt and somewhere around eighty years old like your dad. And also like your dad she looks much younger and she's psychic like Jenna. So by Other I think she means another line of them or something."

Will frowned a little. "I would think we would have heard of it. Maybe they're a line of something other than Faerian, which is entirely possible."

Anna shrugged. "Well we won't know until we get there."

"Alright, let's head up there tomorrow," Josh said.

"Will you call me and fill me in? I'm curious about it now too," Holly inquired.

She nodded and put a hand on her stomach. She was beginning to feel a little queasy having gone a few days without sustenance. "Will? Can we go up to your room for a few minutes?"

"Yeah, what's up?"

She raised her brows and ran her tongue over her teeth.

"Oh shit, that's right. Come on."

They headed inside and Anna heard Holly ask Josh what the deal was.

"Um, well she's a vampire."

There was a pause. "Oh. Right. Didn't really think about that. So, she bites your neck just like in the movies?"

His voice was amused as he answered, "Yup, just like in the movies."

"You eavesdropping?" Will asked as they entered his room.

She flushed guiltily.

"That is such a cool ability, I really wish I had it."

"It is, but it can borderline on invasion of privacy."

"Nah. If you were a mind reader I'd agree with that, but people should always be careful of the things they say out loud. If they're not it's their own fault."

"Glad you feel that way."

He grinned. "Don't worry, I don't say anything aloud I need to hide from you."

She laughed and twined her arms around his neck. "I'm afraid I have to bite you for that."

"Ohhhh, knee slapper," he retorted and dipped his head for easier access.

Chapter Thirty-Six

It was a fairly short drive from Maryland to New Jersey and the trio arrived in the early afternoon having left just after seeing Holly onto her flight.

Jenna threw open the door with a smile stretched across her face and two enormous dogs flanking either side of her.

Will eyed the giants warily and Jenna laughed.

"Don't worry they're friendly," she turned towards the inside of the house, "Harri can you call the beasts?"

"Dominique! Angelique! Come!" A smoky voice commanded and the dogs went bounding off.

"Come on in! I'm so glad you guys came!"

They followed the bouncing Jenna inside, Anna smiling widely at her friends' apparent happiness. Since Jenna wasn't generally the bouncy type it was evident that her aunt was a positive influence. Jenna had described Harriet over the phone, so she was prepared for the elegant woman whose appearance and style seemed to belong in a 1940's smoky bar with a microphone in one hand and a glass of chardonnay in the other. Or maybe a cigarette attached to one of those long holders that women used to use.

Harriet was studying Anna with a bemused expression. "Vampire is not the word that comes to mind when looking at you sweetie. Fairy princess is more apt."

Anna smiled looking down at her attire. She was wearing a pale pink sweater that clung to her small frame and a blousy light green skirt. Her translucent sandals seemed to accentuate her little feet and her pink painted toenails peeped out from the straps. She could definitely see the pixie impression.

"My niece on the other hand, now she looks like a vampiress don't you think?"

Anna grinned at Jenna's mock insulted expression, but looking her over she had to agree. Jenna had straightened her long black hair and it curved around her face and down her back in a very flattering way. Her nearly violet eyes were brought out by the dark eyeliner and mascara she wore, and her lips were painted a wine color. Her outfit was stunning. A low cut blouse the same shade as her lips accentuated her generous breasts and small waist. Her pants were sheer black and looked tailored, fitting snugly around her ample booty, but loose and flowing down her legs and nearly covering the shiny black shoes she wore.

"You look incredibly sexy Jenna, seriously, if I were a guy I would want to do you." She glanced at the brothers and saw that Will definitely agreed but Josh...well he looked appreciative of her appearance, but it was more in the way someone might acknowledge their attractive sister.

Jenna was blushing under their scrutiny, "Enough of that, let's get comfy so my aunt can tell you what you came to hear."

They went in the living room and settled down. Anna snuggled up to Josh on the large couch and Will sat on the other end. Jenna and Harriet sat across from them on the love seat.

"I swear you could be mother and daughter," Anna stated.

The two dark heads bobbed in unison, "We get that a lot," Jenna told her.

"Although I prefer older sister," Harriet added with a wink as she lit a cigarette and leaned back crossing her legs. "Jenna told me you seemed certain she was not of Faerian blood?" She directed this at Will.

He lifted a shoulder slightly. "Faerian women are healers," he stated. "Even if you discount the fact that they generally have Anna's physical traits she doesn't fit the profile without that ability."

Harriet had a smug looking smile on her face, obviously enjoying the fact that she was about to school the know-it-all with things he *didn't* know. "And I don't either, isn't that right?"

Will didn't comment, just looked at her expectantly.

"In your legends and ancestral history it talks about two groups of Faerian females who left their island home in search of mates. What it fails to tell you is that a short while later a group of Faerian males left the island in search of *them*." She paused to let that sink in. "Of course it's not in your history because the males never found the females. Eventually they gave up the search and joined a migrating people in France, a people we know of as Gypsies." She paused again and this time the trio on the couch became animated.

"That makes so much sense!" Anna declared. "Gypsies are fortune tellers and even in the movies they look like the two of you!"

Will and Josh were smiling and shaking their heads. Josh spoke up, "So your line sprung from these males and they had the gift of prophecy?"

"That's right, we're soothsayers. Like you we can see Beschatten Sie Männer, or shadow men, and we live long lives, but instead of the gift of healing, our females can see the future, or at the very least sense it." She put out her cigarette and leaned back, the smug smile still in place.

"So how did you find about all of this?" Anna asked.

"Ahh. Well most of my life I thought I was crazy. The Faerian blood was passed to me from my mother's line but her abilities remained dormant throughout her life, as is often the case, particularly these days. My father was a very religious man and he believed I was plagued by demon influences. When I was young they put me through shock treatment, then eventually on medications to treat Schizophrenia. The medications did serve to dull my abilities, I rarely saw demons once I became a regular user. But my life was no life at all. For sixty years I was little more than a zombie. If you've ever smoked marijuana then you might've experienced the state I was in constantly. Stoned, though not in a good sense. Then one day I received a phone call from a woman with a French accent who claimed she was a distant cousin and that she'd dreamt of me. At first I was convinced the call was a hallucination but then the woman, Dominique Moreau, traveled from France and came to my door. She was an older version of me, like I am of Jenna."

"At one hundred and thirty years old she appeared to be climbing up on sixty, and she was still very attractive," she smiled at Jenna, "it's what we have to look forward to dear. Anyway, she told me of our ancestry and I learned I wasn't crazy after all." She smiled brilliantly, "It was the finest day of my life, and the first day of it as far as I'm concerned. To find out that not only was I sane but I still had a good seventy years left to actually live! It was a heavenly second chance. And I'm certainly not wasting it, am I hon?"

She posed the question to Jenna who shook her head emphatically. "My aunt has the fullest life of anyone I know, well present company excluded of course, but she owns her own shop filled with herbs and natural soaps, and she does a little fortune telling on the side. She has an amazing group of friends as well. They're upbeat, eccentric, and all of them either own their own businesses or their spouses do. I swear they live the way Americans should, loving their work and using their talents to enjoy their lives! Thomas Jefferson would be proud."

"So these friends," Will jumped in, "are any of them like us?"

Harriet shook her head slightly, "Not Faerians, no, though they are more in tune with the spiritual world than most people. I was looking for others like myself when I came upon Ms. Georgina's Rare and Unusual Books. George and I became fast friends, which is quite fitting, George and Harri, don't you think? Well she was already acquainted with a number of likeminded people, she has a book club you see, and I decided this was the place for me to make a life. I opened up my own store right next to George's, and the rest is history as they say."

"What happened to Dominique?" Josh asked.

"Oh, she stayed with me while my mind cleared of all the drugs and then returned to France. She is nearing the end of life now, still sharp as a tack but she claims she's ready for the next adventure. We keep in touch by phone and letters and I intend to make a trip out to see her sometime in the next year. I think perhaps Jenna and I will go together," she looked at her niece who was elated by the news.

Anna bolted upright from her relaxed position on the couch. "I think I saw her!" she exclaimed.

"Who?"

"Dominique, when we were in Montmarte!" She looked at Jenna, "I was lagging behind you guys and I saw this older woman writing a letter, and as I was watching her she glanced across the road and I followed her gaze and there was a shadow man there! But when I looked back at her she was writing again and I thought I imagined it. She had the same color eyes as..."she looked at the two women, "well both of you."

"Well they don't say it's a small world for nothing," Harriet mused and then perked up. "Well I'll be Goddamned, I think Domini mentioned you in a letter she sent!" She hopped up and went into another room. A few minutes later she came out with stationary, scanning the contents.

"Here it is. It says "I saw one of those dark creatures just now, they still have the power to dampen my mood, though only for a moment. A pretty young girl just walked passed me and then turned and looked back so I waved and she smiled. There's something about her, I feel as if I've seen her before in a dream, though these days my "vision" isn't what it used to be." Harriet looked up at them and grinned. "I would bet my bottom dollar that was you."

"It was, I did look back and she did wave!" Anna loved moments like these, when you could see pieces of the grand puzzle of life fit together in such a way.

"Old Domini will get a kick out of this when I write her next."

Anna suddenly felt strange as she thought about being in France. It had been before everything happened. It was only a few months ago but in a way it felt like years. Time was a funny thing, how it could move so slowly at times and rush by at others.

"Anna, you there?" Jenna waved a hand in front of her eyes and she blinked and laughed.

"La la land, as usual. Actually I was just thinking how France feels like a million years ago."

"I know, for me too."

Harriet clapped her hands together. "I would like to take all of you out for dinner. You can meet some of my friends."

The boys were enthusiastic about the idea of grub, so they wasted no time moving towards the door.

Chapter Thirty-Seven

They spent the next several days with Jenna and Harriet, hanging out with the older woman's friends who were exactly as Jenna had described. At one point she remembered Jenna had mentioned something about involving Jess and asked her about it. She replied that her aunt had the definite sense Jess would be brought in at some point but it was a little hard for both girls to imagine Jess fitting into Harriet's world. She was a small town girl through and through, but then you never knew. Changes could and did occur.

The guys did some exploring of the area on their own. They fit in perfectly and seemed content to hang there for a while. They found several places to make some money shooting pool and after the fourth day they rented a motel room in town. Anna decided to stay with them at night, she was worried they might ditch her if she appeared too comfortable. She really liked Harriet, and of course she loved Jenna, but her place was with the brothers and she couldn't see herself settling anywhere at this point.

A week and a half later they received a call from their dad telling them to head west and Anna found herself saying goodbye to Jenna once again.

"Nevada? Are you going to Vegas?"

"Looks like it."

"You better keep in touch."

"Right back at you."

They exchanged a quick hug and Anna slid into the back of Will's car, leaning through the middle of the seat as they pulled away from the curb.

"So what's going on?" She asked.

"More strange happenings with the teaming up of the possessed. Not clear on the details yet, dad said to get our asses out there, so we're going." Will fiddled with the radio finding a classic rock station.

"Does he know I'm still with you?"

The guys exchanged a look.

"I take that as a no."

"Don't want to hear his shit until we have to," Josh said.

"Whatta you think he'll say?"

Another exchanged look.

"That's getting annoying. Out with it."

Josh sighed, "I'm sure it will be something along the lines of "What the Hell is orphan Annie still doing with you-and-you stupid assholes are gonna get yourselves killed making poor choices and not listening to ME, the MIGHTY ONE."

"Wait, what about what happened in North Carolina? Did he watch the news?"

"Actually, what we heard on the radio about us got turned into some post-traumatic stress thing, apparently the cops didn't want to own up to having lost us so they made it seem like the witnesses were seeing things. Which works out well for us."

"Yeah, but he must have heard something about it."

"Nah, dad doesn't watch the news, or much television at all, he calls it the "brainwasher". He gets his news from the internet and local newspapers."

"Umm...YouTube? Hello, if there was anywhere the witnesses were going to talk about it, it would definitely be on the net."

"That's true, but since he hasn't mentioned it I'm assuming he hasn't heard about it. He's really not the type to neglect to demand answers for something like that."

Will, who was quiet during their back and forth, cleared his throat. "Actually, I might have kept track of the net and who was saying what, and I also might have sent viruses to the blabbermouths' computers."

Josh looked at his brother in surprise, "And you didn't mention this?"

"Well, I thought you'd probably lecture me on freedom of speech and censorship." He flicked a glance at Josh who was scowling, and said defensively, " I was just holding them off, if they decide to say something about it in the future, A, dad won't be looking for it, and B, without pictures no one's gonna believe it, probably they'll convince themselves of their own post-traumatic stress."

"Well, that solves that problem," Anna said diplomatically earning a look of disapproval from Josh. "What, you want your dad to ask why I'm leaping over lines of cars?"

"Not the point."

They settled in silence for a bit. Anna was surprised to find there was a teeny tiny part of her that was looking forward to seeing their father, and not just because it would be fun to see his reaction to his sons' defiance of his wishes. Although there was that too.

Several days later she was questioning her sanity for thinking she ever wanted to see him for *any* reason. He took one look at her seated at the bar and blew up. Way out of proportion as far as she was concerned.

"What the Hell is *she* doing here, I thought I told you to get her ass on a plane!"

"Calm down dad," Will said, hands up in a ward off gesture. "We know how you feel about it, but...

"Calm down? Don't fucking tell me to calm down! She's an accident waiting to happen, you don't let civilians tag along, you know the rules!"

"She's not exactly a civilian," Josh tried.

"Oh bullshit, she's a fucking child!" He turned his fiery gaze on Anna and she cringed. "Tell me, have you done some training, maybe in martial arts or at least weaponry?"

"Well actually...."

"Fuck that, I don't give a rats ass if you did learn how to wield a knife, you'd never get a chance to use it. I know ten year old boys who could take you down without breaking a sweat. You're a liability, and a selfish one at that." He stalked away from her and sat at the opposite end of the bar.

Will followed him and Josh sat down with her.

"Maybe we should tell your dad about me," Anna said quietly. "If we explain the whole story...

Josh shook his head. "Believe me Will and I have talked about this, but dad has always been adamantly opposed to any interspecies mingling, and I know you're gonna say that part of you is human, but it isn't likely he'll see it that way. Sure he might feel sorry for your circumstances, but if he even thought we were letting you drink from us, he would blow a gasket. He's set in his ways. He might look thirty five, but you have to remember that he's actually eighty, men of that age tend to have their opinions set in stone. And he's never been very flexible. Will's gonna tell him what we decided on in the car- that you called us after you learned about Jenna and the male Faerians."

"Yeah, and like *I* said in the car, that might explain why you came to see me, but it doesn't explain why I came with you."

"I know. He'll just have to deal with it."

Half an hour later Jack walked over to them, arms folded across his chest. "Interesting story, I'll allow it's possible, still does not explain what you are doing here, and my son can't seem to explain it either. So maybe you can?"

Anna met his eyes. "You're right, I'm selfish. I cried when they were going to leave, begged them to take me with them in fact."

Jack narrowed his eyes. "Why?"

"Like you said, I'm selfish." She turned away from him and picked up her beer.

"That's it, that's all you have to say?"

Anna glanced at him, "What more can I say? I want to be with them, I guilted them into taking me, case closed."

Jack reached over and took her beer then turned to the bartender, "She's underage you know."

The man frowned, "She showed me an I.D."

"Fake."

"Miss, I'm gonna have to ask you to leave." The man said nervously.

Anna glared daggers at Jack and stood.

"No, no, she doesn't need to leave," Jack told him, "the damage is done, just bring her a coke. She needs to be where I can keep an eye on her."

"Okay, so long as she doesn't do any more drinking," the man cast Anna a scolding look and went to get her the soft drink.

Anna was fuming. He was such a bastard, there was no reason for that except to *be* a bastard. She sat back down and clenched the edge of the bar so she wouldn't be tempted to knock him on his ass.

Josh put a hand on her shoulder and she looked up at him. His eyes widened and he grabbed her hand and pulled her towards the restroom.

"What? I'm not going to do anything, as much as I might want to," she said through clenched teeth.

He leaned in, "Your eyes Anna, they're flashing."

She was startled to hear that. "Really?"

He pushed her gently towards the ladies room and she went inside, staring in wonder at herself in the mirror. Her gums ached a bit, though her teeth hadn't extracted. She rubbed them with her tongue and her eyes flared with that golden light from deep in their depths. Pretty, she thought. Eerie, otherworldly, but really pretty.

As her anger dissipated the light receded. Strong emotion did that? Good to know.

She went back into the bar and saw the boys and their jackass father seated at one of the booths. Well, she didn't have to sit with them to listen. She went back to her place at the bar and tuned in.

"......and that's just the tip of the iceberg. This is going on everywhere, and I mean all over the world. But it's really concentrated in large American and European cities. The Creator has apparently decided the human race is in need of a wakeup call. I've discussed this with a number of others and from their histories as well as ours we've determined that the demon gates are usually watched, if not consistently guarded, by angels. But there are times when the angels seem to be called off duty, whether it's to teach a lesson or the Almighty is just disgusted with us is anyone's guess. Right now we're certain the gateway of Dantalion is open, but we don't know about the others. We know it's happened before but our history is a little sketchy on this, in fact it's as if our ancestors purposely omitted certain details or hid them. I don't know why. So at this point all we can do is be a stop gap measure. Keep an eye on things and take out whomever we can whenever we can."

"Shit." Will leaned back against the seat rubbing his chin. "I remember reading something in our literature about the Guards at the Gates. It wasn't very clear but it definitely made a point about the gateways and the angels that watch over them, and how there were so many gateways to the Jinn's dimension, or wait no-that the demons were constantly moving the first gateway, but that it was much harder to accomplish with the other three."

"Yeah, that's right," Josh put in, "actually it said there was more than one gateway to the first dimension *and* they could be moved which is why we see the Jinn so frequently."

Jack was nodding, "Right. I'll talk to some people and have them look that up in their material, the Guards at the Gates or Moving portals, something of that nature. In the meantime we need to bring a few of the fuckers down. At the moment I've been keeping tabs on a ring of three, one for each of us." He reached into his briefcase and pulled out some papers. He scanned them then pushed them across the table to the boys. Anna shifted so she had a clear view.

Gerald Crenshaw, age thirty seven, nondescript average looks, profession-banker. Jean Lauriat, age forty-one, looked a bit like a linebacker, profession-accountant. Lisa Courier, age thirty two, pretty freckled face, profession-accountant.

Anna thought it was strange how the demons were grouping by profession, since in the case with that Lucien guy he had been a lawyer and the DA and other attorneys were involved.

Josh voiced the sentiment. "Notice a pattern here? First Lucien the lawyer and his lawyer friends, now Gerald the banker and his accountant friends. Why?"

Jack nodded, "Well, if a demon managed to take possession of me and the two of you were being dogged, it stands to reason I could help those possessions along. We already have a bond, couple that with the persuasiveness of demon and since the Dantalion are more powerful it makes it a bit easier for them anyway, and there you go, there's your connection."

"As simple as that, huh?

Jack leaned back against the seat and folded his arms, his expression challenging. "Do you know why murder cases often go unsolved?"

"Enlighten me."

"Because the idiot investigators imagine complicated motives, therefore overlooking the evidence in their face. Most people are not complex, and in my experience demons follow that pattern. These might be a bit more organized and determined than their Jinn predecessors, but it's doubtful there's some big plot centered around law firms and banks. Far more likely these lawyers and bankers are greedy and morally corrupt making them easy marks."

Will's lip twisted in a rueful smile. "Organized and determined to do what exactly?"

"Live in our bodies, but also spit in God's eye I imagine."

"Okay, but the fuckers we've been killing all our lives, what makes them different?"

"Power. They don't have as much. It takes them so long just to get themselves into a body it's far too much work for them to help others of their kind in any big way. Of course they do help, but they might only manage to influence one or two people in the course of their stay. In this case it appears the shitheads are moving much, much quicker."

They were all quiet for a minute, drinking their beers. Anna asked the guy sitting next to her for a cigarette and he obliged. All of the things involving the shadow men, their dimensions and demonic influence was fairly new to her, but the worry on the three hunters' faces gave her a chill of foreboding.

As if on cue the Simon and Garfunkel song Hello Darkness came on the jukebox. She loved the song, but right now it made her feel nervous.

Jack glanced her way and she turned her head quickly.

"About her, exactly when are you going to grow a pair and send her home?"

Anna was watching them out of the corner of her eye and both boys shifted uncomfortably.

Josh spoke up, "I like her company, she reminds me of why we do this, what we're protecting. Will and I form no relationships with anyone, ever. It's nice to have someone who knows who and what we are, who understands to a point, and who's cute and bubbly on top of it. Makes life less lonely and dark."

Will looked impressed by the explanation. Jack, not so much, though there was something in his expression that border lined on understanding.

Jack leaned forward, his posture intense. "This life *is* lonely and hard. Forming attachments like this seems to make life a little sweeter, I know, I've been there, but take it from me, in the end it only makes things lonelier and harder. Imagine if something happened to her, the guilt you would feel. I understand that since she's Faerian it seems different, but she's not equipped for the physical demands of this work. As a healer it would make more sense for her to become a nurse, she could be of real value in a profession like that. She's a beautiful young girl who could have a life, the kind that we're deprived of. Do you really want to see her jaded like we are? If you care for her you should send her home."

Poor Will and Josh, that lecture would make a whole lot of sense if only she weren't a vampire. She couldn't help but like Jack a little bit after that speech, and the fact that he thought she was beautiful made her heart trip a little.

"You're right but the problem is at the moment she's a little lost and being with us helps her make sense of things that she's been wrestling with for years." Josh looked at Will for help.

"Yeah, so we know she can't stay with us forever, but you know just for a little while."

"I believe you said that before." Jack's voice turned flat. "I said my peace so if you're determined to learn the hard way, so be it. Your guilt to wrestle with, not mine." He stood up, strode over to the bar and ordered a whiskey massaging his temples. Anna felt a stab of guilt for causing a potential rift between him and his sons. But what could she do? She really had no other place to go. She stared into her glass of soda and tried to think of alternatives but came up with nada.

Josh and Will came over and sat on either side of her. "Hear everything?" Will asked and she nodded.

"We should go get a room, it's getting late."

Chapter Thirty-Eight

In the next few days Anna went from sympathy for Jack to loathing him above all things. It seemed that since he hadn't been able to talk sense into his sons he was determined to make her as miserable as possible. She knew he was pissing her off for what he considered her own good, but knowing his motives didn't make it more tolerable. It was a constant verbal assault from morning until night.

She sat on the motel bed frowning so hard she could actually feel the corners of her mouth pulling downward. Just the idea of seeing him at breakfast made her want to break something other than her fast. Like his face. No, just his mouth, in fact she could karate chop him in the throat that might put his infuriating voice box out of commission for a while.

Josh came out of the bathroom and looked at her sympathetically. "He...

She looked at him sharply, "If you make one more excuse for that horrible son of a bitch I will kick you in the balls."

Josh shut his mouth and moved his hands in front of his crotch protectively while Will, who had appeared to be sleeping, doubled over the side of the bed his shoulders shaking with laughter.

"It's not funny!" Anna insisted, but felt the corner of her mouth tug. Had she actually just threatened poor Josh's balls? She started to giggle and stomped her foot. "Damn it, I was reveling in my bad mood!"

Josh grinned, "Are my "boys" safe now?"

Anna giggled harder and Will choked. "Oh shit Anna, you are a trip sometimes." He got it together and swiped at his eyes. "I have to hand it to you for having the patience of a saint. If someone did to me what my dad's been doing to you, no part of their anatomy would be safe from my ass whooping. Seriously though," he covered his crotch, "he has the best of intentions."

Anna shot him a warning look, then dropped her shoulders and sighed. "Yeah, yeah, I know. I don't think I can deal with him this morning though, I'm just gonna order in."

"I don't know, I think you should brave it, if you avoid him he'll think he's getting somewhere and turn up the heat. But if you persist eventually he's got to tire out. It's a battle of wills and he thinks he'll win." Will jumped to his feet and headed to the bathroom.

Josh came over and put an arm around her shoulder and she hugged him.

She looked up at his face, "Has he been giving you any more crap about it?"

He shook his head, "He thinks we're both in love with you and that he's better off aiming his attack in your direction."

"That's good, it would be a lot harder if it was putting strain on your relationship with him. I can deal with it as long as that's not the case."

Will came out of the bathroom, "So you coming?"

She blew air out of her mouth in irritation and started to nod when a hot flash snaked up her body making her feel a little dizzy.

"What's that smell?" Will said. "It's like honey and vanilla, you have a new perfume or something?"

Anna pulled away from Josh and sat on the bed.

"Are you okay?" Josh's brows furrowed. "Anna?"

Another hot flash made her lay down and both boys came to her side in concern.

"I don't feel so good all of a sudden." She noticed the honey and vanilla scent as well, it seemed like it was coming from her pores.

"You don't get sick sweetheart, but avoid dad if you want to."

She glared at Will, "I'm not faking, I feel odd."

"You just fed last night."

"It's not that, I don't know what it is." Another hot flash, but this time it seemed to go from her thighs to her belly.

Will stood up, unconvinced. "Well I'm hungry so I'm going downstairs." He saluted them and went out the door.

"Josh, I swear I'm not pretending, if I didn't want to go I'd just say so. I'm not worried about looking like a wuss."

"I know, but maybe you're reacting to the stress of what he's putting you through, you know like an anxiety attack."

Anna looked at him and frowned uncertainly. "Maybe...yeah, that makes sense I guess. Still, I just wanna lie here until it passes. You go, I'll be fine."

"You sure?"

"Definitely, go." Her stomach felt odd, kind of like the butterflies, but also a little like she felt when she used to get hot and bothered with Austin. Which didn't make sense at all.

Josh stood, "Call me if you need me."

"I will."

After a while it subsided. She got up, took a shower, and once she was dressed she felt more like herself. Maybe it *had* been an anxiety attack. She frowned and pictured facing Jack, and though it annoyed her it wasn't enough to make her panic. Whatever, best go and deal, she thought.

When she got to the hotel restaurant she didn't see them so she called Josh.

"You okay?" he answered.

"Yeah fine, I'm at the restaurant, where'd you go?"

"We're meeting a couple of friends of dad's, we're on our way to a casino."

"Oh. You know that's good actually. Since he's probably already got it in his head that I'm avoiding him I might as well take the day off from his delightful company."

Josh snickered. "Yeah, I think you're right, you should go do something fun."

"Okay, I'll see you guys later."

She hung up and chewed on her lip. Fun? What fun could she have by herself? Well there was a new romantic comedy in the theaters and she hadn't been to the movies in forever. She went back to the room and looked up the show times on her laptop. First matinee was at 12:10, three hours away. She decided to go for a walk and see Vegas in the daytime.

It was definitely a different city without all the lights and she was enjoying the sightseeing until another hot flash brought her to her knees. The scent of honey and vanilla filled the air around her. What *is* that? She thought. She forced herself to her feet and hailed a cab.

Once she was back in the room she climbed under the covers and turned on the television. She had no idea what could be happening to her, but it was a little scary. She put on a movie and fell asleep halfway through it.

She opened her eyes to a man hovering over her, brushing his lips against her forehead. He pulled back and she knew his handsome face. "Jack," she whispered. He smiled, his beautiful green eyes filled with lust and trailed kisses down her face causing her to shift in the bed, silk sheets caressing her naked body and sending tremors through her. She felt his lips on her breasts and then he was pulling her nipple into his mouth as she gasped and arched towards him. He moved to the other nipple and she felt his fingers brushing the curls between her legs. She pushed into his hand and he continued to caress her.

A delicious feeling pooled in her lower belly and moved between her legs and down her inner thighs. She moaned and undulated under the feeling of his trailing fingers. He placed soft kisses down her belly then brought his head up and took her lips pushing his tongue between them.

Oh God, she wanted him to fill her, needed him desperately....

She woke and sat straight up in the bed, heart beating frantically. *What the hell?* Her body was tingling all over and the feeling she'd had in her dream was still with her. She was HORNY. The insides of her thighs were all wet.

She jumped out of bed and went in the bathroom. She was shaking and the scent of honey and vanilla was clogging her nose. She turned on the sink and splashed water in her face then looked up at the mirror. Her eyes were exuding amber light and she stared at them in fearful fascination.

She heard the door to the room open and Josh's voice, "Anna, you here?"

She would've liked to answer but a tingling sensation started moving up her calves and it felt sooo good as it made its way up her thighs and straight between them. Phantom fingers stroked her curls and spread her lower lips. "Unng." She was breathing rapidly. *I'm being fingered by a ghost*, she thought incoherently, *a gifted spectral figure, Ohh Godddd.*

Just when she thought she might experience her first orgasm the fingers left her. She sank to the floor with a mixture of relief and sexual frustration. *I think I just got a taste of blue balls.* She laughed shakily.

A knock on the door startled her, "Anna are you in there?"

"Yeah," she squeaked then cleared her throat, "Yes I'll be right out."

She washed her face one last time and emerged with a forced smile.

"You okay, you were in there awhile."

"Oh yeah, no, I mean yeah I'm fine."

Josh arched his brow. "Is that a real yes?"

She took a breath and let it out slowly. "Where's your dad and Will?"

"At the bar downstairs."

She nodded and sunk into the armchair.

"Spill it, what's going on, same as this morning?"

She chewed on her lip and met his intense gaze. "I don't know exactly." She attempted to describe what had just happened to her.

His brows had drawn together while she spoke and now he looked as if something had dawned on him.

"What? You know something, tell me!"

"No, I'm not sure. Will would be a better person to ask, he'd be more likely to know about a vampire's sexuality."

"I don't know if I'm comfortable describing this to him." She frowned, for some reason it was different with

Josh. "In fact it seems to have gone away, so let's not recruit his opinion too hastily, deal?"

"Yeah, deal, but if it happens again...."

"Okay."

"You gonna hang here or come downstairs?"

"I'll go with you, I've been cooped up all day." She made a face when she realized she'd have to endure Jack at his most abhorrent. But she might as well get it over with or she'd just have to go through it tomorrow.

Chapter Thirty-Nine

It was two in the afternoon which surprised her, that meant she'd slept for hours. The dream certainly hadn't seemed that long....*yeah, let's forget the dream okay, about to see him, can't believe my subconscious would be so cruel!*

The hotel bar was relatively crowded for the early hour, though the sign indicating happy hour probably had something to do with it. Jack and Will were busy at a game of pool in the corner.

"I'm telling you," Will was saying, "nine ball is the new eight ball, you really have to get up on the times old man."

Jack snorted a laugh, "Old man, huh? Well this old man can still school you pup, maybe we should take it into the ring."

"Whoa, whoa," Josh put up his hands as he reached the table, "Remember what happened last time? I thought we agreed no more of that."

"Just because my son's a pansy...."

"Pansy my ass!" Will retorted. "Why don't we take this argument to the table?" he flexed his bicep and raised a brow in challenge.

"Give it a rest kid, you can't beat me, you'll just embarrass yourself and pull a muscle trying," Jack smirked.

Anna had to laugh at the macho exchange. "Whew," she said waving a hand in front of her face, "just smell that testosterone."

Jack gave her a scathing look and headed over to the bar.

"Sorry, did I ruin it?" Anna looked at Will apologetically.

"Nah," he said loudly, "he's just scared and using you as an excuse to back down."

Jack flicked a hand gesture over his shoulder. He came back with beers for him and his boys and looked Anna up and down with his typical "you disgust me" expression. "I ordered a Shirley Temple, it should be waiting for you over there." He inclined his head towards the bar.

Will chuckled, "Come on dad, lay off, she can have a beer."

"Little girls have no business drinking big boy drinks."

Anna glared at him. "You know if you're ever in need of my healing prowess I think I might let you bleed awhile before I help."

"As long as that means you're nowhere near the battlefield I'm good with that princess."

God he was an infuriating bastard. She turned and strode over to the bar and sure enough there was a Shirley Temple sitting there. She had to laugh. She picked it up and started to take a swig when a wave of lust washed over her. She dropped the glass and gripped the counter hard.

"You alright miss?" The bartender hurried over and she waved him away with one hand, stammering an apology. She heard laughter coming from the guys.

"Hey barkeep, I think you should cut her off," Jack called.

That might have been funny if phantom fingers were not reaching inside of her most intimate place. She gritted her teeth but a moan slipped through the barrier.

"Miss what's wrong?" The bartender motioned for the guys, ignoring her adamant head shake.

Josh was at her side in seconds. The smell of vanilla and honey filled the space around her and she gritted, "Get me out of here."

But it was too late, the next wave of lust nearly took out her knees and the scent was so strong it drew Will like a stray Tom. *Pheromones*, her mind supplied weakly.

"What's going on?" Will asked.

Josh gave him a look, "We have to get her to the room, *now*."

Jack walked up and Josh tried to dissuade him, "We got this covered dad, I think she got into some bad food."

Jack looked at her doubtfully. "What's that smell?"

Will's eyes widened as something dawned on him. "Oh shit, this is potentially bad."

"Bad?" Anna stammered, "Bad how..." her question faded to a moan as her whole body ignited with the need for sex.

"What the hell is going on?" Jack demanded.

Anna stared up at Jack's handsome face as he hovered over her, "God Jack, I want you so bad right now," she said as the rational part of her brain cowered in disbelief.

All three men stared at her in astonishment. She abruptly burst into tears then crumpled to the ground with the next wave of lust.

She felt arms lift her up and carry her out of the bar and she attempted to wiggle herself into a position to rub that sensitive part of her against any part of him.

"Calm down Anna, try to get a grip," Will whispered.

She continued to wiggle and he crushed her against him to stop her and she was dying for someone to touch her EVERYWHERE, oh God she wanted him to lick and bite and thrust.

They made it to the room and closed the door just in time for her fangs to extract. She bit Will without warning.

"HOLY FUCK, WHAT THE FUCKING HELL!!" Jack bellowed.

Will rushed her into the bathroom and locked the door putting his back against it as she drank. He could hear Josh trying to calm their dad down and doing a piss poor job.

"You need to sit down so I can explain this!" Josh yelled over his ranting.

"Explain this? Explain that Anna is a fucking *bloodsucker*, that my sons are fucking *liars*, do you have any clue what is happening to her right now? No? Well allow me to enlighten you. She's going into heat, which means that every bloodsucker within a three hundred mile radius is going to be heading for this hotel come sundown, all crazy with the desire to fuck her! You need to call one of her leech buddies to come and take her out of here now!"

"She doesn't have any *leech buddies* dad!"

"What the hell do you mean she doesn't have any? There hasn't been any new females in centuries and from what I hear there are few of them left in ratio to males so don't fucking tell me she doesn't have one bloodsucking friend..."

Josh shouted to be heard, "She is nineteen years old dad! She wasn't *born* a vampire, she was a human until three months ago when she was changed!"

There was utter silence for several seconds and then, "Bullshit. Humans can't be turned, they die or become animals."

"We know this dad, we know what normally happens, but she is an exception. We don't know why, she sure as

HELL doesn't know why, and just LOOK AT HER! Have you heard of a female vampire with blonde hair and blue eyes? Or one that can go out in the sun?"

There was a longer silence this time and Will pushed on Anna's face gently, "Enough."

She broke away but continued to gyrate.

"You keep that up and I'm going to lay you down on the tile and strip you."

"Oh please," Anna whined, "please do that."

"Oh shit, shit, shit. Dad?" Will called. "Can I bring her out without fear of you hurting her?"

There was a loud exhalation. "Yeah, bring her."

Will carried her into the room and put her on the bed. She immediately flipped over and writhed against the mattress, the need for sex so great it was painful and getting worse. She let out a whimpering noise and it went on and on as she undulated.

Jack stared at her. "How certain are you about this human turned vampire thing?"

"Well let's see," Will said, "when she sprung us from jail her human friends were driving the getaway car, friends she'd had for years, one of them her high school boyfriend in fact. And then there's the fact that she put her hand on my cut and it healed, not a modern vampiress technique from what I know, oh yeah and of course there's the little matter of her human friend Holly who almost fainted when she found out what Anna had become."

Jack absorbed this with a frown. "How and when did it happen?"

"She was in London on vacation and got jacked from a club and brought to a warehouse of horrors. She got out because when she woke up she still had her mind intact and none of the evil fuckers expected it so she crawled into a space and hid until morning. From there she went home. Her mother died a few years ago and her father is a photojournalist currently working in Haiti or something, I've heard her talk to him on the phone several times. Dad, she's a nineteen year old girl who was turned into a vampire. We're certain."

Jack watched her as she continued writhing and making pained sounds, then squeezed his eyes shut and massaged the lids. "Leave the room boys," he said.

"Why? What are you gonna do?" Josh's voice held an edge.

Jack squared off with his sons. "I'm not going to hurt her, I'm going to help her."

"Whoa, wait a minute, she's a virgin dad," Will said.

Jack raised his brows and looked back at Anna's contorting form. "I'm not gonna take my clothes off, so don't worry about that."

Anna cried out, sounding like a wounded animal.

"I can help her, but you gotta leave unless one of you is romantically involved?" He stared hard at his sons who both shook their heads. "Good, that's good. Now get the hell out."

They left reluctantly and Jack approached the bed staring down at her small writhing form. He climbed up next to her and gently grabbed her head forcing her to look at him.

Her gaze was unfocused at first, but then it cleared, "Please," she whispered desperately.

He kissed her and she plastered herself against him. He slid his hand down into her pants, stroking between her legs. Just like in the dream she began to moan and thrust towards it. She was so wet that his finger pressed into her with ease so he pushed in another and began moving them in and out. Anna thrust her hips viciously while Jack slipped a hand inside her shirt and massaged her breasts, continuing the steady in and out motion between her legs. She cried out and her whole body wracked with tremors, her muscles contracting around his fingers as she came.

Her breathing slowed and she was once again able to think but immediately wished she couldn't. *Jack just fingered me. Oh God, I was like a cat in heat.* She kept her eyes squeezed shut not wanting to see the look of utter contempt she was certain he would have. She felt a sob welling up and did her best to stifle it. She pulled her knees to her chest and hot tears squeezed out of the corners of her eyes.

Jack's voice was quiet and soothing when he spoke. "It's okay sweetheart, it's not your fault. Look at me."

She cracked open her eyes and was shocked to see an expression of compassion on his face. It undid her completely and she began to shake, great heaving sobs pouring out of her, and Jack, the man who despised bloodsuckers and was not real fond of her, gathered her into his arms and rocked her like a child.

Still speaking quietly he told her, "We have to get you out of this city before nightfall. I have a cabin in the wilderness of Montana, we'll go there until this passes."

She was still breathing unsteadily and she looked at him in confusion. "Why?"

"You're in heat and every blood...vampire within three hundred miles is going to be attracted to your pheromones. Which is bad enough, but it makes them a little crazy, and if they're denied, sexual lust can quickly turn to bloodlust. And if they're of the condemned variety it could mean a bloodbath."

She sucked in a breath imagining the carnage that she'd witnessed during her transition taking place in the streets of Las Vegas.

Jack pulled out his phone, purchased plane tickets, then called the boys back in and explained his plan.

"For how long?" Will's voice sounded odd and Anna flushed as she realized he knew what had taken place and what would continue occurring in a secluded cabin.

"As far as I know it shouldn't last more than a few days."

"We'll come with you," Josh said determinedly.

"Well that's up to her I guess." Jack turned towards her and she slowly shook her head. She could not imagine Will and Josh sitting outside the bedroom for days while she was brought to orgasm again and again by their father. She shook her head more forcefully. "Just Jack," she said quietly, not meeting anyone's eyes.

Chapter Forty

From the airport in Bute Montana the drive to Jack's cabin seemed to take eons. Especially when the phantom fingers made their next appearance. She was able to keep it under control as Jack went into a country store for necessities. She watched him come back out carrying grocery bags and it struck her as odd to see him doing something so normal and mundane, especially when hot flashes were curling around her thighs and wrapping around her belly.

She watched the sun go down from the window of the car and it was as if a switch had been flipped. Her coherent mind was left behind in the all-consuming NEED her body was feeling. She was vaguely aware of Jack speaking to her, but couldn't begin to conceive of the words. She felt the car ease to the side of the road, and then Jack's hand was slipping into her panties, and it felt sooo good. She came in seconds and the tension eased, but this time it was only minutes later before she was writhing again. Jack had no choice but to keep driving so he directed her own hand down to her sensitive place. All of the normal embarrassment or shyness disappeared in the strength of her need and she brought herself to climax again and again.

When they reached the cabin the moon was high in the sky. Jack carried her inside and straight to a bed.

For the next several hours he gave her release in every conceivable way without removing an item of his own clothes. Somewhere in the night this fact seemed to make it into her lust soaked brain, and she commanded him to take them off. When he attempted to deny her she became frantic, and he was no match for her wild strength.

His protests grew weaker as she took him in her hand and bent over the evidence of his own arousal. She licked all the way up his shaft and wrapped her fingers around it, finding a rhythm, bringing the round head into her mouth.

"Oh God, that feels so good," he rasped.

She continued it until she felt his whole body tighten then sucked as much of him inside her mouth as she could. He groaned and tangled his hands in her hair, his body convulsing as warm fluid spurted down her throat.

It went on and on this way, night bleeding into morning, and even when the sun was up she continued to need. Several times she tried to insist he push inside of her but he resisted, always distracting her with his fingers or his tongue.

He managed to remove himself from her to get sustenance and tried to coax her to eat as well, but she turned away from the offered food.

For three nights she could think of nothing but her insatiable desire, barely sleeping, drinking only from the vein of her companion. She didn't know who she was, it was as if she'd become an animal in its most basal form.

Around dawn on the third morning she drifted off to sleep, and when she awoke her mind had returned. Jack lay naked and sleeping heavily, his large muscular body moving in rhythm to his deep breathing. She stared at him uncomprehending for several minutes then eased quietly from the bed and located clothing. She spotted a pack of cigarettes on an end table and picked them up, heading out the door onto the porch.

She lit one with trembling hands and settled into the porch swing. Her thoughts were scattered and she was having trouble conceiving a way to go on from here with any semblance of normality. How could she ever look at the man lying inside without recalling in vivid detail all of the intimate things they had done? She cringed as she remembered how she'd tried to get him to take her innocence and felt an overwhelming sense of gratitude for his resistance. There was a slight feeling of rejection there too which she shoved away forcefully.

She decided to shove all thoughts of the past few days away and realized she was looking out at the most beautiful panorama she had ever seen. His backyard was wild and unkempt, summer flowers still hanging on in places though most had dried, but it was the trees that caught and held her in awe. There were so many different varieties stretching out into the woods beyond his property line and the vibrant colors of the leaves gave evidence to autumn's arrival. Everywhere she looked leaves had begun to dress in gowns of purples and pinks and yellows, and the breeze flowing through them made it appear as if they were dancing. She could almost hear them laughing.

A brisk wind lifted her hair and she breathed in deeply. Before she knew what she was doing she leapt from the porch and ran towards the tree line to join in the party.

She stopped at the edge of the woods and peered in. Sunlight was shining through in spots making it look like an enchanted forest straight from a fairy tale. She skipped inside feeling a sheer childlike delight and was overcome with the need to run. As her legs pumped the wind hit her in the face faster and harder...she blurred for the first time.

Her body stopped her right at the edge of a steep ravine. She glanced around in wonder, trying to understand the mechanics of what had just happened, how she'd navigated through the woods without running into anything.

She looked down into the cavern and watched the river rushing by a couple of hundred feet below. The scenery reminded her of a movie she'd seen starring Brad Pitt when he was young. It was so beautiful she was held mesmerized. She sat down on the edge with her feet dangling over the side, musing that if she happened to fall she would survive. It made her feel giddy. As she watched the water swirling and heading away she began imagining what it would be like to jump in and let the water take her. She could see herself landing in the cold liquid then popping out and swimming down the stream.

I bet it would feel like flying, she thought, picturing herself leaping over the side. She stood up slowly and stared. Why couldn't she? A shiver of excitement ran through her.

"What do I have to lose?" she said aloud and the words were carried away from her, adding to the feeling of enchantment. Excitement grew and she leaned forward a little. This time she shouted. "WHAT DO I HAVE TO LOSE?"

The words echoed back to her and her heart sped up.

After a brief mental tug of war she backed up from the edge and ran forward. She grinned widely as she leapt out into the air. It was glorious, she was flying.....and then abruptly she realized she was falling.

Her feet hit the water and she felt bones breaking, her arms came down next, and her elbows snapped, then her face hit and her nose was shoved inside her skull. It felt as if she'd landed on concrete, but then the water came up around her and swallowed her whole. The pain was excruciating, her shattered bones felt like jagged splinters all through her body, and water was filling up her lungs rapidly as she was dragged down and pushed forward. As fast as the water came in it went out again, her body expelling it in an attempt to survive. This process, which continually repeated, was as painful as her shattered limbs.

A few moments later she slammed against a rock and was wedged into a small crevice. She had to pull her head out of the water before her chest exploded from the effort of expelling, and somehow she did it, using her screaming arms to pull herself up onto the rock.

Unconsciousness swallowed her.

When she opened her eyes again the sun had lowered in the sky to the west. Her mind told her it would hurt to move so she slowly flexed her hands and stretched out her arms. No pain. She put her hands underneath her and pushed herself into a kneeling position and still there was no pain. Thinking that maybe her body was in shock or suffering from hypothermia she turned to a sitting position and reasoned. Do vampires get hypothermia? After a few more minutes she decided the answer was no. She had completely healed as if nothing had happened.

She stood up on the rock staring at the water rushing around her in amazement. A human would have died several times over, the impact alone would have done it, let alone the multiple drownings and the slamming into a rock. And here she stood, hale and whole.

She grinned foolishly and raised her arms in the air. "I'M INVINCIBLE!" She shouted into the air then danced a little jig.

She leapt from the rock onto the shore still grinning. Not that she would be tempted to try it again anytime soon. For all she was fine, it had fucking *HURT*. She decided she should try learning her limitations in a less dramatic fashion.

Then she noticed the light was beginning to fade from the sky. "Oh shit," she thought, "Jack."

She stared up at the steep cliff puzzling over how to get back up. There weren't many hand holds and she'd certainly discovered it was too far of a jump. She really didn't want the inconvenience of falling and having to re-mend. Or any more pain, that she definitely wanted to avoid.

She walked alongside it and finally found a place that had plenty of spots to grab hold. She was more cautious than she probably needed to be and twenty minutes later she was standing at the top feeling mighty good about herself. Until she realized she had absolutely no idea where she was, or how she managed to blur there in the first place.

The boys had said something about vampires being able to track a person after they'd taken their blood, but she had no idea how it worked. She took in a great breath of air and was assaulted with a thousand different scents.

Come on Anna, concentrate. She closed her eyes and pictured Jack's handsome face. Recalling his taste and scent she began to run.

She came to a halt, nearly tripping over him.

"Anna!" His voice was a bit high, "Jesus, where did you come from?" He blinked rapidly and then his eyes narrowed. "More importantly, *where the HELL have you been?*"

She opened her mouth and shut it again, watching as his expression grew darker and darker. He was furious.

He grabbed her by the shoulders and shook her. "I've been going out of my FUCKING mind, I thought one of them came and took you, and all I could do was wait here with my thumb up my ass!"

By "them" she could only assume he meant bloodsucking fiends like her. Now how to explain without further pissing him off.

"I....I blurred for the first time and I....got lost."

"Got lost," he repeated staring at her.

She nodded. "When I stopped I had no idea where I was."

"And it took you all day to get back." His voice was flat and full of doubt.

She nodded again, trying to make her expression earnest.

"You're lying," he stated.

She bit her lip and her hands fidgeted under his scrutiny. "Well I did blur for the first time and I didn't know where I was."

He stared at her harder, waiting.

"And then...." she trailed off, biting down on her lip harder.

"What. Anna. Then. What." His words were clipped and she could feel his eyes boring holes into her. He grabbed her shoulders and forced her to look up at him.

She looked away and mumbled, "I stopped at the edge of a ravine and got it in my head that I could jump into the river."

He released her. "How high up?" His voice was quietly menacing.

"Not that high."

"Anna."

"A couple hundred feet."

He took that in and seemed to look her over for injuries.

"I healed," she offered.

"How bad was it?"

"Pretty bad I guess. Not sure exactly, I managed to pull myself onto a rock and pass out. When I woke up I was all better." She heard him take in a ragged breath and cringed, waiting for him to yell, but instead he walked away. The door to the cabin slammed and she winced.

He came back out a few minutes later and flopped onto the swing, lighting a cigarette. He said nothing and didn't look at her.

She walked onto the porch and stopped in front of him. "I'm sorry Jack," she said quietly.

He glared at her and let out a stream of smoke.

"I didn't know that would happen."

He continued to glare at her the way he had in the days preceding her "come out". She grew exasperated with the feeling that she was a little girl being reprimanded by her father...and made the mistake of telling him that.

The cigarette flew off the porch and she found herself lying on the grass on her back, an enraged Jack looming over her. His teeth were clenched when he spoke. "I should drag you over my knees and spank the living daylights out of you, unfortunately you're stronger than me and I probably couldn't hold you there." He pushed away from her and stood glaring down.

His eyes were so full of accusation and condemnation she couldn't help but feel like she *was* a child, and reacted like any child would. She burst into tears.

A female's tears were the undoing of all good men and Jack was no exception. He pulled her into his arms.

"You scared the hell out of me," he whispered into her hair. "For better or worse you were tossed into my life, and I care about what happens to you."

Her tears ebbed and she looked up at him. In a trembling voice she said, "It hurt so bad Jack, I will never do anything so stupid again. Nothing could be more effective in dissuading me like having my bones shatter and drowning."

His expression tightened and he clenched his teeth again. She buried her head into his chest and felt him relax and sigh.

He gave her one last squeeze then led her up to the porch and they sat.

"So, you're back to yourself again?" He looked at her in a way that told her he wasn't referring to her fall.

She nodded, flushing.

He put his hand on her cheek. "No need to feel like that. What happened was not in your control."

She nodded slightly and suddenly she was exhausted. Emotionally and physically wiped out.

"I'll make us something to eat," Jack stated and they went inside.

He prepared breakfast food and after they'd eaten Anna asked him if he knew how often she'd have to deal with heat.

"From what I've learned, females go into it about three times a year if they're unmated, more often if they are." He settled in an armchair and indicated that she sit across from him on the couch. "I called Will today and he filled me in on all the details of your transition. I've run into vampires like those in the past and they are dangerous. More dangerous than demons because they're so difficult to kill and supernaturally strong, though their inability to go out in sunlight does give us some advantage when dealing with them. It's widely believed in our circle of hunters that there are few vampires left who have not either turned to the practice of draining humans or been hunted and killed by those who have. Particularly females, in fact the last known breeding female was murdered over a century ago. Those that remain are evil to the core. At one point we thought that maybe these vampires were possessed but have since learned it isn't possible. They just chose to either ally with demons are call a truce with them."

Anna felt a bit deflated hearing this even though Will and Josh had alluded to some of the same things. But they hadn't been sure and Jack seemed to be more knowledgeable.

Noting her expression he added, "I didn't say all of them. There are still some that do the job they were created to do. Some males anyway." He seemed to be contemplating something, struggling with it in fact.

"What is it?" Anna asked.

He took a breath. "I think we should get some sleep and head back to Nevada in the morning. I don't want to give you misinformation, and I'd like to check on a few things before we continue this discussion."

Anna was agreeable to that, having been tired since before they'd eaten.

She climbed under the covers and looked over at Jack who had settled in on the small sofa. She bit down on her lip then gathered the courage to ask, "Will you sleep with me tonight, just hold me?" Her voice sounded pitiful and she felt a blush climb her cheeks. Jack crawled in beside her and pulled her in to his chest from behind. The warmth of his body coupled with the strength of his character made her feel secure and she was out in minutes.

Chapter Forty-One

Jared was perched atop the steeple of an old abandoned church staring out over the city of London. He'd been feeling restless for days and couldn't pinpoint what the problem might be. He was adequately fed, he'd pumped himself into several human females, and he'd challenged and devastated one male vamp after another in the No Holds Barred fighting ring they had set up under one of their nightclubs.

He was used to feeling listless with only lust and the occasional bout of fury to break up the monotony. This was different, this was almost like anxiety. From somewhere in the depths of his mind he recalled some old prophecies concerning the second millennium. He'd thought of them in the past but had always dismissed them as being something he no longer wished to be a part of.

Let the human race fall, let demons run rampant on the earth, why the fuck should he care? It was their own fault, their own selfishness and basic immorality that would bring about such things. Not that he was any better, but he didn't care much about that either. Life had lost its value for him at the end of the sixteenth century, the night his mother and father had breathed their last breath.

He had lost everything he'd ever cared about and vowed never to care again. And now that every last female of his kind was nothing more than a demon with a body, there really didn't seem to be any pressing reason for him to change his mind now.

He'd made the error of visiting one of those females recently. Since sex with a vampiress was so much more intense and satisfying then it was with human women there was a definite appeal, and Terrina had always made it apparent she wanted him as a regular lover. She'd even gone so far as to try and find ways to blackmail and coerce him to stay. He'd always laughed at her efforts. What could she possibly use against someone who cared for nothing including himself?

This time she had invited a human female-a semi attractive brunette and judging by her perfume and attire likely a whore-to join them in the middle of their interlude. She told him she wanted to watch, so he had driven into the woman from behind while Terrina lay on her stomach on the bed. Then she'd crawled over to the brunette and started drinking from her and before he'd realized what was intended the woman went limp while he was still buried inside of her.

He'd pulled out in horror and ripped Terrina from the female's throat but it was too late, and a moment later he'd been thrown across the room.

He'd heard the act of drinking a human to death drastically increased a vampire's abilities but he'd never witnessed it before.

She was on him a second after he hit the wall and it took every ounce of strength in his two hundred and eighty pound frame to pin her to the floor. She was snapping and writhing in his grip for thirty minutes before her strength began to wane and he was able to let go with one hand and strike her, which he did repeatedly until she stopped fighting him. At that moment she'd looked up at him with a smile that had made his insides shrivel and said "Fuck me barbarian, batter me with your body." He'd pushed away from her in disgust as he'd contemplated ending her life. She'd turned pleading and then vicious, calling him a "human sympathizer" which was the highest form of insult for those that had turned.

He hadn't responded, just finished dressing and blurred from her place of dwelling. The entire thing had disturbed him profoundly, though he wasn't sure if he was more disturbed by what had happened or by the way he'd felt about it. Being mostly numb and comfortably heartless the idea that he cared even in a small way about the death of that human grated on him. He tried to convince himself that the woman had been worthless trash, but couldn't quite do it.

His thoughts veered to the small band of vampires he'd witnessed tearing apart demons several years back. Since fallen vampires weren't fond of those who didn't join their ranks the demon hunters kept a low profile so he didn't know who they were or where they lived.

Jared clenched his fists and shook his head violently. Why the hell was he thinking about this now? He'd made a point not to in the past, to ignore the evil surrounding him, his indifference was his cloak. He was not fucking interested in where the demon hunters lived, he was not one of them anymore and never would be again.

He leapt from his perch landing on the sidewalk fifty feet down. He walked several blocks through the seedier parts of London and was once more reminded of why the human race was no longer his concern as a gang of skin heads covered in snake tattoos made the unfortunate mistake of accosting him.

"Fancy coat and shoes, bet you got some green in your wallet. Why don't you hand it over and we'll let you be on your way." The man who spoke wasn't the biggest in the group, but he had the air of "leader."

Jared regarded them with the contempt they deserved and gave them one chance to change their minds. He growled low in his throat as he spoke, "You don't want this fight, go down the road and find another."

Two of the men who were nearly as large as he was began to laugh. "Big fucking man, are you?" One of them took a step forward.

Jared moved so quickly the others would later claim they hadn't seen him move at all. He broke both the man's arms and shattered his kneecaps, tossing him to the side like the bag of trash he was. Two more men came at him with blades. He flashed in, removing their knives which he used to sever the Achilles tendons on one leg apiece. Their screams of pain caused the remaining four to change their minds and run. But they'd had their chance.

Jared leapt over them landing in their path and watched with mild satisfaction as the color drained from their faces.

"We're sorry," one babbled, "we made a mistake, we'll just be on our way now."

He gave one slow shake of his head then grabbed the man and threw him against the side of a building with just enough force to knock him out cold. The others were backing away, looking frantically for an escape and he stalked towards them like a panther tracking its prey. He felt his fangs extract in his mouth and knew his eyes were flashing. He dimmed himself slightly so they wouldn't recognize what he was.

One broke from the group and he leapt in front of him, pulling his shoulders from their sockets as he ripped him from the sidewalk. He launched the writhing body into his fleeing buddies knocking them off their feet. He leapt again landing on two of them and stood with one foot on each back as he grabbed the third by his shirt and lifted him into the air.

The man wet his pants as he hung there and Jared threw him onto the sidewalk in disgust. The two beneath his feet were pleading for mercy. He bent down and bounced both of their faces off the road, hearing the satisfying crunch of their noses breaking.

Then he stepped off of them, pulled out a cigarette and lit it. Mercy. He had shown them mercy. All of them would live. Humans. Not fucking worth it. He strode away without a backwards glance.

Chapter Forty-Two

Anna and Jack were finally reunited with the boys and she reveled in the suffocating hugs she received from them both.

"It's good to be home," she quipped making them all laugh considering they were in a shabby hotel room. Jack had been really quiet while they were traveling and Anna though he was most likely regretting the things that had taken place between them. It did make their relationship a little awkward. Especially since she was now a bit infatuated with the man. She glanced at him and took in his appearance feeling a peculiar melting in her belly.

"So," Will spoke up, "I've been talking to Richard and Isaac and they tell me they've found another group like the bankers who are less cautious when they're out on the town. They think we could take them out fairly easily if we team up, so I'm thinking we should head out to Colorado. These fucks in Vegas are too well guarded right now, we can't get to 'em. And we can keep tabs on them from anywhere."

Josh was nodding his agreement and Anna said, "I'm game."

Jack looked at her and drew in a breath. "Actually Anna...." he trailed off.

"Oh come on dad," Josh jumped in, "she can handle herself in the field. She's stronger, faster, and way more difficult to kill than all of us put together."

Jack shook his head, "That's not it."

Anna shrank back, her heart filling with pain. "It's because of us and what we did?"

"No. Shit. Just let me explain, stop jumping to conclusions all of you." He braced himself and said, "Anna needs to be with her own kind, at least for a while."

That was met by stunned silence, followed quickly by violent protests.

"Let me finish!" Jack commanded. He waited until they were quiet and his tone softened. "I know of some vampires who are still on our side, that still perform the duty they were created for."

Utter silence.

"Years ago in Europe I met up with a trio of hunters, Faerians, who were helping me with some research and they had some friends. Vampire friends they traded information with and sometimes went to for help with possessed individuals that were proving themselves difficult to deal with. From what I was told they were the real deal. Demon hunters who were bound to the cause by faith and duty."

"Wait a fucking minute," Will cut in angrily, "are you telling us that you have non-human friends? After all these years of adamantly stating that none of them can be trusted?"

Josh had grown very still and looked like he might explode.

Jack snorted, "I'm not saying that at all. They're friends of friends, not friends of mine."

Josh bolted to his feet. "How can you nonchalantly fucking suggest we send Anna to some vamps just because a few people you know in Europe say they're okay? You don't trust them or we would have heard about them by now!"

Jack stood up, "Look, I have serious prejudice against all manner of things, which is not necessarily right. At the time I regarded them with one eye shut, didn't matter what they appeared to be, they were bloodsuckers therefore I didn't like them. But my attitude has gone through a bit of readjustment over the past several days." He looked at Anna and his boys did too.

She met his eyes. "I guess that should be flattering," she said quietly. "But it doesn't change the fact that there is no possible way I will go to England, in fact that happens to be the very last place on the face of this world that I want to go."

She was sitting on the bed, feet crossed with her legs pulled up against her chin. All three guys were struck by how young and vulnerable she looked, particularly since her eyes were shining with tears that wanted to fall.

Jack crossed the room and sat down next to her, draping a large arm across her shoulders. He brushed her hair from her face and said, "I know you don't sweetheart. I know you're afraid, but it's the safest thing for you right now."

She peered up into his bright green eyes. "Why?" she asked in a small voice.

"I told you the remaining female vampires are evil. They have a deep seated hatred towards any of their kind who have chosen to remain on our side, but they are outmatched in strength by males so they target females, and especially healers. The last of the females who still fought for us was of the black-haired, violet eyed, more aggressive variety. Fair haired healers like you were eliminated much earlier on. When they get wind of your existence, which is inevitable, you will be in danger. And my boys and I are not equipped to protect you. And that's only part of the problem. You're not just a female vampire, you are a breeding female which the race has not seen in well over a century. Every male of your species will want you in some way."

She frowned up at him. "But why do they have to find out about me? No one knows I exist. When I go into heat I can just go to Montana, it worked this time, and like you said it's only three times a year."

"Even if it were possible to hide your identity, we aren't going to live forever," Jack swept his hand indicating himself and his boys who were currently seated and staring down at their laps.

"But there are more vampires in Europe than there are here, wouldn't that put me in greater danger?"

"Not if you had protection."

Anna's lips were trembling now. It didn't matter if his reasoning made sense, she didn't want to go. She didn't want to leave everyone again.

"No," she said firmly.

"Anna..."

"NO! I don't want to go! I don't want to leave everything and everyone I know and love to live with vampires who may or may not be trustworthy! Even if they fight demons and don't prey on humans, I don't want to leave here!" The tears started sliding down her face and her voice shook. "I don't want to leave you."

Jack moved away from her and his tone was firm, "That isn't something you have a say in. I will be leaving to meet up with men in Los Angeles next week."

Anna felt a sharp pain of rejection in the cold set of his face and words. She jumped to her feet and ran into the bathroom slamming the door.

Josh stared daggers at his father. "You callous son of a bitch," he growled.

"Excuse me?"

"You heard me. You just spent the last three days doing God knows what with her, and even if intercourse didn't come into it she was completely innocent before this. And now you tell her that not only do you not want her, you want to ship her off to a place that's tied to horror in her mind?" Josh's voice was beginning to rise and he got to his feet. "You are a heartless, selfish fucking *asshole*!"

Jack stood up and leaned in towards his son, his tone menacing. "Is that how you see me?"

Josh stood his ground, "How else can I see you? You can spout all the bullshit you want about her best interests, but in the end she's just a problem in need of a solution, instead of a girl in need of help. She doesn't fit into your life so you put her out of it, well go a-fucking-head, in fact why wait until next week, leave now! I happen to love Anna, and I won't let you bully her into doing something you deem as right the way you bully everyone else!"

Will sat silently through the exchange waiting for an explosion that would bring him in as peacekeeper. He understood his father's motivations but he also agreed that Anna deserved to be treated more gently.

Jack surprised both of his sons with his next words. "You're right, I am being selfish."

"You admit it?"

"Yeah. Even though I think my reasons are valid, they're as much for me as they are for her." He stood up and went to the bathroom door, knocking softly.

The lock disengaged and he went in. She had been listening to the exchange and her face was wet with tears. She was sitting on the closed lid of the toilet and he sat down across from her on the edge of the tub.

"Tell me what you're thinking, how you're feeling," he asked gently.

"I don't know," her voice hitched, "Confused. Scared. Hurt. I don't want you to leave me." She felt her chest tighten and she bit back a sob.

"Why?" he asked softly.

She tried to convey her feelings with her eyes, but the question hung in the air. She looked at his handsome face and felt like she was being pulled apart.

"I want to be with you," she said, tensing for rejection.

"I want that to."

She looked up in surprise, then furrowed her brows and waited for the "but".

"In fact I haven't wanted anything as much in a long, long time. Yet it isn't right. I don't want to tell you all the things you already know or expect me to say. I know how much anyone despises being told what they feel, after all how can anyone possibly know better than we do what's inside our own hearts?" He reached over and ran a finger down her hairline and across her lips making her shiver. "You are so beautiful."

He withdrew his hand and looked at her sadly. "I could tell you how my heart belongs to Elena and how there will never be another for me. I could tell you that my life belongs to the cause and there's no room for anything else. But no matter how much truth there is to these things, they are not precisely what is stopping me. When I was with you for these past three days there were times that I wanted to claim you as mine so strongly it took every ounce of my will not to." He paused then, looking at her, wanting her to see the sincerity of his words.

She waited and he continued. "A long time ago, when I was younger than my boys are now, I traveled through Europe on a quest for knowledge. There were so many things about our world that I wanted to learn, things that my ancestors could only allude to. It's been years since I thought about this, but because of you and all that's happened I remembered this book I came across." He paused and looked into space, drawing the memory in closer. "It was in a museum of sorts, not the version we have here in America, but a rundown old house owned by a woman who collected unusual artifacts. It was a book of prophecies, though none that the world would ever accept as anything but the rantings of a crazy person. Even to me some of what was said seemed farfetched. But there was one prophecy concerning a female vampire that sticks out in my mind. It said she would come forth to unite the allies of old and breathe new life into the race and that her mate would be a warrior from another time who had lost his way but would rise up and lead. It mentioned a battle between good and evil of potentially epic proportions and it dated the fulfillment to be in the beginning of the second millennium. I don't recall anything more, but....I believe that you might be that female." He paused and took a breath. "And I am not that male."

Anna chewed on her lip and spoke in a small voice. "But you don't know if that was really a prophecy, you don't know if it's true."

"No. But what I do know is there is a reason this happened to you. That God has a plan for you, a higher purpose that does not include an aging hunter. You will likely live for a very, very long time, long after I'm gone. I know it's a hard thing for you to hear, that you don't want to think of losing everyone that you love, but it's something you need to face. If you continue to ignore your own kind in favor of humans you will end up alone. And that is unacceptable to me because I care for you deeply, and I want to make sure you're safe and have a chance at a life filled with more joy than pain."

Anna nodded miserably. She knew the truth of what he said, and that he was right. After all she had left Austin for those very reasons. In her heart of hearts she believed that there must be a reason for this. And she'd always believed in a soul mate. But it was still hard for her to let everything go, to let her humanity go in a sense.

She looked at Jack and saw that his face was pained and etched with worry. She got up and kneeled between his legs lying her head down on his thigh, "I know you're right. But it's really hard."

He stroked her hair. "Yes. It is."

She looked up at him and managed a weak smile.

He put his hand under her chin and leaned down to kiss her lightly on the mouth then pulled her to her feet. "If you're not ready right now it can wait. Since no one knows about you yet you would probably be safe going on to Colorado with the boys."

But not with him, she thought, he was leaving her no matter what. She stared at him and made her decision. "If you can get them to come here then I'm willing to meet them. But I'm not going there."

He nodded. "Fair enough. I'll make some calls."

Chapter Forty-Three

Leo Matridan sank his head into his hands and rubbed his eyes wearily. He'd been up for thirty six hours straight, pouring over his ancestral history along with some other old books and documents he and his brother Bret had collected in the past fifty years. At the age of seventy-two he looked to be a man in his thirties, but in his soul he felt much older.

The demons were changing their M.O. In the past several months there had been more and more cases where they were not just taking over individuals but groups of individuals linked by their occupations. They were teaming up and being far more cautious making the hunters' job extremely difficult.

The door to his used book store jingled and in walked Finn, another hunter and close friend, his usual upbeat demeanor clouded. He had also been doing research, had in fact just come back from Kazikstan after hearing a rumor that an old hunter lived there in seclusion.

Finn's red hair was unkempt, his beard scraggly, his face beginning to show the signs of age that hunter's wore after a century had passed.

"Any luck?" Leo inquired.

Finn snorted and blew out a puff of air in irritation. "The old basta'd was there all right, but he couldn't tell me a thing that I doon' already know." His Irish brogue was thicker than usual, a stark contrast to Leo's refined English. "Wha' about you, didja find anything?"

"Bits and pieces of things, mostly conjecture." He frowned up at his friend. "I still haven't heard from Michael. It's beginning to worry me, he usually doesn't take this long to return my calls, and if anyone knows anything it will be him. Matthias has to have run into something in the centuries of his life."

Finn nodded in agreement. The phone on Leo's desk rang, the vibration rattling the papers around it. The two exchanged a hopeful look as Leo pressed talk. "Hello?"

"Leo?"

"Who's this?"

"Jack McClaron. Been a long time."

Leo's brows shot up and he leaned back in his chair looking at Finneus. He put the phone on speaker so his friend could listen in. "Jack McClaron, I'll be damned. I take it you've run into some strange demon activity?"

"Yeah, I have, but that isn't the reason for my call."

"Oh?"

"If you don't mind I have some questions I need to ask before I get into it."

Leo lifted a brow at Finn. "Sure. Fire away."

"Are you still friendly with the leeches?"

Leo chuckled. "I am, and as always they are not fond of that label."

"Sorry, old habits die hard. So they're still fighting on our side then?"

"Jack my man, vampires are no more likely to change sides than humans are."

"I'd like to say that was encouraging."

Leo chuckled again, "Michael and the boys are firmly on our side as always."

"As far as you know, every female vampire has been turned, is that right?"

"That's right, either turned or murdered, Michael's mother was the last of the good ones. But you know that, we've discussed it before. Why do you ask?"

"I'm getting there. I wondered if you'd ever heard about a prophecy involving a female of their kind, something along the lines of saving their race from extinction?"

Leo grew quiet. "I've heard it. Though most say the sources of these prophecies are suspect. Again, why do you ask?"

Jack took a deep breath. "Because for the past couple months a female vampire has been living and working with my boys."

Leo and Finn stared at each other in shocked silence, Leo clutching the phone tightly. "Where did she come from?"

"Have you ever heard of a human surviving the transition with their mind intact?" Jack asked quietly.

"No, it's never happened, it doesn't happen, what are you saying Jack that you have a human woman-turned vampire?"

"That's precisely what I'm saying. Though she's more of a girl than a woman. She's only nineteen years old. It happened over the summer in your city at some fucked up vampire version of a dogfight using people instead."

"The Gaming Dungeons." Leo breathed. "We know of them, but we've never been able to pinpoint a location because they're constantly moving. Christ, are you sure about this? When did you find out about her?"

"My boys kept her identity from me considering my long standing prejudices. They passed her off as a Faerian, a healer, which is in fact what she was before this happened. Then a few days ago....she went into heat. I managed to get her to a remote location so she wouldn't attract a horde of blood suckers, but she can't stay hidden forever. I'm no match for a single vampire, let alone a lust crazed army of them. Not to mention the females who would want her dead."

Leo rocked back in his chair, shaking his head in disbelief. "Look Jack I'm glad you called. This is unbelievable news. She'll definitely need the protection of her own race. Problem is I've been waiting to hear from Michael for a week, and until he calls I can't pass the information on. Is there anything else you can tell me so that when he gets back to me I can fill him in?"

"Yeah, actually, there is one other thing. She drinks from humans and it has no effect on her, it seems to be the same for her to do that as it would for a vampire to take from their own."

"You're sure?"

"Absolutely. She's in complete control, there's no drug like side effects and it has no effect on her daytime abilities."

"This just gets stranger and stranger. Okay Jack, as soon as I hear from Michael I'll relay this to him and have him contact you directly. Same number?"

"Yeah, same."

"I'll be in touch." He pressed end, shaking his head in amazement.

"So whatta ya think?" Finn cocked his head to the side and locked eyes with his friend.

"If Jack says there's a human-turned-vampire, then there is. He's not the type to jump to hasty conclusions. So what I think is that the world just got a whole lot more interesting. Something big is on the horizon." He met his friend's eyes, his lip curling. "I believe we have a new direction for our research. Ancient prophesies."

Chapter Forty-Four

It was three days later when Jack received a call from a shell shocked vampire.

"Is this Jack McClaron?"

"Depends on who's asking."

"My name is Michael, I'm a friend of Leo's. He filled me in on the things that you told him."

Jack shot a glance at Anna who was playing a game of cricket with Josh. She pulled her arm back and hit the bullseye, another hat trick, and Josh threw down his darts in mock anger.

"We'd like you and your friends to come to the states. She's not eager to return to England at this point after suffering so much there."

"Of course. Just say when and where."

"Denver Colorado, whenever you can get here." Jack had made the trip with them after all, wanting to have things settled with Anna before taking his leave.

"I'll send you a text with our arrival details within the hour."

Jack hung up the phone and approached Anna and Josh, waving Will over from the corner where he was deep in conversation with Mac, another hunter and long time family friend.

"I just spoke with Michael, they are booking a flight as we speak." He had filled them in on his conversation with Leo so they were prepared for the news.

Anna looked at him nervously.

"It's going to be fine sweetheart, you'll see." They had refrained from touching over the past few days, Jack was determined not to further complicate the issues. He reached out to her now and gave her shoulder a reassuring squeeze. Josh put an arm around her waist and challenged her to a game of 301, wanting to keep her anxiety at a minimum.

"Make it three players," Will put in, and Jack smiled at the fine young men he'd raised. Despite their difficult lives they had compassionate souls. He and Mac joined in as well and they spent the rest of the evening entertaining and distracting the innocent little vampire.

The text came forty-five minutes after the phone call, stating their guests would be arriving the following day at 4pm. They would meet at a quiet upper class club in the ritzy part of Denver. What happened from there remained to be seen.

***

Anna spent the day of their imminent arrival on pins and needles. She'd called Jenna to fill her in on the details, having already told her everything that had happened between her and Jack. Well, not everything, but she'd given her the gist. Jenna had wanted to be there to meet the vamps, but her aunt had decided they were going to France in a couple of days so she didn't have the time.

"If you end up going to England, I'll come and see you," she'd said, "It looks like Harri and I will be staying for a month or more."

"That would be fantastic, *if* I were going to England which I'm probably not," she'd countered. Jenna had made a sound of the "we'll see" variety and they'd exchanged love and hung up.

She stared at the clock, 2:30, a couple more hours and she'd be meeting her own kind. Own kind. She didn't really feel like that fit, how could they be her kind if she was born and raised a human? And Jack had pointed out some differences recently, like the fact that she didn't get off on human blood. Face it Anna, you're a freak, even in the vampire world.

She frowned and scolded herself. Where's your sunny outlook? Not a freak, just unique. Ooo, that rhymes. She giggled. According to Jack she was special. He believed her to be the fulfillment of an ancient prophecy, a uniter of good against evil. She definitely liked the idea of that, it was certainly better than thinking she was just an accident, a mistake. *Special, that's me*, she thought and smiled brightly.

"What are you grinning about?" Josh asked as he crossed the room.

"Oh you know, the usual, how great I am, amazing, special, unique. Definitely not a freak."

He was smiling at her list until the last part. He gave her a dark look, "Don't even think it Anna, you are *not* a freak."

"A freak?" Will walked in and looked at Anna with concern.

"I said that I *wasn't* a freak, not that I was, chill out you two. I know that I'm a fountain of wondrous awesomeness," she grinned widely and snatched Will's coke from him taking a long swig.

"You're lucky you don't have germs," he told her snatching it back.

"Says you. Don't you know that wondrous awesomeness is code for icky germiness?"

"A fountain of icky germiness, hmm, I've met a few people who fit that description." Will grinned.

"Yeah, the women you love and leave." Josh laughed and leapt out of the way of his brother's retaliation.

"At least I get some lovin', unlike my brother the priest."

"It's monk, get it straight," Josh countered.

"Straight? I'm not the one who needs to work on that," Will snorted and went over to the television.

Anna caught Josh with an odd look on his face which he wiped away quickly, but it was too late, his expression had made her wonder. Was Josh gay? She glanced at Will and thought about Jack. Poor Josh, if he *was* gay that would not be an easy closet opening.

Jack sauntered into the room, "We might as well head out. We can get something to eat while we wait for them."

Anna nearly panicked. *Not ready!* She thought, her stomach tightening. But would another hour make a difference? No. *Face your fears Anna, head on, you've done pretty well with it this far.*

They went in Will's car, Anna and Josh in the back, and she cuddled up to her friend.

"It's gonna be fine Anna, if they're creeps we'll send them packing. Don't worry." He put his arms around her and she held him tightly.

"Uptown" Denver was breathtaking. In fact the entire city was enormously appealing with the surrounding mountains. Naturally the upscale parts were exceptional. She had asked why they'd decided on this location, the guys weren't usually the upper crust type. Jack had explained that it was always safer to be in classier environments, it generally put people, and other things, on their best behavior.

She was wearing a simple dress that matched the turquoise color of her eyes, though a few shades lighter. It was expensive but not flashy, with straps that clasped behind her neck and a neckline that dipped down showing just a little cleavage. It was clingy on her upper body but light and airy from her waist down to where it cut off just above her knees. She had curled the tips of her normally straight hair and fastened a silver butterfly hairclip just above her right temple. She'd even applied a little makeup- a very light shade of shimmery pink on her lips, blue eyeliner that accented her eyes and just a touch of color on her cheekbones. The guys had told her she looked beautiful and she had to admit that she did look very pretty. She still believed the term "beautiful" was reserved for women with voluptuous curves like Jenna and Jess.

The guys were wearing Khaki pants and dress shirts, though they'd forgone ties as that would have been overkill for the smoky tavern bunch. They looked extremely handsome, all of them with their unique features that blended to make for some serious head turners.

They were led to a table by a very formally attired and well-spoken waiter, and once seated they wasted little time in ordering.

When their appetites were sated they ordered drinks and sat back making small talk.

Their guests arrived at nearly 5pm and they could not have been mistaken, at least by anyone who knew of their existence, for anything other than what they were. They were five *absolutely stunning* male specimens, otherworldly in their masculine beauty. When they reached the table every eye was on her making her nervous. Each one of them took a turn clasping her hand to their lips after they gave their names.

Time warp, she thought, *I have just been dropped into the early 1900's.* She struggled with her blush and tried not to giggle like a schoolgirl.

They were seated in one of those booths that wrapped all the way around and she pushed herself tightly into Josh's side as they filed in. One of them, Seth, pulled up a chair at the head and she noticed there was something that separated him from the others. Maybe it was just that his hair was long and he had a light beard where the rest of them were clean shaven. His rugged handsomeness made him appear less alien than the other four.

The one seated next to her, Michael, turned to her and smiled. His eyes held the look of someone absolutely enthralled. They were a beautiful shade of vivid dark blue, framed by long dark lashes. The color of his hair was similar to Jack's chocolate shade, and it was wavy and full, the kind you wanted to run your hands through. When they were walking over to the table she'd judged them all to be over six feet tall, ranging in their physiques from muscular and slim to muscular and broad. Michael was of the latter version. She smiled back at him and he took her hand and kissed it again continuing to look at her in a way that made her feel revered and uncomfortable at the same time.

"We're all extremely honored to meet you," he told her, and she glanced at the others who were nodding their agreement.

The waiter came up to the table.

"We'll have three bottles of your best Merlot," Michael told him.

"Very good, sir."

When the beverage was served the McClarons' engaged the males in conversation giving her a chance to look them over more thoroughly. Two of them, Matthias and Coderin, had blonde hair, the first one a shade very similar to her own with startling emerald green eyes flecked with blue and a.....lip ring? Yup, *and* an eyebrow ring. She also saw what appeared to be a tattoo of some kind on his neck, appearing just above his shirt line. Big guy. Big *big* guy.

The other blonde had no piercings and eyes the color of amber, almost yellow, with streaks of orange running through them. She had never seen eyes that color in her life, she imagined most people would assume they were contacts. He was more boyishly handsome than the rest, probably the dimples were to blame. He also had a leaner body as did the dark haired male sitting beside him. Tyros. His eyes were the color of dark chocolate, just a shade lighter than his pupils. Iridescent gold rings circled his irises making him appear even more exotic than the others. His dark brows were slanted lending him a menacing appearance and the watchfulness in his eyes added to the effect. He could definitely play a vampire on one of those teenage pop culture series and be an instant heartthrob. An air of danger with a sexy face and body-perfect for the teenage crush.

Then there was Seth. The good looking smart ass from the series Lost came to mind, only with a much more powerful body. He was also the tallest of the group, about six and a half feet. His hair was dark gold, almost brown, and she thought if it wasn't tied back it would hang just above his shoulders. His eyes were a mixture of gold and teal, he had high cheekbones and gave the impression of a cross between a pirate and a warrior. He caught her staring and grinned, revealing perfect white teeth. His smile was a bit feral yet somehow disarming. She didn't always like facial hair on a guy, but on him, neatly trimmed the way it was, it only added to his appeal. Her eyes kept being drawn back to him, trying to figure out why he seemed so different than the rest.

Michael leaned into her and whispered, "He's a Lyncane."

She furrowed her brows and he smiled. "Seth. He's not a vampire, he's a Lyncane."

"Lyncane?" she whispered in question. She glanced at Seth who was smiling at her in amusement, obviously hearing her question.

"You've never heard the term?" Michael seemed genuinely surprised.

She shook her head.

He smiled at his friend before turning to her. "Humans depict the Lyncane as the Werewolf."

And she thought she knew everything by now. So wrong. She stared at Seth in awe. "Does he actually turn into a wolf?" she whispered.

Michael nodded still smiling. "When the need arises."

"Wow. That's cool."

All but Tyros erupted with laughter having listened in on the exchange.

"She thinks you're cool, I think I'm jealous," Coderin joked.

"Yeah, that's just until she smells his dog breath, than "cool" will change to "foul"," Matthias quipped.

Anna felt heat rise in her cheeks. Cool? How much sillier could she make herself appear?

"Knock it off guys, you're embarrassing her," Seth continued to smile, "don't let them fool you, they all wish they were as cool as me." He had a slight Irish brogue and she found herself relaxing and smiling back. For some reason that particular accent always seemed friendly.

"Yeah it's my dream to shed," Matthias retorted. Anna looked at Josh and Will and saw they were equally intrigued. Apparently she wasn't the only one surprised to learn of werewolves. Or at least to find one sitting at their table which Will confirmed with his next statement.

"We thought the Lyncane were extinct and last I heard they were enemies of the vampire."

Seth grinned, flashing his teeth again and Anna could see the wolfishness about him. "That's what the Lyncane want people to think. Most of my kind have chosen to live their lives raising their families in seclusion and don't involve themselves with the dark ones anymore. I'm an exception."

"So how did you come to be an exception?" Jack, ever suspicious of non-humans, was regarding him warily.

"My family moved from Ireland to the outback of Australia over a century ago. Since we tend to have long lives, several centuries or so, we have to either live in remote places or move around. The McKellar's chose seclusion so they could remain in one place. But every new generation has to go out into the world at some point to find their mate. I came to London just after I hit maturity seventy years ago, and met Michael in a tavern. We struck up a conversation and when I learned about his ongoing battle against the dark ones I decided it was the life for me and joined him. That about sums it up."

Anna had a million questions she wanted to ask the vampires and the Lyncane, but she decided this was not the place for it. She felt Michael's eyes on her again and turned to him. "How long are you going to stay?" she asked.

"As long as it takes to convince you to come back with us."

Whoa. She leaned back slightly and looked at him.

He explained, "We couldn't possibly leave you here unprotected, you are way too important."

She swallowed hard. The term breed mare came to mind, why else would she be important? All of a sudden she was struck with fear that they had plans to share her.

Nervousness assailed her as she looked around at the intimidating lot. "I don't think that I'm the one from the prophecy," she declared.

Michael cocked his head to the side, "No?"

"No. I think I'm a fluke. You know, an accident."

"Why do you say that?"

Why indeed? Just a couple of hours ago she wanted to be the special one. "I don't know, it's too much responsibility," she said weakly.

There was understanding in his eyes and he spoke to her gently. "You don't have to worry about things like that. If it's a matter of fate than what is supposed to happen will, you don't have to live in fear of making the wrong choice. But no matter what, going with us *is* the right choice. It's far too dangerous for you to live without protection. Your friends," he looked up at the McClaron's, "they care very much for you and would no doubt protect you with their lives, but it might come to that kind of cost if you stayed with them."

Damn. Double damn. If there was anything that might have talked her into leaving, the image of her beloved McClaron's dying in an attempt to protect her was definitely it. She had been in denial for the past few days, thinking that she would find a way to keep things as they were. A part of her had known all along that this was yet another turn in the road that she would have to make.

"Where do you live?" she asked in hopes that he painted a lovely picture complete with an in-ground pool.

"Our home, the place we go to rest and regroup, is on the outskirts of London, in the country. It's been in my family for hundreds of years."

She must have made a face as she pictured an antique because he smiled reassuringly.

"It's modernized, it has every convenience. I'm certain you'll like it there. You can select any room you like and decorate it to suit you."

Talk about assuming the victory. But....did she really have a choice? "Sounds lovely." Sounding English already, she thought, and inwardly sighed, knowing her decision was made.

She looked over at her guys, especially Jack, and thought she could not do another teary departure. It's not as if she wouldn't see them, and she planned on bugging them with phone calls on a daily basis. Well maybe not Jack. She'd already managed to analyze herself out of her crush on the handsome Irishman. She'd convinced herself it was just the intimacy and insanity of the days they'd spent together that had made her feel that way. Which was mostly true.

The group decided to move their gathering to a tavern down the street.

"The wine left a sour taste in my mouth," Matthias said to Will as they walked outside, "I'm more of a beer and scotch kinda male, you?"

Will grinned, "Hell yeah, I'll order us up a pitcher and some shots."

Anna spent the first part of the evening attached to Josh since she felt her departure was imminent. He'd asked her about it and she'd looked away saying only "I want to do what's best." Mentally she'd added *for you and your brother.*

Throughout the night she observed the males with fascination. Matthias and Will hit it off right away and she found that the gorgeous vampire had a similar sense of humor to Will's. Seth seemed comfortable in any situation, bantering with Will and Matthias, talking more seriously with Jack and Michael, who incidentally seemed to have a personality similar to Austin's only a great deal more cultured and polite. Coderin appeared to be most comfortable with Seth, it almost seemed he was trying to emulate the wolf-man. Tyros, well he just sat alone and watched. Aloof was the best word to describe him, she had yet to see him interact with anyone aside from his brief greeting.

"Let's go see what dad and Michael are talking about so intensely," Josh suggested, handing her another beer.

Anna considered and shook her head, "I think I'll try and talk to the loner." She nodded in the direction of Tyros.

"Okay, I'll be over there if you need me."

She walked slowly towards the brooding male and felt his eyes rake over her. His expression didn't indicate what he felt about her one way or another.

"Hi," she said with a smile.

He stared at her.

"Do you mind if I sit?" She pointed at the stool beside him and he lifted one shoulder slightly.

She took a sip of her beer and swiveled towards him. "Have you been to America before?"

He turned towards her and regarded her silently for a moment. "No."

"Not a big talker?"

This earned her a slight curl of his lip. "What gave you that impression?"

She smiled again. "So what's it like, fighting demons?" Her one experience had not given her much to go on.

"It's....immensely satisfying."

She frowned a little, waiting for more.

His lip curled again. "Ripping apart their flesh and knowing that the deed has taken their existence forever.....is satisfying."

Anna was beginning to get the "creeper" vibe from Tyros. "I attempted it once." She told him just to fill the silence.

His eyes raked over her again and an eyebrow went up.

"It didn't go very well, though Will assured me that I did destroy it."

His expression didn't change. "What happened?"

She looked down. "It brought me to hell in my mind. Not an experience I'd be eager to repeat."

"They can do that if your mind is weak."

She jerked her head back up. OUCH. That wasn't a nice thing to say. In retrospect talking to the loner might not have been the best idea.

"Well," Anna said hopping off the stool, "It was....nice talking to you." She walked two steps when she heard him say "liar" in just above a whisper. She turned to find him staring at her in challenge.

She met and held his gaze, then shrugged. "You're right, nice was the wrong word."

He have her half a smile for that. "So what is the right word?"

"Words actually. Mildly unpleasant. That describes it."

He smiled widely and it transformed his face into something hauntingly beautiful. "I appreciate honesty." His smile faded as quickly as it had come.

"I'll remember that. For the next time we talk."

He lifted a brow and she winked before going to see what Matthias and Will were laughing about.

"So I say to the fucker, 'tell you what, we'll both swim under the ship and he who comes up first gives their loot to the other. And he goes, 'Ain't no one can hold their breath longer than me, you're on!' And fuck if he didn't hold his breath until he passed the hell out, damned determined bloody asshole! So I haul the bastard out of the water give him mouth to mouth, the whole nine, and while he's still coughing up the sea he sputters, "That don't count you brought me up, I didn't come up on my own!"

Will doubled over with laughter.

Matthias grinned and downed another shot, then poured himself a beer, draining the last of the pitcher. He put his glass down and glanced at her. "Hey there, you have a nice talk with our resident freak?"

Anna winced. "He can hear you."

"And?"

"He's not so bad."

"Compared to a demon possessed gargoyle you mean?"

"I take it the two of you are not friends."

"Virus doesn't have friends."

"But he lives with you, right?"

Matthias made a face. "In a manner of speaking."

She quirked an eyebrow.

"We all go back to one house and sleep occasionally."

"Otherwise where do you go?"

"When we're not taking out demons? Where ever we feel like going."

"So-you work together, sort of live together, but don't hang out together?"

He barked a laugh. "Some of us hang out. I occasionally hang with Michael and Seth. And of course wherever Wolfie goes Code-red goes too, so...." he shrugged.

Anna glanced at Seth and sure enough Coderin was sticking by his elbow. "Is he gay?"

Matthias erupted in laughter at that. "Nah, though I like to give him shit like that, it's just a little idol worshipping."

Will was still grinning and he jumped in, "So how long were you on the high seas?"

"On and off for a century and a half. Treasure hunting is a hell of a blast. Of course most of the time the bastards robbed other ships for their loot, which was fine by me, I just kept the killing in check. There was never a reason to hurt anyone when I could just zip in and take what we wanted and leave without anyone the wiser. They called me the Phantom Pirate."

"Nice."

So he'd been a pirate minus the killing and hopefully the raping. That was definitely an exciting past.

"So sweetheart, you coming back to England with us?"

Will looked at her, interested in the answer.

"I guess I don't have much of a choice. My presence in people's lives puts them in danger."

"I'm sure Michael-Angel-O will be thrilled with that decision."

"But not you?"

Matthias looked her over slowly, his eyes growing heavy lidded. In a sexy voice he asked, "Do you want me to be?"

She flushed and looked down.

Will's expression changed dramatically. "Hey, Anna's a good girl and a close friend, don't fucking treat her like that."

Matthias looked at him in surprise then turned back to her. "I apologize. Spend too much time with whores you forget how to treat a lady."

Anna shrugged and smiled. "It's okay, guys will be guys."

"You forgot to add Thank God for that," Matthias told her grinning.

"No I didn't," she said grinning back.

He laughed. "Nicely done." He poured himself another shot then held the bottle up to her in offering.

"No thanks, I'll let you get back to your pillaging stories," she meandered over to Josh again.

She listened in to Will and Matthias for a minute to see if they'd talk about her. They did.

"She's innocent you know," Will was saying. "*Innocent*."

The emphasis made her cheeks burn.

"Serious? Didn't she just go through heat?"

"Yeah, but my dad....he helped her out without taking that from her."

"Shit. I have just gained all kinds of respect for that man. Do you have any idea how difficult that would be, to resist a vampiress in heat?"

"I have some idea. My old man is a rock. They don't make them any stronger."

"No kidding."

Will poured his own shot and tipped his head in the direction of his father's table. "Michael, he seems solid."

"Oh fuck yeah, that boy is as solid as they come. I've got nothin' but love for him, he's the anchor to our band of misfits. Though I gotta say Wolfie comes in a close second. A lot more wild because of his animal nature, but grounded at the same time. I can easily see His Hairiness with a couple of brats bouncing on his knees. All it'll take is the appearance of his mate and he'll be domesticated. Of course he has a strong family still living so that helps. And then there's Code-red. Now there's an interesting story." He leaned back in his chair eyeing the amber eyed vampire.

"He was among the last born, about fourteen years before Michael, who is only a hundred and thirty by the way, a mere adolescent in our world. Anyway Code's mother was being hunted by a vicious vampiress called Sandrayna." He said her name like there was dirt on his tongue. "One night the bitch caught up with them and his mother fled with seventeen year old Coderin who was still several years away from being able to tear that bitch apart. Vampires don't come into their own until they reach about twenty-five, until then they're not much different than humans. Anyway, she flees and finds an underground cave where she puts her son in hyberstasis, know what that is? Yeah, only there was one serious problem with this-he was too young to turn on his own internal clock, meaning he needed someone to wake him up. Of course she intended to do that once it was safe, but she never came back, the assumption being she was killed. Cody boy was in stasis for the full one hundred years, which is the maximum length we can go under. So about twenty five years ago he woke up and found his world had drastically changed. He actually lived with some humans for a while, passing himself off as a teenager--which is the other thing, his aging process didn't continue while in stasis, so when he climbed out of that cave he was still seventeen. We age until about mid to late twenties right, so yeah he lived with humans until he ran into us at a bar about fifteen years ago. So essentially he's still a kid, vampirically speaking."

Anna was loving Matthias at the moment, being able to learn so much about the males she would be staying with. It definitely eased her mind to know that for the most part they were good.

"Shit, that would've been nuts to wake up after a hundred years, especially this past century, so many changes. So what about creepy over there, what's his story?" Will nodded at Tyros.

Matthias followed the direction of his nod and looked at Tyros for a long moment, then shook his head. "No one really knows. He just showed up one day about five years ago, said he wanted to help us in our mission to take out the evil ones. One thing I can say about him is that he's a vicious fighter, and since it looks like war is coming our way that's a damn good quality."

"How does that work exactly, what you do?"

"At this point the demons are mostly child's play. Occasionally we'll come across a big enough gathering to have our hands full for a second, but they're not physically powerful. It's just the mind shit you have to worry about, they reach inside and try to warp you. For most of us one or two are easy, you build walls against them in your head, a kind of mental fortress. You'll still come away with that sick diseased feeling-although with Anna around that will change. Generally we have to get some R&R between attacks, let the evil dissipate, but a healer can merely touch you and it's gone. She'll be an asset, especially if things are going like we think."

"Which is what? You mentioned war, what do you think is happening?"

"The second gateway has moved and it hasn't been found, on top of which we think the Guards have absconded. The Dantalion are a bitch. They have the mental powers of the Jinn coupled with physical strength and speed. It's been a long time since I've seen any real battle, but it looks like that's about to change."

"We thought it was something like that. I know you guys deal with them in their basic form, but even their possession of humans is changing."

"Hell yeah. They're much more aggressive and they team up."

Anna shifted her focus to Michael, Jack, and Seth who were talking about the same things.

"What we really need to know is why this happened or happens. What about this particular time is different?" Jack looked to Michael.

"Every hundred years the potential for it is there since the time vampires were first created. At that time all the doorways were wide open and demons ran rampant through the world. The why's we don't know, but we were created to take care of the problem and angels were put at three of the gates once they were closed again."

"All right, so every one hundred years the demons attempt to move the doorways, but is it the Angels that find them or vampires?"

Michael shook his head slightly. "Matthias is the only one who was around the last time the Dantalion got through, and all he did was fight the fight. He was basically a soldier in the army who followed orders but wasn't privy to all of the reasons behind them. There are ancients of our kind who are supposedly involved in the process, as far as we know these ancients locate the doorways and they, with the help of the angels, get them closed again. The problem is so many of our kind were hunted down and killed by fallen vampires or human mobs who equate all vampires with evil, that much has been lost. We once had detailed accounts written down, but no one knows where these accounts are. So unfortunately we're about as much in the dark as you are."

"Damn." Jack said, leaning back in his chair.

Michael looked up and smiled warmly as Anna walked over to them. She smiled back thinking that if there were ever a man to fall in love with it would be him. Considering the things Matthias had said a girl could not go wrong. She sat down next to Josh and pictured herself spending eternity with the vampire, and faltered.

I shouldn't have made that Austin comparison, she thought. But that was the problem, he did remind her of Austin. On top of which she felt no spark when she looked at him. *Don't be ridiculous, you just met him*, she scolded. *And Jack is here muddying your thinking.* Her eyes scooted over to Jack and saw he'd returned to the bar, along with Seth and Coderin.

Josh asked Michael several questions about his demon slaying process and she listened to the exchange watching Michael's expressions. He was beautiful, how could she not be attracted to him? But she wasn't. She could already see him in Josh's role, growing to love him quickly but not in the fireworks, want to take her pants off for him kind of way. Matthias inspired more excitement in her but he didn't seem right either.

Oh Jesus, she thought, *are you really going to look at every vampire as a potential mate and then discard him based on a couple of hours? No more thinking about it*, she decided, *things like that should just happen.* She heard her phone ringing from the deep recesses of her purse and pulled it out.

"Anna?"

"Jess! How are you, I haven't talked to you in forever!"

"I know, I miss you. And my sister. Speaking of which, have you talked to her lately?"

"This morning actually, why what's up?"

"My parents are flipping out. Apparently she messaged them that she was going to France with Aunt Harriet- they thought she was with you this whole time, did you know that? Anyway they messaged her back a bunch of crap and she ignored it then ended up turning off her phone. And I wanted to go with her.

"Wait, what? You want to go with her? What about Nate?"

"He's an idiot who I never want to see again. But that's not why I want to go, I want to meet Aunt Harriet, I want to find out about where we came from. I've been...well, a week ago I went to this party with some girls I met at work. Since Marina moved to Buffalo to live with Macey I've had to make a few new friends, or at least people I can spend time with. Anyway, they wanted to play with a Ouiji board, and you know how I am about that stuff, it scares me. So I just watched, but apparently you don't have to participate for something to happen, you just have to be there." She sounded distraught and Anna could tell she'd begun to cry.

"What happened?"

"I can see them now, the shadow things. I'm afraid to leave the house because I hate seeing them. But I don't want to be with my family because they wouldn't understand, they would think I was crazy or possessed like Aunt Harriet. I would stay at your house, but I'm afraid to be alone. I want my sister and I can't reach her!" Her voice was sky rocketing.

So that's what Harriet had sensed. "Okay, calm down sweetie and listen to me. They cannot hurt you. They cannot touch you. They are only shadows, they have no power unless someone gives it to them. And you can shut them out. It's just like turning a light switch on and off in your head. The next time you see one squeeze your eyes shut and will it away-when you open them again it'll be gone. It might take a few tries but with some effort you can do it, and pretty soon it becomes second nature."

"I know, I heard you talking about that before," she was crying her words coming out garbled, "but I can't help being scared."

"I know babe." Anna paused and thought it over. "Here's what I want you to do. Go to my house. In the upstairs hallway closet on the top shelf way in the back is a box. There's about three thousand dollars in cash, I want you to take it and go to Harriet's. They're leaving in two days, so you have time. It's only about a five or six hour drive for you and I'm sure Jenna will check her messages, so just call and let her know you're on your way."

"I don't know if I can drive there by myself," she sniffled.

"Sweetie it's dark right now, I'm sure you'll feel better about the idea tomorrow morning."

"Yeah, I guess so. Thank you, I'll only use the money I need, I won't...

"Stop right there! You are not to even think twice about the money. I don't care about money I care about you, so use every last cent because I won't accept it back."

"Okay, you don't have to bite off my head," she grumbled.

Anna giggled, "Sorry. Anyway, you're going to France! That's awesome!"

"Well, if they'll let me."

"Of course they will! And guess what? I'm going to England so we can all meet up!"

"You are? To England? When, with who?"

"Soon and with....it's a long story, but they're like me. And they're good."

"Really, you met other vampires? How do you know they're good, remember that Jake guy seemed good...

"Jess, trust me, they're not like Jake."

"Guys or girls?"

It really had been too long since they'd talked. "Males. Four vampires and a werewolf," she giggled as she said the last.

"Uh Uh! A werewolf? You're teasing me."

"You're right. Werewolf is a human term, they're actually called Lyncane."

"Are you serious!?"

"As a heart attack."

"So you're going to England with...wow, are they cute?"

Anna laughed, leave it to Jess. "Cute. Yeah, that would be an understatement. In fact....let me take a few pictures and send them to you."

Anna snuck a bunch of pictures making sure to include them all then hit send.

A minute later Jess was exclaiming loudly in her ear. "Oh my GOD, they're gorgeous! Especially the one sitting alone at the bar, he is sooo hot!"

Anna glanced at Tyros. Figured she would go for him...though actually he *was* Jess's type, she generally went for lankier guys. Anna had never heard her gush over a large framed man. Not that Ty was small by any stretch, he was at least six foot two and though he wasn't overtly buff it was obvious he had a nice firm body, rangier muscles instead of bulky.

"Are all vampires good looking?"

"You know, I'm not sure. All the ones I've seen have been. I guess they have good genetics."

"So which one do you like?"

Anna laughed, "I don't know. I haven't known them long enough to figure that out yet."

"What about Will and Josh, aren't you going to miss them? I heard they were really cute too."

Anna looked at the McClaron's feeling a slight tug in her heart. "Yes, I will definitely miss their cute selves. But I'll keep in touch."

"Okay, well I guess I better go pack. You know what, I feel so much better now! I can't wait to go to France, and I can't wait to see you, and I'll be able to meet your new friends, right?" All evidence of fear and worry had flown from her voice, making Anna smile.

"Of course."

"Yay! I'll call you when I get to my aunt's house."

"You better. I love you."

"Love you too!"

When Anna hung up she realized every vampire in the room could have listened to her conversation if they wanted. It was a very good thing she hadn't elaborated on her thoughts and feelings. She peered around and saw that Tyros was staring at her. So he had listened?

She walked over to him. "Were you eavesdropping?"

"Your friend thinks I'm hot."

"Yup."

"Do you have a picture of her?"

She pulled the saved photos up on her phone and looked for one of Jess. There was a great one of her posing by the lake and she held it out to him. He stared at it for a moment and smiled a little. "She's very pretty."

"I know. All my friends are. In fact my dad used to joke that I must be prejudiced against ugly people since everyone I hang out with is attractive."

"Are you?"

Her brows drew together. "Am I what?"

"Prejudiced against ugly people."

She laughed. "No, of course not. That would make me shallow."

"And you're not shallow?"

She frowned. "You really need to work on your people skills."

"Isn't that what I'm doing? I'm asking you questions, carrying on a conversation. How else does someone work on it?"

"Okay. Fair enough. And no I don't believe I'm shallow. I love people for who they are not for what they look like. My friends just happen to be amazing people who look amazing."

He cocked his head to the side, his dark eyes flashing subtly as if considering. He eyed her neck and said abruptly "Will you let me take your vein?"

Her eyes widened. "Um. I don't know. I've never, well except when I was turned and I was forced to, I've never done that. You guys are the first vampires I've ever met."

Michael appeared over her shoulder looking a little angry. "No, she will not let you take her vein."

"I'm sorry, I wasn't aware you had claimed her."

"I haven't...Tyros you should know that sharing a vein is intimate, not done lightly, especially when you first meet someone." He sounded like someone patiently scolding a child.

"Is it?" Anna asked.

Michael looked at her. "Things have been different for you. I'm aware of you taking from the McClaron's, but in our culture we take from animals and only from the veins of those we're intimate with."

Tyros looked away.

"Come over and sit with us Anna."

"I'm okay Michael, I appreciate your concern, but Tyros and I are working on his people skills."

Tyros looked back at her, his expression unreadable.

"Are you sure?" Michael looked at Tyros warily.

"Absolutely."

He frowned but nodded once and walked away.

"Where were we?" Anna asked.

"Interrupted."

"So how long have you...."

"I'm done working on people skills for today," he shifted his focus away, his long lashes shielding his eyes.

"You're dismissing me?"

"Yes."

She bit her lip and sighed before turning away from him and heading back over to Josh. He was seated in a comfortable chair, leaning back and looking about as tired as she was feeling. His lap looked comfortable and she thought, *Why not, I'll be gone soon*. She climbed onto him and curled up like a cat. He immediately put his arms around her and she noticed she'd drawn a number of eyes but didn't care, she just wanted to be comfortable for one last night.

PART TWO
Chapter Forty-Five

Anna's first few days in England were a highly educational experience.

The first thing she learned was that a female vampire had certain interesting advantages. No one could force a female to give their vein or to have sex. If a male attempted either without permission they would be struck by the most intense pain a being could experience. It started in their head, an acute pain akin to a severe toothache and then if it were related to sex it would travel down the body and center in their groin. If it was related to their vein it would run through their blood. This pain would last for three straight days unless the female released them from it with the words "You are forgiven." Although it wasn't the words that mattered, it was the intent behind them. And if the female was a virgin? A male couldn't attempt it without expressing love-and again it was the intent that mattered, not the words, with one exception. If a vow was made.

The vow of a vampire was iron clad and it could be made about all manner of things. You would start with the words, I vow this to you, or for you, or on behalf of, and then you can put anything in it you wanted, finishing it up with words in the ancient language of the vampire. Montadade Basillade Chrisenade Tahallum. Loosely translated it meant with my heart, my soul and my life, I swear this, and after the words were uttered it would seal the vow.

Some otherworldly force would compel the person who made the vow to keep it, but if for some reason they broke it they would suffer agony similar to the kind experienced for violating females. Anna asked how this worked but wasn't given a precise answer. It just was.

In addition to vows, there were also a vast number of spells, but few knew them in their entirety, at least nowadays. This crew knew one however, a protection spell or ward, and Michael's home was enveloped in it. It had to be performed yearly, but apparently it made it impossible for anyone to come in who was not invited. This particular spell was where the myth that vampires could not enter a place uninvited had come from. At some point along the line, when many vampires had "turned" or "fallen"- the term differed depending on who you were talking to- vampires still true to their purpose invoked this spell to protect their homes from them.

On her second day there they brought her with them to meet Leo, Finn, and Brett, the Faerian hunters who were mutually acquainted with Jack. Leo owned a rare and used bookstore and the crew assembled in a back room to discuss the things that were going on in the world of demons.

Michael and the others filled the hunters in on what they'd discussed with the McClaron's, so basically it was a repeat of the night she'd met them-with one new element-weaponry. She learned that vampires took the fangs of their dead, partially so that humans who came across the bodies would not be aware of what they were looking at, but more importantly because these teeth retained their power to destroy demons.

Ages ago vampires had fashioned all kinds of weapons with their fangs, using them against more physically powerful demons, but also distributing it among the humans who battled with them. Anna told them about the Mistress and the necklace that she wore and they explained that it was "spelled" and that long ago a number of these medallions had been created so that non-Faerians could "see".

At that point Anna began imagining great battles of old, where vampires and humans fought side by side against their common enemy. She loved the idea of that, it connected them all in a way she hadn't known before.

The males didn't currently have any of these weapons, but they'd heard there were still some pieces in the possession of vampires who had turned. Apparently these condemned vamps had made pacts with demons and were holding onto the weapons as a favor. But Matthias thought that for the right price they might be willing to part with them. The problem was they'd also vowed never to give or sell them to other vampires who might use them, which meant that either the Faerian hunters or humans would need to do the bartering. Leo thought they should hire out, but it was tricky. Fallen vampires couldn't be trusted and it would not be known whether the weaponry was authentic until it was tested.

This discussion went on for awhile then turned to the several groups of possessed humans in the area as well as the increasing amounts of demons who were running in packs. It was more and more common in urban areas to see the shadows gathered in groups and not necessarily dogging humans. This was a highly disturbing development, and they debated the reasons without coming up with anything concrete.

After they left the bookstore they took her on a hunt, not for demons but animals. She thought it would be gruesome, but found it was almost beautiful. Their movements were graceful and quick, and the animals didn't appear to suffer. Michael explained that their fangs released a chemical that acted as a calming agent and was even pleasurable...something she already knew of course.

She attempted to drink the blood of a deer but the taste made her gag, so they had her try a number of others but it was always the same, she just couldn't stomach it. In the end they decided she would drink from them instead, taking turns between them so unnatural attachments didn't result.

On the third and fourth days Michael stayed with her while the others went off to other things. She asked him about how her healing powers worked and she learned that when it came to dissipating the effects of demons, it worked fairly quickly and painlessly. Unfortunately it was different for physical injuries. Just as she'd felt that fleeting pain over healing Will's arm, anytime she used it for that she would experience the pain of the one she was healing, even taking on their ailments in a mental way. For instance if she healed someone of cancer she would contract the disease herself for a bit, suffering whatever the individual had suffered. She decided it made sense as it reduced the desire to spend time in hospitals playing God.

She also asked about their names, since she hadn't heard them use a last name, and he'd told her although they did have them they were alien to the human race. In fact their first names were just pseudonyms for their actual names. With the exception of Seth McKellar. She tried to learn more about the Lyncane, but Michael told her she'd need to ask Seth, something she planned to do if the wolf-man ever hung around for more than a few minutes.

On the fifth day they went to another meeting with Leo's group and afterward Michael brought her back to the house, sat her down, and outlined some rules. She was not to go out after sunset or before sunrise. During the day she could only leave the property if she were accompanied. When she was out in the day she couldn't talk to anyone she didn't know, which meant anyone but them or those they knew and deemed okay. He explained in the kindest of tones that she was far too precious and valuable to risk exposure or danger.

A week later she was bored out of her skull since the males, Michael included, were generally gone all night and either slept most of the day or went out—to where she didn't know, but she recalled Matthias telling Will they led fairly separate lives.

She stretched out on the hammock Coderin had brought home to her the day before and tried to call Jenna and Jess for the tenth time that afternoon. Voice mail again. She looked around and sighed. The males had been out all night as usual but at least most other mornings she was useful for a moment as they often needed her healing touch after tangling with demons. She hadn't seen them yet this morning, so at the moment she just felt like someone under house arrest. She understood their concerns, but she hadn't had this much restriction since she was a child and it was driving her batty.

Dad, she thought suddenly, *better check in*. She dialed and it rang several times then went to his voice mail. "Hey dad, just calling to say hello and I love you. Call me when you can." She hung up and sighed.

Jenna and Jess were somewhere in France with their eccentric relations. She'd spoken to them several days ago and they seemed to be having a wonderful time. A visit from them would definitely help with the tedium, but for some reason neither of them had their phones on today.

She decided to call Josh and he answered on the first ring.

"Anna!"

"Hey, what're you doing?"

"Not much, just dragged myself out of bed. Are you loving British life?"

She gritted her teeth. "Mmm, I don't think that I would go as far as love."

"Why, what's up?"

She briefly explained her rules and he chuckled.

"A house full of Jack McClaron's, huh?

"Yup, pretty much. Hey, have you ever heard about vampire weaponry?"

"Yeah, I know a little about it."

Anna launched into a thorough description of the fang powered tools and Josh had her explain it to Will as well.

"Shit, that would be seriously handy to have," Will's voice elevated in excitement, "Do you think they'll get a hold of any, because we could definitely use them over this way."

"I'm not sure what their plans are, I know they talked about it, but to be honest they are keeping me out of the loop. Like your brother said, I live with a house full of Jack McClaron's. They treat me like a little girl. But I will ask them for you."

"Awesome, keep us posted."

"I will."

Josh got back on, "Sorry to cut this short but we have to head out. Call me later?"

"Okay. Love you guys."

"We love you too."

She hung up and thought, Well that wasted a whole fifteen minutes. She looked towards the empty house and was struck again by how large it was. With ten bedrooms, four bathrooms and two large sitting rooms, it was the closest thing to a mansion she'd ever been in. The inner décor was both beautiful tasteful, in fact other than the bathrooms and the kitchen which were newly renovated, most of the house was filled with well maintained antiques making it look like a throwback from another time.

Outdoors there was a massive wraparound porch and the property was immense. The game of hide and seek that could commence there....

Her phone rang. Jenna, finally.

"Sorry Anna, we didn't have our phones with us this morning!"

"Not a problem."

"You called a gazillion times, what's going on, something wrong?"

"A gazillion might be a wee bit of an exaggeration," Anna joked.

"You're not one to call over and over."

"Ech, I know, I'm just bored to tears."

"Still under house arrest?"

"Yup."

"Okay, we're going to head out there tomorrow. We've got your address and Harri says to expect us in the afternoon."

"She's coming? I thought she was staying with..."

"Are you kidding?" Jenna broke in, "Do you actually think she'd pass up a chance to meet a house full of handsome vampires, and a werewolf? Riigght."

Anna giggled, "Gotcha, so I'll see you girls tomorrow?"

"Yup, can't wait!"

"Me either, I'm going nuts!"

Chapter Forty-Six

The following day the girls arrived at four in the afternoon and Anna skipped over to them wrapping them in a big group hug. Michael, Seth, Tyros and Coderin were in one of the sitting rooms and they stood to greet the women when they entered. Anna couldn't help but grin at the looks on her friends' faces as they took in the gorgeous group. Only Matthias was absent, having taken off on a mission to locate weaponry the day before.

After the formalities Anna gave them a tour around the large house and showed them to the rooms they'd be staying in. They settled onto the bed in the room Jess claimed and Jess immediately started gushing over her housemates, especially Tyros.

"They are some fine looking men," Jenna agreed.

"Are you currently interested in any one of them in particular, love?" Harriet asked.

Anna shook her head.

"Hmm, to be on the safe side I'll tumble the wolf, doubtful you'll end up with him."

"Aunt Harriet!" Jess exclaimed, eyes wide.

"What? Honey, I'm not too old for sex, I can assure you."

Jess continued staring wide eyed at her aunt as Anna and Jenna laughed.

"Go for it," Anna said, "I like Seth but there's no chemistry."

Harriet waggled her eyebrows and the girls laughed harder.

"What about Tyros?" Jess asked.

Anna frowned. "I'm not sure that's a good idea, he's...no one really knows anything about him and they're all a little wary. Whenever he's around, Michael tends to hover like he doesn't trust him around me."

"Oh. Well, maybe I can get him to talk to me, tell me about himself."

Anna shook her head and smiled. "Just be careful." She didn't want to say too much since it was more than possible he was listening to them right now.

For the next hour the girls filled her in on their trip to that point, how much they loved Dominique and how amazing Paris was when you were with someone who knew where to shop and eat, and then Anna filled them in on everything she'd learned so far.

When she was finished Jenna eyed her. "So who do you drink from?"

"Well, initially they had me try out animal's blood which is what they drink exclusively, but the taste of it made me gag and they think it might lack something for me, some kind of nourishment I need. So now I alternate between them."

"Even Seth?"

"Yup, his blood tastes different though."

At their raised brows, she elaborated.

"A human's blood tastes like....honey roasted peanuts would be the best comparison, with the salty and the sweet. A vampire's blood is like wine, fruity and flowery. And then there's Seth, his is like a mixture of different spices, hard to describe."

"That is so weird yet somehow cool," Jess commented.

After a few more minutes they decided to go and join the guys. Harriet wasted no time conveying her interest to Seth who assumed the look of a male who would be getting sexed up.

Anna and Jenna wandered outside and walked around the property discussing how much things had changed in the last several months.

"Anna!" Michael called from the doorway, "can I talk to you for a minute?"

"Sure." She started in his direction and Jenna told her she'd wait outside.

She walked inside and Michael shut the door behind her.

"What's up?"

"I'm not sure your friend should be alone with Tyros."

Anna frowned. "I think we should give him the benefit of the doubt. Maybe Jess's conversation will be good for him. Not that I want them locked in a room or something...where are they?"

"They're taking a walk."

"I didn't see them come out."

"They went out the back."

Anna cocked her head to the side and zeroed in on Jess's voice.

"So what's it like to kill demons?" Jess was asking. Anna cringed waiting for the strange and creepy answer he'd given her at the bar.

"You don't want to hear about that, it's disturbing."

Impressive, seemed he was getting better at people skills.

"Okay," Jess said, "then tell me something else about you, what's your life like when you're not slaying demons?"

"Hunting demons is pretty much it."

"Oh come on, there must be something."

"Well, I have sex occasionally, I drink occasionally, I play pool occasionally."

"So basically the same stuff as human guys do."

There was a pause. "I guess so."

Anna looked at Michael who was obviously listening too. "Sounds like they're just talking, nothing worrisome yet."

"All right, I'll just keep an eye on the situation," Michael told her.

He was looking at her in an odd way and she had the feeling he wanted to say something but was holding back. She started to ask him when she heard a scream from the front lawn.

She and Michael bolted out the door to find Matthias had tackled Jenna to the ground and now had a hand at her throat.

"HEY, WHAT ARE YOU DOING?" Anna was yelling as Michael grabbed Matthias's shoulder.

Matthias's eyes were feral, lit with that inner light. He blinked several times as it registered that Anna and Michael were pulling him off the woman. He let go of her and backed away.

"*What the hell Matthias?*" Michael was gaping at him.

"I thought...I thought she was a vampiress." He looked back at Jenna. Anna had her cradled in her lap and was busy healing the bone in her wrist that he'd broken in the tackle, as well as her bruised neck.

Anna had to grit her teeth to keep from crying out. She could feel the injuries, the cracked bones and injured neck as if she were the one it had happened to. And she could feel them mending, not a particularly pleasant sensation either.

"That's Anna's friend Jenna," Michael spoke slowly, looking at him like he'd gone berserk.

Matthias stared at the girl. She had the hair color and nearly the eye color of a vampiress, and when he'd seen her she had reminded him of someone from his past. Someone he despised. Now that he was clear headed he wondered how he could have mistaken her, she didn't smell like a vampire. Although vampires who drank human blood on a regular basis did tend to smell a lot like humans, so it was actually an honest mistake.

"I'm okay," Jenna said, sounding a little dazed as she struggled to her feet. "Wow, broken bones freakin' hurt!"

Anna mentally nodded her agreement. Her wrist throbbed a bit and she absently rubbed her neck.

"But it's healed right?" Matthias asked.

"Well yeah, that's what Anna does after all." Jenna stared at him while she waited for an apology. He was different than the others with piercings on his lip and eyebrow, strange symbols tattooed on his neck and blonde spiky hair making a striking contrast to his tanned skin. He looked like a rock star. An extremely gorgeous one.

He ran a hand up the back of his head and shifted on his feet, then raised his brows in a brief "whoops" kind of way.

"Aren't you going to apologize?" Michael stared hard at Matthias.

"Right, yeah. Sorry about that." He glanced at her briefly before striding into the house.

Jenna watched him go and when the door closed her brows snapped together. "Right, yeah, *sorry about that*? That's all he has to say? He broke my wrist and practically crushed my throat! Not to mention he scared the hell out of me, I thought he was one of the condemned vampires! I mean look at him, he looks like a freak, with his piercings and tattoos! My life flashed before my eyes!"

Anna looked at her friend apologetically. What the hell was wrong with Matthias? She glanced at Michael.

"I'm sorry Jenna, I don't know what's wrong with him, maybe something happened over the last couple of days," Michael looked puzzled and upset.

Jenna frowned. "Fine. But he's an asshole in my book." Inside she was truly shaken. His attack had brought back an old memory, and the fact that he didn't even feel bad? Totally unacceptable.

They went inside and Michael was summoned to a meeting.

***

Anna put a finger to her lips and sat outside the study with Jenna, listening in on the males' conversation.

"The weaponry is basically a dead end, at least here in London," Matthias was saying.

"So no one has any?" Coderin sounded disappointed.

"Yeah, someone does, or at least...okay let me just tell you what happened. I went to a few of the twisted vampire lairs, you know the clubs they own or have claimed. I asked around, talked money, and this one vamp they call Paulo said if anyone had weapons like that it would be Jared. I asked around about him and was told he's not someone to fuck with, definitely didn't need money, and as far as any of them knew his only vices are fucking and fighting in that No Holds Barred underground ring they have. They all seemed wary of him, and that's saying something coming from those evil fuckers. Anyway I tracked him down to a bar called Stoke's. The dude just looks dangerous, he's easily the largest vamp I've ever seen. I was thinking maybe I could get him to gamble his weapons in the ring, so I sat down by him and tried striking up a conversation. He was definitely not what I'd call friendly. At any rate I finally got around to asking about the weapons, if there was any price he would part with them for. He looked at me like I was a bug he wanted to squash and told me in no uncertain terms that if he were to have anything like that there was nothing anyone could offer him that he couldn't get himself. So yeah that was a big fat No."

"Did you suggest the gamble?" Coderin asked.

"I thought better of it. Look I'm no coward, but the guy's built like a brick shit house and he's probably high on human blood, and those kind of guys have no problem with cheating, so all he's gotta do is drain a human before the fight and he's on the vampire version of steroids meets PCP. You know the odd thing is that he looked familiar, like someone I knew from another time but I can't put my finger on it. At any rate the vague association I have with that notion stands right by the one I've got now- bad motherfucker."

"What about finding out where he keeps them and busting in?" Coderin asked hopefully.

He really wanted those weapons, he reminded Anna of a twelve year old boy who desperately wanted a BB gun.

"Yeah, see no one knows where he lives, in fact it's a sore point with the females I guess, that he's never taken any of them to his place. It's like a competition they're having with no winners. And even if we did find out where his place is, pretty damn likely it's protected like ours."

"So I guess we'll tell Leo it's a no go for now. What else we got going on?" Seth was not one to dwell on failures.

Jenna was tugging on Anna's sleeve and she led her friend upstairs. She told her what she'd heard, and as she was relaying it a thought crossed her mind. *I could help*. If women are one of his vices, and vampire women are in short supply....she shook her head. *What am I crazy?* she thought, then right on the heels of that...*but I'm so useless just sitting around here.*

"You know," she told Jenna, "sex with a vampire is supposed to be ten times what it is with a human."

"Who are you thinking of having sex with?" her friend quirked a brow and smiled slyly.

"Hey, where's Harriet?" Tell Jenna her idea? What was she thinking?

"I'm pretty sure she was in that room with them, and nice try but you can't distract me," she said pointedly.

"I wasn't thinking of having sex, just maybe using that fact to get something...."

Jenna looked confused. "Like what?"

Harriet waltzed into the room looking at Anna in a strange way.

Anna looked between the two. "Never mind, it's a really bad idea."

"What is hon?"

"Nothing, I was just....I'd like to help with something you know? I just feel like I'm a burden, and I'm frustrated."

"I think we should all take a drive and Anna can tell us what's on her mind." Harriet suggested.

There was a peculiar glint in her eyes that caused goose bumps to raise on Anna's arms.

"Wait, where's Jess?"

"Don't worry, my niece is doing just fine with the odd one. Last I checked they were huddled on the back porch and seemed quite involved in their conversation."

"A drive, not sure they'll let me do that."

"Oh they will, we'll just say we're going out for ice cream."

Chapter Forty-Seven

Michael grudgingly let her go and Anna felt elated. *Wow, that's all it takes to make me happy now, just let me go for a drive.*

When they were a good distance away Harriet spoke. "Tell us what you were thinking sweetie."

Anna took a deep breath and blew it out. "Okay, you heard everything about the weapons and how they can't get to them, well I was just thinking about what I could do to help."

"Like what?" Jenna raised her brow.

"Like maybe I could...."she frowned and thought it through a little. "Well he said that the females are in competition to find out where Jared lives. And I know that males like to have sex with vampire females when they get a chance. And since no one can take me by force, vein or sex, especially since I'm still a virgin, I was just thinking that maybe I could flirt his location out of him. Get him to take me to his place, let him think that we're going to get it on, then blur out of there and at least they'd know where to find him. Or maybe I'd get lucky and he'd have a weapon or two on display and I could snatch them...."

"Whoa, wait, are you nuts? Talk about flirting with danger, *Matthias* is afraid of this vampire which pretty much says it all. No way." Jenna shook her head.

Anna started to nod and Harriet surprised them both. "I think it's worth a try."

Jenna was having a day of incredulous expressions. "*What?*"

"Women are so underrated, a fact that despite our supposed rights has not changed much over the centuries, and yet there are plenty of women in history who accomplished incredible feats." She looked at Anna appraisingly. "Do you think you can act?"

Anna thought about it. "You mean like a condemned vampiress?"

Harriet nodded.

"I think if I changed my hair and got some contacts and a sexy outfit I could put on a bit of a show. It's not as if he'd suspect, all vampire females have turned as far as everyone knows, and I could just say I've been in America, hanging out in Vegas."

Harriet was nodding. "So no one can take your vein without permission...how does that work exactly, do they have to ask and you say yes or no, or can you say yes and mean no?"

Anna chewed on her lip. "I get what you're saying. I think maybe if he asks and I smile invitingly but inside my head I am saying Hell no....maybe that would work, since it's more than just words."

"I don't get it," Jenna said, "What does that have to do with anything?"

"Remember I told you that if a vamp tries to force a female they will suffer tremendous pain...

"Oh!" she cut in, "I see where this is going, so you get him to take you back to his place, get a little frisky and he goes for your vein and you knock him out with pain. Then you can get the weapons and get out."

"Right! This could work!" Anna was starting to feel a little excited.

"What if he's not interested in your vein, what if he goes straight for sex?" Jenna worried.

"Well, it's the same idea just a little more detailed. Either way I'll knock him out with pain as you said. Then when I get back to Michael's I can release him and change back to my own look, he'd have a hell of a time finding out who I am."

"So when would you do this?"

"Tomorrow night? Then you girls can be my alibi with my overprotective housemates."

"So what we would need to do," Harriet put in, "is say that we're taking you out on the town for the day and into the evening...that you need to get out and let down your hair so to speak. We'll get you a make-over and figure out a place for us to wait as you attempt this."

"I'm surprised you're so supportive of this idea." Anna eyed her, remembering the strange look. "Did you see something?"

"Not exactly. Just a feeling that this is something you need to do."

"Then it's settled."

They decided to get ice cream after all then drove back to the house. Anna warned them not to say a word about it when they got there since the males could eavesdrop the same as she could.

They encountered Jess on the way to their rooms and her eyes had stars in them.

"So, what have you and Tyros been doing?" Anna teased.

"Ty is misunderstood," she began, leading Anna over to the bed by her elbow. "He had a tough life, he told me some things about it in confidence so I can't repeat it to you, but what I can say is that he's a really great guy. Based on the way he grew up his decisions to be a hunter and work on the side of good means he IS good, through and through."

"Oh come on, you can't say something like that and not dish a little," Anna prodded.

"No really, I promised it would stay between us. But I really like him. And I think he likes me too."

Jenna rolled her eyes. "You do realize he's a vampire right? Not a guy you can marry, have kids with and live happily ever after."

"I know that! Why do you always have to be so condescending?"

"Oooh, big word, Jess has been working on her crossword puzzles."

"Sometimes you can be a real bitch!" Jess snapped.

Anna jumped in to neutralize. "Guys, come on, that's enough. There's nothing wrong with Jess making a friend, and don't call her stupid that pisses me off too."

"Whatever. She does always make smart choices, doesn't she?" Jenna's voice dripped sarcasm.

"You know what..."

"No, and I don't care what," Jenna cut Jess off, "I'm going downstairs."

Jenna entered the kitchen scowling. Her sister had a real problem with being attracted to assholes. Nate had turned out to be one just like every other guy she'd ever really liked, and now she was interested in a vampire with a tortured soul. If she was going to pick one of the immortals to mack on, couldn't it be Coderin? He was sweet and still seemed young. Nope, had to go right for the messed up one.

"You know, if you frown like that too often you'll get those disgusting lines in your forehead," Matthias was leaning against the doorframe, arms folded across his chest.

"Oh, you." Jenna turned her back on him and opened the fridge pulling out a can of soda.

"You know that shit will go straight to your ass and thighs, and you definitely don't need it."

Jenna choked on the soda. "Excuse me, did you just call me fat?"

"No, just trying to help you avoid it."

"I know a way you can help me, by removing yourself from my presence. Asshole." She turned her back on him again.

"I think you like my presence."

"You are delusional."

"I saw the way you looked at me when I put you on the ground."

She whirled on him, "Which look, the one where my face was wracked with pain from the wrist you *broke*, or when it was draining of color while you choked me to death?"

"Nope, you didn't even feel the pain for a few seconds, you were so enamored with the male hovering over you."

Jenna laughed exaggeratedly, "Oh my God, you are insane, seriously, even if you hadn't hurt me and failed to show remorse, you are not my type."

Matthias raked his gaze over her slowly, and to her immense displeasure she could feel a blush climbing up her neck.

He smiled lazily, "No, I don't affect you at all, it just got hot in here I suppose."

"You're ogling me, it embarrasses me when anyone does that, idiot."

"You must be embarrassed often."

Jenna narrowed her eyes, "Was that a compliment?"

"You have tits that most guys want to bury their face in and an ass they want to squeeze and bite and slap. It's just a fact."

"Okay, you know what? You're a dick. A sleazy, inconsiderate shithead, and I'm done talking to you." She looked around and realized he was blocking the only exit. Damn it.

He was still looking her over with that smile.

"I would like to leave the kitchen now." she said between clenched teeth.

"What's stopping you?"

"You're in my WAY!"

"I'm afraid I'm comfortable and I don't feel like moving. But I might consider it if you paid a toll."

"A toll, uh huh, right, ANNA!!" She cried.

Anna showed up behind Matthias.

"Hey, is Jenna in there?"

He turned and looked at her over his shoulder. "Yup."

"Uh, she just yelled for me."

"Yup."

"So can I go in?"

"NO!" Jenna cried, "I want out, and he's blocking me."

Anna furrowed her brows. "And *why* are you trapping my friend in the kitchen exactly?"

"No reason. I just feel like standing here."

"Um, can't you just move for a second?"

"Sure, as soon as she pays the toll."

"Which is?"

"Standard. A kiss."

"Hell NO!" Jenna said angrily, "I would not kiss you to save your life you ASSHOLE, let me out!"

"Matthias?" Anna pleaded.

"Sorry Banana, but this is between me and her."

"So you're saying I have to yell for Michael?"

Matthias pinned her with a look that made her shrink backwards. "If you do that, you and I will no longer be friends."

"But...she's my friend and..."

His tone lightened. "I'm not going to hurt her, I just want a kiss, you know the whole kiss and makeup concept? I mean we did have a rough start, what with me causing her pain and bungling the apology."

Anna stared at him. Jenna was ranting in the kitchen saying he still hadn't apologized that he'd just insulted her, but Anna decided that no matter what was going on here he wouldn't hurt her, not again anyway. After another moment of consideration she nodded and left.

Matthias turned back to Jenna with a self-satisfied smirk.

"She did NOT just leave me here."

"I'm pretty sure she's not worried about your safety."

Jenna snorted. Infuriating male, horrible terrible.....He's taking off his shirt. Why is he....*Oh my God, he has the most beautiful chest I have ever seen, I just want to run my hands over the tattoos, what are they anyway, hieroglyphics?* She couldn't stop staring.

"Like what you see huh?"

The smug tone in his voice snapped her out of it. She marched up to him, stood on her tiptoes and kissed him hard enough to hurt. "There, I kissed you, now let me by," she hissed.

He grabbed her chin and brought his mouth to hers, pressing a hand to her back. At first she resisted, keeping her lips pinched together, but then he started tracing a finger down her neck and she shivered and relaxed, letting him fully take her mouth...and then a tickly feeling started in her lower stomach and she panicked. She brought a knee up hard into his groin, managing to startle him into stepping backwards, giving her just enough room to push by him and run for the stairs.

"Low fucking blow!" He yelled behind her.

She knew that even if he had felt pain it was brief being a vampire and all, and then wondered why she would care. She burst into the room where the girls were sitting and pointed a finger at Anna in accusation.

"I'm sorry Jenna, really I am, but I couldn't overpower him and you should have seen how he looked at me when I threatened to rat on him, and I have to live here, I don't need any enemies.....

Jenna held up her hand. "Okay. I forgive you. But him, him I don't forgive, in fact I hate his freakin' guts."

"Did you kiss him?" Jess asked with a big smile.

Anna cringed and Jenna glared at her. "Thanks for filling my sister in. *He* kissed *me*, and it was gross, and I don't want to talk about it ever again, got it?" She stomped over to her suitcase and pulled out some jammies then stomped across the hall to the bathroom slamming the door shut.

"Do you really think it was gross?" Jess asked Anna, looking at the bathroom door.

Anna shook her head smiling a little. Jenna had been deeply flushed, something she had never seen on her face before. Usually that chic would just shoot her middle finger at guys who made perverted remarks or checked her out too openly.

"I think she likes him or she wouldn't be so pissed," Jess stated.

"Shh," Anna admonished, "if she hears you say that, she'll blow a cork."

Jess nodded, grinning.

Anna flopped back on the bed. It was hard for her to dwell on Jenna's feelings when she was feeling all kinds of nervous about her plan. If Harriet hadn't had one of her "feelings" about it, she probably would have chickened out. She sat up and hopped off the bed.

"I'm tired, I'm going to hit the hay," she told Jess and bent down to kiss her on the cheek.

Chapter Forty-Eight

The following day Harriet told Michael and Seth- whose room she had been seen coming out of in the morning by Jess, the resident peeping Tom- that she and her nieces were stealing Anna for the day and into the evening, and that they shouldn't worry, they would keep to well lit places. Michael didn't like it but Seth, who was in a particularly good mood, rallied for them.

"Come on, she needs to get out of the house. Besides she's with a group and no one knows about her, how much trouble can she get in?"

Michael sighed. "Okay, but keep your phones on."

Jess had spent the morning with Tyros and almost bowed out of coming, but Jenna forcefully insisted.

They set out to a salon they'd found on the net and when they were far enough away from the house they filled Jess in on the plan. She was instantly worried and even hearing that Harriet had had a "feeling" didn't alleviate her concern.

"I don't think it's a good idea," she kept repeating.

Jenna rolled her eyes. "Listen Miss Queen of bright ideas, she's doing this, so enough with the broken record."

"Hey, if you were the one just hearing about it, you'd be thinking the same thing."

"Actually you're right," Anna put in, "Jenna was pretty adamantly against it until Harriet intervened." Anna raised a brow at Jenna daring her to disagree.

"Yeah, but since we're all on board with this then Jess can just be quiet and go with the flow."

"So I'm not allowed to have an opinion about anything?"

"Girls, girls, stop." Harriet said from the driver's seat. "Listen to me. I don't know what the outcome will be, I didn't have a vision. It's just when I was walking into the room and I overheard Anna I had this feeling, this fated feeling. You are meant to do this Anna, but I can't promise it will be all candy and roses."

Anna nodded. Good enough.

Once at the salon Anna sat nervously in the chair while they worked in the dye. She was so used to her moonlight hair it felt like she was removing an appendage. Of course it wasn't permanent, in fact the dye the stylist recommended was a sixty day temp job which would start to fade from her roots in a week. She was also having some curls put in for body, and the final touch was a very temporary and non-toxic dye for her eyebrows. When it was finished she stared at herself in the mirror.

"Once I get the contacts we might pass for sisters," she told Jenna.

While they were there she decided to have them apply her make up as well.

After that they picked up her "new eyes". She paid five grand for them because she needed something that blended, a vampire's sight would pick up the edges of a normal contact too easily.

Next was clothing and she tried on one sexy outfit after another, grinning at herself in the mirror while the girls made catcalls. In the end it was Harriet who picked out the most suitable attire and when she stood in front of the mirror she did not know the person looking back at her.

Along with her wavy raven hair and purple eyes, she was wearing dark maroon lipstick, black mascara and liner, and dark purple shadow. Her neck up was shocking enough, but her outfit made the complete package. Snug black leather pants hugged her small bottom and a shimmery purple blouse sculpted her body with a neckline that dipped into her cleavage. She had purchased a push up bra that nearly pressed her boobs right out of her shirt, and last but not least she wore a pair of black leather high heeled shoes.

"Oh my God Anna," Jess was exclaiming, "If I hadn't seen you do this and you passed me on the street? I would not know you. You look really hot!" She pinched Anna's butt and made a kitty noise in her throat.

"I do look pretty sexy, don't I? And I finally got my Batgirl outfit."

Jenna laughed. "Yeah, holy shit!"

She was so amazed by the change in her appearance she had difficulty pulling her gaze from the mirror.

They left the boutique and went to a park that was relatively empty. Now that she had successfully accomplished making herself look the part, it was time for her to work on acting it. Harriet began the instruction, showing her how to walk the walk.

"It's all in the hips," she told her and Anna followed the older woman's movements until the others agreed she had it down.

She worked on her facial expressions next, Jess coaching her on how to give a guy the once-over while keeping her eyes a bit narrow and a half smile on her face. She managed to affect it well enough to appear sexy, and even a little bit evil. She was feeling pretty good about herself until it came time for talking. She could not make herself sound all "badass sexy vampire bitch" without erupting into giggles.

"See, this is why Austin dubbed you the indestructible fairy, how can you possibly pull off bat woman giggling like an adolescent?" Jenna goaded.

But even when she managed to minus the giggles she felt foolish.

"I think the less talking the better," Harriet declared, "You'll take a pack of cigarettes in with you and only speak when you need to. All right, I think we're ready so why don't we go find a place to get some drinks before the "show"."

They chose a club on the brightly lit side of town and Anna ordered up two shots and a beer in hopes of calming her nerves.

"Hey, why doesn't Anna practice on some of the men in here?" Jess suggested.

They decided that wasn't a bad idea and pretty soon she was dancing with one guy after another, all of them vying for her attention and buying her drinks.

She broke free from one of them and beamed at her friends, "I'm not too bad at this!"

"Of course not, why would you be honey, you're gorgeous," Harriet raised an eyebrow.

"Thanks, but normally my appearance does not have men falling over themselves to get to me."

"That's because you don't choose it," Jess told her, "A little makeup and a suggestive smile is all it takes for a pretty girl to attract attention, I should know."

They left the club at ten o'clock and headed for the bar called Stokes with their fingers crossed that he would be there, or someone could direct her to where he was. It would royally suck if all their preparation was for nothing.

When she mentioned that possibility Jenna said, "Not true, all you have to do is change back into normal clothes, wash your face, take out your new eyes and we can just tell your housemates that you wanted to dye your hair for a change of pace. Then we can try again another day."

"True I guess, but the black will make them suspicious, and I'm pretty sure they won't like it."

"Too bad!" Harriet exclaimed. "You are a woman and they are *not* your fathers'. If you want black hair to sister up with Jenna and me, then who are they to nay say?"

"Yeah Anna, they'll have no reason to think anything else."

She nodded. "Okay, so if we don't find him tonight we keep trying, but I really, really hope we do."

Chapter Forty-Nine

They parked down the street from Stokes trying to determine the best place for them to wait when Anna was hit with a sudden inspiration.

"I know I can always blur back to Michael's but...what if I were to take your vein Jenna, that way I could track and blur to you if I needed to?"

Jenna raised her eyebrows and shrugged. "Sure." She moved her head to the side and Anna laughed.

"I'll use your wrist, the neck might be a little weird. Actually this could serve more than one purpose since it's probably not a bad idea for him to smell human blood on me."

Anna took Jenna's wrist and watched her friend's face as she drank. She seemed to be having a pleasant experience judging by the rhythm of her breathing.

"What did it feel like?" Jess asked Jenna when she was finished.

"It felt like I was being tickled by a feather up and down my arms."

"Okay, I'm ready," Anna announced.

"So what do we say, good luck? Or go get 'em tiger?"

"That'll work."

She stepped out of the car feeling pretty good. Her nervousness had melted away with the liquor and the blood. She could do this, she could definitely do this. She was going to kick some ass and take down names.

She walked into the bar keeping her head high and meeting the eyes of everyone she saw. There were a number of male vampires inside as well as a group of human females and she swept her gaze over them.

She started to head towards the counter when she saw *him* and felt like the wind had been knocked out of her, freezing her feet to the floor in the process. *Oh God,* she breathed, staring at the beautiful male. The one who looked like a statue of a Greek warrior god, with eyes the color of ice and shimmering golden hair. *The one who had ripped off Jake's head and thrown it against a wall.* She stood frozen thinking, *please don't let him be Jared*, but she knew that it was. That *this* was the mammoth muscular warrior Matthias did not dare go up against in a fight. She made her feet move and changed direction, heading over to the juke box. She gathered herself, just barely remembering to keep her stance cool and confident. As she flipped through the music she could feel a number of eyes on her back and she started to lose her nerve.

Come on Anna, she coaxed, *they need those weapons.* She could do this for Will and Josh and Jack. *You're not a meek little child anymore you're a strong vampire female.*

She chose a couple of goth rock songs then strode over to the bar and ordered a beer. She purposefully placed herself two stools from the towering male, and if he hadn't noticed her before, he did now. She could feel his eyes all over her, and it was as if he had fingers attached to his gaze. Her body was filling with heat so quickly it nearly made her lose her nerve once more. She steeled herself against the impulse to run and turned to face him instead. She inwardly congratulated herself when she met and held his gaze, allowing a smile to slowly come across her face.

"You must be Jared." She said his name with emphasis. When his eyes narrowed a bit she let her smile grow a touch wider then picked up her beer, making the act of putting her lips on the bottle sensual as she sucked its contents. In her mind she was cheering herself on wildly. She pulled a cigarette from her pack and lit it, taking a drag and letting the smoke slide through her pursed lips. He didn't answer and she had a feeling it was purposeful, meant to unnerve her.

"Not a particularly talkative male are you?" She quirked an eyebrow, taking another drag of her cigarette.

He stared at her a moment longer taking a swallow of his own drink. "Most of those I encounter have nothing of value to say."

Anna tried not to stare. His voice was as beautiful and masculine as the rest of him, like the strum of a guitar and a drum beat blending perfectly. She mulled over how to respond. She could dazzle him with her wit and intelligence....yeah right, or just...."You're right of course, I find words to be exhausting myself. So I'm going to cut to the chase."

He lifted a brow and she felt another shiver course through her.

She pressed on. "I haven't been in London for a very long time, and upon arrival I find you are a subject of interest and competition." She pushed the tip of her cigarette into the ashtray and slid off the bar stool, then walked over and stood in front of him. She decided to wait him out this time.

He was studying her intensely. "Go on." He said finally, his ice blue eyes narrowing.

She tried to think of what to say next but the sharpness of his gaze was muddling her thoughts. She pulled it together and managed, "Hmm. I think I've changed my mind," with a slight tremor. She turned and started to walk away and nearly ran into his massive chest. *How did he move that quick*, she thought nervously. His hands settled on her shoulders, then snaked their way down her arms and back up again. She looked up at him and lifted a brow.

He put a hand under her chin and stared at her hard. "Who are you?"

"Terasa."

"I've never heard of you."

"You wouldn't have. I have kept myself.....apart."

"In America?"

She nodded.

"No one mentioned a female visiting from the States."

"I haven't been here long."

He released her chin and took a step back from her. She had a feeling that a vampire female would not back down so she took a step forward and brazenly placed her hands on his chest. She could feel the muscles rippling under her touch and barely suppressed a shiver.

He caught her wrists and turned her around, shoving her towards the hallway that led to the restrooms. Once they were there he spun her around once more and pinned her against the wall. He put his hands under her ass, lifting her to his middle and her body *exploded* in sexual reaction. When he pressed his mouth to hers she almost forgot who she was and what she was doing there. He was kneading her bottom while rubbing his enormous erection in tight circles against her leather clad crotch and she couldn't think beyond the sensations it was causing. He moved his hand to cup a breast through her blouse and squeezed her nipple with two fingers. The sharp pain shocked her out of her trance.

She pulled back from him. "No," she said shakily. "Not unless you take me to your place."

His brows drew together. "My place?"

She nodded and forced her voice to steady. "That's right. No female has seen where you live and since I'm the new girl I want to make a statement. We go to your place, or I find someone else."

He still had her pressed firmly against him. She ground her hips lightly and he growled deep in his throat and then they were gone. He blurred so fast it felt as if they'd disappeared and then reappeared in front of a small stone cottage.

He still had her legs wrapped around his waist as he carried her through the door and she craned her neck to look around him before he reluctantly set her down.

"My place," he said with a sweep of his arm.

Her heart was beating wildly and she forced herself to calm down and take stock. "His place" would've been very cozy if it wasn't so sparsely furnished, she noted, thinking it did not look like the lair of an evil vampire. In his living room to the left was a fieldstone fireplace, one couch and a large screened T.V. To the right there was a small kitchen and an eating area, one table and one chair. She took note of two closets and walked slowly through the living room, pushing open a door to a large clean bathroom.

She turned to face him and found him watching her, still studying. Her movements? Her reactions? Her heart was thudding against her breastbone, unnerved by the way she'd responded to him. She kept repeating "condemned" in her mind like a mantra. So what if he had looked like suffering the first time she'd seen him, he had not put a stop to the horror, had not tried to help her. He was most certainly in the "turned" vampire's grouping.

You're here to get some weapons. Don't let him confuse you again.

He took a step toward her, then another, his gaze never wavering from her face. His stride made her think of a lion stalking its prey. She concentrated on the thought she was supposed to be projecting: *No, you can't take my vein. No, you can't*...He reached her and her heart sped to an alarming rate. A slow smile spread across his face as he placed a hand on her racing organ and her thoughts stuttered. Pure sex, this male was Pure. Sex.

His arm snaked behind her neck and he grabbed a fistful of hair, then put his hand under her bottom again and lifted. He didn't stop at his waist this time, he brought her up eye level with him so her legs were spread wide, her knees straddling his chest.

And then in a movement so fast it was like a cobra strike, he sank his teeth into her neck. He was *not* knocked to the floor in unimaginable pain, and as soon as he began sucking she could not imagine telling him to stop.

She'd often wondered what it would feel like since she'd never been on the receiving end...and now she knew. Nothing had *ever* felt so good. She could feel an orgasm ripping up through her body and ground against his chest. She cried out as waves of sensation washed through her. The scent of vanilla and honey filled the air, the first time she'd smelled it since she was in heat.

He pulled back and his eyes were glorious. Lit with that inner light the ice was broken into tiny diamonds. He carried her into his bedroom and as he tossed her on the bed she vaguely realized she was in trouble. She wanted him more than anything else in the entire world.

Her body was still trembling from climax, her mind on hiatus as he fell on top of her and ripped her blouse away, snapping her bra in one fluid motion. His hot breath on her nipples was almost enough to make her come again. As he sucked them, first one then the other, her mind fractured completely. He leaned back and tore his own shirt off, and God in Heaven, glorious, incredible, absolutely fucking beautiful did not do his massive body justice.

He smiled slightly as he took in her appreciation, then yanked on her leather pants and slid them off. He stripped his own pants off and.....*That won't fit in me!!* Her mind finally came back and slammed against her brain. Austin had been big. Jared was inhuman. *I can't do this*, she thought, and then realized, *He* can't do this. Without love for her or breaking the virgin clause with a vow, he would be....she felt her legs get pushed backwards and him guiding himself to her slick entrance. He slid up and down and she watched wide eyed as if it were happening to someone else. His fingers caressed then slid in and she gasped. He pulled them out and replaced them with the enormous head of him.

She shouted "NO!" just as he was pressing in, and the next thing she knew he was lying on the floor, his arms wrapped around his legs, howling in pain. She stared at him in shock. She hadn't yelled no for herself. In that instant she hadn't wanted this to happen to him, but it was too late. *I could free him right now and explain*....EXPLAIN WHAT?!

What the hell was *wrong* with her, this was a fallen vampire who could pop her head off her shoulders like a dandelion! She snapped herself out of it and pulled her pants back on. Since her shirt was ruined she had to use his and it flowed around her like an ill made nightgown.

Her mind was going numb yet somehow she managed to continue moving. She looked down at him and the noises pushing through his lips were terrible, causing guilt to gnaw at her stomach. He seemed to focus on her for a moment and fury warred with the agony in his eyes. She was suddenly afraid he might fight through the pain to get at her.

She flipped the light on in his room and pulled open his closet, darting glances behind her to make sure he wasn't getting up. She couldn't reach the top shelf so she blurred to the kitchen for a chair, then came back in and climbed up. There were two leather sacks all the way in the back and she pulled on them. One was weighty, the other flew towards her with the force of her yank.

She reached into the light sack and pulled out what appeared to be leather gloves with fangs exuding from them like claws. *Jackpot,* she thought feeling a little giddy. She shoved them back into the bag and pulled the object out of the heavier sack. It was a bludgeoning weapon, a club with fangs coming out of it like spikes. She shoved it back in and jumped from the chair.

She looked down at his contorted form. She felt guilt sneaking up on her again and shook it off violently. *Preys on humans, drinks them to death.* She turned away from him and headed for the other two closets she'd spotted in the living room.

The first closet was empty but she hit pay dirt in the second. Hanging on a nail just inside the door was a leather sack that contained a battle axe with fangs projecting off the sides and one protruding from the front. She grabbed it and raced out the front door, wanting to get back to Michael's as soon as possible and release him from his pain, condemned vampire or not.

Focusing on Jenna's scent, she blurred.

***

Anna stopped outside of a bar and hid the weapons underneath the enormous shirt, cradling them with one arm. She eyed the sign which stated The Haunt, and peered in the doorway. Should she dim? She'd have to undim for them to see her. Which would be more conspicuous, she wondered, walking in as if she owned the place with a tent for a shirt that did nothing to conceal the bulges beneath it, or appearing out of thin air, even if just for a second?

A second. Every second she wasted was one more second *he* had to suffer. She closed her eyes tightly for a moment, willing away her guilt. *Okay, no dimming, just walk in and let them see you, then walk out again.*

The moment she crossed the threshold she spotted Jenna who jumped to her feet, then turned and went back outside. Seconds later they were with her and she patted the sacks beneath her shirt.

"Got 'em," she grinned.

"Oh my God, you did it! You actually did it!" Jenna was ecstatic.

"That was quick!" Jess stated grinning, "How did you do it so fast?"

"What time is it?"

"You've only been gone an hour," Harriet told her. She was smiling as well.

"Look, we've gotta go now. I left him in a state of horrible pain, and no matter what he is I can't bring myself to let him suffer like that for long."

As soon as they were in the car they began firing questions at her. She opened her mouth to answer and froze, her mouth drying up. *Oh shit*, she thought, *I let him drink from me, he can track me.* Not good. Not good at all.

Jenna grabbed her arm. "What? What is it, you're face just turned white as a ghost!"

She stared at her friend unblinking, then took a breath. "I, oh crap, I screwed up."

"What do you mean, you've got the weapons...

"He drank from me."

"What?!?"

"I thought that's how you put him in his state of pain!" Jenna exclaimed.

She flushed and forced herself to explain. When she was finished she stared at her hands. "I don't know what was wrong with me, it's like my body wasn't connected to mind, in fact my mind wasn't connected....it was like when I went into heat." She finished lamely.

"It's all right honey. You still got the weapons. And Michael's house is protected, he can't get in," Harriet spoke to her in the rearview mirror reassuringly.

She nodded weakly knowing full well her housemates would not be happy.

They pulled in the driveway and as soon as they were safely on the porch she let the others rush inside. She stared out at the night and thought about Jared, remembering vividly his contorting form. *Because of me*, she thought and whispered fervently, "You are forgiven."

An instant later he appeared directly in front of her on the walkway and her heart slammed against her chest. His eyes were shooting off flames, his fangs bared in a snarl, and she watched in numb shock as he lifted his arms in the air with a roar and brought them back down again, shaking the ground beneath her feet.

Coderin burst out on to the porch, took one look at the irate vampire and hauled her inside.

The girls were standing in the middle of the sitting room, their faces pale.

"That was him?" Jess asked fearfully. Another tremor rocked the ground. "How is he doing that?" she squeaked.

Anna shook her head, unable to speak. Her heart was still pounding with fear, and when the house shook once more she nearly dropped to her knees.

"What the hell is going on, why do you look like that?" Coderin demanded, looking her over, lingering on her face. "Who is that, and why is he so fucking piss...what do you have?" He focused on the leather bags she held dangling from her fists and understanding lit his face. "Whoa, you have the weapons? Holy shit!" His boyish face broke into a grin and she smiled shakily in return.

Tyros, who was standing across the room leaning against the wall, spoke up. "Not bad, but you do realize Michael, Matthias, and even Seth are going to be oh, just a little pissed at you for putting yourself in danger, not to mention leading that monstrosity here. And something tells me they won't like your new look much either."

She gave him a pained look. "Thanks, thanks for that, I wasn't already worried or anything."

"Oh come on!" Coderin said to Tyros. "She got the weapons, that kicks ass!" He turned back to her, "Let me see them."

Anna handed them over and he pulled them out one at a time laying them reverently on the coffee table.

Jess went to Tyros and tugged him over to them.

"Hate to break up this little viewing, but shouldn't someone call and warn the others about Senor Scary," he said casually.

Coderin looked up, his worshipful expression transforming into alarm. He whipped out his cell phone and punched in speed dial.

"Michael, you can't come back to the house tonight."

"What? Why, what's going on?"

"Are Seth and Matthias with you?"

"Yeah, they're here. Speak."

"Anna....may have did something." He looked at her with the expression of a brother ratting out his sister and she gave him a small smile of understanding.

"Did what?" Michael's voice flattened out.

"Before you get mad, know that what she did was very brave and pretty kick ass."

"Coderin."

"Well, I don't have the details on how this was accomplished yet, but somehow she is here with three very old, very vampire weapons."

Complete silence for a drumbeat. Then Anna heard Matthias say "How the fuck??" Then Seth, "Uh, why can't we come to the house?"

"Well it seems she may have been followed home...and what followed her may be angry enough to shake the ground outside."

"Put Anna on the phone." Michael's voice was deadly.

He held the phone out for her with an expression of sympathy.

She took it and spoke quickly, "I know you're angry, but I wanted to help."

"*How* did you help, exactly?"

"I got the weapons."

"No, I don't mean *how did you help*," he enunciated the words like he was speaking to a child, "I mean, *how the hell did you do it?*"

She had never heard Michael swear before which definitely didn't bode well, and her explanation wasn't likely to make it better. She looked around the room for help and Harriet held out her hand.

"Hello Michael."

"I want to speak to Anna."

"Anna's a little nervous about explaining."

A pregnant pause. "Then you explain."

"First I want you to know that this is partially my fault. In fact I doubt she would have gone through with her plan if not for me. You see, I overheard her talking about it, and I felt it was something she had to do. And I never doubt my intuition."

Another pause and Anna could feel the animosity in it.

"You still haven't said what she did."

Harriet gave her a reassuring look before continuing. "Her plan didn't go exactly as intended. She meant to coax her way into Jared's house and deny him when he tried to bite her, which in my understanding would have put him out of commission and given her a chance to search his dwelling to lift the items in question. But as it turns out he did drink from her, which is why he is here. However she did accomplish her mission as she was able to get the weapons no one else could acquire. I understand your anger, it was a gamble, but my intuition has never been wrong. Even this vampire being here seems fated somehow, though I can't say why."

There was a full ten seconds of silence this time before Michael responded. "We'll be there in the morning." The phone went dead.

Anna looked at the floor.

"Don't worry, they'll get over it. I definitely think it was brave," Coderin smiled reassuringly and she smiled gratefully back.

They didn't feel any more tremors, but none of them were particularly interested in going out on the porch to look around. They settled in the sitting room with some music and beer and Anna spent the hours until she went to bed worrying about what the following day would bring.

Chapter Fifty

Jared prowled around the perimeter of the house seething with rage. He couldn't decide who he was more furious with-*that bitch* who had tricked him and caused him more pain than he'd experienced in seven centuries of life, or himself for not being more *fucking careful*. He had given his cock the reigns and the consequences had been...indescribably horrific.

Who in the fuck was she? He'd never heard of her, not one word uttered about a vampiress holed up in America. As far as he and everyone else he'd ever encountered knew, the only females were on this continent. And the male who had hauled her inside was also unfamiliar. From America as well?

His mind went back to his recent agony and his hand went to his crotch reflexively. He had never experienced anything remotely like it. In his seven hundred years of life, he had never touched a female who didn't want him. Which was immensely fucking puzzling since she *had* fucking wanted him! She'd been soaking wet when he'd touched her and he had smelled her arousal. She'd cried out "NO" just as he was attempting to enter, but that was *bullshit*. It didn't work that way, they had to mean it in the fiber of their being, not just say the fucking word!

There was one thing he knew for certain, he would never again touch another female without first eliciting a vow from them. He frowned slightly, wondering why she hadn't made him suffer out the full three days. Did she think he would show her mercy for that? If that were the case, she had made a terrible mistake. His hands clenched into fists, trembling with the desire to strangle her. *I am going to squeeze her fucking throat until it shatters and then put a knife through her black fucking heart.*

He thought about the pierced up vamp who'd come to ask him about his weapons and knew he must be linked to her. Another death he would mete out. Maybe he was her lover. Good, he would kill her in front of the fuck first. He continued prowling around the house as if he could find an entrance. The estate was well protected, and considerately so, it actually warned someone first before it shocked them to their knees. Right at the porch steps he'd heard a shrill buzzing in his ears to alert him that he was about to be fried. He had not bothered with that at his own place, no one came to visit him anyway and if someone did they would not be welcome. They would find that out in a big hurry, no warning first.

After a while his fury died down a bit and he made himself comfortable in a group of trees where he could monitor both the front and back entrances. He concentrated for a moment and felt himself dim.

This was not the dimming they used for humans, that version didn't even require effort. This was his own special brand which he'd dubbed deep dimming. No beings on earth could sense him in this state. Unfortunately it only lasted up to seventy-two hours and then it would be three days before he could use it again. But he didn't think it would take seventy-two hours to get at them. Sooner or later they would cautiously leave, and not sensing him they would think they were safe. He would wait through the day as well, since he couldn't be sure that all of the vampires dwelling within would be unable to go out in sunlight.

He stared at the house and after a couple of hours without any signs of movement his thoughts drifted.

Following each hyberstasis he had eventually run into someone from his past. Many had tried to coax him back into the fight, but he had always declined. As time passed he found fewer and fewer of those he recognized. Some had turned, though no one he'd ever been close to. And some had disappeared like him, dead or living he couldn't say. Most had been killed by either a human mob or other vampires who had turned. He'd heard the stories of the females who had hunted down and killed every last member of their sex who refused to turn and knew his association with them should make him feel shame. He thought perhaps his pain tonight had been a punishment for that association but it didn't matter, it was *nothing* compared to the punishment he would deliver.

The last time he'd been close to as furious as he was at the moment he'd killed the half-turned shit in the gaming dungeon-and he'd taken care of that problem in much the same way he would take care of this one. He stared at the house once more, wishing someone would grow a pair.

Come out, come out, where ever you are.

***

Shortly after sunrise a car pulled up the driveway and he sat up, fully alert.

It parked in front of the porch and two male vampires, the pierced one among them, and a Lyncane climbed out. A Lyncane, *what the hell*? He'd heard rumors that they were extinct or at the very least had settled in the far reaches of the earth. And they certainly were no longer friends of the vampire, hadn't been in centuries.

The trio ran up the porch steps and disappeared into the house leaving Jared to sit there puzzling. So there were at least two vampires who could be out in the sun and they were buddies with a wolf. What was going on here? Suddenly he was not certain of anything.

***

Inside the house Michael had taken on the posture of a very angry father. Anna was prepared for this reaction as all the males in her life did this to her at one time or another.

"I don't care if Harriet had a *feeling,* it was a reckless and *foolish* thing to do. Do you even understand what that male could have done to you? Do you think he couldn't have raped you? He could have tortured a vow from you that would have given him your body, you are just lucky he was taken off guard!"

Anna sighed. "I know. I'm sorry."

Michael shook his head. "And now he can track you where ever you go for the next week, which means you can't leave this house for any reason."

"Except during the day...

"No, not at all. We don't know for certain he's fully turned and even if he is he could have one of those half-turned assholes lying in wait. Which means we're going to have to find another place to stay after the week is up." Michael swept his eyes around the room and Anna suddenly felt terrible. They would have to move? He would have to leave his home because of her?

"I'm so sorry Michael," she said and this time really meant it. "I don't know what else to say."

He looked at her and sighed. "Well, I guess we should take a look at what we've traded our living arrangements for."

Coderin leapt to his feet and swept his arm to indicate the weapons on the table.

Matthias picked up the battle axe and unsheathed it completely. "My God, this is ancient. I fought with one like this in the only real battle I was ever in. You know I thought he looked familiar, I would be willing to bet this was his or a relative's at least. God it's a shame he defected if he fought with weapons like these....." Matthias shook his head and passed the axe to Seth.

"I was wondering if we could send one to the McClarons'," Anna asked.

"Yes, of course," Michael said.

Matthias was looking at her oddly. She had removed her contacts and her hair was tied up with a bandanna wrapped around it, but a black lock had escaped the confines of the material.

"So you disguised yourself at least, huh?" Matthias stated.

She nodded, and Jess jumped in to describe what she'd looked like.

"Well at least she shouldn't be recognized once we manage to get ourselves situated somewhere else," Seth said.

"Take your hair down, I want to see it," Matthias ordered.

She did as he asked.

"That's a terrible look for you." Matthias said wrinkling his nose.

"You're such an asshole," Jenna said from across the room and he winked at her in reply. She snorted and looked away.

"It will start to fade next week and be gone in two months so I won't have to live with it forever," Anna said defensively.

"Actually honey, you could get rid of it sooner if you wanted, there's a shampoo sold at shops like mine that pulls the dye from your hair," Harriet told her.

"Oh good, I'll have to pick that up when I get off house arrest," she replied. She saw Michael frown and felt instantly guilty. "I didn't mean anything by that," she said quickly, "you're the one who really has to suffer for my actions."

He was looking at her with the fatherly expression again. "It's alright Anna, you wanted to help and you did, we have the weapons. I berated you for things that might have happened, but the simple fact is your safe and maybe all of us will enjoy a change of scenery."

He was such a nice vampire, why couldn't she go wild for him? That made her think of the night before and she slammed the mental door quickly. Last night she'd absolutely refused to think about it, and she wasn't going to start now.

She smiled at Michael, then on impulse crossed the room and kissed him on the cheek. He blushed. It was so cute she had the urge to pinch the cheek she'd kissed.

"Are you blushing Michael Angel-O?" Matthias laughed loudly, "Christ you need to get laid."

Michael turned away and Anna was embarrassed for him. She gave Matthias a scathing look and Jenna expounded. "Way to go Matthias, I knew you were a kick your friends in the balls kind of guy." She shot him a disgusted look and to Anna's surprise Matthias actually appeared regretful. Mildly, but it was there.

Anna looked away and noticed that Tyros and Jess had gone missing again. She was becoming increasingly curious about them and the things they talked about. Or were they talking? Anna worried a little about that one, Jess was not known to be a "no" kind of girl. Then again, what did it hurt if they were messing around? Well, besides the fact that if there was genuine affection it would only end in heartbreak.

She watched as Harriet and Seth left the room and felt a laugh bubble up. For some reason the idea of Aunt Harriet sleeping with the wolf struck her as hilarious, meanwhile Jenna was still throwing castrating looks Matthias's way. There was definitely something up there too.

Anna wandered out of the room thinking of ways to keep busy for the next seven days. She wasn't sure how long her friends would be staying, but she had a feeling Michael would insist they stay until that time was up. In effect she had put them all on house arrest.

His face, eyes incandescent with fury blinked into her mind, and she shivered. She had no doubt that if he had been able to get to her she would no longer be living. She wondered if he would continue coming back every night just waiting for the opportunity to get his hands on her. She shivered again, but there was something other than fear in that shiver, something she had to once again shut the door on.

The males left before the sun went down, not wanting to be accosted by Jared even grouped up. The girls had strict instructions not to set one foot in the yard, as if they needed them. None of them, including her, wanted anything whatsoever to do with the ground shaker. They ended up pulling out a monopoly board and wasting away the hours battling over real estate.

***

Jared watched as the males filed out. Piercings, wolf, the dark haired one, the boyish looking blonde who'd yanked her inside and one other...he blinked as another face from long ago teased the edges of his consciousness before fading away. He shook his head to clear it and took stock. Four vampires and a wolf, all out in daylight. They climbed into the SUV and because of the wolf Jared couldn't make the assumption they didn't possess the power to blur. Lyncane could only move that fast in their wolf form, so they might just be driving for his sake.

He was torn between following them and waiting to see if the female would emerge. He had a feeling she wouldn't, certainly not in daylight. No matter what was going on, *there was no fucking way* she was an unturned female, that little fact would not have escaped an entire population of vampires. But even when the sun went down, he was sure she wouldn't dare risk his fury.

He decided to follow the males. He kept pace with the vehicle, and listened in.

"Leo's going to wig the fuck out when he sees these," piercing was saying.

Jared saw that "these" were his weapons and nearly overturned the SUV in the middle of the highway. Unfortunately it was light out and there were humans everywhere. At least he would be able to keep track of where his things were going.

"I think Finn will be the most excited, he's an ancient weaponry connoisseur. And these are beautiful." The boyish one was lovingly stroking the handle of his battle axe. Jared envisioned sinking it into the little shit's skull.

"They are fine weapons, well made. I can understand why the bastard would be pissed. Especially if they were originally his or he inherited them." This from the wolf. Wise assessment, unwise reference.

"Nah, he probably stole them himself," boyish one stated. Battle axe. In the skull.

"It doesn't make a difference whether they were his or whether they're stolen. They're doing no good stored in a closet. Our guys can use them for the benefit of all."

Jared faltered, dropping behind the vehicle. Benefit of all? They couldn't be hunters. *Of course they could be*, his mind whispered, *and you've known it since you saw them this morning*.

Doesn't make a difference, he thought borrowing the arrogant prick's words, *they stole from me*. Machiavellian ends justify the means bullshit did not wash with him, *especially* if they were hunters.

They pulled up to a curb in front of a rare and used book store and filed out looking around themselves carefully. Satisfied there was nothing to harm them they ushered inside. Jared made to follow and a siren screech sounded in his head.

They had the place protected. *FUCK*. He wouldn't even be able to *hear* what was going on. So much for learning anything concrete. He blurred back to the house to wait them out.

Chapter Fifty-One

At the bookstore Leo and Finn were fawning over the weapons.

"Finally, we can take them down when it does the most good!" Finn was handling the axe with adoration.

"We promised to send one to Jack, so you'll have to choose between the axe and the club."

"Oh, we'll take the axe. We get the claws too?" At Michael's nod, Leo slipped his hands in them.

"So where's your brother? We haven't seen him around lately." Seth inquired.

"Brett is somewhere in Siberia tracking down a lead. He's been very mysterious about it."

"Well, I hope he finds what he's looking for, I'm sure it can only benefit."

"Yeah, if he's not wasting his time. Tonight we plan on taking down a couple of possessed SOB's. They've been making routine visits to an abandoned warehouse. Interested?"

Michael raised an eyebrow. "Need our help?"

"Nah, just figured I'd ask in case you were looking for something to do."

"Maybe. We'll call if we decide to. And of course call us if you need to."

"Why don't we go shoot a few games, we've got time to kill," Finn suggested.

"Sounds good!" Matthias clapped his hands together, "Prepare to be taken down."

They left the store and headed downtown to a bar.

***

Later that night the males were tracking a few demons when Michael's phone went off.

"Leo?"

"Shit Michael, something strange is going down here. We're outside of the warehouse and there's a whole troop of demons on the roof, and a number of human demons as well."

"Give us the location, we're on our way."

Leo rattled it off and they blurred, Michael taking Seth with him, and found themselves on the outskirts of a bad neighborhood on an abandoned street.

They located the two hunters standing in the shadows of a building. They gestured towards the roof of the warehouse opposite.

"Holy hell, there's at least two dozen of them up there," Seth bared his teeth in preparation.

They advised Leo and Finn to stay out of this one since they hadn't had time to train with their new weapons and then leapt up to the roof and were on the demons before they knew what hit them. It went well at first but after the initial surprise the demons started fighting back, and along with stronger mental abilities this new breed could fight physically.

They were still holding their own when Coderin shouted and pointed at the sky. They looked up in unison and it was as if there was a rip in the fabric of the world. A small army of demons rained down from it.

Chapter Fifty-Two

Anna was just putting up another hotel on their ongoing monopoly game when she was jolted by a feeling of dread. At first she thought that she was sensing Jared outside, but then Michael's face flashed before her eyes. *What the*...she felt pain and realized she'd drank from him today. She jolted to her feet, her eyes wild.

"Anna? What's wrong?"

"Michael, he's in trouble, he's hurt!"

"You can sense that?"

She nodded frantically. "I have to go!"

"No!" Jenna jumped to her feet, "you can't, that psycho is out there, and besides if Michael's hurt...

But Anna didn't hear her, she ran out the door and leapt from the porch blurring the instant her feet hit the walkway.

She found herself on a deserted street looking up at the roof of a building. She couldn't quite make her eyes understand what she was seeing. It looked like a battle was raging and there were shadow men everywhere. She leapt up to a corner of the building where there wasn't any action and saw Coderin and Michael lying still.

Tyros and Matthias were fighting back to back, ripping and tearing the things apart, but despite the frequency of their blows and the ferocity on their fanged countenances they seemed to be getting weaker. She looked around for Seth, anxiety shortening her breath. She spotted him in wolf form, bleeding from several gashes. In fact they were all bleeding. She had to do something, but what? She saw a horrific demon, unlike anything she'd seen before looming over Michael and leapt for it.

"Anna, NO!" Matthias was fighting his way over to them while she tore at the demon in a frenzy. She could feel it trying to get inside her mind, but this time she was prepared and walled it. Just when she thought she was getting the better of it, another one slammed into her, yanking her off.

She felt something oozing from her and then her mind was being ripped at...

Someone grabbed her forearm and pulled her from the demon, leaping from the roof onto the sidewalk below. She was dropped on the cement and found herself looking up into bewildered ice blue eyes.

"Why did you jump in the fight, what could possibly be in it for you?" Jared demanded. As he glared down at her his eyes flickered in surprised confusion. Instead of violet, he was staring into turquoise eyes ringed with gold.

Anna stared up at the behemoth, mouth working, no words coming. Her mind was still pushing away the darkness that had crept in. She looked back at the roof and found her voice, "Help them, please help them, please..." she started to get up and he shoved her back down.

She stared up at him and made a rash decision, the words coming out in a rush. "If you help them, I vow to let you use my body however you see fit," she paused, trying to remember the words. "Montadade Basillade Chrisenade Tahallum!"

He gazed down at her, a war raging in his features. He probably feels the demons are just doing the job for him, Anna thought miserably. Why would a condemned vampire even be tempted to help, when he could just bring her home and torture her into submission.....but then he leapt.

She stared after him in surprise and then leapt up too, crouching down in a corner out of the way. She watched in amazement while he diced up the demons as if they were nothing more than the shadows they appeared to be. He ripped apart one right after another, and when several teamed up and jumped him, he shook them off like ants, then turned and ripped them apart as well. Matthias, who was still battling, kept glancing at him with an expression of recognition and awe.

The demons began to retreat. They were backing off and staring at Jared, distorted features full of fear and hate. He said something in a language Anna didn't know, and they took off in a flurry.

She rushed forward with the intention of healing her friends but he caught her, and in a blink they were plunging into his house. Inside his bedroom he spun her to face him and his eyes were once more incandescent, but this time there was black in their depths as well. *After effects of the demon attack*, she acknowledged.

"You have to take me back, I have to help them…" she was cut off by a stinging slap to her face.

His voice sounded alien and demonic as he spoke through clenched teeth. "*Open your mouth again and I will Shatter. Your. Jaw.*"

She bit down on her lip and reached out to touch him, intending to heal the damage the demons had wrought, but he grabbed her wrists before she could and spun her around roughly. Her shins slammed into the bed frame and he bent her over the edge of the mattress, using his free hand to rip her pants down.

She had a moment to think of the irony that the nearly unrape-able was about to be raped before his massive shaft slapped down against the cleft of her ass causing her stomach to clench with fear.

He leaned forward and snarled into her ear, "*Hands out in front of you.*"

She obeyed, her heart tripping like a frightened sparrow. Gooseflesh broke out all over her as he ripped away the remainder of her clothing exposing her skin to the cool air. He covered her breasts with his large palms and something inside of her shifted in response. She had the crazy thought that whatever it was, it was irrevocable.

The warmth from his hands as he massaged her flesh soothed the tension knotting her stomach and she was glad he was behind her. From this position she could pretend there was warmth in his expression as well.

This is not how it's supposed to be, she thought as an image of Austin's gentle face blazed into her consciousness. Tears stung the back of her lids and she blinked them away. *Ante up*, she shouted internally, *you brought this on yourself*!

His palm slid down her belly and cupped her sex, large fingers sifting, and suddenly the fear gave way to something else. As his probing found her entrance she gasped.

Why does he make me respond like this? She wondered in confusion. His continued exploration heightened her sensations until her body *ached* for him, filling with a craving so intense she was suddenly on the verge of begging him to relieve it.

He hissed something in her ear and lifted off her, using his knees to spread her wide. She pressed her forehead down into the blankets, bracing for penetration. The enormous head of him began nudging into her and her breath came out in little panicky bursts.

A guttural sound burst from him and with one powerful thrust he tore through her barrier. She cried out into the rumpled blanket and there was the briefest of pauses before he pulled out only to plunge in deeper.

Oh my Goddd, she thought incoherently, *how can something hurt so much but feel so good at the same time?* The strange feeling of craving soared higher with each brutal thrust and she strained backwards towards him, searching for release.

He growled again dropping down on his forearms, and pinned her arms against her head. The feel of his warm breath by her ear caused a tingling sensation to travel down her neck and mewling sounds broke free of her mouth. His rhythm increased in tempo, his pelvis slamming faster and harder against her bottom and when he sank his fangs into her neck she came so hard a cry tore from her throat and tears sprung to her eyes. Her inner muscles contracted violently and she felt his legs shuddering against her.

When she stopped twitching he flipped her over onto her back and pushed her knees backward, spreading her wide. His eyes were flashing, his full lips curved in a soundless snarl as he pressed into her. He slid a hand under her head and gripped her hair then proceeded to fuck her so hard she feared the bed would break apart beneath her. Waves of pleasure crashed through her as he continued the assault, centering in her bottom and spreading down her thighs to her toes. She reached up and gripped his shoulders as he rode, hanging on for dear life.

Something in his eyes began to change as she pulled the darkness from them, and he made a strangled sound as he continued to thrust. He took her mouth with his and she felt him grow even larger and knew he was about to come.

His eyes registered a shocked disbelief just before his release. His neck strained backwards with the force of it and he roared at the ceiling, the pulsing of him sending her over the edge once more with a startled cry.

When he was finished he stood there breathing heavily, his eyes wild and unfocused. She felt something compress inside of her as she stared up at his heaving body. He was so devastating to her senses she found it difficult to breathe. *He's so impossibly beautiful*, she thought as she took in his broad form, every inch rippling with muscle. Even her imagination could not have conjured up a male so perfect. She could barely bring herself to focus on his face. *Fallen Angel*, she thought, but even that description fell short somehow.

He finally met her eyes and began slowly shaking his head as if in denial. He pulled out of her and backed up a few steps, continuing to stare at her as if he'd just woken from a vastly disturbing dream. He blinked rapidly and gave his head one last hard shake, then turned and strode from the room.

She lay there a few minutes longer, trying to get her bearings. Her world had just been thoroughly turned inside out. Shouldn't have been a new feeling, but this was. Shakily she pulled herself up and leaned over the side of the bed. She managed to salvage her pants enough for a return trip home but her shirt was once again demolished.

She swung her legs over the side of the bed and dropped to the floor spotting another shirt of his in the corner. She picked it up and slipped it over her head breathing in a scent she couldn't identify though it was somehow familiar. Like the forest in winter. *His scent*, she thought, her throat constricting for reasons she couldn't explain.

She had thrown his other shirt away but had a feeling this one would end up under her pillow. She felt hysterical laughter bubbling up and shoved it back down, but that made the tears come. She clamped her sliding emotions as tightly as possible and stood in the middle of the hard wood floor wondering where he'd gone.

She stretched out her senses and listened intently but was greeted by silence. *Too quiet*, she thought, *unnaturally so*. *No, not unnatural*, she realized with a sudden chill, *instinctual.* Like the world was holding its breath so it wouldn't attract the attention of an enraged and dangerous predator.

She walked slowly through the house then proceeded outside and looked around. He was gone. She stood in the middle of his lawn trying to decide what to do then an image of her injured male friends filled her mind. She darted one last look at his house and blurred home.

***

She burst through the door and Jenna greeted her frantically, pulling her into a desperate hug. "Oh my God, we didn't know...

"Where are they, are they here, are they okay?" Anna cut in, her voice climbing.

Jenna took her arm and led her into the living room where Matthias and Seth were trying to coax Michael and Coderin out of their coma like states. Tyros was seated in a corner and he tracked her movements with eyes flashing like emergency flares. Jess was kneeling beside him rubbing his neck. Anna rushed over and placed her hands on Michael and Coderin, focusing all of her concentration on the task. She could feel terror and madness and she focused harder, stripping it away from them like mental mummy wrap.

The two males began making whimpering noises and she felt a surge of relief, hers or theirs she wasn't sure. And then they were back.

Michael sat up first, Coderin shortly after. Their eyes were wide, but awareness was seeping in. She closed her eyes tightly for a moment letting the horror of what they felt flow through and out of her. Her stomach was clenching and she willed herself not to lose its contents.

Finally their breathing became normal. "Okay, I'm okay," Michael said, and Coderin nodded weakly.

She noticed Matthias was looking at her strangely and then Michael focused on her and his eyes widened.

"He mated with you," came his incredulous whisper.

Anna's brows shot up, "What? What do you mean?"

"His scent is pouring off you," Matthias answered.

Anna shook her head in disbelief. Mated? They must just be talking about sex because they couldn't mean that he'd claimed her as his one and only. But then she recalled the shocked look on his face and suddenly knew what it had been about. "I thought the mating bond was a choice," she gasped out.

"It is," Michael gritted, his eyes flashing with anger.

But Matthias shook his head "No...," he said slowly, "not always. It's very rare but occasionally it's a compulsion. I've heard of males who didn't realize it would happen until the moment before release. Supposedly that indicates a soul mate, stronger than any other bond."

Anna shook her head firmly, "No, that can't be true."

"Don't worry Anna," Michael said through clenched teeth, "he meant to do it."

Her brows drew in.

"If he's bonded with you he can track you where ever you go. Protection wards won't work, he can come right into this house, on top of which he can take your body whenever he wants, no permission required. *That bastard!*" Michael's hands clenched into fists.

Matthias held up a hand. "You're getting ahead of yourself Michael," he stated and Seth nodded agreement.

Michael turned to him, eyes narrowing. "What do you mean?"

"If it wasn't for him we might not be here right now. I was losing steam and there were still too many, I wouldn't have lasted much longer."

Once again Seth nodded, this time adding, "I've never seen anyone fight like he did."

Michael's expression changed to confusion. He'd been out since before Jared had arrived so he hadn't known the male had fought with them.

But Anna couldn't let them think he'd done it out of the kindness of his heart.

"He only helped you because I vowed to give him my body if he did," she said quietly.

They all turned to her.

Michael's fists clenched again. "That *motherfucker*!"

Michael had just said motherfucker, this night kept getting more twisted.

"Hold on," Matthias held up a hand once more, "What exactly happened Anna? You jumped on top of the demon attacking Michael..."

"She did *what*?"

"...and then you were thrown to the ground and the next thing I know you were yanked up and off the roof by Jared, and a couple minutes later he was tearing demon ass apart. They were afraid of him and started retreating, then he shouted something in the old language and they scattered. I saw you running towards us and he yanked you up in mid-stride and disappeared."

She bit her lip. "When he pulled me off the roof the first time he demanded to know why I was helping, what was in it for me. I couldn't speak at first then I begged him to help you and tried to get up but he threw me back down. That's when I gave him the vow. I didn't think he'd go for it, but he leapt up, and the rest you saw."

"And he took you back to his place?"

She nodded.

Jenna, Jess, and Harriet had been quiet throughout the entire exchange, but at this point Jenna burst in, "Did he hurt you?"

Anna looked at her. How to answer that? "He....no. I responded." She felt her face heat and looked away. "Then at the end right before he, you know, he looked startled, and then afterward he looked like someone who'd just had a vision of his own death. Then he left." She felt tears welling again and stamped them down.

They were all silent for a moment. "I don't think he's fallen," Matthias said finally. Anna looked at him in surprise.

"I don't think a fallen vampire would have been compelled to help us for any reason. He could have just taken Anna and tortured a vow from her."

Her thoughts exactly.

"I'm not even sure it's possible for a fallen vamp to bond," he added.

Michael looked away.

"And there's one other thing. He is LeJariende'Dachielle."

Even Tyros looked up at that.

"What? How do you know?" Michael asked, his voice thick.

"Because when I was a child he visited the village I lived in with my aunt. He was courting a female there, the blonde and blue eyed healer variety. From what I remember she was a sweet soul. Then one day a mob of humans led by a demon possessed man burned our village to the ground. LeJarien came in like a violent storm, saving me and my aunt and some of the others, but it was too late for his female. He killed every last human in the mob. Then I heard not too many years later his mother was killed by humans as well, which in turn ended his father's life. He disappeared after that, some thought he was killed, while others thought that he'd turned because of his hatred for humans. But a male like that doesn't turn. And a turned male doesn't save others without serious gain for themselves. Which is why he wanted to know what was in it for Anna, because he assumes she turned. And why wouldn't he? There are no unturned females left as everyone knows, on top of which she dressed herself up like a member of the damned, tricked him, put him in the kind of intense pain only hell can match, and stole his belongings."

Anna shrank from his words. Put like that it seemed she was the bad guy in the situation. Was she?

"Hey, easy," Seth said sharply. "Anna had no way of knowing who he was let alone any of those other things. She's only a child, she was just trying to help. If we were certain the male was fallen we wouldn't feel any remorse over his pain or loss of belongings, and she was definitely under that impression."

Anna appreciated the defense, but she couldn't help thinking there was truth to what Matthias said.

"Why do you all know his name?" she asked quietly.

Matthias turned to her, his expression still accusing. "He's only one of the greatest warriors of all time.

Arguably the greatest warrior since vampires began to breed."

Anna sucked in a breath and glanced at Jenna who was looking at Matthias very strangely. Stricken.

"Jenna, what is it?"

She looked at Anna and shook her head forcefully, looking down at the floor.

Anna looked back at Matthias and said quietly, "You're right to view me that way. What I did was thoughtless, I should have considered he might not be a member of the damned. If I had, I would never have put him through that, or taken what was rightfully his. Even if he was turned, I'm not so sure what I did could be completely justified."

His face softened a bit and he nodded at her. "So he just left you in his house alone?"

She nodded weakly.

He seemed to be considering the entire situation.

Michael took the opportunity to speak. "Okay Matthias, I don't want to fight with you on this, the male is clearly and understandably a hero of yours, but you speak as if you know these things as fact. And although evidence suggests he's not turned, other than a very old memory you aren't certain of who he is. Nothing is certain yet, it remains to be seen."

Matthias looked like he was going to argue but thought better of it.

Anna's phone rang from the depths of her bag on the table and she stared at it for a moment before digging in and pulling it out.

Dad! Damn, she hadn't made her weekly call...."Hello?"

"Hi...honey. I haven't heard from you, so I got a little worried."

She stared down at the floor. His voice made her want to cry again so she bit her lip. "I'm sorry dad, I've just been so busy the time flew."

"No, it's okay, it's not as if I couldn't call you, which I did. So everything's fine?"

Emotion welled up in her, fine wasn't quite the word. "Yeah it's..." her voice broke a little.

"What's wrong?" his voice filled with alarm.

She forced herself to laugh. "No, no, I just stubbed my toe, ouch that hurt! Really everything's good."

"Okay. So how are your musician friends?"

God, she hadn't even told him she'd left the country again. "They're great, having a blast. Jenna and Jess joined me too."

"Oh good! That's good, I'm glad to hear that. Well, I'll let you get back to your friends. Tell them I said hello. I love you."

"I love you too." She swallowed thickly as she hung up. She realized the room was silent and when she glanced up all of the males were looking at her with varying degrees of sympathy and sadness.

Matthias cleared his throat. "I never even thought about the fact that your family is still living."

"Just my dad, I'm an only child and my mom died several years ago." She'd told Michael her history but she hadn't spent much time with the others.

"I'm sorry," he said, and the others murmured the same.

She managed a smile. "I'm okay. Really. I just...my dad makes me feel...," she trailed off and they seemed to understand.

"Why don't we all get some much needed sleep," Seth suggested. "Then I think tomorrow we should relax for a day."

They headed for their rooms and Jenna asked Anna if she wanted to talk, but she shook her head. She needed to sort through her feelings alone first.

It took her a long time to find sleep, her mind going over and over the night's events. Her heart felt sore and a little empty. She had kept his shirt on, using it as a nightgown. The scent of him filled her nostrils and her body responded to it in ways she couldn't put into words.

LeJariende'Dachielle. An ancient warrior. The moment Matthias had said it she'd heard Jack's voice in her mind telling her about the prophecy, about the mate she was intended to have. It certainly would make sense of why she responded to him so strongly.

She finally drifted off, his face looming in her mind.

Chapter Fifty-Three

Jared sat on a hilltop overlooking a town outside of Dublin. There were few lights, indicating that this was not a metropolis. It was a peaceful scene, a stark contrast to the turmoil going on inside of him. When he'd left his house he'd barely had the presence of mind to throw on clothes.

How could he have bonded with her? What sort of cruel joke was this, that after centuries of being alone, of wishing to be so, he would end up bonding with a fallen female?

Stop lying to yourself, you know she isn't fallen. He drew in a breath of irritation.

He pictured her in his mind, her small feminine body, delicate elven features, brilliant blue eyes ringed with gold...the eyes of a healer. He shook his head hard. He didn't know how it was possible that she had gone undiscovered. Of course that was how she had survived, wasn't it?

And yet why stay hidden for centuries and show up in London now? And expose herself so fucking recklessly! That last thought made him grind his teeth together in anger. In part for what she had done to him, but also for the danger she'd placed herself in.

What kind of fools were those males to allow it? Or plan it, or whatever the *hell* had happened to bring her into the bar that night. If he learned they *had* sent her to perform the theft he would curse the fact that he didn't leave them to their fates on the rooftop.

And she had been a virgin. That fact kept blowing his mind. Not only had she been well hidden, she'd been untouched. And he'd taken it from her so roughly. If it weren't for the fact that he could smell her desire...No, that was a lie. He would have taken her even if she hadn't wanted him, he'd been too far gone with the effects of the demons in combination with his anger and lust.

Those eyes, he thought again. Obviously she'd been wearing contact lenses when they met, but he'd never seen a female with her particular combination. Warrior females had black hair and violet eyes and healers were fair haired with her shade of blue. She must have dyed it as part of the disguise. But the idea that not only was she an unturned female but a healer as well...the last known of her kind had died centuries ago. Yet when she'd grabbed onto his shoulders he had felt the darkness recede. And she'd begged to be allowed to go back to her friends. To heal them?

He sunk his head in his hands. He didn't need this. *He didn't fucking Want This!* Even now he could feel her presence. Less than in London, but he could still feel it. And he was being drawn there, pulled as if by an enormous invisible magnet. Thoughts were tumbling around in the back of his mind, particularly the fact that she was in a house full of males. Rage boiled up in him as he imagined them touching her, *he would tear the arms off of any who fucking DARED!* She was HIS.

But rebellion was in the forefront of his thoughts. *I don't give a damn who touches her, I will NEVER accept this.* Let them touch her and break the bond, he would deal with the pain, it would be far better than this.

Then another thought slammed into him. Those males kept either pushing her into, or at least allowing her near danger. Panic rushed through him, the need to go and make sure she was safe.

Shit. Shit. SHIT.

Long buried feelings were shoving their way to the surface. His indifference was no longer providing a cloak.

He forced himself to stay put. But eventually he knew he would weaken and the magnet would draw him, the instincts were just too strong.

Chapter Fifty-Four

For the next couple of days Anna found herself moping. She kept trying to get involved in conversations, but quickly lost interest or got distracted. She'd asked a lot of questions about mated males, and from what everyone seemed to know....Jared must loathe her. Intensely, as he was fighting one of the strongest known forces of nature. A bonded male supposedly couldn't stand to be parted from his female, and though sometimes it was necessary, they wouldn't feel right or whole again until she was near. Particularly since they had the overwhelming instinct to protect their mate from any and all perceived dangers. But if something were to happen to her...wouldn't he die too? That was a question she'd asked and was answered in the affirmative. Maybe he didn't care, she thought. If he *was* LeJariende'Dachielle then he'd forsaken his old life. Maybe he wanted death.

She decided she was going out that night, she had to get her mind off this....or maybe find him? If only she'd drank from him or paid more attention to where his house was when she was there. Last night she had stood outside trying to figure out how to retrace her steps but it eluded her. And she couldn't track him since she hadn't drank from him. She'd asked why, if they were bonded, couldn't she sense him and learned that until she drank from him for the first time, the connection was incomplete. On her end at least.

She couldn't believe how desperately she wanted him to look at her with tenderness, to pull her into his arms with something other than lust. Like passion or...*dream on Anna*. And she *was* dreaming on, constantly. There was no other male in the world that she could imagine herself with now. She'd always thought that she would be struck by lightning when she found her soul mate. Turns out she was right.

She got the girls together and they headed out on the town. No one even tried to stop her, it seemed that her loss of innocence had changed things. Or maybe, she thought hopefully, it was because they thought that Jared would take care of her if the need arose.

Even though she wanted to see him she couldn't go to the vampire hangouts, especially with the girls. So they settled on a lively club downtown. Her sole mission for the night was to get hammered. Sooo drunk that thinking would be a chore, and she set about it with a vengeance.

A few hours later she was dancing with some guy, her hands draped over his shoulders to hold herself up. She was slurring and her vision was getting a little funny. The guy, whose breath was on her neck at the moment, said something she didn't understand. She started to ask for a repeat, when suddenly she was yanked from him and taken to the back of the club into a deserted hallway.

Mr. Fury Eyes we meet again, she thought and giggled. He clearly didn't think anything was funny.

"What were you doing with that human?" he hissed, "were you going to let him fuck you?"

She looked at his face and there were two of them, she couldn't decide which one to look at so she kept shifting back and forth.

"You're drunk." He said flatly.

"Um. Yup. I am super duper wasted," she giggled again.

"Stay right here." he commanded. He strode away and came back several minutes later. She was still standing there bopping her head to the music and shifting her feet.

"Where are the males you stay with?" he demanded.

She half focused on him. "Dunno. Prob'ly out fightin shadow men."

"Do they know you're here?" he growled.

"Um," she wrinkled her forehead trying to concentrate and failed miserably. "I think...maybe."

"Are you here alone?"

She shook her head.

"Who's with you?" His voice was icy.

"Jenna and Jess, and Harri," she ticked them off on her fingers.

"Bring me to them."

She walked unsteadily back towards the dance floor, her vision fading in and out. The amount of alcohol she'd consumed would have killed a human. Straight liquor all night. It was the only way for a vampire to hold onto any kind of buzz for long, their bodies' purged alcohol far more quickly than humans.

She attempted to survey the room, what was she looking for again? Oh yeah, the girls. She got dizzy with the back and forth motion and stumbled. Arms caught her and swept her up.

She laid her head against his solid chest and she could hear his heart pounding and the sound of his shallow breaths. He was most definitely pissed off.

"Anna!" A familiar voice rang out. She turned her head and saw the blurry form of Jess hurrying over then stopping several feet away to stare at the male holding her.

"Anna?" His voice rumbled.

Oh yeah she'd lied about her name too.

"Are you going to hurt her?" Jess's voice was shaky.

"Who are you?" he demanded.

"I'm her friend."

"You're a *human*." He said the word like it was corrosive.

"What are you doing with her?" Jess kept her distance, but her voice had gained strength.

"Whatever I'd like. She's mine."

"But she doesn't want to be! It's not fair that you can make that choice for her!"

Anna vaguely thought Jess had it wrong, the first part and most likely the second too.

"She said this?"

"Yes! It's Michael she belongs with, he loves her. He would be good to her!"

"Who is *Michael*?" His voice was ominous.

"He wants to break the bond or whatever it is, and she does too."

What?? Anna squirmed in his arms, wanting to deny her friend's words but having trouble making sound come out of her mouth.

He released her suddenly and she dropped onto the floor. Jess rushed forward and bent down glaring up at him.

"Tell this *Michael* to hurry up and be done with it."

Anna watched him stride away and pain filled her chest. She looked at Jess in disbelief. Where'd she come up with that?

"Come on, get up." Jess tugged her to her feet and she tried to locate him, wobbling back and forth unsteadily. But he was gone.

"Why'd you say that? I don't want..."

Jess wasn't listening, she was pulling her towards the front of the bar. Jenna and Harriet were waiting there, relief on their faces when they saw them coming.

Anna stumbled again, and Jenna ran forward to catch her. "Whoa, I think we need to get you home."

She allowed them to lead her outside to the car. When she was seated in the back she tried desperately to make her thoughts coherent but the struggle made her head hurt and she squeezed her eyes shut.

She woke to someone lifting her and her hopes soared for a moment, then his scent hit her nose and it was wrong. She cracked her eyes open and saw Michael's grim face. *Why had Jess said those things*, she thought distantly then slid back to unconsciousness.

She awoke the following morning and rubbed her eyes against the light that was streaming through the windows of her bedroom. Although she wasn't suffering from a hangover, her body having rid itself of toxins in the night, her insides felt hollowed out. She recalled what had happened and wanted to cry, or scream with frustration.

She decided to go find Jess and demand she explain why she had made those declarations. She ran into Jenna first and asked where her sister was.

"Somewhere with Tyros again," she answered, rolling her eyes.

Anna sighed. She had to find Jared. Had to tell him that Jess was wrong, that she didn't feel that way. But how?

"What's on your mind?" Jenna asked in concern.

"Nothing, I just…I don't feel like talking about it."

"Okay. Let me know when you do."

To Anna's relief Michael was gone for the day. She wondered if he had said something to Jess to give her those ideas but found the idea of confronting him difficult.

When Jess finally turned up she was upset. Jenna asked her what was wrong but she shook her head and went straight to her room locking the door. After a long tense moment Anna decided against breaking it down, her friend apparently had problems of her own. Instead she waited until Jenna was distracted by her aunt, pocketed the purple contacts, and slipped out the door.

She blurred to a clothing store and changed her outfit. She chose all black, and covered herself with an oversized black leather jacket. She was determined to find him, and the only place she knew to look was that bar called Stokes. She figured going in disguise would be a wise choice since she still had to worry about others identifying her, but she felt it wouldn't be particularly wise to show off her body.

It was still light outside, so encountering a bar full of the "damned" would not be an issue. Unfortunately it was also unlikely that he'd be there, but she still had to try. Maybe she could leave word with the bartender that she was looking for him. She contemplated writing a note then decided against it. As long as the barkeep passed on her inquiry he should come looking for her. She hoped.

There were only a few people in the bar when she arrived, and of course none were him. She went up to the counter and ordered a beer, hunching her shoulders to ward off interest. It didn't work, one of the patrons came to sit beside her instantly.

"Who are you?" he asked and she refrained from answering, keeping her eyes forward. His scent indicated he was a vampire, and she began to nervously reconsider this plan. She signaled the bartender and he came towards her.

"Do you know Jared?"

The barman lifted a brow.

"If you see him could you tell him that Anna is looking for him?"

He stared at her for a moment and nodded.

She got up and started for the door when a hand came down on her arm.

"An American accent? I thought all females resided in England."

She yanked her arm free and continued walking. He followed her outside and she tensed. She couldn't blur with so many people on the street, shit! She scanned up and down for a cab, ready to spring into action if he attempted to touch her again. She could still feel his presence and she snuck a glance at him. His brows were furrowed, and...holy shit she knew him! Paulo, she remembered, the Italian vampire that had hit on her at the rave the night she'd been turned. Her insides tightened with fear and she quickly looked away, ducking her head. Her heart sped up as she imagined him pointing a finger and shouting I KNOW YOU and then relaxed slightly as she recalled her disguise.

From her peripheral she could see him looking at the sky then back at her with an expression of surprise and curiosity. It dawned on her that she was outside in the daylight, an incredibly strange thing for him to see. Shit. She really had to go. She saw a cab coming down the street and hurried to it. Yanking open the door she jumped in and told the driver to "Go".

She glanced out the window and Paulo remained on the sidewalk staring after her. She figured that considering he'd been at the place Jake had taken her he probably drank from humans on a regular basis so it wasn't likely he could blur after her. That thought made her feel a bit safer. But she was no longer an unknown. Highly unlikely he wouldn't spread the news of what he'd seen.

All she could do now was hope that Jared got her message, or that he came to her anyway.

Chapter Fifty-Five

Jared made his way through the Black Forest in Germany thinking that he needed to board a flight to a far distant place. Although he felt her presence even less here than in Dublin, all the instinctual mated feelings were a constant. It had been two fucking days, why hadn't she broken the bond? What was this *Michael* waiting for? He pictured the group of males he had seen, wondering which one was him, fluctuating between the desire to rip off his head and the desire to demand the male release him from this.

He wished he could drink himself into a stupor the way she had. He shook his head in exasperated anger as he walked into a cabin, one of many isolated places he had in the world, and settled into the old worn armchair. Tonight he would hunt for large game and forget about the little lying thief who had torn his carefully maintained world apart. And if she hadn't released him by sunrise he would get on a plane to Greenland.

Chapter Fifty-Six

A couple of days later Harriet announced that they needed to get back to France. Jess seemed eager to go, though her eyes held a sadness that was mildly concerning, especially since nothing ever affected Jess for longer than a few minutes. She still refused to tell anyone what had happened and Tyros had disappeared leading everyone to believe the worst. Just before they left Jess handed Anna a sealed envelope.

"Would you give this to him when he comes back?" Anna nodded and put it in her purse. She tried once more to find out what was wrong, but Jess just shook her head.

Anna had purchased and used the dye remover, and it was comforting to have her hair color back although she still retained some curl. Seth told her she looked like a medieval princess and she decided the waves weren't so bad.

She gathered with her friends in the front room of the house to say their goodbyes, and as she watched them go a part of her wanted to leave with them. But she knew her place was still here. They assured her they would return before they went back to the states, probably in a few weeks, and that made it a little easier.

She watched from the window as the car drove out of sight, then turned to the males who had assembled for the farewell. The night before she had decided she was going to sit them down and tell them what her feelings were in regards to Jared. She did not want Michael to hope for something that would never be, and she wanted their help in finding him.

No one noticed the car that was sitting at the end of the street watching the house for the past two days.

When the women climbed into their rental and headed for the train station, they were not aware of being followed.

Paulo lived to fuck the vampire females in London, and there was nothing he wouldn't do to that end. He had kept himself restrained from making the final plunge, from draining a human of life, only to be of use to those he desired.

On the train he sat a car away, keeping an eye on the daylight female. Her black hair and purple eyes had made him suspicious at the bar, and when she'd asked about Jared he'd known what she was. He had been shocked when she'd walked out into the sun. At first when he'd gone to Terrina and Alyssa they had not believed him, stating it was impossible. But after a little digging they'd discovered that Jared had recently left Stokes with a female who had an American accent.

Paulo had tracked down the cab driver by his license plate that same night and learned where he'd taken her. He'd quickly discovered the home was protected and there were a number of males living within, males who did not drink from humans and therefore retained their powers in daylight.

Paulo was given the task of watching the house and delivering the female to them, for which he would be rewarded immensely. His cock lengthened and hardened just thinking of the many things they had promised if he was successful.

The females exited the train in France and Paulo followed at a discreet distance. He was curious about the other two who appeared to be human as one looked like no vampire he'd ever seen and the other, though bearing a resemblance to the female who'd called herself Anna, was far too old to be. He puzzled over that resemblance, than dismissed it. Anna was wearing more form fitting clothes this afternoon, and her curves were delicious. He truly hoped she would choose to turn rather than die, one more female for him to enjoy.

They climbed into a cab and he followed in another. A short drive later they were pulling up in front of a small cottage. He paid the driver and climbed out, perching himself out of sight down the street, trying to decide his next move. He would have to wait until dark for his abilities to return to him.

When evening finally came the female and the attractive human girl came out of the house and began walking. They were discussing a place they would go for a late dinner and what they would do afterwards. They settled on catching a cab from the restaurant to a club across town, and his plan came together.

He waited by the restaurant until he saw them exit then hailed a cab and with a friendly smile affected a French accent. "Girls, I have one for you," he opened the door of the taxi and they looked at each other and grinned. They slid into the car and he slid in next to them.

"Where are you headed?" His handsome face had fooled many an innocent victim, and they were no different...then it struck him. They were both human. He inhaled deeply and pinned the dark haired girl with an intense stare. He had followed the wrong female. He felt anger building, and his expression must've shown it.

"Um, driver, can you let us out at the next-

He leaned in. "If you finish that statement or alert him in any way to a problem, I will kill him," he whispered.

She shut her mouth.

"Where is Anna?" he demanded.

"Who?" she asked, her voice shaky.

The driver interrupted, "Where are you going?"

Paulo managed to smile, "Just drive for a bit, we haven't decided yet."

He turned back to the girls. "She's still at that house in England?" he bit out.

"I don't know what you're talking about." Jenna managed to push the tremor out of her voice. Jess had gripped her arm on the other side, her fear climbing.

Paulo sat back, gaining control of his anger and thought about the situation. Perhaps this was fortuitous, he could get information from these two and use them as bait.

He told the driver to take them downtown. When the cab stopped he ordered the girls out, and once on the sidewalk he blurred them to a shady part of the city. He located an empty building and pulled them inside, taking the dark haired one by the throat.

He turned to the other who was exuding terror from her pores. "Answer my questions or your friend dies."

Eyes wide with fear Jess swallowed and nodded.

Paulo tied the hands of the dark haired girl behind her back, and as he drew out a handkerchief to gag her he again cursed the fact that his abilities during the day were no better than a human's. If not for that he would have seen her more clearly. The one who called herself Anna had much more delicate and childlike features, and her eyes had been a different shade of violet.

He turned to the other girl who was still seated on the floor as he'd instructed.

"What are your first and last names?" He was greeted with silence so he made a show of pulling a dagger from his bag and turning it over in his hands. "I don't. like. repeating myself." He pronounced the words slowly, in a chillingly quiet voice.

"Jessica and Jenna Richmond," she answered, her voice shaking.

"Related? How?"

"S..sisters."

"What is your relationship with the vampire female?"

"F..friend."

"You are Americans, yes?"

She nodded.

"From what state?"

"New York."

"How long have you known the female?"

"About s..se...seven years." Tears were beginning to slide down her face and Paulo grimaced.

"What are the names of the males that share the house in London with her?"

Jess took a shaky breath and spoke barely above a whisper, her eyes on Jenna. "Michael, Seth, Matthias, Coderin, and....Tyros."

"Five of them? Are any of these her lover?"

Jess shook her head.

"Is Jared her lover?"

"J...just once."

"Do any of the five feed from her?"

"No."

He raised his brows doubtfully.

"She drinks from them but not the other way around."

He was quiet for a moment wondering about the disgustingly high moral fiber of this group of males, making a note of it. "These males, they are hunters, yes?"

Jess nodded.

"Is she as well?"

"They don't let her, it's too dangerous."

"Does she feed from the two of you?"

Jess shook her head. He raised a brow, she shook her head again.

"Why does she have you around then?"

"We...we're Faerian."

His eyes widened briefly at this. "Healers?"

She shook her head, "We're from the male line."

His brows drew together. "Male line? I've never heard of such a thing. What abilities do you have?"

"We can see the shadow men. And some of us have visions."

"You have visions?"

Jess shook her head.

"Your sister then?"

She looked at the floor without answering.

He glanced at Jenna. He could think of nothing else to ask at the moment. Time to call his females.

He spoke to Terrina in Italian, explaining the situation and filling her in on the details of his question and answer session.

He pressed end and set about tying the girls securely around the wrists and ankles then placed a gag on the one he'd questioned. Hoisting one over each shoulder he blurred back to London.

***

The vampiress glided across the floor, fangs bared, eyes flashing. "Incompetence, *sheer stupidity*," she hissed, disgust written across her feline features.

She lowered herself into her expensive Italian armchair and tapped her long red fingernails against the glossy wood. After a minute her anger began to fade as she considered the situation. "Perhaps it will work in our favor. From what he said about the males guarding her she might have been impossible to get to. With her friends as hostages...yes, this might be for the best."

The one to whom she spoke nodded with feigned interest. Terrina was rabidly bent on this new female's demise and Alyssa knew why it was so, Jared had been seen leaving the bar with her. She liked being under the male herself, but she had not developed Terrina's obsession with him. In her opinion it would be better to try and convince the female to turn rather than kill her, but she doubted Terrina would give her that choice.

The two vampiress' had nearly the same shade of eyes and hair color, but that was where the similarity ended. While Terrina was tall and fierce, Alyssa was petite and docile. Secretly she thought that Jared preferred her smaller stature, a fact she would never mention to the stronger female, not and keep her pretty eyes in her face. Much stronger females had ended up beneath the ground for less. Terrina was no one to trifle with. Alyssa was content to act as the complacent sidekick and reap the benefits of the wealthy life they lived. Extravagant shopping sprees, wild dancing, fucking males and drinking the human drug had kept her entertained and occupied for centuries.

There was one small thing about her that no one knew and certainly her housemate could never know. She had only killed once. Three hundred years ago she had been given the choice to die or to turn. She had only been 26 years at the time and too weak and timid to take a stand. So she had drank the man to death and lost the sun forever. What she had never understood was that it didn't seem to have changed her as severely as all the others. She pretended she was as indifferent and cruel as they were and yet...yet she had never killed another human in all those years.

She glanced at Terrina who had hopped off her perch on the chair and was pacing the room again.

"I do believe that I will refrain from killing the female right away," she said, "I'll send for the traitorous bastard first, let him watch while I remove her head from her little neck."

Alyssa frowned. "Why would he care? Just because he screwed her doesn't mean it will bother him," she pointed out.

The other female glared in her direction. "I have reason to believe the male has more feelings than anyone knows about. He still walks in the sun."

She continued to pace and plot until Paulo arrived with his two abused and frightened deliveries. He dumped them on the floor at Terrina's feet and she glanced from one to the other with undisguised disgust.

She turned to Paulo, her mouth set in a grim line. "Which is the one you interrogated?" He pointed to Jess's shaking form.

"Then I will speak to the other."

She bent down and hauled Jenna into a sitting position. Jenna's eyes sparked both fear and defiance as she studied the vampiress. The female cupped Jenna's face with one hand then curved her long red fingernails into the gag and yanked it from her mouth.

"You will call your vampiress and I will speak to her and negotiate your release." She pulled a knife from her bag to cut the rope on Jenna's right hand then pressed her phone into it.

Jenna stared at the device for a moment then looked up at her captor's face and smirked. She gripped the offensive electronic and in a swift motion hurled it against the far wall, shattering the encasement.

Terrina blinked in disbelief and her lip curled. "That wasn't wise." She struck Jenna, splitting her lip wide open.

Jess cried out from her fetal position on the floor, the sound muffled behind her muzzle, but Jenna just wiped the blood across her sleeve and glared at her assailant.

Terrina raised an eyebrow. "I see why you chose to question the other one," she said to Paulo, then turned to Alyssa. "Give that one your phone," she instructed.

After Jess's bonds were cut she shakily dialed the number avoiding Jenna's accusatory look. It went straight to voice mail. She tried twice more with the same result and Terrina snatched the phone from her hand, her anger mounting.

She handed the phone back to Alyssa. "We'll try again later," she spat. "For now..." She walked to the center of the room and looked back at the two girls speculatively. "It's not really necessary for us to have two of them, is it?" Terrina glanced at Alyssa who shrugged indifferently.

Terrina picked her knife back up and turned it over and over in her hand. She shifted her gaze from one girl to the other. "I think that the more loyal of the two and one who has visions will be of more value to the female." She turned toward Jenna and watched her face drain of color. She smiled slowly and nodded at her as she spoke, "Besides, I think I will rather enjoy seeing that one's expression as her sister dies."

Jess cried out, trying to scramble backwards and Terrina laughed, stepping on her hair.

"NO!" Jenna yelled struggling against her bonds. "We're both valuable, Anna......" Terrina stopped her midsentence by seizing her throat and throwing her into the wall.

She turned back to Jess who had flipped over and was attempting to crawl away and with a cruel smile she walked over until she was straddling her.

"Pathetic," she spat, then bent down and grabbed her by the hair and hauled her up against her chest.

She smiled widely at Jenna as she slid the knife across Jess's neck, drawing her tongue across the blood welling up from the long cut.

Jess gasped soundlessly and Jenna screamed, trying desperately to get to her feet. She was promptly pushed back down by Alyssa's heeled shoe and the female spoke so quietly it sounded like the rustle of dead leaves. "There's nothing you can do, she gets off on others' suffering."

Terrina ran her tongue back and forth the length of the wound and Paulo, who had been quietly observing the scene, stepped up beside her and whispered, "There's no reason for waste, let me have her."

She licked her lips and stared into the girl's terrified eyes then looked back at Paulo and shrugged. "I suppose, but it will be your payment since you botched the job so badly."

He nodded and hoisted Jess over his shoulder, then strode through the door of the house and was gone.

"What is he doing with her?" Jenna demanded in a strangled voice, her breath coming out in little screams.

"Oh it's of no consequence to you, she is minutes from death," Terrina said dismissively.

Jenna blinked away the tears that were forming and pushed her grief aside, overcome by the need to keep her head clear. She trembled as she stared at the unholy bitch, burning her face in her mind while a cold rage washed through her. *I will kill you,* she silently vowed, *I will murder you and smile exactly like you did as you take your last breath.*

Alyssa caught the murderous look in Jenna's eyes and felt a brief spark of sympathy. "I think you should try and call the female again." She held out her phone to Terrina.

Terrina nodded, relishing the scent of pain coming from the girl on the floor, amused by the anger. She took the phone and tried several times. It became obvious that the phone would likely remain off until morning and she growled in frustration. It appeared her transaction would have to wait until the following night. Refastening the human's gag she threw her up on her shoulder and strode out of the room. She reached a door and yanked it open, revealing a steep stairwell leading down into the dark. She dropped the girl on the top step and gave her a push, watching her roll down into the basement. She stood glaring down at her for a moment then slammed the door with a resounding thud.

Chapter Fifty-Seven

Anna sat outside on the porch lost in thought. She'd had trouble sleeping and it was still over an hour before the sun would begin its ascent into the sky. Michael had not been happy with the news that she wanted to stay mated to Jared. His reaction caused her to suspect that he *had* said something to make Jess believe what she'd said.

Surprisingly Matthias was her biggest supporter. He seemed vehemently against breaking the bond, making comments about how painful it would be and causing Anna to wonder if he'd experienced it. He also seemed confident that when some time had passed and she had yet to break it, Jared would return to find out why.

She kept replaying their night together, and each time she was filled with longing and desire like she'd never known before. Not even when she was in heat, *that* had been mindless. This went much deeper.

Seth burst out onto the porch, startling her. He held his phone out, worry creasing his brow.

She took the phone. "Hello?"

"Anna?" It was Harriet and she sounded panicky.

Anna shot to her feet, "What is it?"

"The girls, they did not come home last night. They went out to dinner and told me they'd planned to visit a club. I went to bed early and when I woke up they weren't here. They're not answering their phones, something must have happened. I can't see anything, I've tried, but my visions are forsaking me."

Dread curled in Anna's stomach. During the night she'd had a dream about Jenna, she couldn't recall it but she remembered being afraid. Oh God, how stupid! She'd drank from her, it wasn't just a dream, it was a link like the one she'd had with Michael! She sat frozen for a moment before she realized-*I drank from her, I can track her.*

"Harriet, I'll find them. I'll keep you posted." She hung up as the males were filing out, led by Seth who'd overheard.

"I drank from Jenna," she told them feeling wobbly, "I can find them."

Matthias gripped her arms to steady her. "Okay, here's what we'll do. The three of us will drink from you so we can follow as you track." He turned to Seth, "I think it would be smart to bring a car, you can track us through our phones." Seth nodded, grabbing the keys.

Anna nodded and Matthias took her wrist. When they'd all taken from her she walked into the yard and concentrated as hard as she could. After a moment she sensed the direction and leapt off the porch letting her body take over.

***

Anna was surprised to find herself stopping so soon. She had thought they were headed for France, instead they found themselves in a posh corner of London where gated estates stretched down a long street.

The gate they were standing in front of was made of cast iron and stood ten feet tall. Matthias hissed for them to back away from it, there were security cameras sweeping the sidewalk near to where they stood.

"I would be willing to wager this place is owned by our kind." Michael stated. "The upside is they're likely unable to navigate the daylight, with any strength at least. Unfortunately even if we get past the gates the house is likely protected."

Anna did not think there could be any upsides to her friends being abducted by fallen vampires. Her stomach turned over and over at the thought of what might be done to them.

An SUV turned down the street and Coderin flagged Seth to a stop down the road. He parked and joined them, glaring at the property.

"So what's our assessment?"

Matthias and Michael looked at Anna, then away.

"I'm guessing that we're all thinking my friends were taken as bait to get to me," she said quietly.

"Females?" Seth asked.

The others frowned and Anna felt her stomach clench harder. If the captors were male at least there were more things to negotiate and less reason for them to kill anyone. Females.....not good.

"Okay," Matthias said finally, "I'm going to check the perimeter, find a place to get inside the gates without being seen."

Twenty minutes later Matthias returned frowning. "There's no way in without triggering a silent alarm. They have beams shooting up much farther than any of us can leap."

"So what now?" Anna asked anxiously.

"Do you have your phone?"

Her eyes widened and she shook her head as she realized she'd left it turned off in her room. "I'll go get it."

"I'll come with you," Michael stated and instructed the rest of them to stay and watch for any activity. Particularly day walking vampires like the one that must have followed the girls in the first place.

Paulo, an accusing voice whispered in Anna's mind, *him or someone he told about you. And you never told anyone about your attempt to reach Jared, did you? If you had, the males would have been on alert and this would not have happened.* She felt tears coming and raced into a blur before anyone could see.

She and Michael reached the house and she leapt up the stairs to her room, grabbing her phone. She turned it on and there were several missed calls from late last night, unknown number, no messages. *It was them*, she thought miserably, *I caused their abduction and didn't even have my phone on when they needed me.*

She spun to race back downstairs and collided with Michael.

"Slow down," he commanded, "Matthias wanted you to have your phone in case they call, but I believe that call won't come until near or after sundown. They won't risk negotiations in the daylight while they're weak."

She looked up into his face and her body started shaking. He gathered her into his arms and spoke soothingly. "It's not your fault, you couldn't have known."

She shook her head denying his words. "I put them in danger, they wouldn't have even been here if not for me, and no one would have known about my existence if I hadn't taken it upon myself to get those weapons..." *not to mention what you don't know*, her mind whispered desolately.

Michael was stroking her hair. "I believe things happen for a reason, you have to trust me on this, guilt will not solve a problem nor will it ever change anything."

She nodded, swallowing thickly.

He tipped her head up, "Everything will be okay."

He said it with such confidence that she had to believe him. She smiled gratefully and he smiled back, a dazzling grin that transformed his face. She realized he didn't smile nearly enough.

His smile receded and a look came into his eyes that Anna recognized all too well, and suddenly she needed to get back to the others. She said as much and pulled free of his grip, dashing out the door and blurring back to the waiting males.

"Where's Michael?" Coderin asked after she'd told them about the missed calls.

"He should be right behind me." She felt a pang, but took Michael's advice and refused to feel guilty. His feelings were not her fault, she had never done anything to encourage them.

He showed up several minutes later and avoided looking at her.

"Fuck, I hate standing around with my thumb up my ass!" Matthias said irritably.

"I agree, but what choice do we have?" Seth looked at the gates again. "If only it wasn't so likely the house was protected, it wouldn't matter if they knew we were coming, they wouldn't be any match for us."

They decided to take the SUV and find a nearby tavern they could wait in. A few blocks away they found one that suited. The males played pool and Anna watched numbly, trying not to think about what might be happening to her friends.

They're fine, she told herself, *they're needed to get at me, so they're fine*. She prayed she was right and held tightly to the vague connection she still felt with Jenna.

Shortly before sunset Anna's phone rang and she stared at the unknown number with dread as she answered.

"Hello?"

"Have you been expecting my call?" The voice on the other line brought up images of Medusa, making her shiver.

She forced anger and strength into her voice. "Where are my friends?"

"We'll come to that, but first tell me the location of the five males who protect you."

"Four," Anna said automatically.

"I was told there were five."

"There were, but one disappeared a couple of days ago and hasn't returned." *Why am I telling her this?* She winced.

"I see." There was the sound of a pen scratching on paper and then, "Mm. What's the missing male's name?"

"Tyros."

"Very well, your stories match."

She asked one of the girls, Anna thought and felt relief course through her.

"So these four, they are with you now?"

"What is the point of this question?" Anna asked.

"Well I'm afraid I can't have your protectors interfering with our deal, so here is what I propose: the four of them will go to a club called Vassaggo's at nine pm where they will be watched by some friends of mine, whilst you, my sweet, will come to a bar called Stokes. I believe you are familiar with the place?" Her voice was dripping with acid covered honey. "I will bring your little friend with the bad attitude to that location. Once we're there she can leave in a cab you'll have waiting for her while you and I become...acquainted."

Anna felt her heart being squeezed, "I won't participate in any deal that doesn't involve the safety of both of my friends," she said tightly.

"I'm afraid that won't be possible. The one called Jess is dead."

Anna's grip on the phone tightened, her knuckles whitening as the color drained from her face to match them. Then she abruptly released it and put both hands over her mouth tightly, breathing through her fingers and shaking her head in vigorous denial. She dropped to her knees and leaned forward until her head touched the back of a chair, her breath whistling through her fingers in labored heaves.

Matthias retrieved the phone. "YOU BITCH! *Do you think you won't pay for this*?" he hissed.

"*Careful*," she hissed back, "I may decide to bide my time and wait for another opportunity to make Anna's acquaintance and just keep this other one as a pet until I tire of her."

Anna looked at Matthias in terror, shaking her head. She climbed to her feet and held her hand out for the phone with a beseeching look. He handed it over reluctantly, his face mottled with anger.

"Don't hurt her," she rasped, "I'll do whatever you want."

"Oh how sweet. You care so much for these worthless little humans. Then I suppose I shall see you in Stokes at ten. Don't be late," she sang and the line went dead.

Coderin wrapped his arms around Anna, and Seth closed in on her from the other side, putting his face next to her ear. "She may be lying," he whispered, "she may just want you upset so you'll act rashly. It makes very little sense for her to kill Jess, it would be wiser for her to have more than one avenue to get at you."

Anna felt some of her tension ease. She looked up into the wolf man's eyes and saw they appeared very canine indeed, as if he were about to change. "Do you think so?" she asked shakily.

He nodded, "Don't lose hope." Then he turned to the others. "I have reason to believe that she doesn't know exactly who we are, or more importantly what we look like."

"What reason is that?" Michael asked.

"Because she called us five males, she didn't mention Dog, did she?"

Anna looked around and they were all nodding vigorously.

Matthias was growing excited. "No fucking way she wouldn't have made a scathing remark."

"So, we get Leo to replace one of us at the bar...

Matthias volunteered automatically. "I'll grab Jenna when they attempt to leave."

"Wait! What about Jess? If you do that it will piss them off and she could suffer for it!" Anna looked around feeling panicky all over again.

"You're right. Damn, I'll have to grab the bitch instead. Likely whatever fuckheads' she's in league with will not want to lose their female slut. We'll negotiate her for the girls."

"Why can't we replace two of you, you know with that other hunter Finn, then you can grab the vampiress *and* Jenna."

Seth shook his head, "We may be able to convince them that we have one human in our midst but two would be pushing it."

Anna bit her lip. Well, it was better than nothing, either way they would have to negotiate for Jess...she hoped. Oh she really hoped.

After further discussion they decided that Anna would not go to Stokes unless ten o'clock came around and the vampires hadn't emerged from the house, indicating they didn't buy Leo's presence or were waiting for Anna to be seen at the bar. Instead she would wait several blocks over at a crowded place for word on what to do next.

At nine fifty she received a text message, Matthias had met with success and was now en route to Michael's with the female scourge.

She blurred back there to find Matthias having a hell of a time holding the furious female down. The other males arrived several seconds later and rushed in to help pin her to the floor. Matthias drove a fist into her face and her nose exploded. She howled in pain before it began to mend.

"I can continue doing that all night without growing tired of it, so I suggest you accept the fucking situation," he growled into her contorted face.

She let out a hiss but stopped fighting and changed tactics. "Well, aren't we all clever? Who would've thought that a *Dog* would be among you, it certainly made it plausible for the *human* animal to be in your little group." Her eyes were narrowed into furious slits. "So I suppose you intend to trade me for the girl."

"*Girls*," Anna snarled leaning over her.

"Oh, you didn't believe my claim? It's unfortunate really, her death was accidental…."

Matthias plowed his fist into her face again, just as Anna's expression fell.

When her nose and cheekbone mended from the blow she hissed, "Whatever is done to me I will be certain to have my…

Matthias didn't wait for her to finish the threat before breaking her face once more. As she squealed and writhed he leaned in close to her, "I wouldn't open my mouth again unless asked to do so."

She shot him a venomous look but stayed silent.

"*This* is what you are going to do. You will call whomever it is that currently has Jenna..."

Matthias was cut off by the sound of a phone ringing from inside the female's purse. Coderin fished it out and flipped it open. "Hello?"

"Who's this?" A female voice demanded.

Matthias had clapped a hand over the bitch's mouth and she was struggling violently.

"You have something we want," Coderin stated.

"And you have taken Terrina."

"That's right."

"Look, I don't want any trouble with you. I was not involved in the death of the other one, all of this is Terrina's doing."

"Coderin!" Matthias held a hand out for the phone as the others continued to restrain the now livid female. He spoke quickly, "If what you're saying is true, then we have no argument with you. Release the girl and you'll hear nothing more from us."

Terrina began to thrash and Coderin had to stretch out over her to keep her from breaking free. "This strength she has..." he trailed off at a sharp look from Matthias who glanced briefly at Anna.

"Oh it is true," the other female was saying, "she's angry because your female was seen with Jared and she wants him for herself. I will put the human in a car and send her to you, but all of you must vow that you will not seek to harm me."

Matthias looked around the room and everyone nodded for him to go on. He gave her the vow and the others followed suit.

"I will send her now."

The phone went dead and Matthias smiled triumphantly. He locked eyes with the female whose expression had changed to fear.

Anna stood over Terrina, rage welling up from the bottom of her soul. This creature had taken Jess's life. She wondered if she had her friend's blood running through her veins and thought that draining it back out sounded like a perfectly fitting idea. She said as much in a voice she didn't recognize as her own.

Matthias closed a hand on her shoulder. "We have to wait for Jenna."

Thirty minutes later a car pulled up the driveway and the group tensed. Anna couldn't bring herself to stop seething down at the abomination, so Matthias went outside.

He led Jenna through the door and she stopped to survey the scene. She met Anna's pain filled eyes, her own filled with ice cold fury.

"*She's mine*," Jenna hissed, "I kill her. I kill the *evil murdering bitch*."

Matthias left the room and returned with a dagger. He stretched his hand out to her, the knife lying loosely in his palm. Something in his face conveyed the desire for her to understand her decision. She met and held his stare then closed her hand around the hilt of the knife. "Show me what to do."

The others continued to restrain the vampiress but Coderin released her mouth allowing her to make her final pleas.

"If you do this, you will be hunted down by males who revere me," she screeched.

Jenna leaned in close and spat, "And I will take great pleasure in killing each and every one of them."

Coderin replaced his hand muffling her outraged curses while Matthias went down on one knee and put his hand over her breastbone, showing Jenna where to aim. "You have to twist violently and continue doing it until her body stops all movement," he told her.

He helped the others hold Terrina still as Jenna knelt down and gripped the dagger tightly with both hands. "Jess," she whispered and closed her eyes briefly then raised her hands up and brought the knife down hard, twisting it sharply.

The female's face contorted and her eyes rolled back inside her head. Her body thrashed violently for several long minutes while Jenna continued to twist.

She finally went limp but Jenna continued to lean into the knife, tremors racking her body as she stared down at the dead female. Anna dropped onto her knees beside her and placed a hand over hers squeezing hard, a tropical storm of grief welling up.

The silence in the room was shattered a moment later when Jenna screamed down at the corpse, no words just a fevered, anguished, furious sound, pushing the knife in deeper.

She finally let go and spun into Anna, throwing her arms around her shoulders. They sobbed together, terrible silent tears that felt as if they would never stop. They were vaguely aware of the corpse being removed from their presence, and a while later they felt large hands on their shoulders as the males knelt around them to offer comfort.

They moved into the smaller living room, Anna and Jenna curled up on one couch with the males sitting listlessly on the other. The front door flew open with a sudden bang and the males leapt into attack mode racing from the room.

Several seconds later they ushered Aunt Harriet in. She stopped short when she saw the anguished girls. She closed her eyes and crossed her hands over her heart, head bent forward, concentrating on her inner sense and intuition. After a moment she opened her eyes and sat down beside her niece on the couch. Grabbing Jenna's hand she stated, "She's alive sweetheart. I feel her and I had a vision of her on the way here…I don't have a sense of what it meant, but I know that she still breathes."

Epilogue

Jared stood on the border of Misiones and Brazil, the mist off the Mocona Falls bathing his body with its refreshing cool spray. The water pouring down sounded like continuous thunder. It was the first place he'd been that helped accomplish what he'd set out to do....ignore her existence. He was far enough away now that he couldn't feel her, but he'd discovered during his journey that no matter the distance the ancestral pull to care for and protect his mate was a constant. In fact the moment he no longer sensed her he was struck with a nearly crippling urge to get closer again, to know she was safe.

But here the constant roaring of the water seemed to fill his mind and vibrate his body, fading all else into the background. He had made camp early that morning intending to wait there as long as it took for her to sever the tie between them.

He eased his towering frame to a sitting position and stretched his arms behind him on the bed of leaves and myriad river debris, staring into the shimmering endless swirl of water. Then closing his eyes he willed his mind to be lost in it.

***

Author's Note

Dear Reader,

Reborn is the first book in my debut series Allies Of Old. I'm incredibly excited to share this world with you and truly hope that the characters have come alive for you as they have for me. I am currently putting the finishing touches on the second book, Renewal, slated to appear on Amazon in 2019.

The success of this series, as of all book series, depends on reader support, so if you enjoyed Reborn please recommend it to your friends, and leave your review at Amazon.com

You can find me at linnetmclaughlin.com

Made in United States
North Haven, CT
29 January 2023